11-1-71 OS-I

2.50

TWO LITTLE SAVAGES

Being the ADVENTURES *of Two* BOYS
Who Lived as INDIANS *and*
What They LEARNED.

WITH OVER TWO HUNDRED DRAWINGS

Written & Illustrated
By

ERNEST THOMPSON SETON

AUTHOR of *Wild Animals I have Known*, Lives of the *Hunted*,
Biography of a GRIZZLY, *Trail of the* SANDHILL STAG, *etcetera*
& NATURALIST *to the Government of* MANITOBA.

DOVER PUBLICATIONS, INC.

NEW YORK

This new Dover edition, first published in 1962, is an unabridged republication of the work first published by Doubleday Page & Company in 1903.

International Standard Book Number: 0-486-20985-7

Manufactured in the United States of America

Dover Publications, Inc.
180 Varick Street
New York 14, N. Y.

To
WOODCRAFT
by one who owes it
many lasting
PLEASURES

Preface

BECAUSE I have known the torment of thirst I would dig a well where others may drink.

E. T. S.

The Chapters

Part I

Glenyan & Yan

Part II

Sanger & Sam

Part III

In the Woods

Part I

Glenyan ❧ Yan

I

Glimmerings

YAN was much like other twelve-year-old boys in having a keen interest in Indians and in wild life, but he differed from most in this, that he never got over it. Indeed, as he grew older, he found a yet keener pleasure in storing up the little bits of woodcraft and Indian lore that pleased him as a boy.

His father was in poor circumstances. He was an upright man of refined tastes, but indolent—a failure in business, easy with the world and stern with his family. He had never taken an interest in his son's wildwood pursuits; and when he got the idea that they might interfere with the boy's education, he forbade them altogether.

There was certainly no reason to accuse Yan of neglecting school. He was the head boy of his class, although there were many in it older than himself. He was fond of books in general, but those that dealt with Natural Science and Indian craft were very close to his heart. Not that he had many—there were very few in those days, and the Public Library had but a poor representation of these. "Lloyd's Scandinavian Sports," "Gray's Botany" and one or two Fenimore Cooper novels, these were all, and Yan was devoted to them. He was a timid, obedient boy in most things, but the unwise command to give up what was his nature merely made him a disobedient boy—turned a good boy into a bad one. He was too much in terror of his father to disobey openly, but he used to sneak away at all opportunities to the fields and woods, and at each new bird or plant he found he had an exquisite thrill of mingled pleasure and pain—the pain because he had no name for it or means of learning its nature.

The intense interest in animals was his master passion, and thanks to this, his course to and from school was a very crooked one, involving many crossings of the street, because thereby he could pass first a saloon in whose window was a champagne advertising chromo that portrayed two Terriers chasing a Rat; next, directly opposite this, was a tobacconist's, in the window of which was a beautiful effigy of an Elephant, laden with tobacco. By going a little farther out of his way, there was a game store where he might see some Ducks, and was sure, at least, of a stuffed Deer's head; and beyond that was a furrier shop, with an astonishing stuffed Bear. At another point he could see a livery stable Dog that was said to have killed a Coon, and at yet another place on Jervie Street was a cottage with a high veranda, under which, he was told, a chained Bear had once been kept. He never saw the Bear. It had been gone for years, but he found pleasure in passing the place. At the corner of Pemberton and Grand streets, according to a schoolboy tradition, a Skunk had been killed years ago and could still be smelled on damp nights. He always stopped, if passing near on a wet night, and sniffed and enjoyed that Skunk smell. The fact that it ultimately turned out to be a leakage of sewer gas could never rob him of the pleasure he originally found in it.

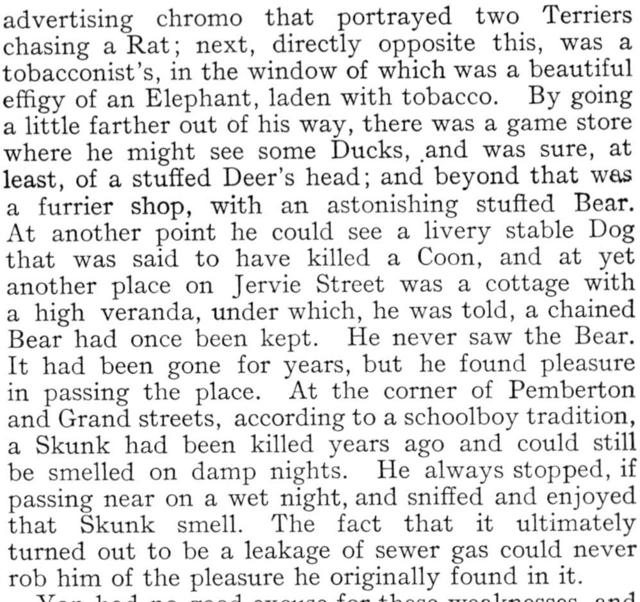

Yan had no good excuse for these weaknesses, and he blushed for shame when his elder brother talked "common sense" to him about his follies. He only knew that such things fascinated him.

But the crowning glory was a taxidermist's shop kept on Main Street by a man named Sander. Yan spent, all told, many weeks gazing spellbound, with his nose flat and white against that window. It contained some Fox and Cat heads grinning ferociously, and about fifty birds beautifully displayed. Nature might have got some valuable hints in that window on showing plumage to the very best advantage. Each bird seemed more wonderful than the last.

There were perhaps fifty of them on view, and of these, twelve had labels, as they had formed part of an exhibit at the Annual County Fair. These labels were precious truths to him, and the birds:

Osprey	Partridge or Ruffed Grouse
Kingfisher	Bittern
Bluejay	Highholder
Rosebreasted Grosbeak	Sawwhet Owl
Woodthrush	Oriole
Scarlet Tanager	* * * * * * *

were, with their names, deeply impressed on his memory and added to his woodlore, though not altogether without a mixture of error. For the alleged Woodthrush was not a Woodthrush at all, but turned out to be a Hermit Thrush. The last bird of the list was a long-tailed, brownish bird with white breast. The label was placed so that Yan could not read it from outside, and one of his daily occupations was to see if the label had been turned so that he could read it. But it never was, so he never learned the bird's name.

After passing this for a year or more, he formed a desperate plan. It was nothing less than to *go inside.* It took him some months to screw up courage, for he was shy and timid, but oh! he was so hungry for it. Most likely if he had gone in openly and asked leave, he would have been allowed to see everything; but he dared not. His home training was all of the crushing kind. He picked on the most curious of the small birds in the window—a Sawwhet Owl, then grit his teeth and walked in. How frightfully the cowbell on the door did clang! Then there succeeded a still more appalling silence, then a step and the great man himself came.

"How—how—how much is that Owl?"

"Two dollars."

Yan's courage broke down now. He fled. If he had been told ten cents, it would have been utterly beyond reach. He scarcely heard what the man said. He hurried out with a vague feeling that he had been in heaven but was not good enough to stay there. He saw nothing of the wonderful things around him.

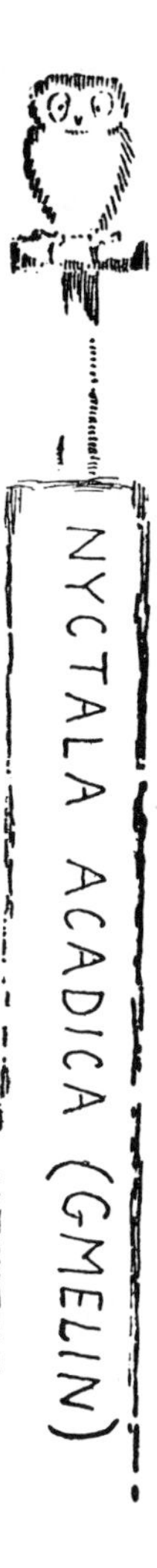

II

Spring

YAN, though not strong, revelled in deeds of brawn. He would rather have been Samson than Moses—Hercules than Apollo. All his tastes inclined him to wild life. Each year when the spring came, he felt the inborn impulse to up and away. He was stirred through and through when the first Crow, in early March, came barking overhead. But it fairly boiled in his blood when the

Wild Geese, in long, double, arrow-headed procession, went clanging northward. He longed to go with them. Whenever a new bird or beast appeared, he had a singular prickling feeling up his spine and his back as though he had a mane that was standing up. This feeling strengthened with his strength.

All of his schoolmates used to say that they "liked" the spring, some of the girls would even say that they "dearly loved" the spring, but they could not understand the madness that blazed in Yan's eyes when springtime really came—the flush of cheek—the shortening breath—the restless craving for action—the chafing with flashes of rebellion at school restraints—the overflow of nervous energy—the bloodthirst in his blood—the hankering to run—to run to the north, when the springtime tokens bugled to his every sense.

Then the wind and sky and ground were full of thrill. There was clamour everywhere, but never a word. There was stirring within and without. There was incentive in the yelping of the Wild Geese; but it was only tumult, for he could not understand why he was so stirred. There were voices that he could not hear—messages that he could not read; all was confusion of tongues. He longed only to get away. "If only I could get away. If—if—— Oh, God!" he stammered in torment of inexpression, and then would gasp and fling himself down on some bank, and bite the twigs that chanced within reach and tremble and wonder at himself.

Only one thing kept him from some mad and suicidal move—from joining some roving Indian band up north, or gypsies nearer—and that was the strong hand at home.

III

His Adjoining Brothers

YAN had many brothers, but only those next him in age were important in his life. Rad was two years older—a strong boy, who prided himself on his "common sense." Though so much older, he was Yan's inferior at school. He resented this, and delighted in showing his muscular superiority at all opportunities. He was inclined to be religious, and was strictly proper in his life and speech. He never was known to smoke a cigarette, tell a lie, or say "gosh" or "darn." He was plucky and persevering, but he was cold and hard, without a human fiber or a drop of red blood in his make-up. Even as a boy he bragged that he had no enthusiasms, that he believed in common sense, that he called a spade a spade, and would not use two words where one would do. His intelligence was above the average, but he was so anxious to be thought a person of rare sagacity and smartness, unswayed by emotion, that nothing was too heartless for him to do if it seemed in line with his assumed character. He was not especially selfish, and yet he pretended to be so, simply that people should say of him significantly and admiringly: "Isn't he keen? Doesn't he know how to take care of himself?" What little human warmth there was in him died early, and he succeeded only in making himself increasingly detested as he grew up.

His relations to Yan may be seen in one incident.

Yan had been crawling about under the house in the low wide cobwebby space between the floor beams and the ground. The delightful sensation of being on an exploring expedition led him farther (and ultimately to a paternal thrashing for soiling his clothes), till he discovered a hollow place near one side, where he could nearly stand upright. He at once formed one of his schemes—to make a secret, or at least a private, workroom here. He knew that if he were to ask permission he would be refused, but if he and Rad together were to go it might receive favourable consideration on account of Rad's self-asserted reputation for common sense. For a wonder, Rad was impressed with the scheme, but was quite sure that they had "better not go together to ask Father." He "could manage that part better alone," and he did.

Then they set to work. The first thing was to deepen the hole from three feet to six feet everywhere, and get rid of the earth by working it back under the floor of the house. There were many days of labour in this, and Yan stuck to it each day after returning from school. There were always numerous reasons why

Rad could not share in the labour. When the ten by fourteen-foot hole was made, boards to line and floor it were needed. Lumber was very cheap—inferior, second-hand stuff was to be had for the asking—and Yan found and carried boards enough to make the workroom. Rad was an able carpenter and now took charge of the construction. They worked together evening after evening, Yan discussing all manner of plans with warmth and enthusiasm—what they would do in their workshop when finished—how they might get a jig-saw in time and saw picture frames, so as to make some money. Rad assented with grunts or an occasional Scripture text—that was his way. Each day he told Yan what to go on with while he was absent.

The walls were finished at length; a window placed in one side; a door made and fitted with lock and key. What joy! Yan glowed with pleasure and pride at the triumphant completion of his scheme. He swept up the floor for the finishing ceremony and sat down on the bench for a grand gloat, when Rad said abruptly:

"Going to lock up now." That sounded gratifyingly important. Yan stepped outside. Rad locked the door, put the key in his pocket, then turning, he said with cold, brutal emphasis:

"Now you keep out of my workshop from this on. *You* have nothing to do with it. It's mine. I got the permission to make it." All of which he could prove, and did.

Alner, the youngest, was eighteen months younger than Yan, and about the same size, but the resemblance stopped there. His chief aim in life was to be stylish. He once startled his mother by inserting into his childish prayers the perfectly sincere request: "Please, God, make me an awful swell, for Jesus sake." Vanity was his foible, and laziness his sin.

He could be flattered into anything that did not involve effort. He fairly ached to be famous. He was consuming with desire to be pointed out for admiration as the great this, that or the other thing—it did not matter to him what, as long as he could be pointed out. But he never had the least idea of working for it. At school he was a sad dunce. He was three grades below Yan and at the bottom of his grade. They set out for school each day together, because that was a paternal ruling; but they rarely

"Gazing spellbound in that window"

" He already knew the Downy Woodpecker "

reached there together. They had nothing in common. Yan was full of warmth, enthusiasm, earnestness and energy, but had a most passionate and ungovernable temper. Little put him in a rage, but it was soon over, and then an equally violent reaction set in, and he was always anxious to beg forgiveness and make friends again. Alner was of lazy good temper and had a large sense of humour. His interests were wholly in the playground. He had no sympathy with Yan's Indian tastes—"Indians in nasty, shabby clothes. Bah! Horrid!" he would scornfully say.

These, then, were his adjoining brothers.

What wonder that Yan was daily further from them.

IV

The Book

BUT the greatest event of Yan's then early life now took place. His school readers told him about Wilson and Audubon, the first and last American naturalists. Yan wondered why no other great prophet had arisen. But one day the papers announced that at length he had appeared. A work on the Birds of Canada, by . . . , had come at last, price one dollar.

Money never before seemed so precious, necessary and noble a thing. "Oh! if I only had a dollar." He set to work to save and scrape. He won marbles in game, swopped marbles for tops, tops for jack-knives as the various games came around with strange and rigid periodicity. The jack-knives in turn were converted into rabbits, the rabbits into cash of small denominations. He carried wood for strange householders; he scraped and scraped and saved the scrapings; and got, after some months, as high as ninety cents. But there was a dread fatality about that last dime. No one seemed to have any more odd jobs; his commercial luck deserted him. He was burnt up with craving for that book. None of his people took interest enough in him to advance the cash even at the ruinous interest (two or three times cent per cent) that he was willing to bind himself for. Six weeks passed before he achieved that last dime, and he never felt conscience-clear about it afterward.

He and Alner had to cut the kitchen wood. Each had his daily allotment, as well as other chores. Yan's was always done faithfully, but the other evaded his work in every way. He was a notorious little fop. The paternal poverty did not permit his toilet extravagance to soar above one paper collar per week, but in his pocket he carried a piece of ink eraser with which he was careful to keep the paper collar up to standard. Yan cared nothing about dress—indeed, was inclined to be slovenly. So the eldest brother, meaning to turn Alner's weakness to account, offered a prize of a twenty-five-cent necktie of the winner's own choice to the one who did his chores best for a month. For the first week Alner and Yan kept even, then Alner wearied, in spite of the dazzling prize. The pace was too hot. Yan kept on his usual way and was duly awarded the twenty-five cents to be spent on a necktie. But in the store a bright thought came tempting him. Fifteen cents was as much as any one should spend on a necktie—that's sure; the other ten would get the book. And thus the last dime was added to the pile. Then, bursting with joy and with the pride of a capitalist, he went to the book-shop and asked for the coveted volume.

He was tense with long-pent feeling. He expected to have the bookseller say that the price had gone up to one thousand dollars, and that all were sold. But he did not. He turned silently, drew the book out of a pile of them, hesitated and said, "Green or red cover?"

"Green," said Yan, not yet believing. The bookman looked inside, then laid it down, saying in a cold, business tone, "Ninety cents."

"Ninety cents," gasped Yan. Oh! if only he had known the ways of booksellers or the workings of cash discounts. For six weeks had he been barred this happy land—had suffered starvation; he had misappropriated funds, he had fractured his conscience, and all to raise that ten cents—that unnecessary dime.

He read that book reverentially all the way home. It did not give him what he wanted, but that doubtless was his own fault. He pored over it, studied it, loved it, never doubting that now he had the key to all the wonders and mysteries of Nature. It was five years before he fully found out that the text was the most worthless trash ever foisted on a torpid public. Nevertheless, the book held some useful things; first, a list of the bird names; second, some thirty vile travesties of Audubon and Wilson's bird portraits.

These were the birds thus maligned:

Duck Hawk	Shore Lark
Sparrow Hawk	Rose-breasted Grosbeak
White-headed Eagle	Bobolink
Great Horned Owl	Meadow Lark
Snowy Owl	Bluejay
Red - headed Woodpecker	Ruffed Grouse
Golden-winged Woodpecker	Great Blue Heron
Barn-swallow	Bittern
Whip-poor-will	Wilson's Snipe
Night Hawk	Long-billed Curlew
Belted Kingfisher	Purple Gallinule
Kingbird	Canada Goose
Woodthrush	Wood Duck
Catbird	Hooded Merganser
White-bellied Nuthatch	Double-crested Cormorant
Brown Creeper	Arctic Tern
Bohemian Chatterer	Great Northern Diver
Great Northern Shrike	Stormy Petrel
	Arctic Puffin
	Black Guillemot

But badly as they were presented, the pictures were yet information, and were entered in his memory as lasting accessions to his store of truth about the Wild Things.

Of course, he already knew some few birds whose names are familiar to every schoolboy: the Robin, Bluebird, Kingbird, Wild Canary, Woodpecker, Barn-swallow, Wren, Chickadee, Wild Pigeon, Humming-bird, Pewee, so that his list was steadily increased.

V

The Collarless Stranger

Oh, sympathy! the noblest gift of God to man. The greatest bond there is twixt man and man.
The strongest link in any friendship chain.
The single lasting hold in kinship's claim.

The only incorrosive strand in marriage bonds.
The blazing light where genius lights her lamp.
The ten times noble base of noblest love.
More deep than love—more strong than hate—the biggest thing in all the universe—the law of laws.
Grant but this greatest gift of God to man—this single link concatenating grant, and all the rest are worthless or comprised.

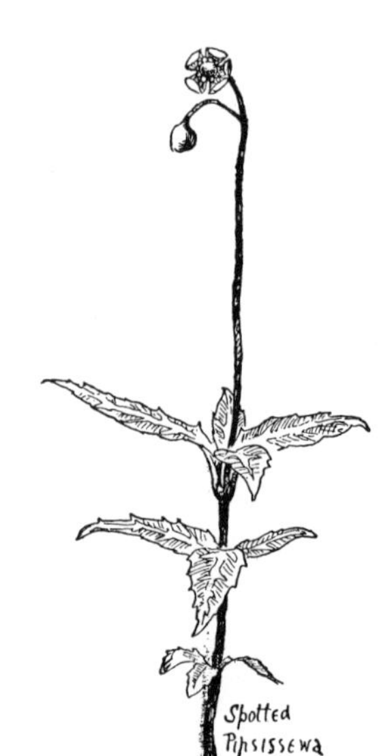

EACH year the ancient springtime madness came more strongly on Yan. Each year he was less inclined to resist it, and one glorious day of late April in its twelfth return he had wandered northward along to a little wood a couple of miles from the town. It was full of unnamed flowers and voices and mysteries. Every tree and thicket had a voice—a long ditch full of water had many that called to him. "*Peep-peep-peep,*" they seemed to say in invitation for him to come and see. He crawled again and again to the ditch and watched and waited. The loud whistle would sound only a few rods away, "*Peep-peep-peep,*" but ceased at each spot when he came near—sometimes before him, sometimes behind, but never where he was. He searched through a small pool with his hands, sifted out sticks and leaves, but found nothing else. A farmer going by told him it was only a "spring Peeper," whatever that was, "some kind of a critter in the water."

Under a log not far away Yan found a little Lizard that tumbled out of sight into a hole. It was the only living thing there, so he decided that the "Peeper" must be a "Whistling Lizard." But he was determined to see them when they were calling. How was it that the ponds all around should be full of them calling to him and playing hide and seek and yet defying his most careful search? The voices ceased as soon as he came near, to be gradually renewed in the pools he had left. His presence was a husher. He lay for a long time watching a pool, but none of the voices began again in range of his eye. At length, after realizing that they were avoiding him, he crawled to a very noisy pond without showing himself, and nearer and yet nearer until he was within three feet of a loud peeper in the floating grass. He located the spot within a few inches and yet could see nothing. He was utterly baffled, and lay there puzzling over it, when suddenly all the near Peepers stopped, and Yan was startled by a footfall; and looking around, he saw a man within a few feet, watching him.

Yan reddened—a stranger was always an enemy; he had a natural aversion to all such, and stared awkwardly as though caught in crime.

The man, a curious looking middle-aged person, was in shabby clothes and wore no collar. He had a tin box strapped on his bent shoulders, and in his hands was a long-handled net. His features, smothered in a grizzly beard, were very prominent and rugged. They gave evidence of intellectual force, with some severity, but his gray-blue eyes had a kindly look.

He had on a common, unbecoming, hard felt hat, and when he raised it to admit the pleasant breeze Yan saw that the wearer had hair like his own—a coarse, paleolithic mane, piled on his rugged brow, like a mass of seaweed lodged on some storm-beaten rock.

"F'what are ye fynding, my lad?" said he in tones whose gentleness was in no way obscured by a strong Scottish tang.

Still resenting somewhat the stranger's presence, Yan said:

"I'm not finding anything; I am only trying to see what that Whistling Lizard is like."

The stranger's eyes twinkled. "Forty years ago Ah was laying by a pool just as Ah seen ye this morning, looking and trying hard to read the riddle of the spring Peeper. Ah lay there all day, aye, and mony anither day, yes, it was nigh onto three years before Ah found it oot. Ah'll be glad to save ye seeking as long as Ah did, if that's yer mind. Ah'll show ye the Peeper."

Then he raked carefully among the leaves near the ditch, and soon captured a tiny Frog, less than an inch long.

"Ther's your Whistling Lizard: he no a Lizard at all, but a Froggie. Book men call him *Hyla pickeringii*, an' a gude Scotchman he'd make, for ye see the St. Andrew's cross on his wee back. Ye see the whistling ones in the water put on'y their beaks oot an' is hard to see. Then they sinks to the bottom when ye come near. But you tak this'n home and treat him well and ye'll see him blow out his throat as big as himsel' an' whistle like a steam engine."

Yan thawed out now. He told about the Lizard he had seen.

"That wasna a Lizard; Ah niver see thim aboot here. It must a been a two-striped *Spelerpes*. A *Spelerpes* is nigh kin to a Frog—a kind of dry-land tadpole, while a Lizard is only a Snake with legs."

This was light from heaven. All Yan's distrust

was gone. He warmed to the stranger. He plied him with questions; he told of his getting the Bird Book. Oh, how the stranger did snort at "that driveling trash." Yan talked of his perplexities. He got a full hearing and intelligent answers. His mystery of the black ground-bird with a brown mate was resolved into the Common Towhee. The unknown wonderful voice in the spring morning, sending out its "*cluck, cluck, cluck, clucker,*" in the distant woods; the large gray Woodpecker that bored in some high stub and flew in a blaze of gold, and the wonderful spotted bird with red head and yellow wings and tail in the taxidermist's window, were all resolved into one and the same—the Flicker or Golden-winged Woodpecker. The Hang-nest and the Oriole became one. The unknown poisonous-looking blue Hornet, that sat on the mud with palpitating body, and the strange, invisible thing that made the mud-nests inside old outbuildings and crammed them with crippled Spiders, were both identified as the Mud-wasp or *Pelopæus*.

Vanessa antiopa

A black Butterfly flew over, and Yan learned that it was a Camberwell Beauty, or, scientifically, a *Vanessa antiopa*, and that this one must have hibernated to be seen so early in the spring, and yet more, that this beautiful creature was the glorified spirit of the common brown and black spiney Caterpillar.

The Wild Pigeons were flying high above them in great flocks as they sat there, and Yan learned of their great nesting places in the far South, and of their wonderful but exact migrations without regard to anything but food; their northward migration to gather the winged nuts of the Slippery Elm in Canada; their August flight to the rice-fields of Carolina; their Mississippi Valley pilgrimage when the acorns and beech-mast were falling ripe

What a rich, full morning that was. Everything seemed to turn up for them. As they walked over a piney hill, two large birds sprang from the ground and whirred through the trees.

"Ruffed Grouse or 'patridge," as the farmers call them. There's a pair lives nigh aboots here. They come on this bank for the Wintergreen berries."

And Yan was quick to pull and taste them. He filled his pockets with the aromatic plant—berries and all—and chewed it as he went. While they walked, a faint, far drum-thump fell on their ears. "What's that?" he exclaimed, ever on the alert.

The stranger listened and said:

"That's the bird ye ha' just seen; that's the Cock Partridge drumming for his mate."

The Pewee of his early memories became the Phœbe of books. That day his brookside singer became the Song-sparrow; the brown triller, the Veery Thrush. The Trilliums, white and red, the Dogtooth Violet, the Spring-beauty, the Trailing Arbutus—all for the first time got names and became real friends, instead of elusive and beautiful, but depressing mysteries.

Flowering Dogwood

The stranger warmed, too, and his rugged features glowed; he saw in Yan one minded like himself, tormented with the knowledge-hunger, as in youth he himself had been; and now it was a priceless privilege to save the boy some of what he had suffered. His gratitude to Yan grew fervid, and Yan—he took in every word; nothing that he heard was forgotten. He was in a dream, for he had found at last the greatest thing on earth—sympathy—broad, intelligent, comprehensive sympathy.

That spring morning was ever after like a new epoch in Yan's mind—not his memory, that was a thing of the past—but in his mind, his living present.

And the strongest, realest thing in it all was, not the rugged stranger with his kind ways, not the new birds and plants, but the smell of the Wintergreen.

Smell's appeal to the memory is far better, stronger, more real than that of any other sense. The Indians know this; many of them, in time, find out the smell that conjures up their happiest hours, and keep it by them in the medicine bag. It is very real and dear to them—that handful of Pine needles, that lump of Rat-musk, or that piece of Spruce gum. It adds the crown of happy memory to their reveries.

And yet this belief is one of the first attacked by silly White-men, who profess to enlighten the Redman's darkness. They, in their ignorance, denounce it as absurd, while men of science know its simple truth.

Yan did not know that he had stumbled on a secret of the Indian medicine bag. But ever afterward that wonderful day was called back to him, conjured up by his "medicine," this simple, natural magic, the smell of the Wintergreen.

Trailing Arbutus

He appreciated that morning more than he could tell, and yet he did a characteristic foolish thing, that put him in a wrong light and left him so in the

stranger's mind.

It was past noon. They had long lingered; the stranger spoke of the many things he had at home; then at length said he must be going. "Weel, good-by, laddie; Ah hope Ah'll see you again." He held out his hand. Yan shook it warmly; but he was dazed with thinking and with reaction; his diffidence and timidity were strong; he never rose to the stranger's veiled offer. He let him go without even learning his name or address.

When it was too late, Yan awoke to his blunder. He haunted all those woods in hopes of chancing on him there again, but he never did.

VI

Glenyan

OH! what a song the Wild Geese sang that year! How their trumpet clang went thrilling in his heart, to smite there new and hidden chords that stirred and sang response. Was there ever a nobler bird than that great black-necked Swan, that sings not at his death, but in his flood of life, a song of home and of peace—of stirring deeds and hunting in far-off climes—of hungerings and food, and raging thirsts to meet with cooling drink. A song of wind and marching, a song of bursting green and grinding ice—of Arctic secrets and of hidden ways. A song of a long black marsh, a low red sky, and a sun that never sets.

An Indian jailed for theft bore bravely through the winter, but when the springtime brought the Gander-clang in the black night sky, he started, fell, and had gone to his last, long, hunting home.

Who can tell why Jericho should fall at the trumpet blast?

Who can read or measure the power of the Honker-song?

Oh, what a song the Wild Geese sang that year! And yet, was it a new song? No, the old, old song, but Yan heard it with new ears. He was learning to read its message. He wandered on their

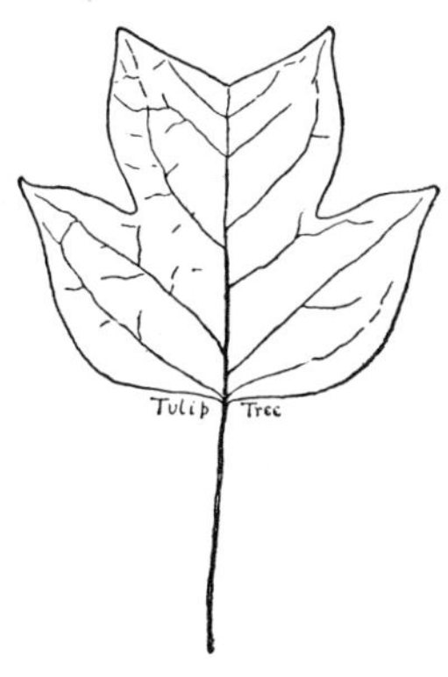

trailless track, as often as he could, northward, ever northward, up the river from the town, and up, seeking the loneliest ways and days. The river turned to the east, but a small stream ran into it from the north: up that Yan went through thickening woods and walls that neared each other, on and up until the walls closed to a crack, then widened out into a little dale that was still full of original forest trees. Hemlock, Pine, Birch and Elm of the largest size abounded and spread over the clear brook a continuous shade. Fox vines trailed in the open places, the rarest wild-flowers flourished, Red-squirrels chattered from the trees. In the mud along the brook-side were tracks of Coon and Mink and other strange fourfoots. And in the trees overhead, the Veery, the Hermit-thrush, or even a Woodthrush sang his sweetly solemn strain, in that golden twilight of the midday forest. Yan did not know them all by name as yet, but he felt their vague charm and mystery. It seemed such a far and lonely place, so unspoiled by man, that Yan persuaded himself that surely he was the first human being to stand there, that it was his by right of discovery, and so he claimed it and named it after its discoverer—Glenyan.

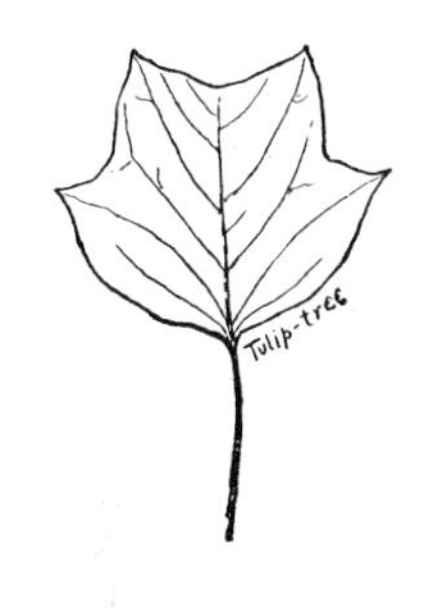

This place became the central thought in his life. He went there at all opportunities, but never dared to tell any one of his discovery. He longed for a confidant sometimes, he hankered to meet the stranger and take him there, and still he feared that the secret would get out. This was his little kingdom; the Wild Geese had brought him here, as the Seagulls had brought Columbus to a new world—where he could lead, for brief spells, the woodland life that was his ideal. He was tender enough to weep over the downfall of a lot of fine Elm trees in town, when their field was sold for building purposes, and he used to suffer a sort of hungry regret when old settlers told how plentiful the Deer used to be. But now he had a relief from these sorrows, for surely there was one place where the great trees should stand and grow as in the bright bygone; where the Coon, the Mink and the Partridge should live and flourish forever. No, indeed, no one else should know of it, for if the secret got out, at least hosts of visitors would come and Glenyan be defiled. No, better that the secret should "die with him," he said. What that meant he did not really know, but he had read the phrase somewhere and he liked the sound of it. Possibly he would reveal it on his deathbed.

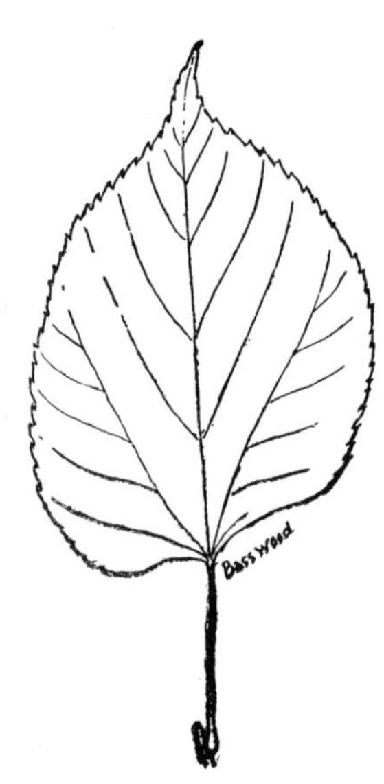

Yes, that was the proper thing, and he pictured a harrowing scene of weeping relatives around, himself as central figure, all ceasing their wailing and gasping with wonder as he made known the mighty secret of his life—delicious! it was almost worth dying for.

So he kept the place to himself and loved it more and more. He would look out through the thick Hemlock tops, the blots of Basswood green or the criss-cross Butternut leafage and say: "My own, my own." Or down by some pool in the limpid stream he would sit and watch the arrowy Shiners and say: "You are mine, all; you are mine. You shall never be harmed or driven away."

A spring came from the hillside by a green lawn, and here Yan would eat his sandwiches varied with nuts and berries that he did not like, but ate only because he was a wildman, and would look lovingly up the shady brookland stretches and down to the narrow entrance of the glen, and say and think and feel, "This is mine, my own, my very own."

VII

The Shanty

HE had none but the poorest of tools, but he set about building a shanty. He was not a resourceful boy. His effort to win the book had been an unusual one for him, as his instincts were not at all commercial. When that matter came to the knowledge of the Home Government, he was rebuked for doing "work unworthy of a gentleman's son" and forbidden under frightful penalties "ever again to resort to such degrading ways of raising money."

They gave him no money, so he was penniless. Most boys would have possessed themselves somehow of a good axe and spade. He had neither. An old plane blade, fastened to a stick with nails, was all the axe and spade he had, yet with this he set to work and offset its poorness as a tool by dogged persistency. First, he selected the quietest spot near the spring—a bank hidden by a mass of foliage. He knew no special reason for hiding it, beyond the love of secrecy. He had read in some of his books "how the wily scouts led the way through a pathless jungle, pulled aside a bough and there revealed a comfortable dwelling that none without the secret could possibly have discovered," so it seemed very proper to make it a complete mystery—a sort of secret panel in the enchanted castle—and so picture himself as the wily scout leading his wondering companions to the shanty, though, of course, he had not made up his mind to reveal his secret to any one. He often wished he could have the advantage of Rad's strong arms and efficacious tools; but the workshop incident was only one of many that taught him to leave his brother out of all calculation.

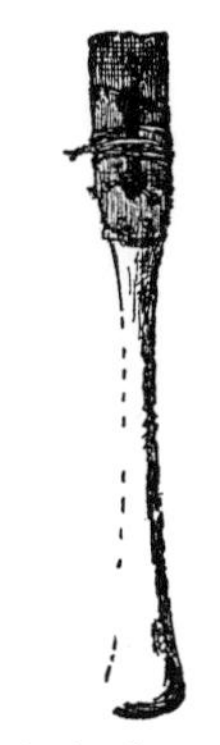

Yan's Shovel

Mother Earth is the best guardian of a secret, and Yan with his crude spade began by digging a hole in the bank. The hard blue clay made the work slow, but two holidays spent in steady labour resulted in a hole seven feet wide and about four feet into the bank.

In this he set about building the shanty. Logs seven or eight feet long must be got to the place—at least twenty-five or thirty would be needed, and how to cut and handle them with his poor axe was a question. Somehow, he never looked for a better axe. The half-formed notion that the Indians had no better was sufficient support, and he struggled away bravely, using whatever ready sized material he could find. Each piece as he brought it was put into place. Some boys would have gathered the logs first and built it all at once, but that was nct Yan's way; he was too eager to see the walls rise. He had painfully and slowly gathered logs enough to raise the walls three rounds, when the question of a door occurred to him. This, of course, could not be cut through the logs in the ordinary way; that required the best of tools. So he lifted out all the front logs except the lowest, replacing them at the ends with stones and blocks to sustain the sides. This gave him the sudden gain of two logs, and helped the rest of the walls that much. The shanty was now about three feet high, and no two logs in it were alike: some were much too long, most were crooked and some were half rotten, for the simple reason that these were the only ones he could cut. He had exhausted the logs in the neighbourhood and was forced to go farther. Now he remembered seeing one that might do, half a mile away on the home trail (they were always "trails"; he never called them "roads" or "paths"). He went after this, and to his great surprise and delight found that it was one of a dozen old cedar posts that had been cut long before and thrown aside as culls, or worthless. He could carry only one at a time, so that to bring each one meant a journey of a mile, and the post got woefully heavy each time before that mile was over. To get those twelve logs he had twelve miles to walk. It took several Saturdays, but he stuck doggedly to it. Twelve good logs completed his shanty, making it five feet high and leaving three logs over for rafters. These he laid flat across, dividing the spaces equally. Over them he laid plenty of small sticks and branches till it was thickly covered. Then he went down to a rank, grassy meadow and, with his knife, cut hay for a couple of hours. This was spread thickly on the roof, to be covered with strips of Elm bark; then on top of all he threw the clay dug from the bank, piling it well back, stamping on it, and working it down at the edges. Finally, he threw rubbish and leaves over it, so that it was confused with the general tangle.

Thus the roof was finished, but the whole of the front was open. He dreaded the search for more logs, so tried a new plan. He found, first, some sticks about six feet long and two or three inches through. Not having an axe to sharpen and drive them, he dug pairs of holes a foot deep, one at each end and another pair near the middle of the front ground log.

The Shanty: front-plan

Into each of these he put a pair of upright sticks, leading up to the eave log, one inside and one outside of it, then packed the earth around them in the holes. Next, he went to the brook-side and cut a number of long green willow switches about half an inch thick at the butt. These switches he twisted around the top of each pair of stakes in a figure 8, placing them to hold the stake tight against the bottom and top logs at the front.

Down by the spring he now dug a hole and worked water and clay together into mortar, then with a trowel cut out of a shingle, and mortar carried in an old bucket, he built a wall within the stakes, using sticks laid along the outside and stones set in mud till the front was closed up, except a small hole for a window and a large hole for a door.

Now he set about finishing the inside. He gathered

moss in the woods and stuffed all the chinks in the upper parts, and those next the ground he filled with stones and earth. Thus the shanty was finished; but it lacked a door.

The opening was four feet high and two feet wide, so in the woodshed at home he cut three boards, each eight inches wide and four feet high, but he left at each end of one a long point. Doing this at home gave him the advantage of a saw. Then with these and two shorter boards, each two feet long and six inches wide, he sneaked out to Glenyan, and there, with some nails and a stone for a hammer, he fastened them together into a door. In the ground log he pecked a hole big enough to receive one of the points and made a corresponding hole in the under side of the top log. Then, prying up the eave log, he put the door in place, let the eave log down again, and the door was hung. A string to it made an outside fastening when it was twisted around a projecting snag in the wall, and a peg thrust into a hole within made an inside fastener. Some logs, with fir boughs and dried grass, formed a bunk within. This left only the window, and for lack of better cover he fastened over it a piece of muslin brought from home. But finding its dull white a jarring note, he gathered a quart of butternuts, and watching his chance at home, he boiled the cotton in water with the nuts and so reduced it to a satisfactory yellowish brown.

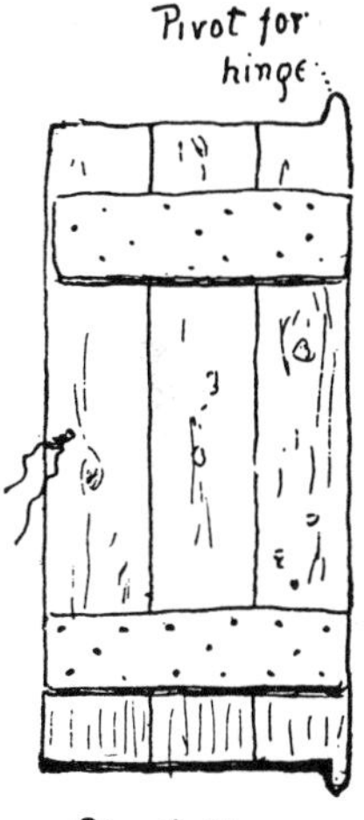

Shanty Door

His final task was to remove all appearance of disturbance and to fully hide the shanty in brush and trailing vines. Thus, after weeks of labour, his woodland home was finished. It was only five feet high inside, six feet long and six feet wide—dirty and uncomfortable—but what a happiness it was to have it.

Here for the first time in his life he began to realize something of the pleasure of single-handed achievement in the line of a great ambition.

VIII

Beginnings of Woodlore

DURING this time Yan had so concentrated all his powers on the shanty that he had scarcely noticed the birds and wild things. Such was his temperament—one idea only, and that with all his strength.

His heart was more and more in his kingdom now; he longed to come and live here. But he only dared to dream that some day he might be allowed to pass a night in the shanty. This was where he would lead his ideal life—the life of an Indian with all that is bad and cruel left out. Here he would show men how to live without cutting down all the trees, spoiling all the streams, and killing every living thing. He would learn how to get the fullest pleasure out of the woods himself and then teach others how to do the same. Though the birds and Fourfoots fascinated him, he would not have hesitated to shoot one had he been able; but to see a tree cut down always caused him great distress. Possibly he realized that the bird might be quickly replaced, but the tree, never.

To carry out his plan he must work hard at school, for books had much that he needed. Perhaps some day he might get a chance to see Audubon's drawings, and so have all his bird worries settled by a single book.

That summer a new boy at school added to Yan's savage equipment. This boy was neither good nor bright; he was a dunce, and had been expelled from a boarding school for misconduct, but he had a number of schoolboy accomplishments that gave him a tinge of passing glory. He could tie a lot of curious knots in a string. He could make a wonderful birdy warble, and he spoke a language that he called Tutnee. Yan was interested in all, but especially the last. He teased and bribed till he was admitted to the secret. It consisted in spelling every word, leaving the five vowels as they are, but doubling each consonant and putting a "u" between. Thus "b" became "bub," "d" "dud," "m" "mum," and so forth, except that "c" was "suk," "h" "hash," "x" "zux," and "w" "wak."

The sample given by the new boy, "sus-hash-u-tut u-pup yak-o-u-rur mum-o-u-tut-hash," was said to be a mode of enjoining silence.

This language was "awful useful," the new boy said, to keep the other fellows from knowing what you were saying, which it certainly did. Yan practised hard at it and within a few weeks was an adept. He could handle the uncouth sentences better than his teacher, and he was singularly successful in throwing in accents and guttural tones that imparted a delightfully savage flavour, and he rejoiced in jabbering away to the new boy in the presence of others so that he might bask in the mystified look on the faces of those who were not skilled in the tongue of the Tutnees.

He made himself a bow and arrows. They were badly made and he could hit nothing with them, but he felt so like an Indian when he drew the arrow to its head, that it was another pleasure.

He made a number of arrows with hoop-iron heads: these he could file at home in the woodshed. The heads were jagged and barbed and double-barbed. These arrows were frightful-looking things. They seemed positively devilish in their ferocity, and were proportionately gratifying. These he called his "war arrows," and would send one into a tree and watch it shiver, then grunt "Ugh, heap good," and rejoice in the squirming of the imaginary foe he had pierced.

He found a piece of sheepskin and made of it a pair of very poor moccasins. He ground an old castaway putty knife into a scalping knife; the notch in it for breaking glass was an annoying defect until he remembered that some Indians decorate their weapons with a notch for each enemy it has killed, and this, therefore, might do duty as a kill-tally. He made a sheath for the knife out of scraps of leather left off the moccasins. Some water-colours, acquired by a school swap, and a bit of broken mirror held in a split stick, were necessary parts of his Indian toilet. His face during the process of make-up was always a battle-ground between the horriblest Indian scowl and a grin of delight at his success in diabolizing his visage with the paints. Then with painted face and a feather in his hair he would proudly range the woods in his little kingdom and store up every scrap of woodlore he could find, invent or learn from his schoolmates.

War Arrow

Odd things that he found in the woods he would bring to his shanty: curled sticks, feathers, bones, skulls, fungus, shells, an old cowhorn—things that interested him, he did not know why. He made Indian necklaces of the shells, strung together alternately with the backbone of a fish. He let his hair grow as long as possible, employing various stratagems, even the unpalatable one of combing it to avoid the monthly trim of the maternal scissors. He lay for hours with the sun beating on his face to correct his colour to standard, and the only semblance of personal vanity that he ever had was pleasure in hearing disparaging remarks about the darkness of his complexion. He tried to do everything as an Indian would do it, striking Indian poses, walking carefully with his toes turned in, breaking off twigs to mark a place, guessing at the time by the sun, and grunting "Ugh" or "Wagh" when anything surprised him. Disparaging remarks about White-men, delivered in supposed Indian dialect, were an important part of his pastime. "Ugh, White-men heap no good" and "Wagh, paleface—pale fool in woods," were among his favourites.

Yan's Necklace

He was much influenced by phrases that caught his ear. "The brown sinewy arm of the Indian," was one of them. It discovered to him that his own arms were white as milk. There was, however, a simple remedy. He rolled up his sleeves to the shoulder and exposed them to the full glare of the sun. Then later, under the spell of the familiar phrase, "The warrior was naked to the waist," he went a step further—he determined to be brown to the waist—so discarded his shirt during the whole of one holiday. He always went to extremes. He remembered now that certain Indians put their young warriors through an initiation called the Sun-dance, so he danced naked round the fire in the blazing sun and sat around naked all one day.

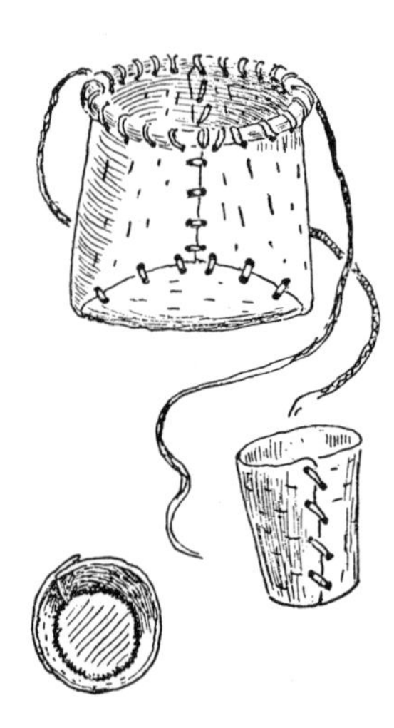

He noticed a general warmness before evening, but it was at night that he really felt the punishment of his indiscretion. He was in a burning heat. He scarcely slept all night. Next day he was worse, and his arm and shoulder were blistered. He bore it bravely, fearing only that the Home Government might find it out, in which case he would have fared worse. He had read that the Indians grease the skin for sunburn, so he went to the bathroom and there used goose grease for lack of Buffalo fat. This did give some relief, and in a few days he was better and had the satisfaction of peeling the dead skin from his shoulders and arms.

Yan made a number of vessels out of Birch bark, stitching the edges with root fibers, filling the bottom with a round wooden disc, and cementing the joints with pine gum so that they would hold water.

In the distant river he caught some Catfish and brought them home—that is, to his shanty. There

Yan's toilet

The Coon track

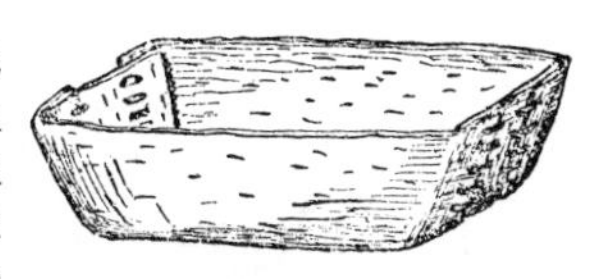

he made a fire and broiled them—very badly—but he ate them as a great delicacy. The sharp bone in each of their side fins he saved, bored a hole through its thick end, smoothed it, and so had needles to stitch his Birch bark. He kept them in a bark box with some lumps of resin, along with some bark fiber, an Indian flint arrow-head given him by a schoolmate, and the claws of a large Owl, found in the garbage heap back of the taxidermist's shop.

One day on the ash heap in their own yard in town he saw a new, strange bird. He was always seeing new birds, but this was of unusual interest. He drew its picture as it tamely fed near him. A dull, ashy gray, with bronzy yellow spots on crown and rump, and white bars on its wings. His "Birds of Canada" gave no light; he searched through all the books he could find, but found no clew to its name. It was years afterward before he learned that this was the young male Pine Grosbeak.

Another day, under the bushes not far from his shanty, he found a small Hawk lying dead. He clutched it as a wonderful prize, spent an hour in looking at its toes, its beak, its wings, its every feather; then he set to work to make a drawing of it. A very bad drawing it proved, although it was the labour of days, and the bird was crawling with maggots before he had finished. But every feather and every spot was faithfully copied, was duly set down on paper. One of his friends said it was a Chicken-hawk. That name stuck in Yan's memory. Thenceforth the Chicken-hawk and its every marking were familiar to him. Even in after years, when he had learned that this must have been a young "Sharp-shin," the name "Chicken-hawk" was always readier on his lips.

But he met with another and a different Hawk soon afterward. This one was alive and flitting about in the branches of a tree over his head. It was very small—less than a foot in length. Its beak was very short, its legs, wings and tail long; its head was bluish and its back coppery red; on the tail was a broad, black crossbar. As the bird flew about and balanced on the boughs, it pumped its tail. This told him it was a Hawk, and the colours he remembered were those of the male Sparrow-hawk, for here his bird book helped with its rude travesty of "Wilson's" drawing of this bird. Yet two other birds he saw close at hand and drew partly from memory. The drawings were like this, and from the picture

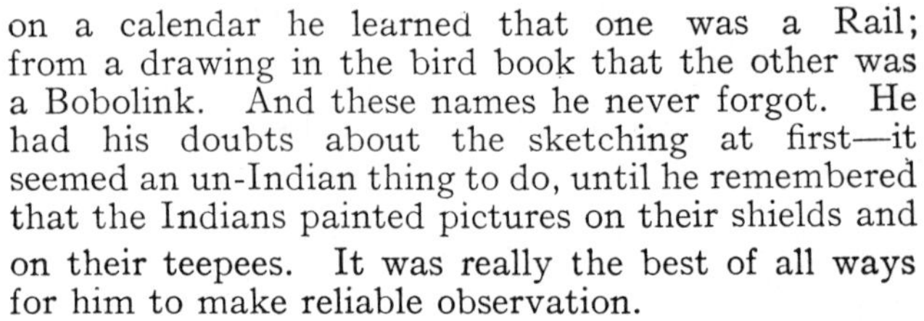

on a calendar he learned that one was a Rail; from a drawing in the bird book that the other was a Bobolink. And these names he never forgot. He had his doubts about the sketching at first—it seemed an un-Indian thing to do, until he remembered that the Indians painted pictures on their shields and on their teepees. It was really the best of all ways for him to make reliable observation.

The bookseller of the town had some new books in his window about this time. One, a marvellous work called "Poisonous Plants," Yan was eager to see. It was exposed in the window for a time. Two of the large plates were visible from the street; one was Henbane, the other Stramonium. Yan gazed at them as often as he could. In a week they were gone; but the names and looks were forever engraved on his memory. Had he made bold to go in and ask permission to see the work, his memory would have seized most of it in an hour.

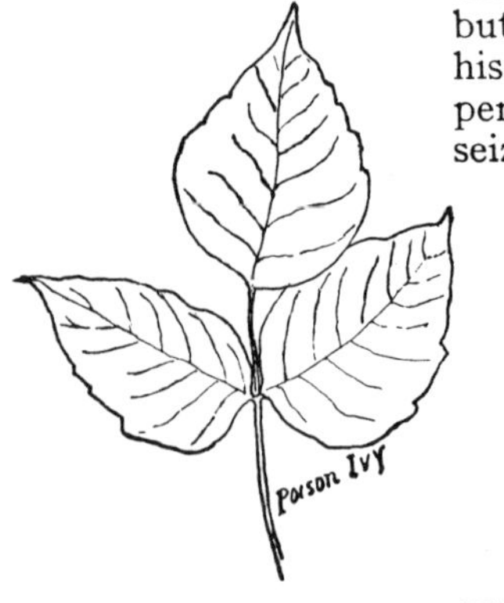

IX

Tracks

IN the wet sand down by the edge of the brook he one day found some curious markings—evidently tracks. Yan pored over them, then made a life-size drawing of one. He shrewdly suspected it to be the track of a Coon—nothing was too good or wild or rare for his valley. As soon as he could, he showed the track to the stableman whose dog was said to have killed a Coon once, and hence the man must be an authority on the subject.

"Is that a Coon track?" asked Yan timidly.

"How do I know?" said the man roughly, and went on with his work. But a stranger standing near, a curious person with shabby clothes, and a new silk hat on the back of his head, said, "Let me see it." Yan showed it.

"Is it natural size?"

"Yes, sir."

"Yep, that's a Coon track, all right. You look at all the big trees near about whar you saw that; then when you find one with a hole in it, you look on the bark and you will find some Coon hars. Then you will know you've got a Coon tree."

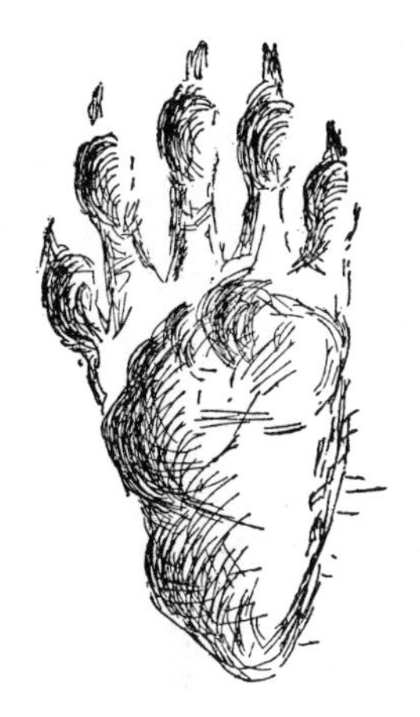

Coon track ..
3½ inches long

Yan took the earliest chance. He sought and found a great Basswood with some gray hairs caught in the bark. He took them home with him, not sure what kind they were. He sought the stranger, but he was gone, and no one knew him.

How to identify the hairs was a question; but he remembered a friend who had a Coon-skin carriage robe. A few hairs of these were compared with those from the tree and left no doubt that the climber was a Coon. Thus Yan got the beginning of the idea that the very hairs of each, as well as its tracks, are different. He learned, also, how wise it is to draw everything that he wished to observe or describe. It was accident, or instinct on his part, but he had fallen on a sound principle; there is nothing like a sketch to collect and convey accurate information of form—there is no better developer of true observation.

One day he noticed a common plant like an umbrella. He dug it up by the root, and at the lower end he found a long white bulb. He tasted this. It was much like a cucumber. He looked up "Gray's School Botany," and in the index saw the name, Indian Cucumber. The description seemed to tally, as far as he could follow its technical terms, though like all such, without a drawing it was far from satisfactory. So he added the Indian Cucumber to his woodlore.

On another occasion he chewed the leaves of a strange plant because he had heard that that was the first test applied by the Indians. He soon began to have awful pains in his stomach. He hurried home in agony. His mother gave him mustard and water till he vomited, then she boxed his ears. His father came in during the process and ably supplemented the punishment. He was then and there ordered to abstain forever from the woods. Of course, he did not. He merely became more cautious about it all, and enjoyed his shanty with the added zest of secret sin.

Indian Cucumber

X

Biddy's Contribution

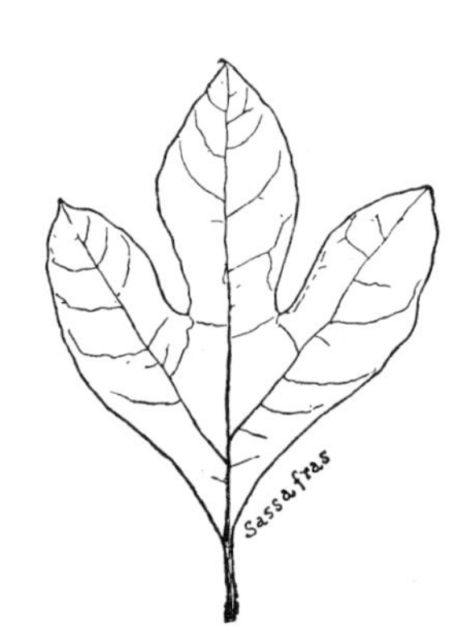

AN Irish-Canadian servant girl from Sanger now became a member of their household. Her grandmother was an herb-doctor in great repute. She had frequently been denounced as a witch, although in good standing as a Catholic. This girl had picked up some herb-lore, and one day when all the family were visiting the cemetery she darted into various copses and produced plants which she named, together with the complaint that her grandmother used them for.

"Sassafras, that makes tea for skin disease; Ginseng, that's good to sell; Bloodroot for the blood in springtime; Goldthread, that cures sore mouths; Pipsissewa for chills and fever; White-man's Foot, that springs up wherever a White-man treads; Indian cup, that grows where an Indian dies; Dandelion roots for coffee; Catnip tea for a cold; Lavender tea for drinking at meals; Injun Tobacco to mix with boughten tobacco; Hemlock bark to dye pink; Goldthread to dye yellow, and Butternut rinds for greenish."

All of these were passing trifles to the others, but to Yan they were the very breath of life, and he treasured up all of these things in his memory. Biddy's information was not unmixed with error and superstition:

"Hold Daddy Longlegs by one leg and say, 'tell me where the cows are,' and he will point just right under another leg, and onct he told me where to find my necklace when I lost it.

"Shoot the Swallows and the cows give bloody milk. That's the way old Sam White ruined his milk business—shooting Swallows.

"Lightning never strikes a barn where Swallows nest. Paw never rested easy after the new barn was built till the Swallows nested in it. He had it insured for a hundred dollars till the Swallows got round to look after it.

"When a Measuring-worm crawls on you, you are going to get a new suit of clothes. My brother-in-law says they walk over him every year in summer and sure enough, he gets a new suit. But they never does it in winter, cause he don't get new clothes then.

"Split a Crow's tongue and he will talk like a girl.

Granny knowed a man that had a brother back of Mara that got a young Crow and split his tongue an' he told Granny it was *just* like a girl talking—an' Granny told me!

"Soak a Horse-hair in rainwater and it will turn into a Snake. Ain't there lots uv Snakes around ponds where Horses drink? Well!

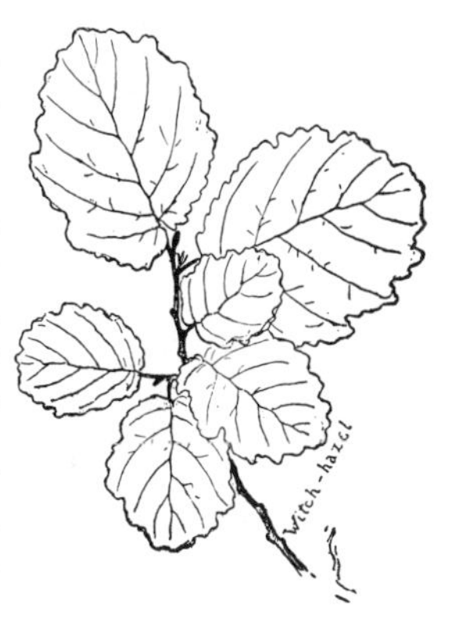

"Kill a Spider an' it will rain to-morrow. Now, that's worth knowin'. I mind one year when the Orangeman's picnic was comin', 12th of July, Maw made us catch twenty Spiders and we killed them all the day before, and law, how it did rain on the picnic! Mebbe we didn't laugh. Most of them hed to go home in boats, that's what our paper said. But next year they done the same thing on us for St. Patrick's Day, but Spiders is scarce on the 16th of March, an' it didn't rain so much as snow, so it was about a stand-off.

"Toads gives warts. You seen them McKenna twins—their hands is a sight with warts. Well, I seen them two boys playing with Toads like they was marbles. So! An' they might a-knowed what was comin'. Ain't every Toad just covered with warts as thick as he can stick?

"That there's Injun tobacco. The Injuns always use it, and Granny does, too, sometimes." (Yan made special note of this—he must get some and smoke it, if it was *Indian.*)

"A Witch-hazel wand will bob over a hidden spring and show where to dig. Denny Scully is awful good at it. He gets a dollar for showing where to sink a well, an' if they don't strike water it's because they didn't dig where he said, or spiled the charm some way or nuther, and hez to try over.

"Now, that's Dandelion. Its roots makes awful good coffee. Granny allers uses it. She says that it is healthier than store coffee, but Maw says she likes boughten things best, and the more they cost the better she likes them.

"Now, that's Ginseng. It has a terrible pretty flower in spring. There's tons and tons of it sent to China. Granny says the Chinese eats it, to make them cheerful, but they don't seem to eat enough.

"There's Slippery Elm. It's awfully good for loosening up a cold, if you drink the juice the bark's bin biled in. One spring Granny made a bucketful. She set it outside to cool, an' the pig he drunk it all

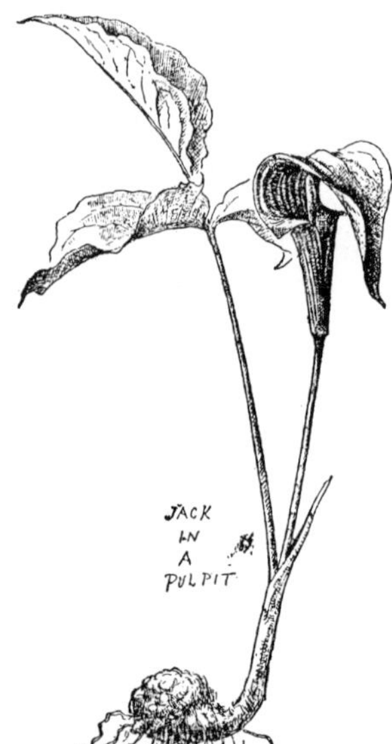

up, an' he must a had a cold, for it loosened him up so he dropped his back teeth. I seen them myself lying out there in the yard. Yes, I did.

"That's Wintergreen. Lots of boys I know chew that to make the girls like them. Lots of them gits a beau that way, too. I done it myself many's a time.

"Now, that is what some folks calls Injun Turnip, an' the children calls it Jack-in-a-Pulpit, but Granny calls it 'Sorry-plant,' cos she says when any one eats it it makes them feel sorry for the last fool thing they done. I'll put some in your Paw's coffee next time he licks yer and mebbe that'll make him quit. It just makes me sick to see ye gettin' licked fur every little thing ye can't help.

"A Snake's tongue is its sting. You put your foot on a Snake and see how he tries to sting you. An' his tail don't die till sundown. I seen that myself, onct, an' Granny says so, too, an' what Granny don't know ain't knowledge—it's only book-larnin'."

These were her superstitions, most of them more or less obviously absurd to Yan; but she had also a smattering of backwoods lore and Yan gleaned all he could.

She had so much of what he wanted to know that he had almost made up his mind to tell her where he went each Saturday when he had finished his work.

A week or two longer and she would have shared the great secret, but something took place to end their comradeship.

XI

Lung Balm

ONE day as this girl went with him through a little grove on the edge of the town, she stopped at a certain tree and said:

"If that ain't Black-cherry!"

"You mean Choke-cherry."

"No, Black-cherry. Choke-cherry ain't no good; but Black-cherry bark's awful good for lung com-

Striped Maple or Moosewood

plaint. Grandma always keeps it. I've been feeling a bit queer meself" [she was really as strong as an ox]. "Guess I'll git some." So she and Yan planned an expedition together. The boldness of it scared the boy. The girl helped herself to a hatchet in the tool box—the sacred tool box of his father.

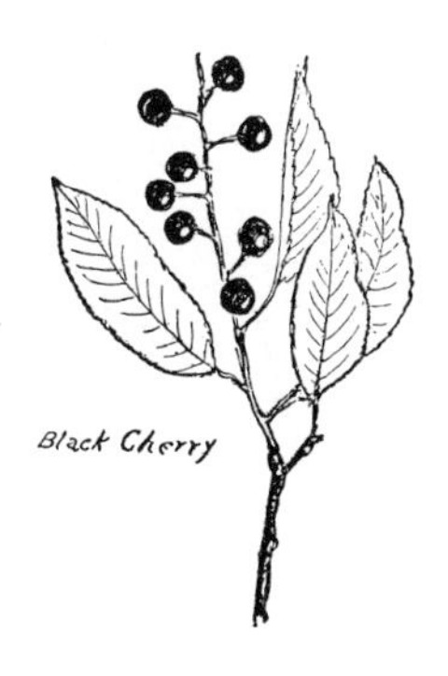
Black Cherry

Yan's mother saw her with it and demanded why she had it. With ready effrontery she said it was to hammer in the hook that held the clothesline, and proceeded to carry out the lie with a smiling face. That gave Yan a new lesson and not a good one. The hatchet was at once put back in the box, to be stolen more carefully later on.

Biddy announced that she was going to the grocery shop. She met Yan around the corner and they made for the lot. Utterly regardless of property rights, she showed Yan how to chip off the bark of the Black-cherry. "Don't chip off all around; that's bad luck—take it on'y from the sunny side." She filled a basket with the pieces and they returned home.

Here she filled a jar with bits of the inner layer, then, pouring water over it, let it stand for a week. The water was then changed to a dark brown stuff with a bitter taste and a sweet, aromatic smell. Biddy added whisky and some sugar to this and labelled it *Lung Balm*.

"It's terrible good," she said. "Granny always keeps it handy. It cures lots of people. Now there was Bud Ellis—the doctors just guv him up. They said he didn't have a single lung left, and he come around to Granny. He used to make fun of Granny; but now he wuz plumb scairt. At first Granny chased him away; then when she seen that he was awful sick, she got sorry and told him how to make Lung Balm. He was to make two gallons each time and bring it to her. Then she took and fixed it so it was one-half as much and give it back to him. Well, in six months if he wasn't all right."

Biddy now complained nightly of "feelin's" in her chest. These feelings could be controlled only by a glass or two of Lung Balm. Her condition must have been critical, for one night after several necessary doses of Balm her head seemed affected. She became abusive to the lady of the house and at the end of the month a less interesting help was in her place.

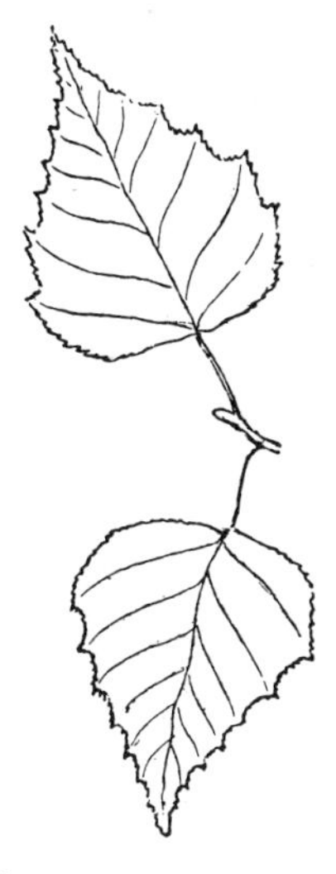
Aspen-leaved or Gray Birch

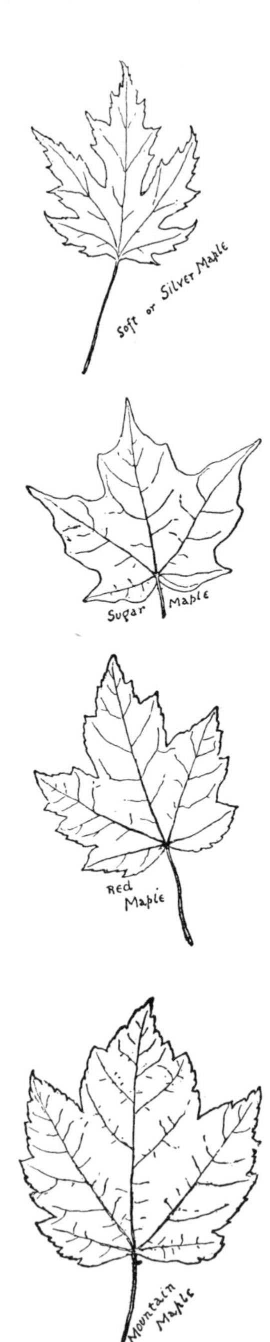

There were many lessons good and bad that Yan might have drawn from this; but the only one that he took in was that the Black-cherry bark is a wonderful remedy. The family doctor said that it really was so, and Yan treasured up this as a new and precious fragment of woodcraft.

Having once identified the tree, he was surprised to see that it was rather common, and was delighted to find it flourishing in his own Glenyan.

This made him set down on paper all the trees he knew, and he was surprised to find how few they were and how uncertain he was about them.

Maple—hard and soft.
Beach.
Elm—swamp and slippery.
Ironwood.
Birch—white and black.
Ash—white and black.
Pine.
Cedar.
Balsam.
Hemlock and Cherry.

He had heard that the Indians knew the name and properties of every tree and plant in the woods, and that was what he wished to be able to say of himself.

One day by the bank of the river he noticed a pile of empty shells of the fresh-water Mussel, or Clam. The shells were common enough, but why all together and marked in the same way? Around the pile on the mud were curious tracks and marks. There were so many that it was hard to find a perfect one, but when he did, remembering the Coon track, he drew a picture of it. It was too small to be the mark of his old acquaintance. He did not find any one to tell him what it was, but one day he saw a round, brown animal hunched up on the bank eating a clam. It dived into the water at his approach, but it reappeared swimming farther on. Then, when it dived again, Yan saw by its long thin tail that it was a Muskrat, like the stuffed one he had seen in the taxidermist's window

He soon learned that the more he studied those tracks the more different kinds he found. Many were rather mysterious, so he could only draw them and put them aside, hoping some day for light. One of the strangest and most puzzling turned out to be the trail of a Snapper, and another proved to be merely the track of a Common Crow that came to the water's edge to drink.

The curios that he gathered and stored in his shanty increased in number and in interest. The place became more and more part of himself. Its concealment bettered as the foliage grew around it again, and he gloried in its wild seclusion and mystery, and wandered through the woods with his bow and arrows, aiming harmless, deadly blows at snickering Red-squirrels—though doubtless he would have been as sorry as they had he really hit one.

Yan soon found out that he was not the only resident of the shanty. One day as he sat inside wondering why he had not made a fireplace, so that he could sit at an indoor fire, he saw a silent little creature flit along between two logs in the back wall. He remained still. A beautiful little Wood-mouse, for such it was, soon came out in plain view and sat up to look at Yan and wash its face. Yan reached out for his bow and arrow, but the Mouse was gone in a flash. He fitted a blunt arrow to the string, then waited, and when the Mouse returned he shot the arrow. It missed the Mouse, struck the log and bounded back into Yan's face, giving him a stinging blow on the cheek. And as Yan rolled around grunting and rubbing his cheek, he thought, "This is what I tried to do to the Woodmouse." Thenceforth, Yan made no attempt to harm the Mouse; indeed, he was willing to share his meals with it. In time they became well acquainted, and Yan found that not one, but a whole family, were sharing with him his shanty in the woods.

Biddy's remark about the Indian tobacco bore fruit. Yan was not a smoker, but now he felt he must learn. He gathered a lot of this tobacco, put it to dry, and set about making a pipe—a real Indian peace pipe. He had no red sandstone to make it of, but a soft red brick did very well. He first roughed out the general shape with his knife, and was trying to bore the bowl out with the same tool, when he remembered that in one of the school-readers was an account of the Indian method of drilling into stone with a bow-drill and wet sand. One of his schoolmates, the son of a woodworker, had seen his father use a bow-drill. This knowledge gave him new importance in Yan's eyes. Under his guidance a bow-drill was made, and used much and on many things till it was understood, and now it did real Indian service by

drilling the bowl and stem holes of the pipe.

He made a stem of an Elderberry shoot, punching out the pith at home with a long knitting-needle. Some white pigeon wing feathers trimmed small, and each tipped with a bit of pitch, were strung on a stout thread and fastened to the stem for a finishing touch; and he would sit by his campfire solemnly smoking—a few draws only, for he did not like it—then say, "Ugh, heap hungry," knock the ashes out, and proceed with whatever work he had on hand.

Thus he spent the bright Saturdays, hiding his accouterments each day in his shanty, washing the paint from his face in the brook, and replacing the hated paper collar that the pride and poverty of his family made a daily necessity, before returning home. He was a little dreamer, but oh! what happy dreams. Whatever childish sorrow he found at home he knew he could always come out here and forget and be happy as a king—be a real King in a Kingdom wholly after his heart, and all his very own.

White Ash

White Elm

XII

A Crisis

AT school he was a model boy except in one respect—he had strange, uncertain outbreaks of disrespect for his teachers. One day he amused himself by covering the blackboard with ridiculous caricatures of the principal, whose favourite he undoubtedly was. They were rather clever and proportionately galling. The principal set about an elaborate plan to discover who had done them. He assembled the whole school and began cross-examining one wretched dunce, thinking him the culprit. The lad denied it in a confused and guilty way; the principal was convinced of his guilt, and reached for his rawhide, while the condemned set up a howl. To the surprise of the assembly, Yan now spoke up, and in a tone of weary impatience said:

"Oh, let him alone. I did it."

His manner and the circumstances were such that every one laughed. The principal was nettled to fury. He forgot his manhood; he seized Yan by the collar. He was considered a timid boy; his face was white; his lips set. The principal beat him with the rawhide till the school cried "Shame," but he got no cry from Yan.

That night, on undressing for bed, his brother Rad saw the long black wales from head to foot, and an explanation was necessary. He was incapable of lying; his parents learned of his wickedness, and new and harsh punishments were added. Next day was Saturday. He cut his usual double or Saturday's share of wood for the house, and, bruised and smarting, set out for the one happy spot he knew. The shadow lifted from his spirit as he drew near. He was already forming a plan for adding a fireplace and chimney to his house. He followed the secret path he had made with aim to magnify its secrets. He crossed the open glade, was nearly at the shanty, when he heard voices—loud, coarse voices—*coming from his shanty.* He crawled up close. The door was open. There in his dear cabin were three tramps playing cards and drinking out of a bottle. On the ground beside them were his shell necklaces broken up to furnish poker chips. In a smouldering fire outside were the remains of his bow and arrows.

Poor Yan! His determination to be like an Indian under torture had sustained him in the teacher's cruel beating and in his home punishments, but this was too much. He fled to a far and quiet corner and there flung himself down and sobbed in grief and rage—he would have killed them if he could. After an hour or two he came trembling back to see the tramps finish their game and their liquor; then they defiled the shanty and left it in ruins.

The brightest thing in his life was gone—a King discrowned, dethroned. Feeling now every wale on his back and legs, he sullenly went home.

This was late in the summer. Autumn followed fast, with shortening days and chilly winds. Yan had no chance to see his glen, even had he greatly wished it. He became more studious; books were his pleasure now. He worked harder than ever, winning honour at school, but attracting no notice at the home, where piety reigned.

The teachers and some of the boys remarked that Yan was getting very thin and pale. Never very robust, he now looked like an invalid; but at home no note was taken of the change. His mother's thoughts were all concentrated on his scapegrace younger brother. For two years she had rarely spoken to Yan peaceably. There was a hungry place in his heart as he left the house unnoticed each morning and saw his graceless brother kissed and darlinged. At school their positions were reversed. Yan was the principal's pride. He had drawn no more caricatures, and the teacher flattered himself that that beating was what had saved the pale-faced head boy.

He grew thinner and heart-hungrier till near Christmas, when the breakdown came.

. . . .

"He is far gone in consumption," said the physician. "He cannot live over a month or two."

"He *must* live," sobbed the conscience-stricken mother. "He must live—O God, he must live."

All that suddenly awakened mother's love could do was done. The skilful physician did his best, but it was the mother that saved him. She watched over him night and day; she studied his wishes and comfort in every way. She prayed by his bedside, and often asked God to forgive her for her long neglect. It was Yan's first taste of mother-love. Why she had ignored him so long was unknown. She was simply erratic, but now she awoke to his brilliant gifts, his steady, earnest life, already purposeful.

XIII

The Lynx

As winter waned, Yan's strength returned. He was wise enough to use his new ascendency to get books. The public librarian, a man of broad culture who had fought his own fight, became interested in him, and helped him to many works that otherwise he would have missed.

"There in his dear cabin were three tramps"

"It surely was a Lynx"

"Wilson's Ornithology" and "Schoolcraft's Indians" were the most important. And they were sparkling streams in the thirst-parched land.

In March he was fast recovering. He could now take long walks; and one bright day of snow he set off with his brother's Dog. His steps bent hillward. The air was bright and bracing, he stepped with unexpected vigour, and he made for far Glenyan, without at first meaning to go there. But, drawn by the ancient attraction, he kept on. The secret path looked not so secret, now the leaves were off; but the Glen looked dearly familiar as he reached the wider stretch.

His eye fell on a large, peculiar track quite fresh in the snow. It was five inches across, big enough for a Bear track, but there were no signs of claws or toe pads. The steps were short and the tracks had not sunken as they would for an animal as heavy as a Bear.

As one end of each showed the indications of toes, he could see what way it went, and followed up the Glen. The dog sniffed at it uneasily, but showed no disposition to go ahead. Yan tramped up past the ruins of his shanty, now painfully visible since the leaves had fallen, and his heart ached at the sight. The trail led up the valley, and crossed the brook on a log, and Yan became convinced that he was on the track of a large Lynx. Though a splendid barker, Grip, the dog, was known to be a coward, and now he slunk behind the boy, sniffing at the great track and absolutely refusing to go ahead.

Yan was fascinated by the long rows of footprints, and when he came to a place where the creature had leaped ten or twelve feet without visible cause, he felt satisfied that he had found a Lynx, and the love of adventure prompted him to go on, although he had not even a stick in his hand or a knife in his pocket. He picked up the best club he could find—a dry branch two feet long and two inches through, and followed. The dog was now unwilling to go at all; he hung back, and had to be called at each hundred yards.

They were at last in the dense Hemlock woods at the upper end of the valley, when a peculiar sound like the call of a deep-voiced cat was heard.

Yow! Yow! Yowl!

Yan stood still. The dog, although a large and powerful retriever, whimpered, trembled and crawled up close.

The sound increased in volume. The yowling *meouw* came louder, louder and nearer, then suddenly clear and close, as though the creature had rounded a point and entered an opening. It was positively blood-curdling now. The dog could stand it no more; he turned and went as fast as he could for home, leaving Yan to his fate. There was no longer any question that it was a Lynx. Yan had felt nervous before and the abject flight of the dog reacted on him. He realized how defenseless he was, still weak from his illness, and he turned and went after the dog. At first he walked. But having given in to his fears, they increased; and as the yowling continued he finally ran his fastest. The sounds were left behind, but Yan never stopped until he had left the Glen and was once more in the open valley of the river. Here he found the valiant retriever trembling all over. Yan received him with a contemptuous kick, and, boylike, as soon as he could find some stones, he used them till Grip was driven home.

. . . .

Most lads have some sporting instinct, and his elder brother, though not of Yan's tastes, was not averse to going gunning when there was a prospect of sport.

Yan decided to reveal to Rad the secret of his glen. He had never been allowed to use a gun, but Rad had one, and Yan's vivid account of his adventure had the desired effect. His method was characteristic.

"Rad, would you go huntin' if there was lots to hunt?"

"Course I would."

"Well, I know a place not ten miles away where there are all kinds of wild animals—hundreds of them."

"Yes, you do, I don't think. Humph!"

"Yes, I do; and I'll tell you, if you will promise never to tell a soul."

"Ba-ah!"

"Well, I just had an adventure with a Lynx up there now, and if you will come with your gun we can get him."

Then Yan related all that had passed, and it lost nothing in his telling. His brother was impressed enough to set out under Yan's guidance on the following Saturday.

Yan hated to reveal to his sneering, earthy-minded brother all the joys and sorrows he had found in the Glen, but now that it seemed compulsory he found keen pleasure in playing the part of the crafty guide. With unnecessary caution he first led in a wrong direction, then trying, but failing, to extort another promise of secrecy, he turned at an angle, pointed to a distant tree, saying with all the meaning he could put into it: "Ten paces beyond that tree is a trail that shall lead us into the secret valley." After sundry other ceremonies of the sort, they were near the inway, when a man came walking through the bushes. On his shoulders he carried something. When he came close, Yan saw to his deep disgust that that something was the Lynx—yes, it surely was *his* Lynx.

They eagerly plied the man with questions. He told them that he had killed it the day before, really. It had been prowling for the last week or more about Kernore's bush; probably it was a straggler from up north.

This was all intensely fascinating to Yan, but in it was a jarring note. Evidently this man considered the Glen—his Glen—as an ordinary, well-known bit of bush, possibly part of his farm—not by any means the profound mystery that Yan would have had it.

The Lynx was a fine large one. The stripes on its face and the wide open yellow eyes gave a peculiarly wild, tiger-like expression that was deeply gratifying to Yan's romantic soul.

It was not so much of an adventure as a might-have-been adventure; but it left a deep impress on the boy, and it also illustrated the accuracy of his instincts in identifying creatures that he had never before seen, but knew only through the slight descriptions of very unsatisfactory books.

XIV

Froth

FROM now on to the spring Yan was daily gaining in strength, and he and his mother came closer together. She tried to take an interest in the pursuits that were his whole nature. But she also strove hard to make him take an interest in her world. She was a morbidly religious woman. Her conversation was bristling with Scripture texts. She had a vast store of them—indeed, she had them all; and she used them on every occasion possible and impossible, with bewildering efficiency.

If ever she saw a group of young people dancing, romping, playing any game, or even laughing heartily, she would interrupt them to say, "Children, are you sure you can ask God's blessing on all this? Do you think that beings with immortal souls to save should give rein to such frivolity! I fear you are sinning, and be sure your sin will find you out. Remember, that for every idle word and deed we must give an account to the Great Judge of Heaven and earth."

She was perfectly sincere in all this, but she never ceased, except during the time of her son's illness, when, under orders from the doctor, she avoided the painful topic of eternal happiness and tried to simulate an interest in his pursuits. This was the blessed truce that brought them together.

He found a confidante for the first time since he met the collarless stranger, and used to tell all his loves and fears among the woodfolk and things. He would talk about this or that bird or flower, and hoped to find out its name, till the mother would suddenly feel shocked that any being with an immortal soul to save could talk so seriously about anything outside of the Bible; then gently reprove her son and herself, too, with a number of texts.

He might reply with others, for he was well equipped. But her unanswerable answer would be: "There is but one thing needful. What profiteth it a man if he gain the whole world and lose his own soul?"

These fencing bouts grew more frequent as Yan grew stronger and the doctor's inhibition was removed.

After one of unusual warmth, Yan realized with a chill that all her interest in his pursuits had been an affected one. He was silent a long time, then said: "Mother! you like to talk about your Bible. It tells you the things that you long to know, that you love to learn. You would be unhappy if you went a day without reading a chapter or two. That is your nature; God made you so.

"I have been obliged to read the Bible all my life. Every day I read a chapter; but I do not love it. I read it because I am forced to do it.

It tells me nothing I want to know. It does not teach me to love God, which you say is the one thing needful. But I go out into the woods, and every bird and flower I see stirs me to the heart with something, I do not know what it is; only I love them: I love them with all my strength, and they make me feel like praying when your Bible does not. They are my Bible. This is my nature. God made me so."

The mother was silent after this, but Yan could see that she was praying for him as for a lost soul.

A few days later they were out walking in the early spring morning. A Shore-lark on a clod whistled prettily as it felt the growing sunshine.

Yan strained his eyes and attention to take it in. He crept up near it. It took wing, and as it went he threw after it a short stick he was carrying. The stick whirled over and struck the bird. It fell fluttering. Yan rushed wildly after it and caught it in spite of his mother's calling him back.

He came with the bird in his hand, but it did not live many minutes. His mother was grieved and disgusted. She said: "So this is the great love you have for the wild things; the very first spring bird to sing you must club to death. I do not understand your affections. Are not two sparrows sold for one farthing, and yet not one of them falls to the ground without the knowledge of your heavenly Father."

Yan was crushed. He held the dead bird in his hand and said, contradictorily, as the tears stood in his eyes, "I wish I hadn't; but oh, it was so beautiful."

He could not explain, because he did not understand, and yet was no hypocrite.

Weeks later a cheap trip gave him the chance for the first time in his life to see Niagara. As he stood with his mother watching the racing flood, in the gorge below the cataract, he noticed straws, bubbles and froth, that seemed to be actually moving upstream. He said:

"Mother, you see the froth how it seems to go up-stream."

"Well!"

"Yet we know it is a trifle and means nothing. We know that just below the froth is the deep, wide, terrible, irresistible, arrowy flood, surging all the other way."

"Yes, my son."

"Well, Mother, when I killed the Shore-lark, that was froth going the wrong way. I did love the little bird. I know now why I killed it. Because it was going away from me. If I could have seen it near and could have touched it, or even have heard it every day, I should never have wished to harm it. I didn't mean *to kill it*, only *to get it*. You gather flowers because you love to keep them near you, not because you want to destroy them. They die and you are sorry. I only tried to gather the Shore-lark as you would a flower. It died, and I **was** very, very sorry."

"Nevertheless," the mother replied, "the merciful man is merciful unto his beast. He who hearkens when the young Ravens cry, surely took note of it, and in His great Book of Remembrance it is written down against you."

And from that time they surely drifted apart.

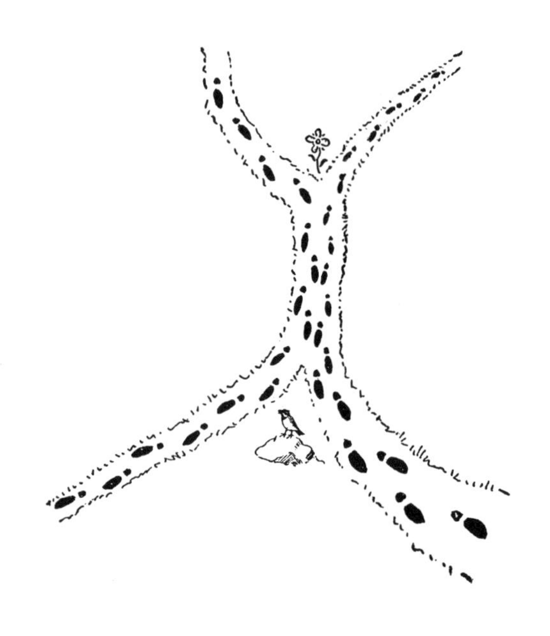

PART II.

SANGER SAM

I

The New Home

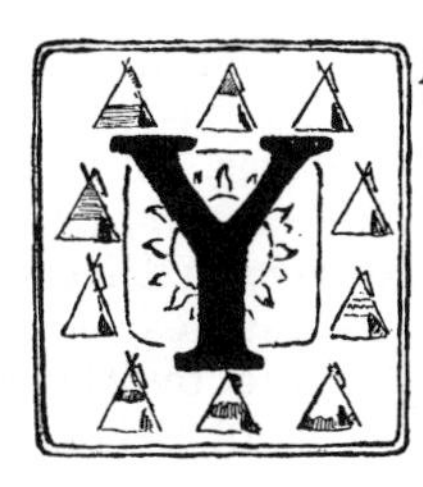

YAN was now fourteen years old, long-legged, thin, and growing fast. The doctor marked this combination and said: "Send him on a farm for a year."

Thus it was that an arrangement was made for Yan to work for his board at the farmhouse of William Raften of Sanger.

Sanger was a settlement just emerging from the early or backwoods period.

The recognized steps are, first, the frontier or woods where all is unbroken forest and Deer abound; next the backwoods where small clearings appear; then a settlement where the forest and clearings are about equal and the Deer gone; last an agricultural district, with mere shreds of forest remaining.

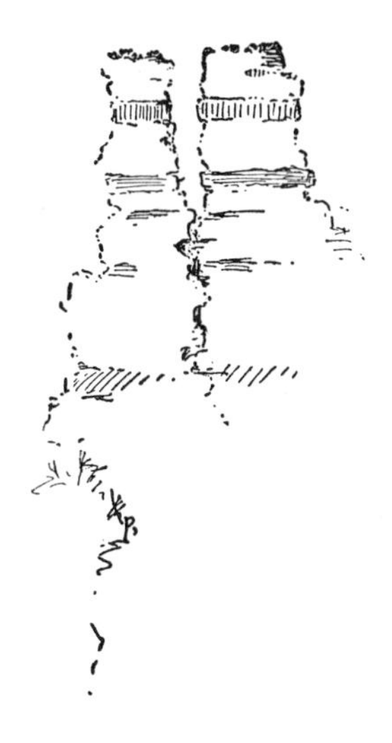

Thirty years before, Sanger had been "taken up" by a population chiefly from Ireland, sturdy peasantry for the most part, who brought with them the ancient feud that has so long divided Ireland—the bitter quarrel between the Catholics or "Dogans" (why so called none knew) and Protestants, more usually styled "Prattisons." The colours of the Catholics were green and white; of the Protestants orange and blue; and hence another distinctive name of the latter was "Orangemen."

These two factions split the social structure in two, vertically. There were, in addition, several horizontal lines of cleavage which, like geological seams, ran across both segments.

In those days, the early part of the nineteenth century, the British Government used to assist desirable persons who wished to emigrate to Canada from Ireland. This aid consisted of a free ocean passage. Many who could not convince the Government of their desirability and yet could raise the money, came with them, paying their regular steerage rate of $15. These were alike to the outside world, but not to themselves. Those who paid their way were "passengers," and were, in their own opinion, many social worlds above the assisted ones, who were called "Emmy Grants." This distinction was never forgotten among the residents of Sanger.

Yet two other social grades existed. Every man and boy in Sanger was an expert with the axe; was wonderfully adroit. The familiar phrase, "He's a good man," had two accepted meanings: If obviously applied to a settler during the regular Saturday night Irish row in the little town of Downey's Dump, it meant he was an able man with his fists; but if to his home life on the farm, it implied that he was unusually dexterous with the axe. A man who fell below standard was despised. Since the houses of hewn logs were made by their owners, they reflected the axemen's skill. There were two styles of log architecture; the shanty with corners criss-cross, called hog-pen finish, and the other, the house with the corners neatly finished, called dovetail finish. In Sanger it was a social black eye to live in a house of the first kind. The residents were considered "scrubs" or "riff-raff" by those whose superior axemanship had provided the more neatly finished dwelling. A later division crept in among the "dovetailers" themselves when a brickyard was opened. The more prosperous settlers put up neat little brick houses. To the surprise of all, one Phil O'Leary, a poor but prolific Dogan, leaped at once from a hog-pen log to a fine brick, and caused no end of perplexity to the ruling society queens, simply paralyzing the social register, since his nine fat daughters now had claims with the best. Many, however, whose brick houses were but five years old, denounced the O'Learys as upstarts and for long witheld all social recognition. William Raften, as the most prosperous man in the community, was first to appear in red bricks. His implacable enemy, Char-less (two syllables) Boyle, egged on by his wife, now also took the red brick plunge, though he dispensed with masons and laid the bricks himself, with the help of his seventeen sons. These two men, though Orangemen both, were deadly enemies, as the wives were social rivals. Raften was the stronger and richer man, but Boyle, whose father had paid his own steerage rate, knew all about Raften's father, and always wound up any discussion by hurling in Raften's teeth: "Don't talk to me, ye upstart. Everybody knows ye are nothing but a Emmy Grant." This was the one fly in the Raften

ointment. No use denying it. His father had accepted a free passage, true, and Boyle had received a free homestead, but what of that—that counted for nothing. Old Boyle had been a "PASSENGER," old Raften an ☞"EMMY GRANT."☜

This was the new community that Yan had entered, and the words Dogan and Prattison, "green" and "orange and blue," began to loom large, along with the ideas and animosities they stood for.

The accent of the Sangerite was mixed. First, there was a rich Irish brogue with many Irish words; this belonged chiefly to the old folks. The Irish of such men as Raften was quite evident in their speech, but not strong enough to warrant the accepted Irish spelling of books, except when the speaker was greatly excited. The young generation had almost no Irish accent, but all had sifted down to the peculiar burring nasal whine of the backwoods Canadian.

Mr. and Mrs. Raften met Yan at the station. They had supper together at the tavern and drove him to their home, where they showed him into the big dining-room — living-room — kitchen. Over behind the stove was a tall, awkward boy with carroty hair and small, dark eyes set much aslant in the saddest of faces. Mrs. Raften said, "Come, Sam, and shake hands with Yan." Sam came sheepishly forward, shook hands in a flabby way, and said, in drawling tones, "How-do," then retired behind the stove to gaze with melancholy soberness at Yan, whenever he could do so without being caught at it. Mr. and Mrs. Raften were attending to various matters elsewhere, and Yan was left alone and miserable. The idea of giving up college to go on a farm had been a hard one for him to accept, but he had sullenly bowed to his father's command and then at length learned to like the prospect of getting away from Bonnerton into the country. After all, it was but for a year, and it promised so much of joy. Sunday-school left behind. Church reduced to a minimum. All his life outdoors, among fields and woods—surely this spelled happiness; but now that he was really there, the abomination of desolation seemed sitting on all things and the evening was one of unalloyed misery. He had nothing to tell of, but a cloud of black despair seemed to have settled for good on the world. His mouth was pinching very hard and his eyes blinking to keep back the tears when Mrs. Raften came into the room. She saw at a glance what was wrong. "He's homesick," she said to her husband. "He'll be all right to-morrow," and she took Yan by the hand and led him upstairs to bed.

Twenty minutes later she came to see if he was comfortable. She tucked the clothes in around him, then, stooping down for a good-night kiss, she found his face wet with tears. She put her arms about him for a moment, kissed him several times, and said, "Never mind, you will feel all right to-morrow," then wisely left him alone.

Whence came that load of misery and horror, or whither it went, Yan never knew. He saw it no more, and the next morning he began to interest himself in his new world.

William Raften had a number of farms all in fine order and clear of mortgages; and each year he added to his estates. He was sober, shrewd, even cunning, hated by most of his neighbours because he was too clever for them and kept on getting richer. His hard side was for the world and his soft side for his family. Not that he was really soft in any respect. He had had to fight his life-battle alone, beginning with nothing, and the many hard knocks had hardened him, but the few who knew him best could testify to the warm Irish heart that continued unchanged within him, albeit it was each year farther from the surface. His manners, even in the house, were abrupt and masterful. There was no mistaking his orders, and no excuse for not complying with them. To his children when infants, and to his wife only, he was always tender, and those who saw him cold and grasping, overreaching the sharpers of the grain market, would scarcely have recognized the big, warm-hearted happy-looking father at home an hour later when he was playing horse with his baby daughter or awkwardly paying post-graduate court to his smiling wife.

He had little "eddication," could hardly read, and was therefore greatly impressed with the value of "book larnin'," and determined that his own children should have the "best that money could git in that line," which probably meant that they should read fluently. His own reading was done on Sunday mornings, when he painfully spelled out the important items in a weekly paper; "important" meant referring to the produce market or the prize ring, for he had been known and respected as a boxer, and dearly loved the exquisite details of the latest bouts. He used to go to church with his wife once a month to please her, and thought it very unfair therefore that she should take no interest in his favourite hobby—the manly art.

Although hard and even brutal in his dealings with men, he could not bear to see an animal ill used. "The men can holler when they're hurt, but the poor dumb baste has no protection." He was the only farmer in the country that would not sell or shoot a worn-out horse. "The poor brute has wurruked hard an' hez airned his kape for the rest av his days." So Duncan, Jerry and several others were "retired" and lived their latter days in idleness, in one case for more than ten years.

Raften had thrashed more than one neighbour for beating a horse, and once, on interfering, was himself thrashed, for he had the ill-luck to happen on a prize-fighter. But that had no lasting effect on him. He continued to champion the dumb brute in his own brutal way.

Among the neighbours the perquisites of the boys were the calfskins. The cows' milk was needed and the calves of little value, so usually they were killed when too young for food. The boys did the killing, making more or less sport of it, and the skins, worth fifty cents apiece green and twenty-five cents dry, at the tannery, were their proper pay. Raften never allowed his son to kill the calves. "Oi can't kill a poor innocent calf mesilf an' I won't hev me boy doin' it," he said. Thus Sam was done out of a perquisite, and did not forget the grievance.

Mrs. Raften was a fine woman, a splendid manager, loving her home and her family, her husband's loyal and ablest supporter, although she thought that William was sometimes a "leetle hard" on the boys. They had had a large family, but most of the children had died. Those remaining were Sam, aged fifteen, and Minnie, aged three.

Yan's duties were fixed at once. The poultry and half the pigs and cows were to be his charge. He must also help Sam with various other chores.

There was plenty to do and clear rules about doing it. But there was also time nearly every day for other things more in the line of his tastes; for even if he were hard on the boys in work hours, Raften saw to it that when they did play they should have a good time. His roughness and force made Yan afraid of him, and as it was Raften's way to say nothing until his mind was fully made up, and then say it "strong," Yan was left in doubt as to whether or not he was giving satisfaction.

II

Sam

SAM RAFTEN turned out to be more congenial than he looked. His slow, drawling speech had given a wrong impression of stupidity, and, after a formal showing of the house under Mr. Raften, a real investigation was headed by Sam. "This yer's the paaar-le-r," said he, unlocking a sort of dark cellar aboveground and groping to open what afterward proved to be a dead, buried and almost forgotten window. In Sanger settlement the farmhouse parlour is not a room; it is an institution. It is kept closed all the week except when the minister calls, and the one at Raften's was the pure type. Its furniture consisted of six painted chairs (fifty cents each), two rockers ($1.49), one melodeon (thirty-two bushels of wheat—the agent asked forty), a sideboard made at home of the case the melodeon came in, one rag carpet woofed at home and warped and woven in exchange for wool, one center-table varnished (!) ($9.00 cash, $11.00 catalogue). On the center-table was one tintype album, a Bible, and some large books for company use. Though dusted once a week, they were never moved, and it was years later before they were found to have settled permanently into the varnish of the table. In extremely uncostly frames on the wall were the coffin-plates of the departed members of the family. It was the custom at Sanger to honour the dead by bringing back from the funeral the name-plate and framing it on a black background with some supposed appropriate scripture text.

The general atmosphere of the room was fusty and religious, as it was never opened except on Sundays or when the parson called, which instituted a sort of temporary Sunday, and the two small windows were kept shut and plugged as well as muffled always, with green paper blinds and cotton hangings. It was a thing apart from the rest of the house—a sort of family ghost-room; a chamber of horrors, seen but once a week.

But it contained one thing at least of interest—something that at once brought Sam and Yan together. This was a collection of a score of birds' eggs. They were all mixed together in an old glass-topped cravat box, half full of bran. None of them were labelled or properly blown. A collector would not have given it a second glance, but it proved an important matter. It was as though two New Yorkers, one disguised as a Chinaman and the other as a Negro, had accidently met in Greenland and by chance one had made the sign of the secret brotherhood to which they both belonged.

"Do you like these things?" said Yan, with sudden interest and warmth, in spite of the depressing surroundings.

"You bet," said Sam. "And I'd a-had twice as many only Da said it was doing no good and birds was good for the farm."

"Well, do you know their names?"

"Wall, I should say so. I know every Bird that flies and all about it, or putty near it," drawled Sam, with an unusual stretch for him, as he was not given to bragging.

"I wish I did. Can't I get some eggs to take home?"

"No; Da said if I wouldn't take any more he'd lend me his Injun Chief gun to shoot Rabbits with."

"What? Are there Rabbits here?"

"Wall, I should say so. I got three last winter."

"But I mean *now*," said Yan, with evident disappointment.

"They ain't so easy to get at *now*, but we can try. Some day when all the work's done I'll ask Da for his gun."

"When all the work's done," was a favourite expression of the Raftens for indefinitely shelving a project, it sounded so reasonable and was really so final.

Sam opened up the lower door of the sideboard and got out some flint arrow-heads picked up in the ploughing, the teeth of a Beaver dating from the early days of the settlement, and an Owl very badly

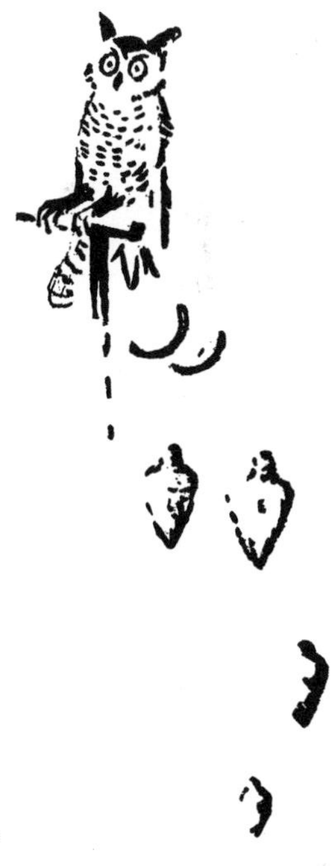

stuffed. The sight of these precious things set Yan all ablaze. "Oh!" was all he could say. Sam was gratified to see such effect produced by the family possessions and explained, "Da shot that off'n the barn an' the hired man stuffed it."

The boys were getting on well together now. They exchanged confidences all day as they met in doing chores. In spite of the long interruptions, they got on so well that Sam said after supper, "Say, Yan, I'm going to show you something, but you must promise never to tell—Swelpye!" Of course Yan promised and added the absolutely binding and ununderstandable word —"Swelpme."

"Le's both go to the barn," said Sam.

When they were half way he said: "Now I'll let on I went back for something. You go on an' round an' I'll meet you under the 'rusty-coat' in the orchard." When they met under the big russet apple tree, Sam closed one of his melancholy eyes and said in a voice of unnecessary hush, "Follow me." He led to the other end of the orchard where stood the old log house that had been the home before the building of the brick one. It was now used as a tool house. Sam led up a ladder to the loft (this was all wholly delightful). There at the far end, and next the little gable pane, he again cautioned secrecy, then when on invitation Yan had once more "swelped" himself, he rummaged in a dirty old box and drew out a bow, some arrows, a rusty steel trap, an old butcher knife, some fish-hooks, a flint and steel, a box full of matches, and some dirty, greasy-looking stuff that he said was dried meat. "You see," he explained, "I always wanted to be a hunter, and Da was bound I'd be a dentist. Da said there was no money in hunting, but one day he had to go to the dentist an' it cost four dollars, an' the man wasn't half a day at the job, so he wanted me to be a dentist, but I wanted to be a hunter, an' one day he licked me and Bud (Bud, that's my brother that died a year ago. If you hear Ma talk you'll think he was an angel, but I always reckoned he was a crazy galoot, an' he was the worst boy in school by odds). Wall, Da licked us awful for not feeding the hogs, so Bud got ready to clear out, an' at first I felt just like he did an' said I'd go too, an' we'd j'ine the Injuns. Anyhow, I'd sure go if ever I was licked again, an' this was the outfit we got together. Bud wanted to steal

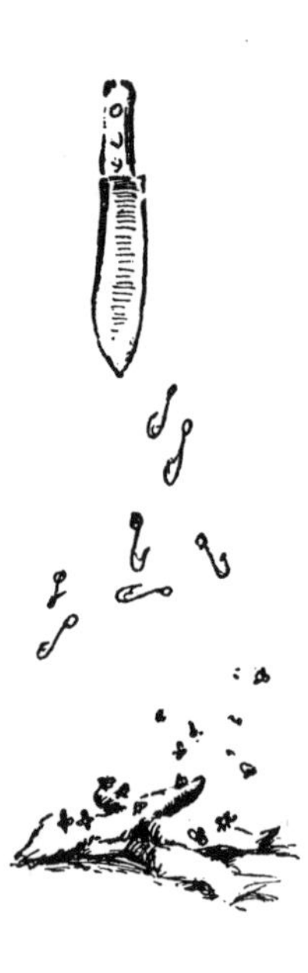

Da's gun an' I wouldn't. I tell you I was hoppin' mad that time, an' Bud was wuss—but I cooled off an' talked to Bud. I says, 'Say now, Bud, it would take about a month of travel to get out West, an' if the Injuns didn't want nothin' but our scalps that wouldn't be no fun, an' Da ain't really so bad, coz we sho'ly did starve them pigs so one of 'em died.' I reckon we deserved all we got—anyhow, it was all dumb foolishness about skinnin' out, though I'd like mighty well to be a hunter. Well, Bud died that winter. You seen the biggest coffin plate on the wall? Well, that's him. I see Ma lookin' at it an' cryin' the other day. Da says he'll send me to college if I'll be a dentist or a lawyer—lawyers make lots of money: Da had a lawsuit once—an' if I don't, he says I kin go to—you know."

Here was Yan's own kind of mind, and he opened his heart. He told all about his shanty in the woods and how he had laboured at and loved it. He was full of enthusiasm as of old, boiling over with purpose and energy, and Sam, he realized, had at least two things that he had not—ability with tools and cool judgment. It was like having the best parts of his brother Rad put into a real human being. And remembering the joy of his Glen, Yan said:

"Let's build a shanty in the woods by the creek; your father won't care, will he?"

"Not he, so long as the work's done."

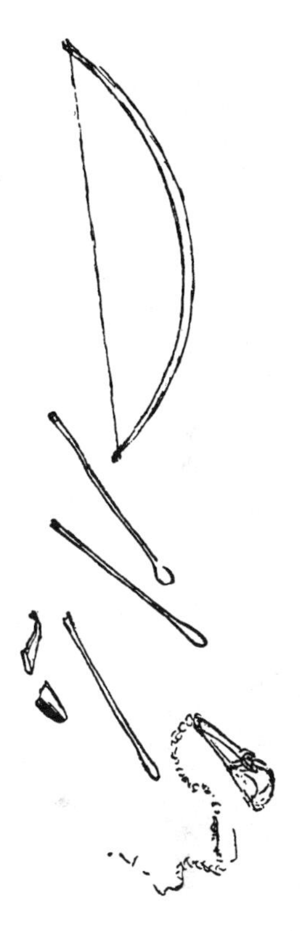

III

The Wigwam

THE very next day they must begin. As soon as every chore was done they went to the woods to select a spot.

The brook, or "creek," as they called it, ran through a meadow, then through a fence into the woods. This was at first open and grassy, but farther down the creek it was joined by a dense cedar swamp. Through this there was no path, but Sam said that there was a nice high place beyond.

The high ground seemed a long way off in the woods, though only a hundred yards through the swamp, but it was the very place for a camp—high, dry and open hard woods, with the creek in front and the cedar swamp all around. Yan was delighted. Sam caught no little of the enthusiasm, and having brought an axe, was ready to begin the shanty. But Yan had been thinking hard all morning, and now he said: "Sam, we don't want to be *White* hunters. They're no good; we want to be Indians."

"Now, that's just where you fool yourself," said Sam. "Da says there ain't nothin' an Injun can do that a White-man can't do better."

"Oh, what are you talking about?" said Yan warmly. "A White hunter can't trail a moccasined foot across a hard granite rock. A White hunter can't go into the woods with nothing but a knife and make everything he needs. A White hunter can't hunt with bows and arrows, and catch game with snares, can he? And there never yet was a White man could make a Birch canoe." Then, changing his tone, Yan went on: "Say, now, Sam, we want to be the best kind of hunters, don't we, so as to be ready for going out West. Let's be Injuns and do everything like Injuns."

After all, this had the advantage of romance and picturesqueness, and Sam consented to "try it for awhile, anyhow." And now came the point of Yan's argument. "Injuns don't live in shanties; they live in teepees. Why not make a teepee instead?"

"That would be just bully," said Sam, who had seen pictures enough to need no description, "but what are we to make it of?"

"Well," answered Yan, promptly assuming the leadership and rejoicing in his ability to speak as an authority, "the Plains Injuns make their teepees of skins, but the wood Injuns generally use Birch bark."

"Well, I bet you can't find skins or Birch bark enough in this woods to make a teepee big enough for a Chipmunk to chaw nuts in."

"We can use Elm bark."

"That's a heap easier," replied Sam, "if it'll answer, coz we cut a lot o' Elm logs last winter and the bark'll be about willin' to peel now. But first let's plan it out."

This was a good move, one Yan would have overlooked. He would probably have got a lot of material together and made the plan afterward, but Sam had been taught to go about his work with method.

So Yan sketched on a smooth log his remembrance of an Indian teepee. "It seems to me it was about this shape, with the poles sticking up like that, a hole for the smoke here and another for the door there."

"Sounds like you hain't never seen one," remarked Sam, with more point than politeness, "but we kin try it. Now 'bout how big?"

Eight feet high and eight feet across was decided to be about right. Four poles, each ten feet long, were cut in a few minutes, Yan carrying them to a smooth place above the creek as fast as Sam cut them.

"Now, what shall we tie them with?" said Yan.

"You mean for rope?"

"Yes, only we must get everything in the woods; real rope ain't allowed."

"I kin fix that," said Sam; "when Da double-staked the orchard fence, he lashed every pair of stakes at the top with Willow withes."

"That's so—I quite forgot," said Yan. In a few minutes they were at work trying to tie the four poles together with slippery stiff Willows, but it was no easy matter. They had to be perfectly tight or they would slip and fall in a heap each time they were raised, and it seemed at length that the boys would be forced to the impropriety of using hay wire, when they heard a low grunt, and turning, saw William Raften standing with his hands behind him as though he had watched them for hours.

The boys were no little startled. Raften had a knack of turning up at any point when something was going on, taking in the situation fully, and then, if he disapproved, of expressing himself in a few words of blistering mockery delivered in a rich Irish brogue. Just what view he would take of their pastime the boys had no idea, but awaited with uneasiness. If they had been wasting time when they should have been working there is no question but that they would have been sent with contumely to more profitable pursuits, but this was within their rightful play hours, and Raften, after regarding them with a searching look, said slowly: "Bhoys!" (Sam felt easier; his father would have said "*Bhise*" if really angry.) "Fhat's the good o' wastin' yer time" (Yan's heart sank) "wid Willow withes fur a job like that? They can't be made to howld. Whoi don't ye git some hay woire or coord at the barrun?"

The boys were greatly relieved, but still this friendly overture might be merely a feint to open the way for a home thrust. Sam was silent. So Yan said, presently, "We ain't allowed to use anything but what the Indians had or could get in the woods."

"An' who don't allow yez?"

"The rules."

"Oh," said William, with some amusement. "Oi see! Hyar."

He went into the woods looking this way and that, and presently stopped at a lot of low shrubs.

Leather-wood

"Do ye know what this is, Yan?"

"No, sir."

"Le's see if yer man enough to break it aff."

Yan tried. The wood was brittle enough, but the bark, thin, smooth and pliant, was as tough as leather, and even a narrow strip defied his strength.

"That's Litherwood," said Raften. "That's what the Injuns used; that's what we used ourselves in the airly days of this yer settlement."

The boys had looked for a rebuke, and here was a helping hand. It all turned on the fact that this was "play hours." Raften left with a parting word: "In wan hour an' a half the pigs is fed."

"You see Da's all right when the work ain't forgot," said Sam, with a patronizing air. "I wonder why I didn't think o' that there Leatherwood meself. I've often heard that that's what was used fur tying bags in the old days when cord was scarce, an' the Injuns used it for tying their prisoners, too. Ain't it the real stuff?"

Several strips were now used for tying four poles together at the top, then these four were raised on end and spread out at the bottom to serve as the frame of the teepee, or more properly wigwam, since it was to be made of bark.

After consulting, they now got a long, limber Willow rod an inch thick, and bending it around like a hoop, they tied it with Leatherwood to each pole at a point four feet from the ground. Next they cut four short poles to reach from the ground to this. These were lashed at their upper ends to the Willow rod, and now they were ready for the bark slabs. The boys went to the Elm logs and again Sam's able use of the axe came in. He cut the bark open along the top of one log, and by using the edge of the axe and some wooden wedges they pried off a great roll eight feet long and four feet across. It was a pleasant surprise to see what a wide piece of bark the small log gave them.

Three logs yielded three fine large slabs and others yielded pieces of various sizes. The large ones were set up against the frame so as to make the most of them. Of course they were much too big for the top, and much too narrow for the bottom; but the little pieces would do to patch if some way could be found to make them stick.

Sam suggested nailing them to the posts, and Yan was horrified at the idea of using nails. "No Indian has any nails."

"Well, what *would* they use?" said Sam.

"They used thongs, an'—an'—maybe wooden pegs. I don't know, but seems to me that would be all right."

"But them poles is hard wood," objected the practical Sam. "You can drive Oak pegs into Pine, but you can't drive wooden pegs into hard wood without you make some sort of a hole first. Maybe I'd better bring a gimlet."

"Now, Sam, you might just as well hire a carpenter —*that* wouldn't be Indian at all. Let's play it right. We'll find some way. I believe we can tie them up with Leatherwood."

So Sam made a sharp Oak pick with his axe, and Yan used it to pick holes in each piece of bark and then did a sort of rude sewing till the wigwam seemed beautifully covered in. But when they went inside to look they were unpleasantly surprised to find how many holes there were. It was impossible to close them all because the bark was cracking in so many places, but the boys plugged the worst of them and then prepared for the great sacred ceremony—the lighting of the fire in the middle.

They gathered a lot of dry fuel, then Yan produced a match.

"That don't look to me very Injun," drawled Sam critically. "I don't think Injuns has matches."

"Well, they don't," admitted Yan, humbly. "But I haven't a flint and steel, and don't know how to work rubbing-sticks, so we just got to use matches, *if* we *want* a fire."

"Why, of course we want a fire. I ain't kicking," said Sam. "Go ahead with your old leg-fire sulphur stick. A camp without a fire would be bout like last year's bird's nest or a house with the roof off."

Yan struck a match and put it to the wood. It went out. He struck another—same result. Yet another went out.

Sam remarked:

"'Pears to me you don't know much about lightin' a fire. Lemme show you. Let the White hunter learn the Injun somethin' about the woods," said he with a leer.

Sam took the axe and cut some sticks of a dry Pine root. Then with his knife he cut long curling shavings, which he left sticking in a fuzz at the end of each stick.

Prayer Sticks

"Oh, I've seen a picture of an Indian making them. They call them 'prayer-sticks,'" said Yan.

"Well, prayer-sticks is mighty good kindlin'," replied the other. He struck a match, and in a minute he had a blazing fire in the middle of the wigwam.

"Old Granny de Neuville, she's a witch—she knows all about the woods, and cracked Jimmy turns everything into poetry what she says. He says she says when you want to make a fire in the woods you take—

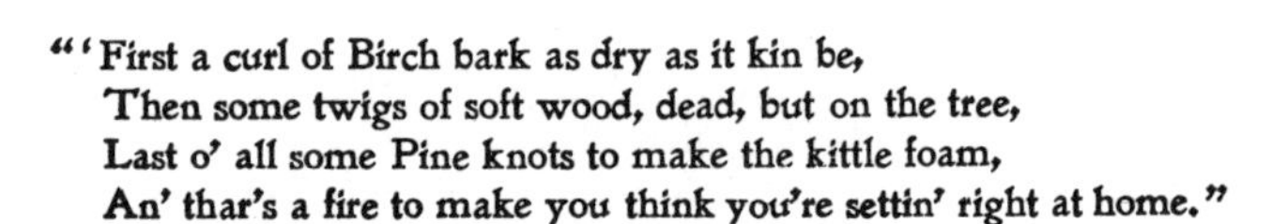

"'First a curl of Birch bark as dry as it kin be,
Then some twigs of soft wood, dead, but on the tree,
Last o' all some Pine knots to make the kittle foam,
An' thar's a fire to make you think you're settin' right at home."

"Who's Granny de Neuville?"

"Oh, she's the old witch that lives down at the bend o' the creek."

"What? Has she got a granddaughter named Biddy?" said Yan, suddenly remembering that his ancient ally came from this part of Sanger.

"Oh, my! Hain't she? Ain't Biddy a peach—drinks like a fish, talks everybody to death about the time she resided in Bonnerton. Gits a letter every mail begging her to come back and 'reside' with them some more."

"Ain't this fine," said Yan, as he sat on a pile of Fir boughs in the wigwam.

"Looks like the real thing," replied Sam from his seat on the other side. "But say, Yan, don't make any more fire; it's kind o' warm here, an' there

seems to be something wrong with that flue—wants sweepin', prob'ly—hain't been swep' since I kin remember."

The fire blazed up and the smoke increased. Just a little of it wandered out of the smoke-hole at the top, then it decided that this was a mistake and thereafter positively declined to use the vent. Some of it went out by chinks, and a large stream issued from the door, but by far the best part of it seemed satisfied with the interior of the wigwam, so that in a minute or less both boys scrambled out. Their eyes were streaming with smoke-tears and their discomfiture was complete.

"'Pears to me," observed Sam, "like we got them holes mixed. The dooer should 'a 'been at the top, sence the smoke has a fancy for usin' it, an' then *we'd* had a chance."

"The Indians make it work," said Yan; "a White hunter ought to know how."

"Now's the Injun's chance," said Sam. "Maybe it wants a dooer to close, then the smoke would have to go out."

They tried this, and of course some of the smoke was crowded out, but not till long after the boys were.

"Seems like what does get out by the chinks is sucked back agin by that there double-action flue," said Sam.

It was very disappointing. The romance of sitting by the fire in one's teepee appealed to both of the boys, but the physical torture of the smoke made it unbearable. Their dream was dispelled, and Sam suggested, "Maybe we'd better try a shanty."

"No," said Yan, with his usual doggedness. "I know it can be done, because the Indians do it. We'll find out in time."

But all their efforts were in vain. The wigwam was a failure, as far as fire was concerned. It was very small and uncomfortable, too; the wind blew through a hundred crevices, which grew larger as the Elm bark dried and cracked. A heavy shower caught them once, and they were rather glad to be driven into their cheerless lodge, but the rain came abundantly into the smoke-hole as well as through the walls, and they found it but little protection.

"Seems to me, if anything, a *leetle* wetter in here than outside," said Sam, as he led in a dash for home.

That night a heavy storm set in, and next day the boys found their flimsy wigwam blown down—nothing but a heap of ruins.

Some time after, Raften asked at the table in characteristic stern style, "Bhoys, what's doin' down to yer camp? Is yer wigwam finished?"

"No good," said Sam. "All blowed down."

"How's that?"

"I dunno'. It smoked like everything. We couldn't stay in it."

"Couldn't a-been right made," said Raften; then with a sudden interest, which showed how eagerly he would have joined in this forty years ago, he said, "Why don't ye make a rale taypay?"

"Dunno' how, an' ain't got no stuff."

"Wall, now, yez have been pretty good an' ain't slacked on the wurruk, yez kin have the ould wagon kiver. Cousin Bert could tache ye how to make it, if he wuz here. Maybe Caleb Clark knows," he added, with a significant twinkle of his eye. "Better ask him." Then he turned to give orders to the hired men, who, of course, ate at the family table.

"Da, do you care if we go to Caleb?"

"I don't care fwhat ye do wid him," was the reply.

Raften was no idle talker and Sam knew that, so as soon as "the law was off" he and Yan got out the old wagon cover. It seemed like an acre of canvas when they spread it out. Having thus taken possession, they put it away again in the cow-house, their own domain, and Sam said: "I've a great notion to go right to Caleb; he sho'ly knows more about a teepee than any one else here, which ain't sayin' much."

"Who's Caleb?"

"Oh, he's the old Billy Goat that shot at Da oncet, just after Da beat him at a horse trade. Let on it was a mistake: 'twas, too, as he found out, coz Da bought up some old notes of his, got 'em cheap, and squeezed him hard to meet them. He's had hard luck ever since.

"He's a mortal queer old duck, that Caleb. He knows heaps about the woods, coz he was a hunter an' trapper oncet. My! wouldn't he be down on me if he knowed who was my Da, but he don't have to know."

IV

The Sanger Witch

The Sanger Witch dwelt in the bend of the creek,
And neither could read nor write;
But she knew in a day what few knew in a week,
For hers was the second sight.
"Read?" said she, "I am double read;
You fools of the ink and pen
Count never the eggs, but the sticks of the nest,
See the clothes, not the souls of men."
—Cracked Jimmy's Ballad of Sanger.

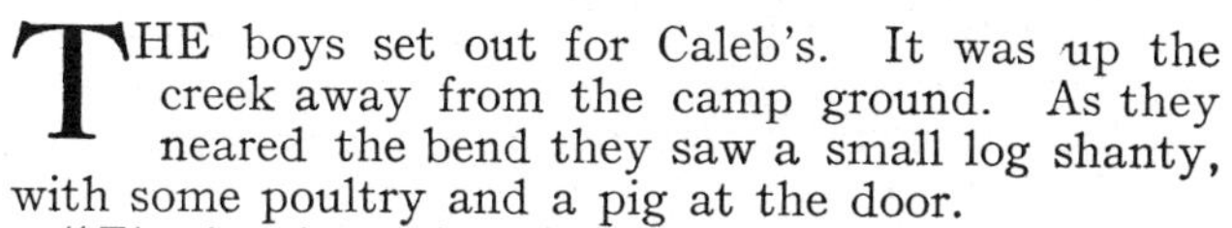

THE boys set out for Caleb's. It was up the creek away from the camp ground. As they neared the bend they saw a small log shanty, with some poultry and a pig at the door.

"That's where the witch lives," said Sam.

"Who—old Granny de Neuville?"

"Yep, and she just loves me. Oh, yes; about the same way an old hen loves a Chicken-hawk. 'Pears to me she sets up nights to love me."

"Why?"

"Oh, I guess it started with the pigs. No, let's see: first about the trees. Da chopped off a lot of Elm trees that looked terrible nice from her windy. She's awful queer about a tree. She hates to see 'em cut down, an' that soured her same as if she owned 'em. Then there wuz the pigs. You see, one winter she was awful hard up, an' she had two pigs worth, maybe, $5.00 each—anyway, she said they was, an' she ought to know, for they lived right in the shanty with her—an' she come to Da (I guess she had tried every one else first) an' Da he squeezed her down an' got the two pigs for $7.00. He al'ays does that. Then he comes home an' says to Ma, 'Seems to me the old lady is pretty hard put. 'Bout next Saturday you take two sacks of flour and some pork an' potatoes around an' see that she is fixed up right.' Da's al'ays doin' them things, too, on the quiet. So Ma goes with about $15.00 worth o' truck. The old witch was kinder 'stand off.' She didn't say much. Ma was goin' slow, not knowin' just whether to give the stuff out an' out, or say it could be worked for next year, or some other year, when there was two moons, or some time when the work was all done. Well, the old witch said mighty little until the stuff was all put in the cellar, then she grabs up a big stick an' breaks out at Ma:

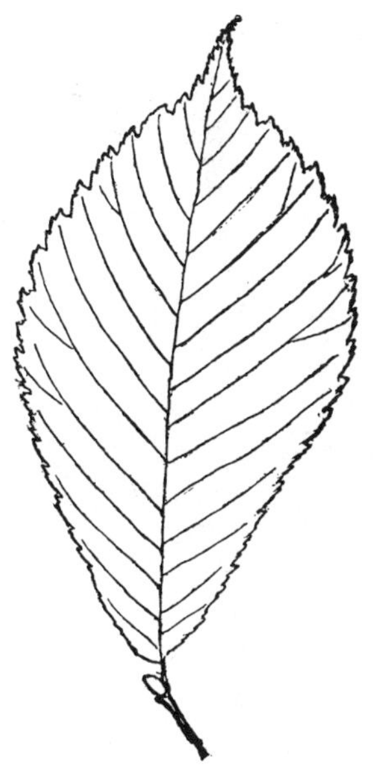

Slippery Elm

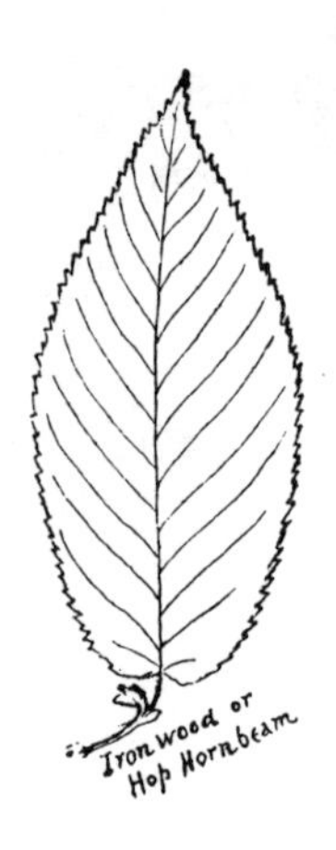

"'Now you git out o' my house, you dhirty, sthuck-up thing. I ain't takin' no charity from the likes o' you. That thing you call your husband robbed me o' my pigs, an' we ain't any more'n square now, so git out an' don't you dar set fut in my house agin'.'

"Well, she was sore on us when Da bought her pigs, but she was five times wuss after she clinched the groceries. 'Pears like they soured on her stummick."

"What a shame, the old wretch," said Yan, with ready sympathy for the Raftens.

"No," replied Sam; "she's only queer. There's lots o' folk takes her side. But she's awful queer. She won't have a tree cut if she can help it, an' when the flowers come in the spring she goes out in the woods and sets down beside 'em for hours an' calls 'em 'Me beauty—me little beauty,' an' she just loves the birds. When the boys want to rile her they get a sling-shot an' shoot the birds in her garden an' she just goes crazy. She pretty near starves herself every winter trying to feed all the birds that come around. She has lots of 'em to feed right out o' her hand. Da says they think its an old pine root, but she has a way o' coaxin' 'em that's awful nice. There she'll stand in freezin' weather calling them 'Me beauties'.

"You see that little windy in the end?" he continued, as they came close to the witch's hut. "Well, that's the loft, an' it's full o' all sorts o' plants an' roots."

"What for?"

"Oh, for medicine. She's great on hairbs."

"Oh, yes, I remember now Biddy did say that her Granny was a herb doctor."

"Doctor? She ain't much of a doctor, but I bet she knows every plant that grows in the woods, an' they're sure strong after they've been up there for a year, with the cat sleepin' on them."

"I wish I could go and see her."

"Guess we can," was the reply.

"Doesn't she know you?"

"Yes, but watch me fix her," drawled Sam. "There ain't nothin' she likes better'n a sick pusson."

Sam stopped now, rolled up his sleeves and examined both arms, apparently without success, for he then loosed his suspenders, dropped his pants, and proceeded to examine his legs. Of course, all boys have more or less cuts and bruises in various stages of healing. Sam selected his best, just below the knee, a scratch from a nail in the fence. He had never given it a thought before, but now he "reckoned it would do." With a lead pencil borrowed from Yan he spread a hue of mortification all around it, a green butternut rind added the unpleasant yellowish-brown of human decomposition, and the result was a frightful looking plague spot. By chewing some grass he made a yellowish-green dye and expectorated this on the handkerchief which he bound on the sore. He then got a stick and proceeded to limp painfully toward the witch's abode. As they drew near, the partly open door was slammed with ominous force. Sam, quite unabashed, looked at Yan and winked, then knocked. The bark of a small dog answered. He knocked again. A sound now of some one moving within, but no answer. A third time he knocked, then a shrill voice: "Get out o' that. Get aff my place, you dirthy young riff-raff."

Sam grinned at Yan. Then drawling a little more than usual, he said:

"It's a poor boy, Granny. The doctors can't do nothin' for him," which last, at least, was quite true.

There was no reply, so Sam made bold to open the door. There sat the old woman glowering with angry red eyes across the stove, a cat in her lap, a pipe in her mouth, and a dog growling toward the strangers.

"Ain't you Sam Raften?" she asked fiercely.

"Yes, marm. I got hurt on a nail in the fence. They say you kin git blood-p'isinin' that way," said Sam, groaning a little and trying to look interesting. The order to "get out" died on the witch's lips. Her good old Irish heart warmed to the sufferer. After all, it was rather pleasant to have the enemy thus humbly seek her aid, so she muttered:

"Le's see it."

Sam was trying amid many groans to expose the disgusting mess he had made around his knee, when a step was heard outside. The door opened and in walked Biddy.

She and Yan recognized each other at once. The one had grown much longer, the other much broader since the last meeting, but the greeting was that of two warm-hearted people glad to see each other once more.

"An' how's yer father an' yer mother an' how is all the fambily? Law, do ye mind the Cherry Lung-balm we uster make? My, but we wuz greenies then! Ye mind, I uster tell ye about Granny? Well, here she is. Granny, this is Yan. Me an' him hed lots o' fun together when I 'resided' with his mamma, didn't we, Yan? Now, Granny's the one to tell ye all about the plants."

A long groan from Sam now called all attention his way.

"Well, if it ain't Sam Raften," said Biddy coldly.

"Yes, an' he's deathly sick," added Granny. "Their own docther guv him up an said mortal man couldn't save him nohow, so he jest hed to come to me."

Another long groan was ample indorsement.

"Le's see. Gimme my scissors, Biddy; I'll hev to cut the pant leg aff."

"No, no," Sam blurted out with sudden vigour, dreading the consequences at home. "I kin roll it up."

"Thayer, thot'll do. Now I say," said the witch. "Yes, sure enough, thayer *is* proud flesh. I moight cut it out," said she, fumbling in her pocket (Sam supposed for a knife, and made ready to dash for the door), "but le's see, no—that would be a fool docther trick. I kin git on without."

"Yes, sure," said Sam, clutching at the idea, "that's just what a fool doctor would do, but you kin give me something to take that's far better."

"Well, sure an' I kin," and Yan and Sam breathed more freely. "Shwaller this, now," and she offered him a tin cup of water into which she spilled some powder of dry leaves. Sam did so. "An' you take this yer bundle and bile it in two gallons of wather and drink a glassful ivery hour, an' hev a loive chicken sphlit with an axe an' laid hot on the place twicet ivery day, till the proud flesh goes, an' it'll be all right wid ye—a fresh chicken iverytoime, moind ye."

"Wouldn't—turkeys—do—better?" groaned Sam, feebly. "I'm me mother's pet, Granny, an' expense ain't any objek"—a snort that may have meant mortal agony escaped him.

"Niver moind, now. Sure we won't talk of yer father an' mother; they're punished pretty bad already. Hiven forbid they don't lose the rest o' ye fur their sins. It ain't meself that 'ud bear ony ill-will."

A long groan cut short what looked like a young sermon.

"What's the plant, Granny?" asked Yan, carefully

" The wigwam was a failure "

"Get out o' this now, or I'll boot ye"

avoiding Sam's gaze.

"Shure, an' it grows in the woods."

"Yes, but I want to know what it's like and what it's called."

"Shure, 'tain't like nothin' else. It's just like itself, an' it's called Witch-hazel.

> "'Witch-hazel blossoms in the faal,
> To cure the chills and Fayvers aall,'

as cracked Jimmy says.

"I'll show you some av it sometime," said Biddy.

"Can it be made into Lung-balm?" asked Yan, mischievously.

"I guess we'll have to go now," Sam feebly put in. "I'm feeling much better. Where's my stick? Here, Yan, you kin carry my medicine, an' be *very* keerful of it."

Yan took the bundle, not daring to look Sam in the face.

Granny bade them both come back again, and followed to the door with a hearty farewell. At the same moment she said:

"Howld on!" Then she went to the one bed in the room, which also was the house, turned down the clothes, and in the middle exposed a lot of rosy apples. She picked out two of the best and gave one to each of the boys.

"Shure, Oi hev to hoide them thayer fram the pig, for they're the foinest iver grew."

"I know they are," whispered Sam, as he limped out of hearing, "for her son Larry stole them out of our orchard last fall. They're the only kind that keeps over. They're the best that grow, but a trifle too warm just now."

"Good-by, and thank you much," said Yan.

"I-feel-better-already," drawled Sam. "That tired feeling has left me, an' sense tryin' your remedy I have took no other," but added aside, "I wish I could throw up the stuff before it pisens me," and then, with a keen eye to the picturesque effect, he wanted to fling his stick away and bound into the woods.

It was all Yan could do to make him observe some of the decencies and limp a little till out of sight. As it was, the change was quite marked and the genial old witch called loudly on Biddy to see with her own eyes how quickly she had helped young Raften "afther all the dochters in the country hed giv him up."

"Now for Caleb Clark, Esq., Q. C.," said Sam.

"Q. C.?" inquired his friend.

"Some consider it means Queen's Counsel, an' some claims as it stands for Queer Cuss. One or other maybe is right."

"You're stepping wonderfully for a crippled boy the doctors have given up," remarked Yan.

"Yes; that's the proud flesh in me right leg that's doin' the high steppin'. The left one is jest plain laig."

"Let's hide this somewhere till we get back," and Yan held up the bundle of Witch-hazel.

"I'll hide that," said Sam, and he hurled the bundle afar into the creek.

"Oh, Sam, that's mean. Maybe she wants it herself."

"Pooh, that's all the old brush is good for. I done more'n me duty when I drank that swill. I could fairly taste the cat in it."

"What'll you tell her next time?"

"Well, I'll tell her I put the sticks in the right place an' where they done the most good. I soaked 'em in water an' took as much as I wanted of the flooid.

"She'll see for herself I really did pull through, and will be a blamed sight happier than if I drank her old pisen brushwood an' had to send for a really truly doctor."

Yan was silenced, but not satisfied. It seemed discourteous to throw the sticks away—so soon, anyway; besides, he had curiosity to know just what they were and how they acted.

V

Caleb

A MILE farther was the shanty of Caleb Clark, a mere squatter now on a farm once his own.

As the boys drew near, a tall, round-shouldered man with a long white beard was seen carrying in an armful of wood.

"Ye see the Billy Goat?" said Sam.

Yan sniffed as he gasped the "why" of the nickname.

"I guess you better do the talking; Caleb ain't so easy handled as the witch, and he's just as sour on Da."

So Yan went forward rather cautiously and knocked at the open door of the shanty. A deep-voiced Dog broke into a loud bay, the long beard appeared, and its owner said, "Wall?"

"Are you Mr. Clark?"

"Yep." Then, "Lie down, Turk," to a black-and-tan Hound that came growling out.

"I came—I—we wanted to ask some questions—if you don't mind."

"What might yer name be?"

"Yan."

"An' who is this?"

"He's my chum, Sam."

"I'm Sam Horn," said Sam, with some truth, for he was Samuel Horn Raften, but with sufficient deception to make Yan feel very uncomfortable.

"And where are ye from?"

"Bonnerton," said Yan.

"To-day?" was the rejoinder, with a tone of doubt.

"Well, no," Yan began; but Sam, who had tried to keep out of notice for fear of recognition, saw that his ingenuous companion was being quickly pumped and placed, and now interposed: "You see, Mr. Clark, we are camped in the woods and we want to make a teepee to live in. We have the stuff an' was told that you knew all about the making."

"Who told ye?"

"The old witch at the bend of the creek."

"Where are ye livin' now?"

"Well," said Sam, hastening again to forestall Yan, whose simple directness he feared, "to tell the truth, we made a wigwam of bark in the woods below here, but it wasn't a success."

"Whose woods?"

"Oh, about a mile below on the creek."

"Hm! That must be Raften's or Burns's woods."

"I guess it is," said Sam.

"*An' you look uncommon like Sam Raften.* You consarned young whelp, to come here lyin' an' tryin' to pull the wool over my eyes. Get out o' this now, or I'll boot ye."

Yan turned very red. He thought of the scripture text, "Be sure your sin will find you out," and he stepped back. Sam stuck his tongue in his cheek and followed. But he was his father's son. He turned and said:

"Now see here, Mr. Clark, fair and square; we come here to ask a simple question about the woods. You are the only man that knows or we wouldn't 'a' bothered you. I knowed you had it in for Da, so I tried to fool you, and it didn't go. I wish now I had just come out square and said, 'I'm Sam Raften; will you tell me somethin' I want to know, or won't you?' I didn't know you hed anything agin me or me friend that's camping with me."

There is a strong bond of sympathy between all Woodcrafters. The mere fact that a man wants to go his way is a claim on a Woodcrafter's notice. Old Caleb, though soured by trouble and hot-tempered, had a kind heart; he resisted for a moment the first impulse to slam the door in their faces; then as he listened he fell into the tempter's snare, for it was baited with the subtlest of flatteries. He said to Yan:

"Is your name Raften?"

"No, sir."

"Air ye owt o' kin?"

"No, sir."

"I don't want no truck with Raften, but what do ye want to know?"

"We built a wigwam of bark, but it's no good, but now we have a big canvas cover an' want to know how to make a teepee."

"A teepee. H-m——" said the old man reflectively.

"They say you've lived in them," ventured Yan.

"Hm—'bout forty year; but it's one thing to wear a suit of clothes and another thing to make one. Seems to me it was about like this," and he took up a burnt stick and a piece of grocer's paper. "No—now hold on. Yes, I remember now; I seen a bunch of squaws make one oncet.

"First they sewed the skins together. No, first thar was a lot o' prayin'; ye kin suit yerselves 'bout that—then they sewed the skins together an' pegged it down flat on the prairie (B D H I, Cut No. 1). Then put in a peg at the middle of one side (A).

Then with a burnt stick an' a coord—yes, there must 'a' been a coord—they drawed a half circle—so (B C D). Then they cut that off, an' out o' the pieces they make two flaps like that (H L M J and K N O I), an' sews 'em on to P E and G Q. Them's smoke-flaps to make the smoke draw. Thar's a upside down pocket in the top side corner o' each smoke-flap—so—for the top of each pole, and there is rows o' holes down—so (M B and N D, Cut No. 2)—on each side fur the lacin' pins. Then at the top of that pint (A, Cut 1) ye fasten a short lash-rope.

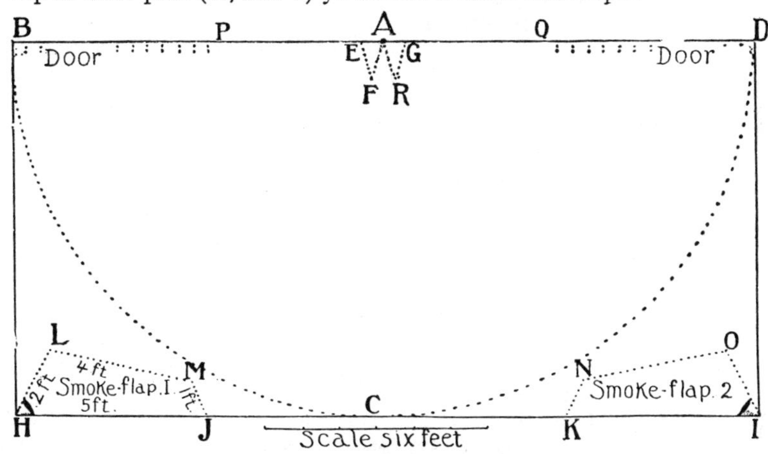

CUT I.—PATTERN FOR A SIMPLE 10-FOOT TEEPEE

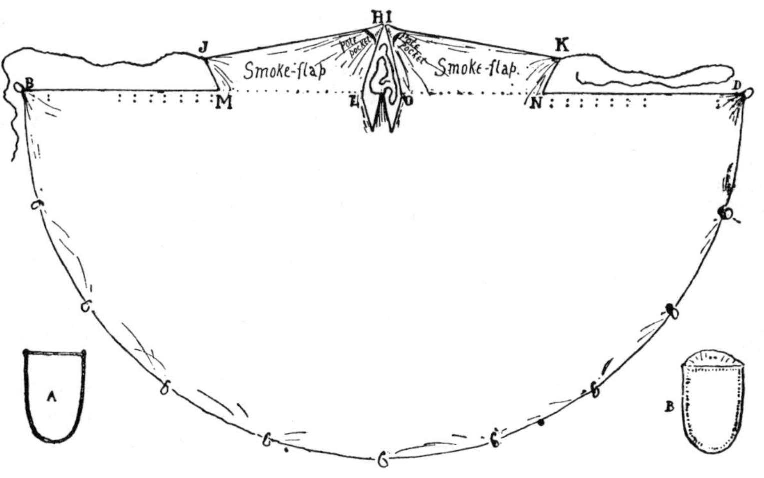

CUT II.—THE COMPLETE TEEPEE COVER—UNORNAMENTED
A—Frame for door B—Door completed

Le's see, now. I reckon thar's about ten poles for a ten-foot lodge, with two more for the smoke-flaps. Now, when ye set her up ye tie three poles together—so—an' set 'em up first, then lean the other poles around, except one, an' lash them by carrying the rope around a few times. Now tie the top o' the cover to the top o' the last pole by the short lash-rope, hist the pole into place—that hists the cover, too, ye see—an' ye swing it round with the smoke-poles an' fasten the two edges together with the wooden pins. The two long poles put in the smoke-flap pockets works the vent to suit the wind."

In his conversation Caleb had ignored Sam and talked to Yan, but the son of his father was not so easily abashed. He foresaw several practical difficulties and did not hesitate to ask for light.

"What keeps it from blowin' down?" he asked.

"Wall," said Caleb, still addressing Yan, "the long rope that binds the poles is carried down under, and fastened tight to a stake that serves for anchor, 'sides the edge of the cover is pegged to the ground all around."

"How do you make the smoke draw?" was his next.

"Ye swing the flaps by changing the poles till they is quartering down the wind. That draws best."

"How do you close the door?"

"Wall, some jest lets the edges sag together, but the best teepees has a door made of the same stuff as the cover put tight on a saplin'-frame an' swung from a lacin' pin."

This seemed to cover the ground, so carefully folding the dirty paper with the plan, Yan put it in his pocket, said "Thank you" and went off. To the "Good-day" of the boys Caleb made no reply, but turned as they left and asked, "Whar ye camped?"

"On the knoll by the creek in Raften's swamp."

"H-m, maybe I'll come an' see ye."

"All right," Sam called out; "follow the blazed trail from the brush fence."

"Why, Sam," said Yan, as soon as they were out of hearing, "there isn't any blazed trail; why did you say that?"

"Oh, I thought it sounded well," was the calm answer, "an' it's easy to have the blazes there as soon as we want to, an' a blame sight sooner than he's likely to use them."

VI

The Making of the Teepee

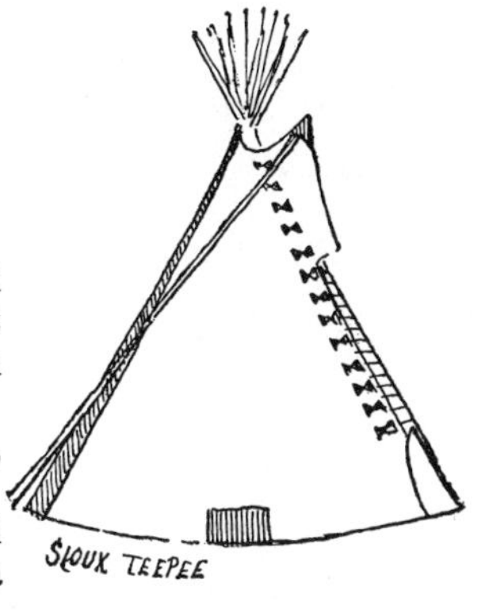

RAFTEN sniffed in amusement when he heard that the boys had really gone to Caleb and got what they wanted. Nothing pleased him more than to find his son a successful schemer.

"Old Caleb wasn't so dead sure about the teepee, as near as I sized him up," observed Sam.

"I guess we've got enough to go ahead on," said Yan, "an' tain't a hanging matter if we do make a mistake."

The cover was spread out again flat and smooth on the barn floor, and stones and a few nails put in the sides to hold it.

The first thing that struck them was that it was a rough and tattered old rag.

And Sam remarked: "I see now why Da said we could have it. I reckon we'll have to patch it before we cut out the teepee."

"No," said Yan, assuming control, as he was apt to do in matters pertaining to the woods; "we better draw our plans first so as not to patch any part that's going to be cut off afterward."

"Great head! But I'm afraid them patches won't be awful ornamental."

'They're all right," was the reply. "Indians' teepees are often patched where bullets and arrows have gone through."

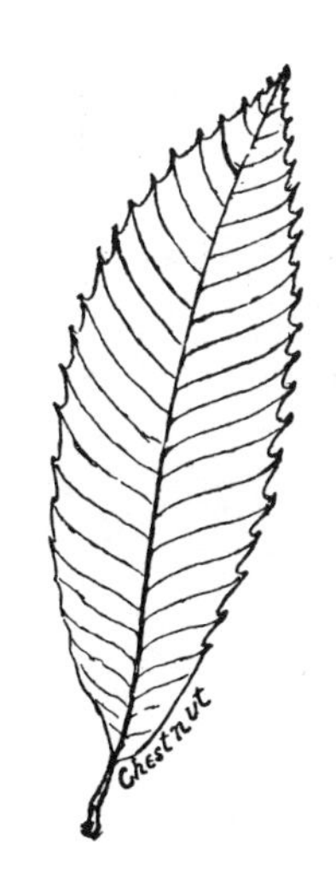

"Well, I'm glad I wa'n't living inside during them hostilities," and Sam exposed a dozen or more holes.

"Oh, get off there and give me that cord."

"Look out," said Sam; "that's my festered knee. It's near as bad to-day as it was when we called on the witch."

Yan was measuring. "Let's see. We can cut off all those rags and still make a twelve-foot teepee. Twelve foot high—that will be twenty-four feet across the bottom of the stuff. Fine! That's just the thing. Now I'll mark her off."

"Hold on, there," protested his friend; "you can't do that with chalk. Caleb said the Injuns used a burnt stick. You hain't got no right to use chalk. 'You might as well hire a carpenter.'"

"Oh, you go on. You hunt for a burnt stick, and if you don't find one bring me the shears instead."

Thus, with many consultations of Caleb's draft, the cutting-out was done—really a very simple matter. Then the patching was to be considered.

Pack-thread, needles and *very l-o-n-g* stitches were used, but the work went slowly on. All the spare time of one day was given to patching. Sam, of course, kept up a patter of characteristic remarks to the piece he was sewing. Yan sewed in serious silence. At first Sam's were put on better, but Yan learned fast and at length did by far the better sewing.

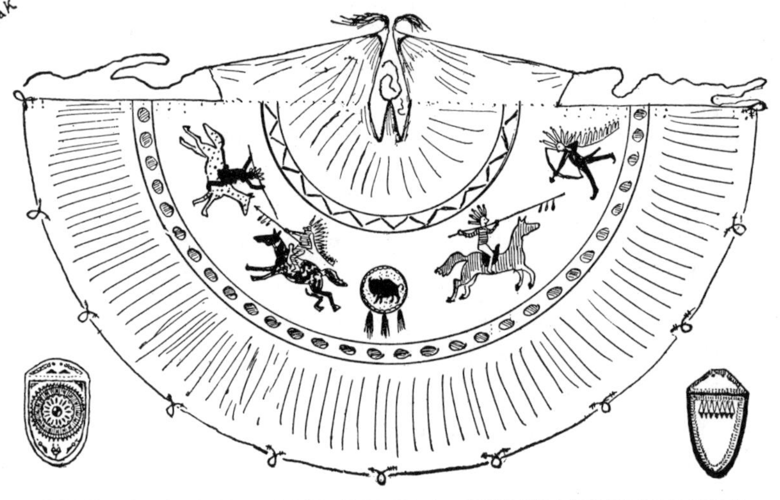

DECORATION OF BLACK BULL'S TEEPEE: (TWO EXAMPLES OF DOORS)

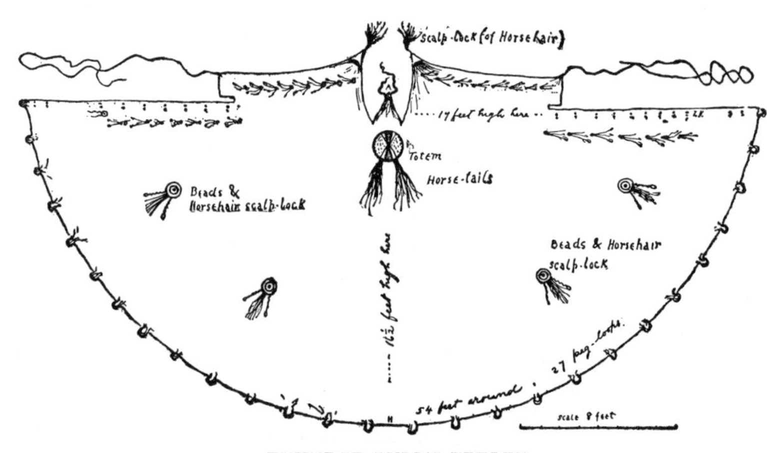

THUNDER BULL'S TEEPEE

That night the boys were showing their handiwork to the hired hands. Si Lee, a middle-aged man with a vast waistband, after looking on with ill-concealed but good-natured scorn, said:

"Why didn't ye put the patches inside?"

"Didn't think of it," was Yan's answer.

"Coz we're goin' to live inside, an' need the room," said Sam.

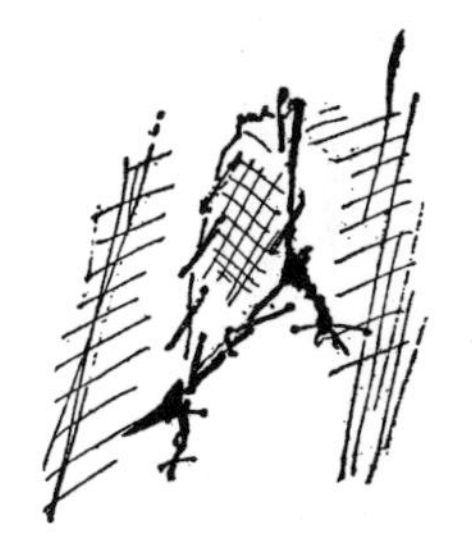

"Why did ye make ten stitches in going round that hole; ye could just as easy have done it in four," and Si sniffed as he pointed to great, ungainly stitches an inch long. "I call that waste labour."

"Now see here," blurted Sam, "if you don't like our work let's see you do it better. There's lots to do yet."

"Where?"

"Oh, ask Yan. He's bossin' the job. Old Caleb wouldn't let me in. It just broke my heart. I sobbed all the way home, didn't I, Yan?

"There's the smoke-flaps to stitch on and hem, and the pocket at the top of the flaps—and—I—suppose," Yan added, as a feeler, "it—would—be—better—if—hemmed—all—around."

"Now, I tell ye what I'll do. If you boys 'll go to the 'Corner' to-night and get my boots that the cobbler's fixing, I'll sew on the smoke-flaps."

"I'll take that offer," said Yan; "and say, Si, it doesn't really matter which is the outside. You can turn the cover so the patches will be in."

The boys got the money to pay for the boots, and after supper they set out on foot for the "Corner," two miles away.

"He's a queer duck," and Sam jerked his thumb back to show that he meant Si Lee; "sounds like a Chinese laundry. I guess that's the only thing he isn't. He can do any mortal thing but get on in life. He's been a soldier an' a undertaker an' a cook. He plays a fiddle he made himself; it's a rotten bad one, but it's away ahead of his playing. He stuffs birds—that Owl in the parlour is his doin'; he tempers razors, kin doctor a horse or fix up a watch, an' he does it in about the same way, too; bleeds a horse no matter what ails it, an' takes another wheel out o' the watch every times he cleans it. He took Larry de Neuville's old clock apart to clean once—said he knew all about it—an' when he put it together again he had wheels enough left over for a new clock.

"He's too smart an' not smart enough. There ain't anything on earth he can't do a little, an' there ain't

a blessed thing that he can do right up first-class, but thank goodness sewing canvas is his long suit. You see he was a sailor for three years—longest time he ever kept a job, fur which he really ain't to blame, since it was a whaler on a three-years' cruise.

VII

The Calm Evening

IT was a calm June evening, the time of the second daily outburst of bird song, the day's aftermath. The singers seemed to be in unusual numbers as well. Nearly every good perch had some little bird that seemed near bursting with joy and yet trying to avert that dire catastrophe.

As the boys went down the road by the outer fence of their own orchard a Hawk came sailing over, silencing as he came the singing within a given radius. Many of the singers hid, but a Meadow Lark that had been whistling on a stake in the open was now vainly seeking shelter in the broad field. The Hawk was speeding his way. The Lark dodged and put on all power to reach the orchard, but the Hawk was after him now—was gaining—in another moment would have clutched the terrified musician, but out of the Apple trees there dashed a small black-and-white bird—the Kingbird. With a loud harsh twitter—his war-cry—repeated again and again, with his little gray head-feathers raised to show the blood-and-flame-coloured undercrest—his war colours—he darted straight at the great robber.

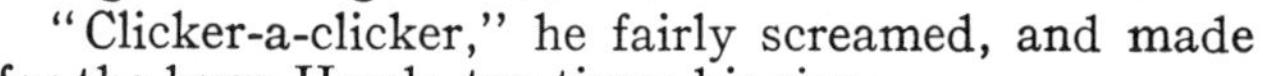

"Clicker-a-clicker," he fairly screamed, and made for the huge Hawk, ten times his size.

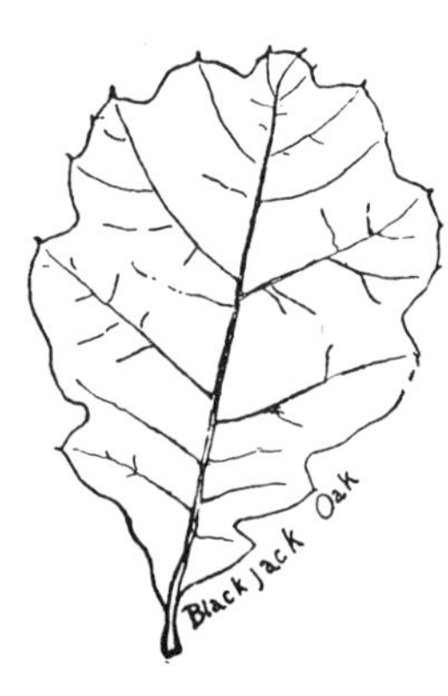

"Clicker-a-clicker!" he shrieked, like a cateran shouting the "slogan," and down like a black-and-white dart—to strike the Hawk fairly between the shoulders just as the Meadow Lark dropped in despair to the bare ground and hid its head from the approaching stroke of death.

"Clicker-a-clicker"—and the Hawk wheeled in sudden consternation. "Clicker-a-clicker"—and the dauntless little warrior dropped between his wings, stabbing and tearing.

The Hawk bucked like a mustang, the Kingbird was thrown, but sprung on agile pinions above again.

"Clicker-a-clicker," and he struck as before. Large brown feathers were floating away on the breeze now. The Meadow Lark was forgotten. The Hawk thought only of escape.

"Clicker-a-clicker," the slogan still was heard. The Hawk was putting on all speed to get away, but the Kingbird was riding him most of the time. Several brown feathers floated down, the Hawk dwindled in the distance to a Sparrow and the Kingbird to a fly dancing on his back. The Hawk made a final plunge into a thicket, and the king came home again, uttering the shrill war-cry once or twice, probably to let the queen know that he was coming back, for she flew to a high branch of the Apple tree where she could greet the returning hero. He came with an occasional "clicker-a-clicker"—then, when near her, he sprung fifty feet in the air and dashed down, screaming his slogan without interruption, darting zigzag with the most surprising evolutions and turns—this way, that way, sideways and downward, dealing the deadliest blows right and left at an imaginary foe, then soared, and did it all over again two or three times, just to show how far he was from being tired, and how much better he could have done it had it been necessary. Then with a final swoop and a volley of "clickers" he dashed into the bush to receive the congratulations of the one for whom it all was meant and the only spectator for whose opinion he cared in the least.

"Now, ain't that great," said Sam, with evident sincerity and pleasure. His voice startled Yan and brought him back. He had been wholly lost in silent admiring wonder of the dauntless little Kingbird.

A Vesper Sparrow ran along the road before them, flitting a few feet ahead each time they overtook it and showing the white outer tail-feathers as it flew.

"A little Graybird," remarked Sam.

"No, that isn't a Graybird; that's a Vesper Sparrow," exclaimed Yan, in surprise, for he knew he was right.

"Well, *I* dunno," said Sam, yielding the point.

"I thought you said you knew every bird that flies and all about it," replied his companion, for the memory of this first day was strong with him yet.

Sam snorted: "I didn't know you then. I was just loadin' you up so you'd think I was a wonderful feller, an' you did, too—for awhile."

A Red-headed Woodpecker, carrying a yellow butterfly, flew on a fence stake ahead of them and peeped around as they drew near. The setting sun on his bright plumage, the lilac stake and the yellow butterfly, completed a most gorgeous bit of colour and gave Yan a thrill of joy. A Meadow Lark on a farther stake, a Bluebird on another, and a Vesper Bird on a stone, each added his appeal to eye and ear, till Sam exclaimed:

"Oh, ain't that awful nice?" and Yan was dumb with a sort of saddened joy.

Birds hate the wind, and this was one of those birdy days that come only with a dead calm.

They passed a barn with two hundred pairs of Swallows flying and twittering around, a cut bank of the road had a colony of 1,000 Sand Martins,.a stream had its rattling Kingfishers, and a marsh was the playground of a multitude of Red-winged Blackbirds.

Yan was lifted up with the joy of the naturalist at seeing so many beautiful living things. Sam felt it, too; he grew very silent, and the last half-mile to the "Corner" was passed without a word. The boots were got. Sam swung them around his neck and the boys set out for home. The sun was gone, but not the birds, and the spell of the evening was on them still. A Song Sparrow by the brook and a Robin high in the Elm were yet pouring out their liquid notes in the gloaming.

"I wish I could be always here," said Yan, but he started a little when he remembered how unwilling he had been to come.

There was a long silence as they lingered on the darkening road. Each was thinking hard.

A loud, startling but soft "Ohoo — O-hoo — O-hoooooo," like the coo of a giant dove, now sounded about their heads in a tree. They stopped and Sam whispered, "Owl; big Hoot Owl." Yan's heart leaped with pleasure. He had read all his life of Owls, and even had seen them alive in cages, but this was the first time he had ever heard the famous hooting of the real live wild Owl, and it was a delicious experience.

The night was quite dark now, but there were plenty of sounds that told of life. A Whippoorwill was chanting in the woods, a hundred Toads and Frogs creaked and trilled, a strange rolling, laughing cry on a marshy pond puzzled them both, then a Song Sparrow in the black night of a dense thicket poured forth its sweet little sunshine song with all the vigour and joy of its best daytime doing.

They listened attentively for a repetition of the serenade, when a high-pitched but not loud "*Wa—wa—wa—wa—wa—wa—wa—wa!*" reached their ears from a grove of heavy timbers.

"Hear that?" exclaimed Sam.

Again it came, a quavering squall, apparently much nearer. It was a rather shrill sound, quite unbirdy, and Sam whispered:

"Coon—that's the whicker of a Coon. We can come down here some time when corn's 'in roastin'' an' have a Coon hunt."

"Oh, Sam, wouldn't that be glorious!" said Yan. "How I wish it was now. I never saw a Coon hunt or any kind of a hunt. Do we have to wait till 'roasting-ear' time?"

"Oh, yes; it's easier to find them then. You say to your Coons, 'Me an' me dogs will meet you to-night at the nearest roastin'-ear patch,' an' sure nuff *they'll* keep the appointment."

"But they're around now, for we just heard one, *and there's another.*"

A long faint "*Lil—lil—lil—lil—lil—li-looo!*" now sounded from the trees. It was like the other, but much softer and sweeter.

"There's where you fool yerself," replied Sam, "an' there's where many a hunter is fooled. That last one's the call of a Screech Owl. You see it's softer and whistlier than the Coon whicker."

They heard it again and again from the trees. It was a sweet musical sound, and Yan remembered how squally the Coon call was in comparison, and yet many hunters never learn the difference.

As they came near the tree whence the Owl called at intervals, a gray blot went over their heads, shutting out a handful of stars for a moment as it passed over them, but making no noise. "There he goes," whispered Sam. "That's the Screech Owl. Not much of a screech, was it?" Not long afterward Yan came across a line of Lowell's which says, "The song of the Screech Owl is the sweetest sound in nature," and appreciated the absurdity of the name.

"I want to go on a Coon hunt," continued Yan,

and the sentence was just tinged with the deep-laid doggedness that was usually lost in his courteous manner.

"That settles it," answered the other, for he was learning what that tone meant. "We'll surely go when you talk that way, for, of coorse, it *kin* be done. You see, I know more about animals than birds," he continued. "I'm just as likely to be a dentist as a hunter so far as serious business is concerned, but I'd sure love to be a hunter for awhile, an' I made Da promise to go with me some time. Maybe we kin get a Deer by going back ten miles to the Long Swamp. I only wish Da and Old Caleb hadn't fought, 'cause Caleb sure knows the woods, an' that old Hound of his has treed more Coons than ye could shake a stick at in a month o' Sundays."

"Well, if that's the only Coon dog around, I'm going to get him. You'll see," was the reply.

"I believe you will," answered Sam, in a tone of mixed admiration and amusement.

It was ten o'clock when they got home, and every one was in bed but Mr. Raften. The boys turned in at once, but next morning, on going to the barn, they found that Si had not only sewed on and hemmed the smoke-flaps, but had resewn the worst of the patches and hemmed the whole bottom of the teepee cover with a small rope in the hem, so that they were ready now for the pins and poles.

The cover was taken at once to the camp ground. Yan carried the axe. When they came to the brush fence over the creek at the edge of the swamp, he said:

"Sam, I want to blaze that trail for old Caleb. How do you do it?"

"Spot the trees with the axe every few yards."

"This way?" and Yan cut a tree in three places, so as to show three white spots or blazes.

"No; that's a trapper's blaze for a trap or a 'special blaze,' but a 'road blaze' is one on the front of the tree and one on the back—so—then ye can run the trail both ways, an' you put them thicker if it's to be followed at night.

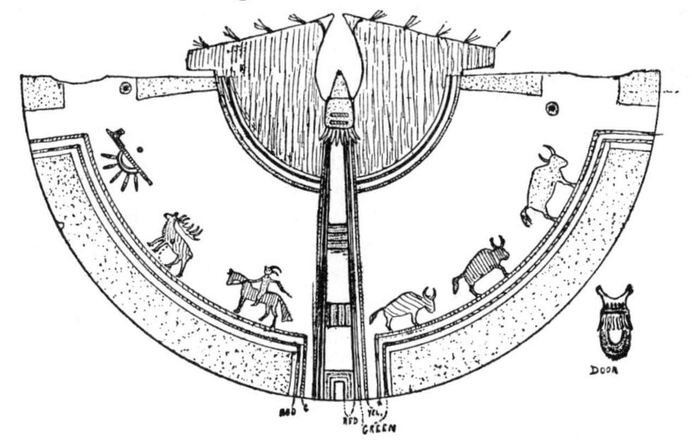

VIII

The Sacred Fire

"TEN strong poles and two long thin ones," said Yan, reading off. These were soon cut and brought to the camp ground.

"Tie them together about eighteen inches higher than the teepee cover——"

"Tie them? With what?"

"'Rawhide rope,' he said, but he also said 'Make the cover of skins.' I'm afraid we shall have to use common rope for the present," and Yan looked a little ashamed of the admission.

"I reckoned so," drawled Sam, "and so I put a coil of quarter-inch in the cover, but I didn't dare to tell you that up at the barn."

The tripod was firmly lashed with the rope and set up. Nine poles were duly leaned around in a twelve-foot circle, for a teepee twelve feet high usually has a twelve-foot base. A final lashing of the ropes held these, and the last pole was then put up opposite to the door, with the teepee cover tied to it at the point between the flaps. The ends of the two smoke-poles carried the cover round. Then the lacing-pins were needed. Yan tried to make them of Hickory shoots, but the large, soft pith came just where the point was needed. So Sam said, "You can't beat White Oak for pins." He cut a block of White Oak, split it down the middle, then split half of it in the middle again, and so on till it was small enough to trim and finish with his knife. Meanwhile Yan took the axe to split another, but found that it ran off to one side instead of going straight down the grain.

Blackfoot

"No good," was Sam's comment. "You must keep *halving* each time or it will run out toward the thin pieces. You want to split shingles all winter to larn that."

Ten pins were made eight inches long and a quarter of an inch thick. They were used just like dress-makers' stickpins, only the holes had to be made first, and, of course, they looked better for being regular. Thus the cover was laced on. The lack of ground-pegs was then seen.

"You make ten Oak pins a foot long and an inch square, Sam. I've a notion how to fix them." Then Yan cut ten pieces of the rope, each two feet long, and made a hole about every three feet around the base of the cover above the rope in the outer seam. He passed one end of each short rope through this and knotted it to the other end. Thus he had ten peg-loops, and the teepee was fastened down and looked like a glorious success.

Piegan

Now came the grand ceremony of all, the lighting of the first fire. The boys felt it to be a supreme and almost a religious moment. It is curious to note that they felt very much as savages do under the same circumstances—that the setting up of the new teepee and lighting its first fire is an act of deep significance, and to be done only with proper regard for its future good luck.

"Better go slow and sure about that fire. It'd be awfully unlucky to have it fizzle for the first time."

"That's so," replied Yan, with the same sort of superstitious dread. "Say, Sam, if we could really light it with rubbing-sticks, wouldn't it be great?"

"Hallo!"

The boys turned, and there was Caleb close to them. He came over and nodded. "Got yer teepee, I see? Not bad, but what did ye face her to the west fur?"

"Fronting the creek," explained Yan.

"I forgot to tell ye," said Caleb, "an Injun teepee always fronts the east; first, that gives the morning sun inside; next, the most wind is from the west, so the smoke is bound to draw."

"And what if the wind is right due east?" asked Sam, "which it surely will be when it rains?"

"And when the wind's east," continued Caleb, addressing no one in particular, and not as though in answer to a question, "ye lap the flaps across each other tight in front, so," and he crossed his hands over his chest. "That leaves the east side high and shuts out the rain; if it don't draw then, ye raise the bottom of the cover under the door just a little—that always fetches her. An' when you change her round don't put her in under them trees. Trees is dangerous; in a storm they draw lightning, an' branches fall from them, an' after rain they keep on dripping for an hour. Ye need all the sun ye kin get on a teepee.

"Did you ever see Indians bring fire out of two sticks by rubbing, Mr. Clark?"

"Oh, yes. Most of the Injuns now carry matches, but in the early days I seen it done often enough."

"Does it take long? Is it hard?"

"Not so long, and it's easy enough, when ye know how."

"My! I'd rather bring fire out of two sticks than have a ten dollar bill," said Yan, with enthusiasm that meant much, for one dollar was his high-water mark of affluence, and this he had reached but once in his life.

"Oh, I dunno'; that depends," was Sam's more guarded response.

"Can *you* do it?" asked Yan.

"Wall, yes, if I kin get the right stuff. Ye see, it ain't every wood that will do it. It's got to be jest right. The Plains Injuns use Cottonwood root, an' the Mountain Injuns use Sage-brush root. I've seen the Canadian Injuns use Basswood, Cedar and dry

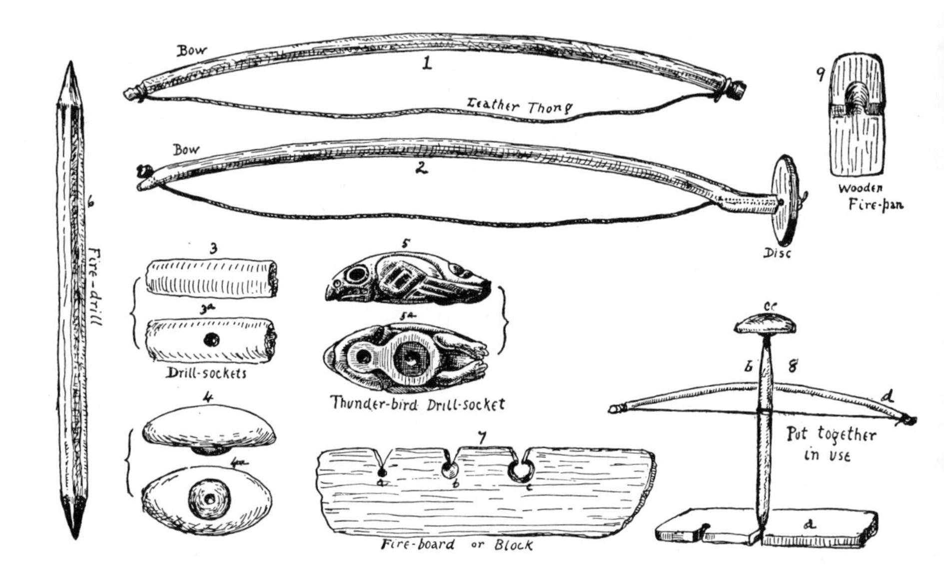

RUBBING-STICKS—FOR FIRE-MAKING

Two tools and two sticks are needed. The tools are bow and drill-socket; the sticks are drill and fire-board.

1. The simplest kind of bow—a bent stick with a stout leather thong fastened at each end. The stick must not spring. It is about 27 inches long and ⅝ inch thick.
2. A more elaborate bow with a hole at each end for the thong. At the handle end it goes through a disc of wood. This is to tighten the thong by pressure of the hand against the disc while using.
3. Simplest kind of drill-socket—a pine or hemlock knot with a shallow hole or pit in it. *3a* is under view of same. It is about 4½ inches long.
4. A more elaborate drill-socket—a pebble cemented with gum in a wooden holder. *4a* is under view of same.
5. A very elaborate drill-socket; it is made of tulip wood, carved to represent the Thunderbird. It has eyes of green felspar cemented in with resin. On the under side (*5a*) is seen, in the middle, a soapstone socket let into the wood and fastened with pine gum, and on the head a hole kept filled with grease, to grease the top of the drill before use.
6. The drill, 12 to 18 inches long and about ¾ of an inch thick; it is roughly 8-sided so the thong will not slip, and pointed at each end. The best wood for the drill is old, dry, brash, but not punky balsam fir or cotton-wood roots; but basswood, white cedar, red cedar, tamarack, and sometimes even white pine, will do.
7. Fire-board or block, about ¾ of an inch thick and any length handy; *a* is notch with pit just begun, *b* shows the pit after once using and in good trim for a second time; *c* shows the pit bored through and now useless; the notch is ⅛ inch wide and ¾ inch deep.
8. Shows the way of using the sticks. The block (*a*) is held down with one foot, the end of the drill (*b*) is put in the pit, the drill-socket (*c*) is held on top in left hand, one end of the bow (*d*) is held in the right hand, while the bow is drawn back and forth.
9. Is a little wooden fire-pan, not essential but convenient; its thin edge is put under the notch to catch the powder that falls.

White Pine, but the Chippewas mostly use Balsam Fir. The easiest way is with a bow-drill. Have ye any buckskin?"

"No."

"Or a strip o' soft leather?"

"I've got a leather shoe-lace," said Yan.

"Rather slim; but we'll double it an' make it do. A cord will answer, but it frays out so soon." Caleb took the lace and the axe, then said, "Find me a stone 'bout the size of an egg, with a little hole into it—like a socket hole—'bout a quarter inch deep."

The boys went to the creek to seek a stone and Caleb went into the woods.

They heard him chopping, and presently he came back with a flat piece of very dry Balsam Fir, a fifteen-inch pin of the same, a stick about three feet long, slightly bent, some dry Pine punk and some dry Cedar.

The pin was three-quarters of an inch thick and was roughly eight-sided, "so the lace would grip." It was pointed at both ends. He fastened the lace to the bent stick like a bow-string, but loosely, so that when it had one turn around the pin it was quite tight. The flat piece of Balsam he trimmed down to about half an inch thick. In the edge of this he now cut a notch one-quarter inch wide and half an inch deep, then on the top of this fire-board or block, just beyond the notch, he made with the point of his knife a little pit.

He next scraped and shredded a lot of dry Cedar wood like lint. Then making a hole half an inch deep in the ground, he laid in that a flat piece of Pine punk, and across this he set the fire-board. The point of the pin or drill was put in the pit of the fire-board, which he held down with one foot; the lace was given one turn on the pin, and its top went into the hole of the stone the boys brought. The stone was held firmly in Caleb's left hand.

"Sometimes," he remarked, "when ye can't find a stone, a Pine knot will do—ye kin make the socket-hole with a knife-point."

Now holding the bow in his right hand, he began to draw it back and forth with long, steady strokes, causing the pin to whirl round in the socket. Within a few seconds a brown powder began to run out of the notch of the fire-board onto the punk. The pit increased in size and blackened, the powder darkened, and a slight smoke arose from the pit.

Caleb increased the pressure of his left hand a little, and sawed faster with the right. The smoke steadily increased and the black powder began to fill the notch. The smoke was rolling in little clouds from under the pin, and it even seemed to come from the heap of powder. As soon as he saw that, Caleb dropped the bow and gently fanned the powder heap. It still smoked. He removed the fire-board, and lifting the punk, showed the interior of the powder to be one glowing coal. On this he laid the Cedar tinder and over that a second piece of punk. Then raising it, he waved it in the air and blew gently for awhile. It smouldered and then burst into a flame. The other material was handy, and in a very short time they had a blazing fire in the middle of the new teepee.

All three were pictures of childish delight. The old man's face fairly beamed with triumph. Had he failed in his experiment he would have gone off hating those boys, but having made a brilliant success he was ready to love every one concerned, though they had been nothing more than interested spectators of his exploit.

IX

The Bows and Arrows

I DON'T think much of your artillery," said Yan one day as they were shooting in the orchard with Sam's "Western outfit." "It's about like the first one I made when I was young."

"Well, grandpa, let's see your up-to-date make?"

"It'd be about five times as strong, for one thing."

"You couldn't pull it."

"Not the way you hold the arrow! But last

winter I got a book about archery from the library and learned something worth while. You pinch the arrow that way and you can draw six or eight pounds, maybe, but you hook your fingers in the string—so—and you can draw five times as much, and that's the right way to shoot."

"Feels mighty clumsy," said Sam, trying it.

"Of course it does at first, and you have to have a deep notch in the arrow or you can't do it at all."

"You don't seem to manage any better than I do."

"First time I ever had a chance to try since I read about it. But I want to make a first-class bow and a lot of arrows. It's not much good going with *one*."

"Well, go ahead an' make an outfit if you know how. What's the best wood? Did the book tell you that?"

"The best wood is Spanish Yew."

"Don't know it."

"An' the next is Oregon Yew."

"Nope."

"Then Lancewood and Osage Orange."

"Try again."

The Archer's Grip

"Well, Red Cedar, Apple tree, Hickory, and Elm seem to be the only ones that grow around here."

"Hain't seen any *Red* Cedar, but the rest is easy."

"It has to be thoroughly seasoned winter-cut wood, and cut so as to have heart on one side and sap wood on the other."

"How's that?" and Sam pointed to a lot of half-round Hickory sticks on the rafters of the log house. "Those have been there a couple of years."

A good one of five feet long was selected and split and hewn with the axe till the boys had the two bow staves, five and one-half feet long and two inches square, with the line of the heart and sap wood down the middle of each.

Guided by his memory of that precious book and some English long bows that he had seen in a shop in town, Yan superintended the manufacture. Sam was apt with tools, and in time they finished two bows, five feet long and drawing possibly twenty-five pounds each. In the middle they were one and one-half inches wide and an inch thick (see page 86). This size they kept for nine inches each way, making an eighteen-inch middle part that did not bend, but their two limbs were shaved down and scraped with glass till they bent evenly and were well within the boys' strength.

The string was the next difficulty. All the ordinary string they could get around the house proved too weak, never lasting more than two or three shots, till Si Lee, seeing their trouble, sent them to the cobbler's for a hank of unbleached linen thread and some shoemaker's wax. Of this thread he reeled enough for a strong cord tight around two pegs seven feet apart, then cutting it loose at one end he divided it equally in three parts, and, after slight waxing, he loosely plaited them together. At Yan's suggestion he then spliced a loop at one end, and with a fine waxed thread lashed six inches of the middle where the arrow fitted, as well as the splice of the loop. This last enabled them to unstring the bow when not in use (see page 86). "There," said he, "you won't break that." The finishing touch was thinly coating the bows with some varnish found among the paint supplies.

"Makes my old bow look purty sick," remarked Sam, as he held up the really fine new weapon in contrast with the wretched little hoop that had embodied his early ideas. "Now what do you know about arrers, mister?" as he tried his old arrow in the new bow.

"I know that that's no good," was the reply; "an' I can tell you that it's a deal harder to make an arrow than a bow—that is, a good one."

"That's encouraging, considering the trouble we've had already."

"'Tisn't meant to be, but we ought to have a dozen arrows each."

"How do the Injuns make them?"

"Mostly they get straight sticks of the Arrow-wood; but I haven't seen any Arrow-wood here, and they're not so awfully straight. You see, an arrow must be straight or it'll fly crooked. 'Straight as an arrow' means the thing itself. We can do better than the Indians 'cause we have better tools. We can split them out of the solid wood."

"What wood? Some bloomin' foreign kind that no White-man never saw nor heard of before?"

"No sir-ree. There ain't anything better 'n White Pine for target and Ash or Hickory for hunting arrows. Which are we making?"

"I'm a hunter. Give me huntin' arrows every time. What's needed next?"

"'Clicker-a-clicker!' he shrieked . . . and down like a dart"

The dam was a great success

"Seasoned Ash twenty-five inches long, split to three-eighths of an inch thick, hot glue, and turkey-wing feathers."

"I'll get the feathers and let you do the rest," said Sam, producing a bundle of turkey-wings, laid away as stove-dusters, and then belied his own statement by getting a block of Ash and splitting it up, halving it each time till he had a pile of two dozen straight sticks about three-quarters of an inch thick.

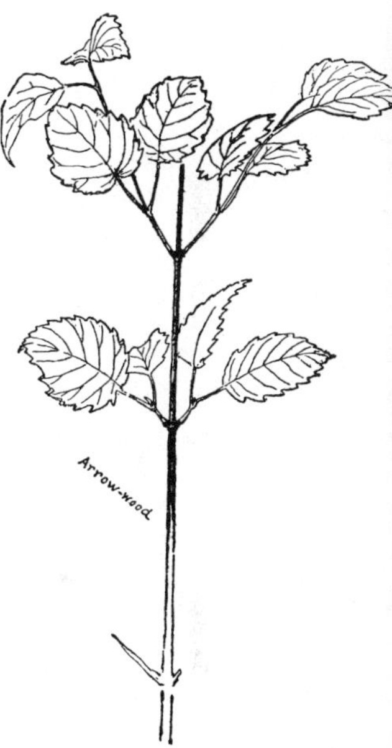

Yan took one and began with his knife to whittle it down to proper size and shape, but Sam said, "I can do better than that," then took the lot to the work-bench and set to work with a smoothing plane. Yan looked worried and finally said:

"Injuns didn't have planes."

"Nor jack-knives neither," was the retort.

That was true, and yet somehow Yan's ideal that he hankered after was the pre-Columbian Indian, the one who had no White-man's help or tools.

"It seems to me it'd be more Injun to make these with just what we get in the woods. The Injuns didn't have jack-knives, but they had sharp flints in the old days."

"Yan, you go ahead with a sharp stone. You'll find lots on the road if you take off your shoes and walk barefoot—awful sharp; an' I'll go ahead with the smoothing plane an' see who wins."

Yan was not satisfied, but he contented himself with promising that he would some day make some arrows of Arrow-wood shoots and now he would finish at least one with his knife. He did so, but Sam, in the meantime, made six much better ones with the smoothing plane.

"What about heads?" said he.

"I've been thinking," was the reply. "Of course the Indians used stone heads fastened on with sinew, but we haven't got the stuff to do that. Bought heads of iron with a ferrule for the end of the arrow are best, but we can't get them. Bone heads and horn heads will do. I made some fine ones once filing bones into the shape, but they were awfully brittle; and I made some more of big nails cut off and set in with a lashing of fine wire around the end to stop the wood splitting. Some Indian arrows have no point but the stick sharpened after it's scorched to harden it."

"That sounds easy enough for me," said Sam; "let's make some of them that way."

So the arrows were made, six each with nail points filed sharp and lashed with broom wire. These were called "War arrows," and six each with fire-hardened wood points for hunting arrows.

"Now for the feathering," and Yan showed Sam how to split the midrib of a turkey feather and separate the vane.

"Le's see, you want twice twenty-four—that's forty-eight feathers."

"No," said Yan, "that's a poor feathering, two on each. We want three on each arrow—seventy-two strips in all, and mind you, we want all three that are on one arrow from the same side of the bird."

"I know. I'll bet it's bad luck to mix sides; arrows doesn't know which way to turn."

At this moment Si Lee came in. "How are ye gettin' on with the bows?"

"Waitin' for arrows now."

"How do ye put on the feathers?"

"White-men glue them on, and Injuns lash them on," replied Yan, quoting from memory from "that book."

"Which is best?"

"Glued on flies better, but lashed on stands the weather better."

"Why not both?"

"Have no sinew."

"Let me show ye a trick. Where's yer glue an' linen thread?"

These were brought, whereupon Si added: "'Pears to me ye oughter put the feathers on last. Better cut the notch first."

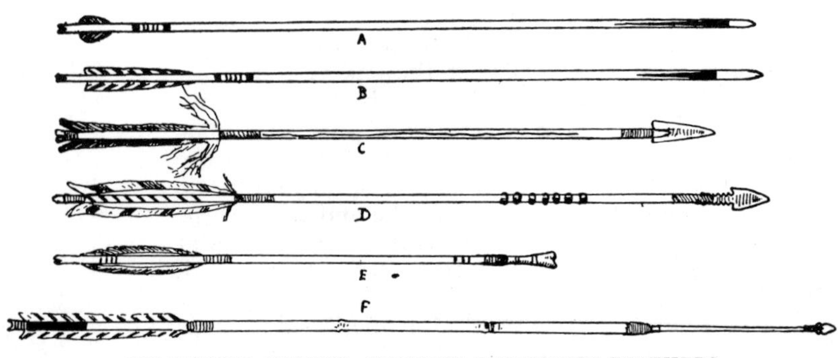

SIX SAMPLE ARROWS, SHOWING DIFFERENT FEATHERS

"That's so; we nearly forgot."

"*You* nearly forgot, you mean. Don't drag *me* in the mud," said Sam, with owlish dignity. A small saw cut, cleaned up and widened with a penknife, proved the best; a notch one-fourth inch deep was quickly made in each arrow, and Si set about *both* glueing *and* lashing on the feathers, but using wax-end instead of sinew.

Yan had marked the place for each feather so that none would strike the bow in passing (see Cut page 86). He first glued them on, then made a lashing for half an inch on the projecting ends of the feather-rib, and another behind, carrying this second lashing back to the beginning of the notch to guard against the wood splitting. When he had trimmed all loose ends and rolled the waxed thread well on the bench with a flat stick, the threads seemed to disappear and leave simply a smooth black ring.

Thus the arrows were made and set away for the glue to dry.

Next day Yan painted Sam's red and blue, his own red and white, to distinguish them as well as guard them from the damp. There was now one more thing, and that was a quiver.

"Do the Injuns have them?" asked Sam, with a keen eye to orthodoxy when it promised to cut short the hard work.

"Well, I should say so; couldn't live without them."

"All right; hurry up. I'm spoiling for a hunt. What are they made of?"

"Oh, 'most anything."

"Haven't got it."

"You're too fast. But some use Birch bark, some use the skin of an animal, and some use canvas now when other stuff is scarce."

"That's us. You mind the stuff left off the teepee?"

"Do till we get better." So each made a sort of canvas bag shorter than the arrows. Yan painted an Indian device on each, and they were ready.

"Now bring on your Bears," said the older boy, and

DESCRIPTION OF SIX SAMPLE ARROWS SHOWING DIFFERENT FEATHERS

A is a far-flying steel-pointed bobtail, very good in wind. *B* is another very good arrow, with a horn point. This went even better than *A* if there were no wind. *C* is an Omaha war and deer arrow. Both heads and feathers are lashed on with sinew. The long tufts of down left on the feathers are to help in finding it again, as they are snow-white and wave in the breeze. The grooves on the shaft are to make the victim bleed more freely and be more easily tracked. *D* is another Omaha arrow with a peculiar owner's mark of rings carved in the middle. *E* is a bone-headed bird shaft made by the Indians of the Mackenzie River. *F* is a war arrow made by Geronimo, the famous Apache chief. Its shaft is three joints of a straight cane. The tip is of hard wood, and on that is a fine quartz point; all being lashed together with sinew.

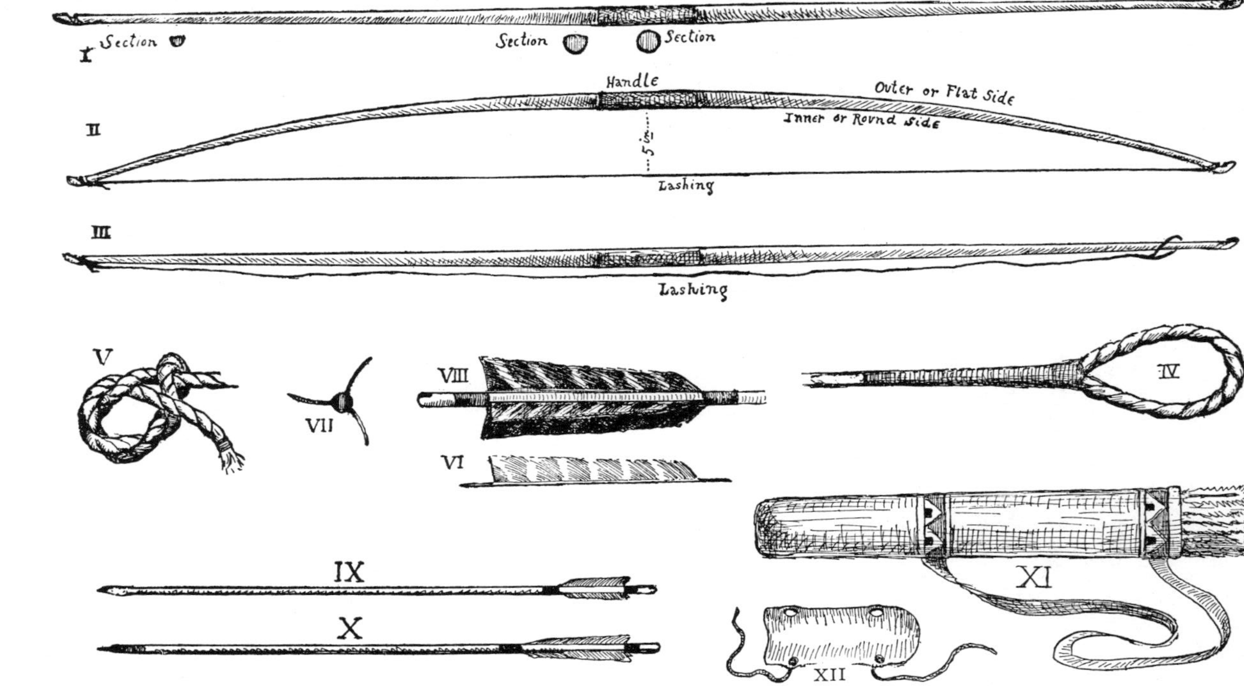

THE ARCHERY OUTFIT (Not all on scale)

I. The five-foot bow as finished, with sections at the points shown.
II. The bow "braced" or strung.
III. The bow unstrung, showing the loop slipped down.
IV. The loop that is used on the upper end of the bow.
V. The timber hitch always used on the lower end or notch of the bow.
VI. A turkey feather with split midrib, all ready to lash on.
VII. End view of arrow, showing notch and arrangement of three feathers.
VIII. Part of arrow, showing feathering and lashing.
IX. Sanger hunting arrow with wooden point; 25 inches long.
X. Sanger war arrow with nail point and extra long feathers; it also is laces 25 inches long.
XI. Quiver with Indian design; 20 inches long.
XII. The "bracer" or arm guard of heavy leather for left arm, with two laces to tie it on. It is six inches long.

feeling a sense of complete armament, they went out.

"See who can hit that tree." Both fired together and missed, but Sam's arrow struck another tree and split open.

"Guess we'd better get a soft target," he remarked. Then after discussion they got a large old corn sack full of hay, painted on it some rings around a bull's eye (a Buffalo's eye, Sam called it) and set it up at twenty yards.

They were woefully disappointed at first in their shooting. It did seem a very easy mark, and it was disappointing to have the arrows fly some feet away to the left.

"Le's get in the barn and shoot at that," suggested Sam.

"We might hit it if we shut the door tight," was the optimistic reply. As well as needing practice, the boys had to learn several little rules about Archery. But Yan had some pencil notes from "that book" and some more in his brain that with much practice gradually taught him: To stand with his heel centres in line with the target; his right elbow in line with the arrow; his left hand fixed till the arrow struck; his right thumb always on the same place on his cheek when he fired, and the bow plumb.

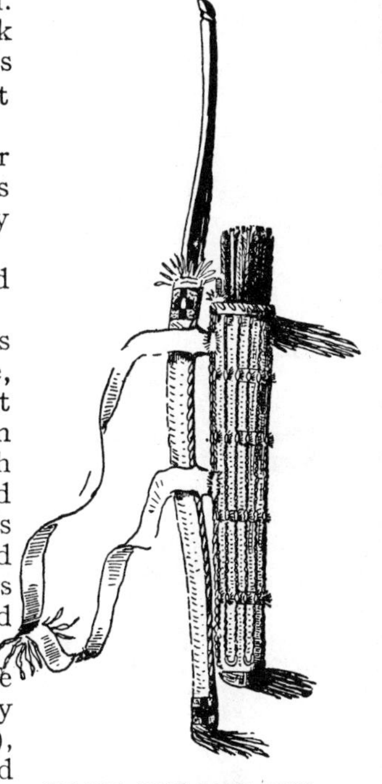

OMAHA BOW-CASE AND QUIVER OF BUCKSKIN AND QUILLWORK

They soon found that they needed guards for the left arm where the bow strings struck, and these they made out of the leg of an old boot (see Cut page 86), and an old glove to protect the fingers of the right hand when they practised very much. After they learned to obey the rules without thinking about them, the boys improved quickly and soon they were able to put all the arrows into the hay sack at twenty yards, increasing the distance later till they could make fair shooting at forty yards.

They were not a little surprised to find how much individuality the arrows had, although meant to be exactly alike.

Sam had one that continued to warp until it was much bent, and the result was some of the most surprising curves in its flight. This he called the "Boomerang." Another, with a very small feather, travelled farther than any of the rest. This was the "Far-killer." His best arrow, one that he called "Sure-death," was a long-feathered Turkey shaft with a light head. It was very reliable on a calm day, but apt to swerve in the wind. Yet another, with a small feather, was correspondingly reliable on a windy day. This was "Wind-splitter."

The one Yan whittled with the knife was called the "Whittler," and sometimes the "Joker." It was a perpetual mystery; they never knew just what it would do next. His particular pet was one with a hollow around the point, which made a whistling sound when it flew, and was sometimes called the "Whistler" and sometimes the "Jabberwock," "which whiffled through the tulgy wood and burbled as it came."

CORRECT FORM
IN SHOOTING

The diagram at bottom is to show the centres of heels in line with target

X

The Dam

ONE hot day early in July they were enjoying themselves in the shallow bathing-hole of the creek, when Sam observed: "It's getting low. It goes dry every summer."

This was not pleasing to foresee, and Yan said, "Why can't we make a dam?"

"A little too much like work."

"Oh, pshaw! That'd be fun and we'd have a swimming-place for all summer, then. Come on; let's start now."

"Never heard of Injuns doing so much work."

"Well, we'll play Beaver while we do it. Come on, now; here's for a starter," and Yan carried a big stone to what seemed to him the narrowest place. Then he brought more, and worked with enthusiasm till he had a line of stones right across the creek bed.

Sam still sat naked on the bank, his knees to his chin and his arms around them. The war-paint was running down his chest in blue and red streaks.

"Come on, here, you lazy freak, and work," cried Yan, and flung a handful of mud to emphasize the invite.

"My festered knee's broke out again," was the reply.

At length Yan said, "I'm not going to do it all alone," and straightened up his back.

"Look a-here," was the answer. "I've been thinking. The cattle water here. The creek runs dry in summer, then the cattle has to go to the barn-yard and drink at the trough—has to be pumped for, and hang round for hours after hoping some one will give them some oats, instead of hustling back to the woods to get fat. Now, two big logs across there would be more'n half the work. I guess we'll ask Da to lend us the team to put them logs across to make a drinking-pond for the cattle. Them cattle is awful on my mind. Didn't sleep all night thinking o' them. I just hate like pizen to see them walking all the way to the barn in hot weather for a drink—'tain't right." So Sam waited for a proper chance to "tackle" his father. It did not come that day, but at breakfast next morning Raften looked straight at Yan across the table, and evidently thinking hard about something, said:

"Yahn, this yer room is twenty foot by fifteen, how much ilecloth three foot wide will it call fur?"

"Thirty-three and one-third yards," Yan said at once.

Raften was staggered. Yan's manner was convincing, but to do all that in his head was the miracle. Various rude tests were applied and the general opinion prevailed that Yan was right.

The farmer's face beamed with admiration for the first time. "Luk at that," he said to the table, "luk at that fur eddication. When'll you be able to do the like?" he said to Sam.

"Never," returned his son, with slow promptness. "Dentists don't have to figger on ilecloth."

"Say, Yan," said Sam aside, "guess *you* better tackle Da about the dam. Kind o' sot up about ye this mornin'; your eddication has softened him some, an' it'll last till about noon, I jedge. Strike while the iron is hot."

So after breakfast Yan commenced:

"Mr. Raften, the creek's running dry. We want to make a pond for the cattle to drink, but we can't make a dam without two big logs across. Will you let us have the team a few minutes to place the logs?"

"It ain't fur a swimmin'-pond, is it, ye mean?" said Raften, with a twinkle in his eye.

"It would do for that as well," and Yan blushed.

"Sounds to me like Sam talking through Yan's face," added Raften, shrewdly taking in the situation. "I'll see fur meself."

Arrived at the camp, he asked: "Now, whayer's yer dam to be? Thar? That's no good. It's narrer but it'd be runnin' round both ends afore ye had any water to speak of. Thayer's a better place, a bit wider, but givin' a good pond. Whayer's yer logs? Thayer? What—my seasoning timber? Ye can't hev that. That's the sill fur the new barrn; nor that—it's seasonin' fur gate posts. Thayer's two ye kin hev. I'll send the team, but don't let me ketch ye stealin' any o' my seasonin' timber or the fur'll fly."

With true Raften promptness the heavy team came, the two great logs were duly dragged across and left as Yan requested (four feet apart for the top of the dam).

The boys now drove in a row of stakes against each log on the inner side, to form a crib, and were beginning to fill in the space with mud and stones. They were digging and filling it up level as they went. Clay was scarce and the work went slowly; the water, of course, rising as the wall arose, added to the difficulty. But presently Yan said:

"Hold on. New scheme. Let's open her and dig a deep trench on one side so all the water will go by, then leave a clay wall to it" [the trench] "and dig a deep hole on the other side of it. That will give us plenty of stuff for the dam and help to deepen the pond."

Thus they worked. In a week the crib was full of packed clay and stone. Then came the grand finish—the closing of this last hole through the dam. It was not easy with the full head of water running,

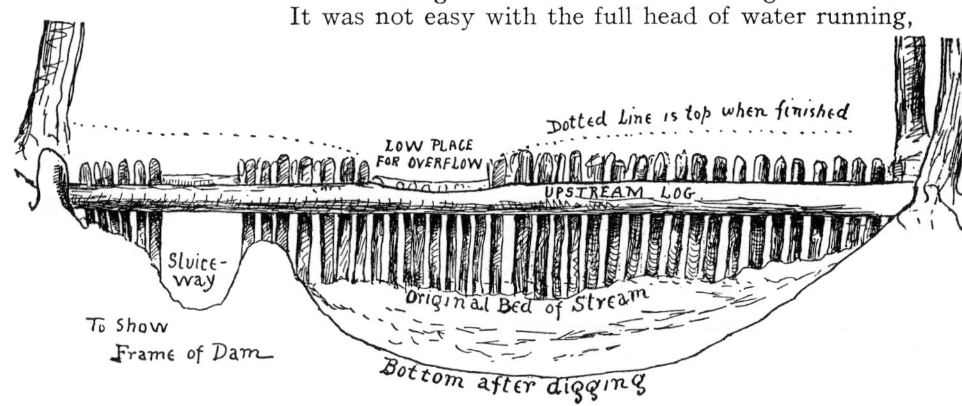

but they worked like beavers and finally got it stopped.

That night there was a heavy shower. Next day when they came near they heard a dull roar in the woods. They stopped and listened in doubt, then Yan exclaimed gleefully: "The dam! That's the water running over the dam."

They both set off with a yell and ran their fastest. As soon as they came near they saw a great sheet of smooth water where the stony creek bottom had been and a steady current over the low place left as an overflow in the middle of the dam.

What a thrill of pleasure that was!

"Last in's a dirty sucker."

"Look out for my bad knee," was the response.

The rest of the race was a mixture of stripping and sprinting and the boys splashed in together.

Five feet deep in the deep hole, a hundred yards long, and all their own doing.

"Now, wasn't it worth it?" asked Yan, who had had much difficulty in keeping Sam steadily at play that looked so very much like work.

"Wonder how that got here? I thought I left that in the teepee?" and Sam pointed to a log that he used for a seat in the teepee, but now it was lodged in the overflow.

Yan was a good swimmer, and as they played and splashed, Sam said: "Now I know who you are. You can't hide it from me no longer. I suspicioned it when you were working on the dam. You're that tarnal Redskin they call 'Little Beaver.'"

"I've been watching you," retorted Yan, "and it seems to me I've run up against that copper-coloured scallawag—'Young-Man-Afraid-of-a-Shovel.'"

"No, you don't," said Sam. "Nor I ain't '*Bald-Eagle-Settin'-on-a-Rock-with-his-Tail-Hangin'-over-the-Edge*,' nuther. In fact, I don't keer to be recognized just now. Ain't it a relief to think the cattle don't have to take that walk any more?"

Sam was evidently trying to turn the subject, but Yan would not be balked. "I heard Si call you 'Woodpecker' the other day."

"Yep. I got that at school. When I was a kid to hum I heerd Ma talk about me be-a-u-tiful *golden* hair, but when I got big enough to go to school I learned that it was only *red*, an' they called me the 'Red-headed Woodpecker.' I tried to lick them, but lots of them could lick me an' rubbed it in wuss.

When I seen fightin' didn't work, I let on to like it, but it was too late then. Mostly it's just 'Woodpecker' for short. I don't know as it ever lost me any sleep."

Half an hour later, as they sat by the fire that Yan made with rubbing-sticks, he said, "Say, Woodpecker, I want to tell you a story." Sam grimaced, pulled his ears forward, and made ostentatious preparations to listen.

"There was once an Indian squaw taken prisoner by some other tribe way up north. They marched her 500 miles away, but one night she escaped and set out, not on the home trail, for she knew they would follow that way and kill her, but to one side. She didn't know the country and got lost. She had no weapons but a knife, and no food but berries. Well, she travelled fast for several days till a rainstorm came, then she felt safe, for she knew her enemies could not trail her now. But winter was near and she could not get home before it came. So she set to work right where she was.

She made a wigwam of Birch bark and a fire with rubbing-sticks, using the lace of her moccasin for a bow-string. She made snares of the inner bark of the Willow and of Spruce roots, and deadfalls, too, for Rabbits. She was starving sometimes, at first, but she ate the buds and inner bark of Birch trees till she found a place where there were lots of Rabbits. And when she caught some she used every scrap of them. She made a fishing-line of the sinews, and a hook of the bones and teeth lashed together with sinew and Spruce gum.

She made a cloak of Rabbit skins, sewed with needles of Rabbit bone and thread of Rabbit sinew, and a lot of dishes of Birch bark sewed with Spruce roots.

"She put in the whole winter there alone, and when the spring came she was found by Samuel Hearne, the great traveller. Her precious knife was worn down, but she was fat and happy and ready to set out for her own people."

"Well, I say that's mighty inter-est-in'," said Sam—he had listened attentively—"an' I'd like nothin' better than to try it myself if I had a gun an' there was lots of game."

"Pooh, who wouldn't?"

"Mighty few—an' there's mighty few who *could.*"

"I could."

"What, make everything with just a knife? I'd like to see you make a teepee," then adding earnestly, "Sam, we've been kind o' playing Injuns; now let's do it properly. Let's make everything out of what we find in the woods."

"Guess we'll have to visit the Sanger Witch again. She knows all about plants."

"We'll be the Sanger Indians. We can both be Chiefs," said Yan, not wishing to propose himself as Chief or caring to accept Sam as his superior. "I'm Little Beaver. Now what are you?"

"Bloody-Thundercloud-in-the-Afternoon."

"No, try again. Make it something you can draw, so you can make your totem, and make it short."

"What's the smartest animal there is?"

"I—I—suppose the Wolverine."

"What! Smarter'n a Fox?"

"The books say so."

"Kin he lick a Beaver?"

"Well, I should say so."

"Well, that's me."

"No, you don't. I'm not going around with a fellow that licks me. It don't fit you as well as 'Woodpecker,' anyhow. I always get *you* when I want a nice tree spoiled or pecked into holes," retorted Yan, magnanimously ignoring the personal reason for the name.

"Tain't as bad as *beavering*," answered Sam.

"Beavering" was a word with a history. Axes and timber were the biggest things in the lives of the Sangerites. Skill with the axe was the highest accomplishment. The old settlers used to make everything in the house out of wood, and with the axe for the only tool. It was even said that some of them used to "edge her up a bit" and shave with her on Sundays. When a father was setting his son up in life he gave him simply a good axe. The axe was the grand essential of life and work, and was supposed to be a whole outfit. Skill with the axe was general. Every man and boy was more or less expert, and did not know how expert he was till a real "greeny" came among them. There is a right way to cut for each kind of grain, and a certain proper way of felling a tree to throw it in any given direction with the minimum of labour. All these things are second nature to the Sangerite. A Beaver is credited with a haphazard way of gnawing round and round a tree till somehow it tumbles, and when a chopper deviates in the least from the correct form, the exact right cut in the exact right place, he is said to be "beavering"; therefore, while "working like a Beaver" is high praise, "beavering" a tree is a term of unmeasured reproach, and Sam's final gibe had point and force that none but a Sangerite could possibly have appreciated.

XI

Yan and the Witch

The Sanger Witch hated the Shanty-man's axe
And wildfire, too, they tell,
But the hate that she had for the Sporting man
Was wuss nor her hate of Hell!
—Cracked Jimmie's Ballad of Sanger.

YAN took his earliest opportunity to revisit the Sanger Witch.

"Better leave me out," advised Sam, when he heard of it. "She'd never look at you if I went. You look too blame healthy."

So Yan went alone, and he was glad of it. Fond as he was of Sam, his voluble tongue and ready wit left Yan more or less in the shade, made him look sober and dull, and what was worse, continually turned the conversation just as it was approaching some subject that was of deepest interest to him.

As he was leaving, Sam called out, "Say, Yan, if you want to stay there to dinner it'll be all right —we'll know why you hain't turned up." Then he stuck his tongue in his cheek, closed one eye and went to the barn with his usual expression of inscrutable melancholy.

Yan carried his note-book—he used it more and more, also his sketching materials. On the road he gathered a handful of flowers and herbs. His reception by the old woman was very different this time.

"Come in, come in, God bless ye, an' hoo air ye,

an' how is yer father an' mother—come in an' set down, an' how is that spalpeen, Sam Raften?"

"Sam's all right now," said Yan with a blush.

"All right! Av coorse he's all right. I knowed I'd fix him all right, an' he knowed it, an' his Ma knowed it when she let him come. Did she say onything about it?"

"No, Granny, not a word."

"The dhirty hussy! Saved the boy's life in sphite of their robbin' me an' she ain't human enough to say 'thank ye'—the dhirty hussy! May God forgive her as I do," said the old woman with evident and implacable enmity.

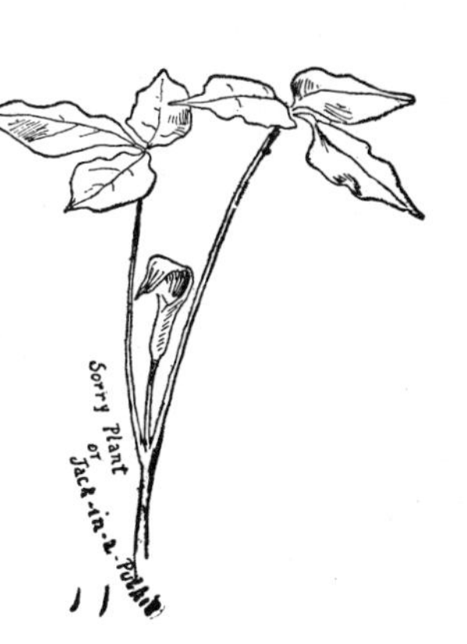

"Fwhat hev ye got thayer? Hivin be praised, they can't kill them all off. They kin cut down the trees, but the flowers comes ivery year, me little beauties—me little beauties!" Yan spread them out. She picked up an Arum and went on. "Now, that's Sorry-plant, only some calls it Injun Turnip, an' I hear the childer call it Jack-in-the-Pulpit. Don't ye never put the root o' that near yer tongue. It'll sure burn ye like fire. First thing whin they gits howld av a greeny the bhise throis to make him boite that same. Shure he niver does it twicet. The Injuns b'ile the pizen out o' the root an' ates it; shure it's better'n starvin'."

Golden Seal (*Hydrastis canadensis*), the plant she had used for Sam's knee, was duly recognized and praised, its wonderful golden root, "the best goold iver came out av the ground," was described with its impression of the seal of the Wise King.

"Thim's Mandrakes, an' they're moighty late, an' ye shure got *thim* in the woods. Some calls it May Apples, an' more calls it Kingroot. The Injuns use it fur their bowels, an' it has cured many a horse of pole evil that I seen meself.

"An' Blue Cohosh, only I call that Spazzum-root. Thayer ain't nothin' like it fur spazzums—took like tay; only fur that the Injun women wouldn't live in all their thrubles, but that's something that don't consarn ye. Luk now, how the laves is all spread out like wan wid spazzums. Glory be to the Saints and the Blessed Virgin, everything is done fur us on airth an' plain marked, if we'd only take the thruble to luk.

"Now luk at thot," said she, clawing over the bundle and picking out a yellow Cypripedium, that's Moccasin-plant wid the Injuns, but mercy on 'em fur bloind, miserable haythens. They don't know nothin' an' don't want to larn it. That's Umbil, or Sterrick-root. It's powerful good fur sterricks. Luk at it! See the face av a woman in sterricks wid her hayer flyin' an' her jaw a-droppin'. I moind the toime Larry's little gurrl didn't want to go to her 'place' an' hed sterricks. They jest sent fur me an' I brung along a Sterrick-root. First, I sez, sez I, 'Get me some b'ilin' wather,' an' I made tay an' give it to her b'ilin' hot. As shure as Oi'm a livin' corpse, the very first spoonful fetched her all right. Oh, but it's God's own gift, an' it's be His blessin' we know how to use it. An' it don't do to just go an' dig it when ye want it. It has to be grubbed when the flower ain't thayer. Ye see, the strength ain't in both places to oncet. It's ayther in the flower or in the root, so when the flower is thayer the root's no more good than an ould straw. Ye hes to hunt fur it in spring or in fall, just when the divil himself wouldn't know whayer to find it.

"An' fwhat hev ye thayer? Good land! if it ain't Skunk's Cabbage! Ye sure come up by the Bend. That's the on'y place whayer that grows."

"Yes," replied Yan; "that's just where I got it. But hold on, Granny, I want to sketch all those and note down their names and what you say about them."

"Shure, you'd hev a big book when I wuz through," said the old woman with pride, as she lit her pipe, striking the match on what would have been the leg of her pants had she been a man.

"An' shure ye don't need to write down what they're good fur, fur the good Lord done that Himself long ago. Luk here, now. That's Cohosh, fur spazzums, an' luks like it; that's Moccasin, fur Highsterricks, an' luks like it; wall, thar's Skunk-root fur both, an' don't it luk like the two o' thim thigither?"

Yan feebly agreed, but had much difficulty in seeing what the plant had in common with the others.

"An' luk here! Thayer ye got Lowbelier, that some calls Injun tobaccer. Ye found this by the crick, an' it's a little airly—ahead o' toime. That's the shtuff to make ye throw up when ye want to. Luk, ain't that lafe the livin' shape of a shtummick?

"Thayer's the Highbelier; it's a high hairb, an' it's moighty foine fur the bowels when ye drink the dry root.

"Spicewood" [Spicebush, *Lindera benzoin*], "or Fayverbush, them twigs is great fur tay—that cures shakes and fayver. Shure an' it shakes ivery toime the wind blows.

"That's Clayvers," she said, picking up a Galium. "Now fwhat wud ye think that wuz fur to cure?"

"I don't know. What is it?"

"Luk now, an' see how it's wrote in it plain as prent—yes, an' a sight plainer, fur I can read them an' I can't read a wurrud in a book. Now fwhat is that loike?" said she, holding up the double seed-pod.

"A brain and spinal column," said Yan.

"Och, choild, I hev better eyes than ye. Shure them's two kidneys, an' that's fwhat Clayver tay will cure better'n all the docthers in the wurruld, an' ye hev to know just how. Ye see, kidney thruble is a koind o' fayver; it's hatin', so ye make yer Clayver tay in *cold* wather; if ye make it o' warrum wather it just makes ye wuss an' acts loike didly pizen. Thayer's Sweatplant, or Boneset" [*Eupatorium perfoliatum*], "that's the thing to sweat ye. Wanst Oi sane a feller jest dyin' o' dry hoide, wuz all hoidebound, an' the docthers throid an' throid an' couldn't help wan bit, till I guv his mother some Boneset leaves to make tay, an' he sweat buckets before he'd more'n smelt av it, an' the docthers thought they done it theirsilves!" and she cackled gleefully.

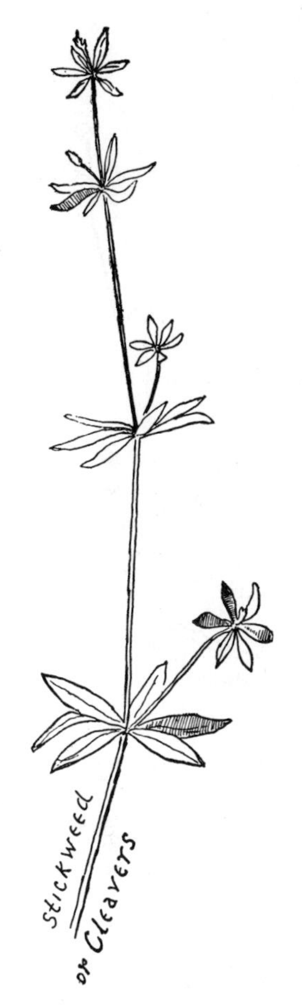

"Thayer's Goldthread fur cankermouth, an' Pipsissewa that cures fayver an' rheumatiz, too. It always grows where folks gits them disayses. Luk at the flower just blotched red an' white loike fayver blotches—an' Spearmint, that saves ye if ye pizen yerself with Spazzum-root, an' shure it grows right next it in the woods!

"Thayer's Wormseed fur wurrums—see the little wurrum on the leaves" [*Chenopodium*], "an' that thayer is Pleurisy root, an' thayer! well, thayer's the foinest hairb that iver God made to grow--that's Cure-all. Some things cures wan thing and some cures another, but when ye don't know just what to take, ye make tay o' that root an' ye can't go wrong. It was an Injun larned me that. The poor miserable baste of a haythen hed some larnin', an' the minit he showed me I knowed it was so, fur ivery lafe wuz three in wan an' wan in three, an' had the sign o' the blessed crass in the middle as plain as that biler settin' on the stove."

Thus she chattered away, smoking her short pipe, expectorating on the top of the hot stove, but with true feminine delicacy she was careful each time to wipe her mouth on the back of her skinny arm.

"An' that's what's called Catnip; sure Oi moind well the day Oi furst larned about that. It warn't a Injun nor a docther nor a man at all, at all, that larned me that. It was that ould black Cat, an' may the saints stand bechuxt me an' his grane eyes! Bejabers, sometimes he scares me wid his knowin' ways, but I hev nothin' agin him except that he kills the wee burruds. He koind o' measled all wan winter an' lay around the stove. Whiniver the dooer was open he'd go an' luk out an' then come back an' meow an' wheen an' lay down—an' so he kep' on, gittin' waker an' worser, till the snow wuz gone an' grass come up, an' still he'd go a-lukin' toward the ayst, especially nights. Then thayer come up a plant I had never sane, right thayer, an' he'd luk at it an' luk at it loike he wanted it but didn't dar to. Thar was some foine trays out thayer in thim days afore the ould baste cut thim down, an' wan av thim hed a big limb, so—an' another so—an' when the moon come up full at jest the right time the shaddy made the sign av the crass an' loighted on me dooer, an' after it was past it didn't make no crass. Well, bejabers, the full moon come up at last an' she made the sign of the shaddy crass, an' the ould Cat goes out an' watches an' watches loike he wanted to an' didn't dar to, till that crass drapped fayer onto the hairbs, an' Tom he jumped then an' ate an' ate, an' from that day he was a well Cat; an' that's how Oi larned Catnip, an' it set me moind aisy, too, fur no Cat that's possesst 'll iver ate inunder the shaddy av the crass."

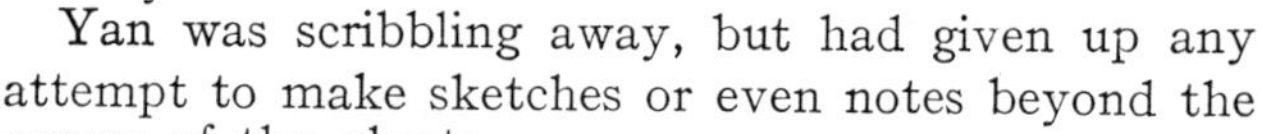

Yan was scribbling away, but had given up any attempt to make sketches or even notes beyond the names of the plants.

"Shure, choild, put them papers wid the names on the hairbs an' save *them;* that wuz fwhat Docther Carmartin done whin Oi was larnin' him. Thayer, now, that's it," she added, as Yan took the hint and began slipping on each stalk a paper label with its name.

"That's a curious broom," said Yan, as his eye fell on the symbol of order and cleanliness, making strange reflections on itself.

"Yes; sure, that's a Baitche broom. Larry makes 'em."

"Larry?"

"Yes, me bhoy." [Larry was nearly sixty.] "He makes thim of Blue Baitche."

"How?" asked Yan, picking it up and examining

it with intense interest.

"Whoi, shure, by whittlin'. Larry's a howly terror to whittle, an' he gets a Blue Baitche sapling 'bout three inches thick an' starts a-whittlin' long slivers, but laves them on the sthick at wan end till thayer all round loike that."

"What, like a fire-lighter?"

"Yis, yis, that's it, only bigger, an Blue Baitche is terrible tough. Then whin he has the sthick down to 'bout an inch thick, he ties all the slivers the wrong way wid a sthrand o' Litherwood, an' thrims down the han'el to suit, an' evens up the ind av the broom wid the axe an' lets it dhry out, an' thayer yer is. Better broom was niver made, an' there niver wuz ony other in th' famb'ly till he married that Kitty Connor, the lowest av the low, an' it's meself was all agin her, wid her proide an' her dirthy sthuck-up ways; nothin' but boughten things wuz good enough fur her, *her* that niver had a dacint male till she thrapped moi Larry. Yis, low be it sphoken, but 'thrapped' 's the wurrud," said the old woman, raising her voice to give emphasis that told a lurid tale.

At this moment the door opened and in came Biddy, and as she was the daughter of the unspeakable Kitty the conversation turned.

"An' sure it's glad to see ye I am, an' when are ye comin' down to reside at our place?" was her greeting to Yan, and while they talked Granny took advantage of the chance to take a long pull at a bottle that looked and smelled like Lung-balm.

"Moi, Biddy, yer airly," said Granny.

"Shure, an' now it was late whin I left home, an' the schulmaster says it's always so walking from ayst to west."

"An' shure it's glad Oi am to say ye, fur Yan will shtop an ate wid us. It ain't duck an' grane pase, but, thank God, we hev enough an' a hearty welcome wid ivery boite. Ye say, Biddy makes me dinner ivery foine day an' Oi get a boite an' a sup for meself other toimes, an' slapes be me lone furby me Dog an' Cat an' the apples, which thayer ain't but a handful left, but fwhat thar is is yourn. Help yerself, choild, an' ate hearty," and she turned down the gray-looking bedclothes to show the last half-dozen of the same rosy apples.

"Ain't you afraid to sleep here alone nights, Granny?"

"Shure fwhat hev Oi to fayre? Thayer niver

wuz robbers come but wanst, an' shure I got theyer last cint aff av them. They come one night an' broke in, an' settin' up, Oi sez, 'Now fwhat *are* yez lukin' fur?'

"'Money,' sez they, fur thayer was talk all round thin that Oi had sold me cow fur $25.

"'Sure, thin, Oi'll get up an' help ye,' sez Oi, fur divil a cint hev Oi been able to set me eyes on sense apple harvest.'"

"'We want $25, or we'll kill ye.'

"'Faith, an' if it wuz twenty-five cints Oi couldn't help it,' sez Oi, 'an' it's ready to die Oi am,' sez Oi, 'fur Oi was confessed last wake an' Oi'm a-sayin' me prayers this minit.'

"Sez the littlest wan, an' he wa'n't so little, nigh as br'ad as that dooer, 'Hevn't ye sold yer cow?'

"'Ye'll foind her in the barrun,' sez Oi, 'though Oi hate to hev yez disturb her slapin'. It makes her drame an' that's bad fur the milk.'

"An' next thing them two robbers wuz laffin' at each other fur fools. Then the little wan sez:

"'Now, Granny, we'll lave ye in pace, if ye'll niver say a wurrud o' this'—but the other wan seemed kind o' sulky.

"'Sorra a wurrud,' sez Oi, 'an' good frinds we'll be yit,' an' they wuz makin' fur the dooer to clayer out whin I sez:

"'Howld on! Me friends can't lave me house an' naither boite nor sup; turn yer backs an' ye plaze, till Oi get on me skirt.' An' whin Oi wuz up an' dacint an' tould them they could luk, Oi sez, 'It's the foinest Lung-balm in the land ye shall taste,' an' the littlest feller he starts a-coughin', oh, a turrible cough—it fair scairt me, like a hoopin' croup—an' the other seemed just mad, and the littlest wan made fun av him. Oi seen the mean wan wuz left-handed or let on he wuz, but when he reached out fur the bottle he had on'y three fingers on his right, an' they both av them had the biggest, blackest, awfulest lukin' bairds—I'd know them two bairds agin ony place—an' the littlest had a rag round his head, said he had a toothache, but shure yer teeth don't ache in the roots o' yer haiyer. Then when they wuz goin' the littlest wan put a dollar in me hand an' sez, 'It's all we got bechuxst us, Granny.' 'God bless ye,' sez Oi, 'an' Oi take it kindly. It's the first Oi seen sense apple harvest, an' it's a friend ye hev in me whin ye nade wan,'" and the old woman chuckled over her victory.

"Granny, do you know what the Indians use for dyeing colours?" asked Yan, harking back to his main purpose.

"Shure, Yahn, they jest goes to the store an' gets boughten dyes in packages like we do."

"But before there were boughten dyes, didn't they use things in the woods?"

"That they did, for shure. Iverything man iver naded the good Lord made grow fur him in the woods."

"Yes, but what plants?"

"Faix, an' they differ fur different things."

"Yes, but what are they?" Then seeing how general questions failed, he went at it in detail.

"What do they use for yellow dye on the Porcupine quills—I mean before the boughten dyes came?"

"Well, shure an' that's a purty yellow flower that grows in the fall out in the field an' along the fences. The Yaller Weed, I call it, an' some calls it Goldenrod. They bile the quills in wather with the flower. Luk! Thar's some wool dyed that way."

"An' the red?" said Yan, scribbling away.

"Faix, an' they had no rale good red. They made a koind o' red o' berry juice b'iled, an' wanst I seen a turrible nice red an ol' squaw made b'ilin' the quills fust in yaller awhile an' next awhile in red."

"What berries make the best red, Granny?"

"Well, 'tain't the red wans, as ye moight think. Ye kin make it of Rosberries or Sumac or Huckleberries an' lots more, but Black Currants is redder than Red Currants, an' Squaw berries is best av them all."

"What are they like?"

"Shure, an' Oi'll show ye that same hairb," and they wandered around outside the shanty in vain search. It's too airly," said Granny, "but it's round thayer in heaps in August an' is the purtiest red iver grew. 'An Pokeweed, too, it ain't har'ly flowerin' yit, but in the fall it hez berries that's so red they're nigh black, an' dyes the purtiest kind o' a purple."

"What makes blue?"

"Oi niver sane none in the quills. Thayer may be some. The good Lord made iverything grow in the woods, but I ain't found it an' niver seen none. Ye kin make a grane av the young shoots av Elder, but it ain't purty like that," and she pointed to a frightful emerald ribbon that Biddy wore, "an' a brown of

Butternut bark, an' a black av White Oak chips an' bark. Ye kin make a kind o' grane av two dips, wan of yaller an wan av black. Ye kin dye black wid Hickory bark, an' orange (bad scran to it) wid the inner bark of Birch, an' yaller wid the roots av Hoop Ash, an' a foine scarlet from the bark av the little root av Dogwood, but there ain't no rale blue in the woods, an' that's what I tell them orange-an'-blue Prattisons on the 12th o' July, fur what the Lord didn't make the divil did.

"Ye kin make a koind of blue out o' the Indigo hairb, but 'tain't like this," pointing to some screaming cobalt, "an' if it ain't in the woods the good Lord niver meant us to have it. Yis! I tell ye it's the divil's own colour, that blue—orange an' blue is the divil's own colours, shure enough, fur brimstone's yaller; an' its blue whin it's burnin', that I hed from his riv'rince himself—bless him!"

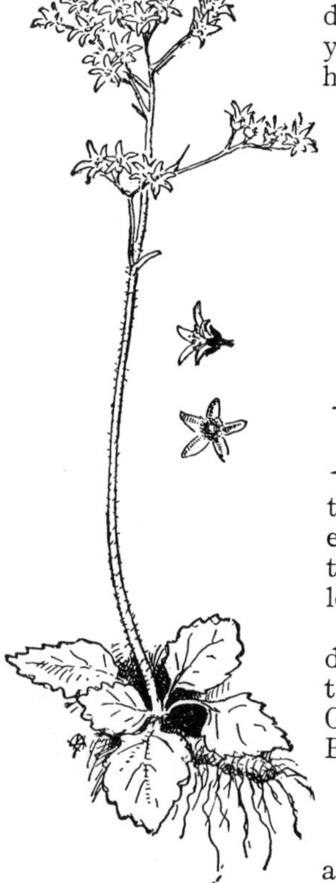

Saxifrage

XII

Dinner with the Witch

BIDDY meanwhile had waddled around the room slapping the boards with her broad bare feet as she prepared their dinner. She was evidently trying to put on style, for she turned out her toes excessively. She spoke several times about "the toime when she resoided with yer mamma," then at length, "Whayer's the tablecloth, Granny?"

"Now, wud ye listen to thot, an' she knówin' that divil a clath hev we in the wurruld, an' glad enough to hev vittles on the table, let alone a clath," said Granny, oblivious of the wreck she was making of Biddy's pride.

"Will ye hav tay or coffee, Yahn?" said Biddy.

"Tea," was Yan's choice.

"Faix, an' Oi'm glad ye said tay, fur Oi ain seen a pick o' coffee sense Christmas, an' the tay Oi kin git in the woods, but thayer is somethin' Oi kin set afore ye that don't grow in the woods," and the old woman hobbled to a corner shelf, lifted down an old cigar box and from among matches, tobacco, feathers, tacks, pins, thread and dust she picked six lumps of cube sugar, formerly white.

"Thayer, shure, an' Oi wuz kapin' this fur whin his riv'rence comes; wanst a year he's here, God bless him! but that's fower wakes ahid, an' dear knows fwhat may happen afore thin. Here, an' a hearty welcome," said she, dropping three of the lumps in Yan's tea. "We'll kape the rest fur yer second cup. Hev some crame?" and she pushed over a sticky-handled shaving-mug full of excellent cream. Biddy, give Yahn some bread."

The loaf, evidently the only one, was cut up and two or three slices forced into Yan's plate.

"Mebbe the butther is a little hoigh," exclaimed the hostess, noting that Yan was sparing of it. "Howld on." She went again to the corner shelf and got down an old glass jar with scalloped edge and a flat tin cover. It evidently contained jam. She lifted the cover and exclaimed:

"Well, Oi niver!" Then going to the door she fished out with her fingers a dead mouse and threw it out, remarking placidly, "Oi've wondered whayer the little divil wuz. Oi ain't sane him this two wakes, an' me a-thinkin' it wuz Tom ate him. May Oi be furgiven the onjustice av it. Consarn them flies! That cover niver did fit." And again her finger was employed, this time to scrape off an incrustation of unhappy flies that had died, like Clarence, in their favourite beverage.

"Thayer, Yan, now ate hearty, all av it, an' welcome. It does me good to see ye ate—thayer's lots more whayer that come from," though it was obvious that she had put her all upon the table.

Poor Yan was in trouble. He felt instinctively that the good old soul was wrecking her week's resources in this lavish hospitality, but he also felt that she would be deeply hurt if he did not appear to enjoy everything. The one possibly clean thing was the bread. He devoted himself to that; it was of poorest quality; one or two hairs looping in his teeth had been discouraging, but when he bit at a piece of linen rag with a button on it he was fairly upset. He managed to hide the rag, but could not conceal his sudden loss of appetite.

"Hev some more av this an' this," and in spite of himself his plate was piled up with things for him to eat, including a lot of beautifully boiled potatoes, but unfortunately the hostess carried them from

the pot on the stove in a corner of her ancient and somber apron, and served him with her skinny paw.

Yan's appetite was wholly gone now, to the grief of his kind entertainer, "Shure an' she'd fix him up something to stringthen him," and Yan had hard work to beg off.

"Would ye like an aig," ventured Biddy.

"Why, yes! oh, yes, please," exclaimed Yan, with almost too much enthusiasm. He thought, "Well, hens are pure-minded creatures, anyway. An egg's sure to be clean."

Biddy waddled away to the 'barrun' and soon reappeared with three eggs.

"B'iled or fried?"

"Boiled," said Yan, aiming to keep to the safe side.

Biddy looked around for a pot.

"Shure, *that's* b'ilin' now," said Granny, pointing to the great mass of her undergarments seething in the boiler, and accordingly the eggs were dropped in there.

Yan fervently prayed that they might not break. As it was, two did crack open, but he got the other one, and that was virtually his dinner.

A Purple Blackbird came hopping in the door now.

"Will, now, thayer's Jack. Whayer hev ye been? I thought ye wuz gone fur good. Shure Oi saved him from a murtherin' gunner," she explained. "(Bad scran to the baste! I belave he was an Or'ngeman.) But he's all right now an' comes an' goes like he owned the place. Now, Jack, you git out av that wather pail," as the beautiful bird leaped into the half-filled drinking bucket and began to take a bath.

"Now luk at that," she shouted, "ye little rascal, come out o' that oven," for now the Blackbird had taken advantage of the open door to scramble into the dark warm oven.

"Thayer he goes to warrum his futs. Oh, ye little rascal! Next thing ye know some one'll slam the dooer, not knowin' a thing, and fire up, an' it's roastin' aloive ye'll be. Shure an' it's tempted Oi am to wring yer purty neck to save yer loife," and she drove him out with the harshest of words and the gentlest of hands.

Then Yan, with his arms full of labelled plants, set out for home.

"Good-boi, choild, come back agin and say me soon. Bring some more hairbs. Good-boi, an' bless ye. Oi hope it's no sin to say so, fur Oi know yer a

Prattison an' ye are all on yez goin' to hell, but yer a foine bhoy. Oi'm turrible sorry yer a Prattison."

When Yan got back to the Raftens' he found the dinner table set for one, though it was now three in the afternoon.

"Come and get your dinner," said Mrs. Raften in her quiet motherly way. "I'll put on the steak. It will be ready in five minutes."

"But I've had my dinner with Granny de Neuville."

"Yes, I know!"

"Did she stir yer tea with one front claw an' put jam on yer bread with the other?" asked Raften, rather coarsely.

"Did she b'ile her pet Blackbird fur yer soup?" said Sam.

Yan turned very red. Evidently all had a good idea of what he had experienced, but it jarred on him to hear their mockery of the good old soul.

He replied warmly, "She was just as kind and nice as she could be."

"You had better have a steak now," said Mrs. Raften, in solicitous doubt.

How tempting was the thought of that juicy brown steak! How his empty stomach did crave it! But the continued mockery had stirred him. He would stand up for the warm-hearted old woman who had ungrudgingly given him the best she had—had given her all—to make a hearty welcome for a stranger. They should never know how gladly he would have eaten now, and in loyalty to his recent hostess he added the first lie of his life:

"No, thank you very much, but really I am not in the least hungry. I had a fine dinner at Granny de Neuville's."

Then, defying the inner pangs of emptiness, he went about his evening chores.

XIII

The Hostile Spy

"WONDER where Caleb got that big piece of Birch bark," said Yan; "I'd like some for dishes."

"Guess I know. He was over to Burns's

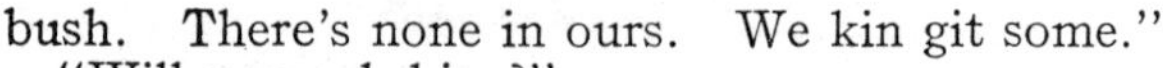

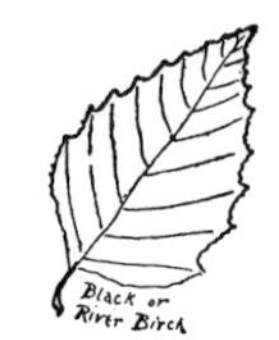

bush. There's none in ours. We kin git some."

"Will you ask him?"

"Naw, who cares for an old Birch tree. We'll go an' borrow it when he ain't lookin'."

Yan hesitated.

Sam took the axe. "We'll call this a war party into the enemy's country. There's sure 'nuff war that-a-way. He's one of Da's '*friends.*'"

Yan followed, in doubt still as to the strict honesty of the proceeding.

Over the line they soon found a good-sized canoe Birch, and were busy whacking away to get off a long roll, when a tall man and a small boy, apparently attracted by the chopping, came in sight and made toward them. Sam called under his breath: "It's old Burns. Let's git."

There was no time to save anything but themselves and the axe. They ran for the boundary fence, while Burns contented himself with shouting out threats and denunciations. Not that he cared a straw for the Birch tree—timber had no value in that country—but unfortunately Raften had quarrelled with all his immediate neighbours, therefore Burns did his best to make a fearful crime of the petty depredation.

His valiant son, a somewhat smaller boy than either Yan or Sam, came near enough to the boundary to hurl opprobrious epithets.

"Red-head—red-head! You red-headed thief! Hol' on till my paw gits hol' o' you—Raften, the Baften, the rick-strick Straften," and others equally galling and even more exquisitely refined.

"War party escaped and saved their scalps," and Sam placidly laid the axe in its usual place.

"Nothing lost but honour," added Yan. "Who's the kid?"

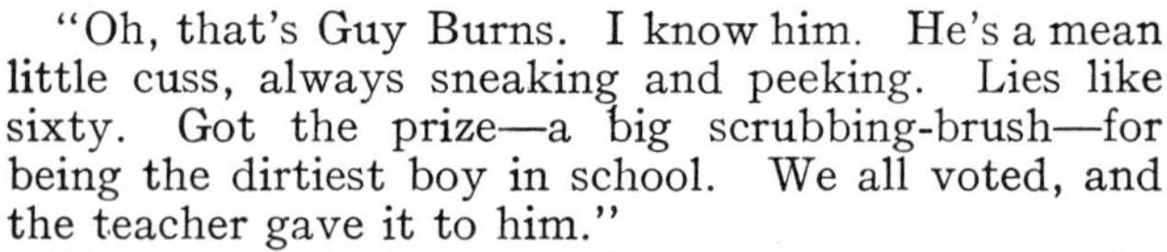

"Oh, that's Guy Burns. I know him. He's a mean little cuss, always sneaking and peeking. Lies like sixty. Got the prize—a big scrubbing-brush—for being the dirtiest boy in school. We all voted, and the teacher gave it to him."

Next day the boys made another war party for Birch bark, but had hardly begun operations when there was an uproar not far away, and a voice, evidently of a small boy, mouthing it largely, trying to pass itself off as a man's voice: "Hi, yer the —— ——. Yer git off my —— —— place —— ——"

"Le's capture the little cuss, Yan."

"An' burn him at the stake with horrid torture,"

was the rejoinder.

They set out in his direction, but again the appearance of Burns changed their war-party onslaught into a rapid retreat.

(More opprobrium.)

During the days that followed the boys were often close to the boundary, but it happened that Burns was working near and Guy had the quickest of eyes and ears. The little rat seemed ever on the alert. He soon showed by his long-distance remarks that he knew all about the boys' pursuits—had doubtless visited the camp in their absence. Several times they saw him watching them with intense interest when they were practising with bow and arrow, but he always retreated to a safe distance when discovered, and then enjoyed himself breathing out fire and slaughter.

One day the boys came to the camp at an unusual hour. On going into a near thicket Yan saw a bare foot under some foliage. "Hallo, what's this?" He stooped down and found a leg to it and at the end of that Guy Burns.

Up Guy jumped, yelling "Paw—Paw—PAW!" He ran for his life, the Indians uttering blood-curdlers on his track. But Yan was a runner, and Guy's podgy legs, even winged by fear, had no chance. He was seized and dragged howling back to the camp.

"You let me alone, you Sam Raften—now you let me alone!" There was, however, a striking lack of opprobrium in his remarks now. (Such delicacy is highly commendable in the very young.)

"First thing is to secure the prisoner, Yan."

Sam produced a cord.

"Pooh," said Yan. "You've got no style about you. Bring me some Leatherwood."

This was at hand, and in spite of howls and scuffles, Guy was solemnly tied to a tree—a green one—because, as Yan pointed out, that would resist the fire better.

The two Warriors now squatted cross-legged by the fire. The older one lighted a peace-pipe, and they proceeded to discuss the fate of the unhappy captive.

"Brother," said Yan, with stately gestures, "it is very pleasant to hear the howls of this miserable paleface." (It was really getting to be more than they could endure.)

"Ugh—heap good," said the Woodpecker.

"Ye better let me alone. My Paw 'll fix you for this, you dirty cowards," wailed the prisoner, fast losing control of his tongue.

"Ugh! Take um scalp first, burn him after," and Little Beaver made some expressive signs.

"Wah—bully—me heap wicked," rejoined the Woodpecker, expectorating on a stone and beginning to whet his jack-knife.

The keen and suggestive "*weet, weet, weet*" of the knife on the stone smote on Guy's ears and nerves with appalling effect.

"Brother Woodpecker, the spirit of our tribe calls out for the blood of the victim—all of it."

"Great Chief Woodpecker, you mean," said Sam, aside. "If you don't call me Chief, I won't call you Chief, that's all."

The Great Woodpecker and Little Beaver now entered the teepee, repainted each other's faces, adjusted their head-dresses and stepped out to the execution.

"The Woodpecker re-whetted his knife. It did not need it, but he liked the sound.

Little Beaver now carried a lot of light firewood and arranged it in front of the prisoner, but Guy's legs were free and he gave it a kick which sent it all flying. The two War-chiefs leaped aside. "Ugh! Heap sassy," said the ferocious Woodpecker. "Tie him legs, oh, Brother Great Chief Little Beaver!"

A new bark strip tied his legs securely to the tree. Then Chief Woodpecker approached with his knife and said:

"Great Brother Chief Little Beaver, if we scalp him there is only one scalp, and *you* will have nothing to show, except you're content with the wishbone."

Here was a difficulty, artificial yet real, but Yan suggested:

"Great Brother Chief Red-headed-Woodpecker-Settin'-on-a-Stump-with-his-Tail-Waggling-over-the Edge, no scalp him; skin his hull head, then each take half skin."

"Wah! Very good, oh Brother Big-Injun-Chief Great-Little-Beaver-Chaw-a-Tree-Down."

Then the Woodpecker got a piece of charcoal and proceeded in horrid gravity to mark out on the tow hair of the prisoner just what he considered a fair division. Little Beaver objected that he was entitled to an ear and half of the crown, which is the essential part of the scalp. The Woodpecker pointed out that fortunately the prisoner had a cow-lick that was practically a second crown. This ought to do perfectly well for the younger Chief's share. The charcoal lines were dusted off for a try-over. Both Chiefs got charcoal now and a new sketch plan was made on Guy's tow top and corrected till it was accepted by both.

The victim had really never lost heart till now. His flow of threats and epithets had been continuous and somewhat tedious. He had threatened to tell his "paw" and "the teacher," and all the world, but finally he threatened to tell Mr. Raften. This was the nearest to a home thrust of any yet, and in some uneasiness the Woodpecker turned to Little Beaver and said:

"Brother Chief, do you comprehend the language of the blithering Paleface? What does he say?"

"Ugh, I know not," was the reply. "Maybe he now singeth a death song in his own tongue."

Guy was not without pluck. He had kept up heart so far believing that the boys were "foolin'," but when he felt the awful charcoal line drawn to divide his scalp satisfactorily between these two inhuman, painted monsters, and when with a final "*weet, weet, weet*" of the knife on the stone the implacable Woodpecker approached and grabbed his tow locks in one hand, then he broke down and wept bitterly.

"Oh, please don't—— Oh, Paw! Oh, Maw! Let me go this time an' I'll never do it again." What he would not do was not specified, but the evidence of surrender was complete.

"Hold on, Great Brother Chief," said Little Beaver. "It is the custom of the tribes to release or even to adopt such prisoners as have shown notable fortitude."

"Showed fortitude enough for six if it's the same thing as yellin'," said the Woodpecker, dropping into his own vernacular.

"Let us cut his bonds so that he may escape to his own people."

"Thar'd be more style to it if we left him thar overnight an' found next mornin' he had escaped somehow by himself," said the older Chief. The victim noted the improvement in his situation and now promised amid sobs to get them all the Birch bark they wanted—to do anything, if they would let him go. He would even steal for them the choicest products of his father's orchard.

Little Beaver drew his knife and cut bond after bond. Woodpecker got his bow and arrow, remarking,

"Ugh, heap fun shoot him runnin'."

The last bark strip was cut. Guy needed no urging. He ran for the boundary fence in silence till he got over; then finding himself safe and unpursued, he filled the air with threats and execrations. No part of his statement would do to print here.

After such a harrowing experience most boys would have avoided that swamp, but Guy knew Sam at school as a good-natured fellow. He began to think he had been unduly scared. He was impelled by several motives, a burning curiosity being, perhaps, the most important. The result was that one day when the boys came to camp they saw Guy sneaking off. It was fun to capture him and drag him back. He was very sullen, and not so noisy as the other time, evidently less scared. The Chiefs talked of fire and torture and of ducking him in the pond without getting much response. Then they began to cross-examine the prisoner. He gave no answer. Why did he come to the camp? What was he doing—stealing? etc. He only looked sullen.

"Let's blindfold him and drive a Gyascutus down his back," said Yan in a hollow voice.

"Good idee," agreed Sam, not knowing any more than the prisoner what a Gyascutus was. Then he added, "just as well be merciful. It'll put him out o' pain."

It is the unknown that terrifies. The prisoner's soul was touched again. His mouth was trembling at the corners. He was breaking down when Yan followed it up: "Then why don't you tell us what you are doing here?"

He blubbered out, "I want to play Injun, too."

The boys broke down in another way. They had not had time to paint their faces, so that their expressions were very clear on this occasion.

Then Little Beaver arose and addressed the Council.

"Great Chiefs of the Sanger Nation: The last time we tortured and burned to death this prisoner, he created quite an impression. Never before has one of our prisoners shown so many different kinds of gifts. I vote to receive him into the Tribe."

The Woodpecker now arose and spoke:

"O wisest Chief but one in this Tribe, that's all right enough, but you know that no warrior can join us without first showing that he's good stuff and clear grit, all wool, and a cut above the average somehow. It hain't never been so. Now he's got to lick some Warrior of the Tribe. Kin you do that?"

"Nope."

"Or outrun one or outshoot him or something—or give us all a present. What kin you do?"

"I kin steal watermillyons, an' I kin see farder'n any boy in school, an' I kin sneak to beat all creation. I watched you fellers lots of times from them bushes. I watched you buildin' that thar dam. *I swum in it 'fore you did*, an' I uster set an' smoke in your teepee when you wasn't thar, an' I heerd you talk the time you was fixin' up to steal our Birch bark."

"Don't seem to me like it all proves much *fortitude*. Have you got any presents for the oldest head Chief of the tribe?"

"I'll get you all the Birch bark you want. I can't git what you cut, coz me an' Paw burned that so you couldn't git it, but I'll git you lots more, an' maybe—I'll steal you a chicken once in awhile."

"His intentions are evidently honourable. Let's take him in on sufferance," said Yan.

"All right," replied the head Chief, "he kin come in, but that don't spile my claim to that left half of his scalp down to that tuft of yellow moss on the scruff of his neck where the collar has wore off the dirt. I'm liable to call for it any time, an' the ear goes with it."

Guy wanted to treat this as a joke, but Sam's glittering eyes and inscrutable face were centered hungrily on that "yaller tuft" in a way that gave him the "creeps" again.

"Say, Yan—I mean Great Little Beaver—you know all about it, what kind o' stunts did they have to do to get into an Injun tribe, anyhow?"

"Different tribes do different ways, but the Sun Dance and the Fire Test are the most respectable and both *terribly hard*."

"Well, what did *you* do?" queried the Great Woodpecker.

"Both," said Yan grinning, as he remembered his sunburnt arms and shoulders.

"Quite sure?" said the older Chief in a tone of doubt.

"Yes, sir; and I bore it so well that every one there agreed that I was the best one in the Tribe," said Little Beaver, omitting to mention the fact that he was the only one in it. "I was unanimously named 'Howling Sunrise.'"

"Well, I want to be 'Howling Sunrise,'" piped Guy in his shrill voice.

"You? You don't know whether you can pass at all, you Yaller Mossback."

"Come, Mossy, which will you do?"

Guy's choice was to be sunburnt to the waist. He was burnt and freckled already to the shoulders, on arms as well as on neck, and his miserable cotton shirt so barely turned the sun's rays that he was elsewhere of a deep yellow tinge with an occasional constellation of freckles. Accordingly he danced about camp all one day with nothing on but his pants, and, of course, being so seasoned, he did not burn.

As the sun swung low the Chiefs assembled in Council.

The head Chief looked over the new Warrior, shook his head gravely and said emphatically: "Too green to burn. Your name is Sapwood."

Protest was in vain. "Sappy," he was and had to be until he won a better name. The peace pipe was smoked all round and he was proclaimed third War Chief of the Sanger Indians (the word *War* inserted by special request).

He was quite the most harmless member of the band and therefore took unusual pleasure in posing as the possessor of a perennial thirst for human heart-blood. War-paint was his delight, and with its aid he was singularly successful in correcting his round and smiling face into a savage visage of revolting ferocity. Paint was his hobby and his pride, but alas! how often it happens one's deepest sorrow is in the midst of one's greatest joy—the deepest lake is the old crater on top of the highest mountain. Sappy's eyes were *not* the sinister black beads of the wily Red-man, but a washed-out blue. His ragged, tow-coloured locks he could hide under wisps of horsehair, the paint itself redeemed his freckled skin, but there was no remedy for the white eyelashes and the pale, piggy, blue eyes. He kept his sorrow to himself, however, for he knew that if the others got an inkling of his feelings on the subject his name would have been promptly changed to "Dolly" or "Birdy," or some other equally horrible and un-Indian appellation.

XIV

The Quarrel

SAY, Yan, I saw a Blood-Robin this morning."

"That's a new one," said Yan, in a tone of doubt.

"Well, it's the purtiest bird in the country."

"What? A Humming-bird?"

"Na-aw-w-w. They ain't purty, only small."

"Well, that shows what you know," retorted Yan, "'for these exquisite winged gems are at once the most diminutive and brilliantly coloured of the whole feathered race.'" This phrase Yan had read somewhere and his overapt memory had seized on it.

"Pshaw!" said Sam. "Sounds like a book, but I'll bet I seen hundreds of Hummin'-birds round the Trumpet-vine and Bee-balm in the garden, an' they weren't a millionth part as purty as this. Why, it's just as red as blood, shines like fire and has black wings. The old Witch says the Indians call it a War-bird 'cause when it flew along the trail there was sure going to be war, which is like enough, fur they wuz at it all the hull time."

"Oh, I know," said Yan. "A Scarlet Tanager. Where did you see it?"

"Why, it came from the trees, then alighted on the highest pole of the teepee."

"Hope there isn't going to be any war there, Sam. I wish I had one to stuff."

"Tried to get him for you, sonny, spite of the Rules. Could 'a' done it, too, with a gun. Had a shy at him with an arrow an' I hain't seen bird or arrow since. 'Twas my best arrow, too—old Sure-Death."

"Will ye give me the arrow if I kin find it?" said Guy.

"Now you bet I won't. What good'd that be to me?"

"Will you give me your chewin' gum?"

"No."

"Will you lend it to me?"

"Yep."

"Well, there's your old arrow," said Guy, pulling it from between the logs where it had fallen. "I seen it go there an' reckoned I'd lay low an' watch the progress of events, as Yan says," and Guy whinnied.

Early in the morning the Indians in war-paint went off on a prowl. They carried their bows and arrows, of course, and were fully alert, studying the trail at intervals and listening for "signs of the enemy."

Their moccasined feet gave forth no sound, and their keen eyes took in every leaf that stirred as their sinewy forms glided among the huge trunks of the primeval vegetation—at least, Yan's note-book said they did. They certainly went with very little

Balsam-fir & fuzz-ball

noise, but they disturbed a small Hawk that flew from a Balsam-fir—a "Fire tree" they now called it, since they had discovered the wonderful properties of the wood.

Three arrows were shot after it and no harm done. Yan then looked into the tree and exclaimed:

"A nest."

"Looks to me like a fuzz-ball," said Guy.

"Guess not," replied Yan. "Didn't we scare the Hawk off?"

He was a good climber, quite the best of the three, and dropping his head-dress, coat, leggings and weapon, she shinned up the Balsam trunk, utterly regardless of the gum which hung in crystalline drops or easily burst bark-bladders on every part.

He was no sooner out of sight in the lower branches than Satan entered into Guy's small heart and prompted him thus:

"Le's play a joke on him an' clear out."

Sam's sense of humour beguiled him. They stuffed Yan's coat and pants with leaves and rubbish, put them properly together with the head-dress, then stuck one of his own arrows through the breast of the coat into the ground and ran away.

Meanwhile Yan reached the top of the tree and found that the nest was only one of the fuzz-balls so common on Fir trees. He called out to his comrades but got no reply, so came down. At first the ridiculous dummy seemed funny, then he found that his coat had been injured and the arrow broken. He called for his companions, but got no answer; again and again, without reply. He went to where they all had intended going, but if they were there they hid from him, and feeling himself scurvily deserted he went back to camp in no very pleasant humour. They were not there. He sat by the fire awhile, then, yielding to his habit of industry, he took off his coat and began to work at the dam.

He became engrossed in his work and did not notice the return of the runaways till he heard a voice saying "What's this?"

On turning he saw Sam poring over his private note-book and then beginning to read aloud:

**"Kingbird, fearless crested Kingbird
Thou art——"**

But Yan snatched it out of his hands.

"I'll bet the rest was something about 'Singbird,'" said Sam.

"Ugh! Heap sassy!

"There stood Raften, spectator of the whole affair"

Yan's face was burning with shame and anger. He had a poetic streak, and was morbidly sensitive about any one seeing its product. The Kingbird episode of their long evening walk was but one of many similar. He had learned to delight in these daring attacks of the intrepid little bird on the Hawks and Crows, and so magnified them into high heroics until he must try to record them in rhyme. It was very serious to him, and to have his sentiments afford sport to the others was more than he could bear. Of course Guy came out and grinned, taking his cue from Sam. Then he remarked in colourless tones, as though announcing an item of general news, "They say there was a fearless-crested Injun shot in the woods to-day."

The morning's desertion left Yan in no mood for chaffing. He rightly attributed the discourtesy to Guy. Turning savagely toward him he said, meaningly:

"Now, no more of your sass, you dirty little sneak."

"I ain't talkin' to you," Guy snickered, and followed Sam into the teepee. There were low voices within for a time. Yan went over toward the dam and began to plug mud into some possible holes. Presently there was more snickering in the teepee, then Guy came out alone, struck a theatrical attitude and began to recite to a tree above Yan's head:

"Kingbird, fearless crested Kingbird,
Thou art but a blooming sing bird——"

But the mud was very handy and Yan hurled a mass that spattered Guy thoroughly and sent him giggling into the teepee.

"Them's the bow-kays," Sam was heard to say. "Go out an' git some more; dead sure you deserve 'em. Let *me* know when the calls for 'author' begin?" Then there was more giggling. Yan was fast losing all control of himself. He seized a big stick and strode into the teepee, but Sam lifted the cover of the far side and slipped out. Guy tried to do the same, but Yan caught him.

"Here, I ain't doin' nothin'."

The answer was a sounding whack which made him wriggle.

"You let me alone, you big coward. I ain't doin' nothin' to you. You better let me alone. Sam! S-A-M! S-A-A-A-M!!!" as the stick came down again and again.

"Don't bother me," shouted Sam outside. "I'm writin' poethry—terrible partic'lar job, poethry. He only means it in kindness, anyhow."

Guy was screaming now and weeping copiously.

"You'll get some more if you give me any more of your lip," said Yan, and stepped out to meet Sam with the note-book again, apparently scribbling away. As soon as he saw Yan he stood up, cleared his throat and began:

"Kingbird, fearless crested——"

But he did not finish it. Yan struck him a savage blow on the mouth. Sam sprang back a few steps. Yan seized a large stone.

"Don't you throw that at me," said Sam seriously. Yan sent it with his deadliest force and aim. Sam dodged it and then in self-defense ran at Yan and they grappled and fought, while Guy, eager for revenge, rushed to help Sam, and got in a few trifling blows.

Sam was heavier and stronger than Yan, but Yan had gained wonderfully since coming to Sanger. He was thin, but wiry, and at school he had learned the familiar hip-throw that is as old as Cain and Abel. It was all he did know of wrestling, but now it stood him in good stead. He was strong with rage, too—and almost as soon as they grappled he found his chance. Sam's heels flew up and he went sprawling in the dust. One straight blow on the nose sent Guy off howling, and seeing Sam once more on his feet, Yan rushed at him again like a wild beast. A moment later the big boy went tumbling over the bank into the pond.

"*You* see if I don't get you sent about your business from here," spluttered Sam, now thoroughly angry. "I'll tell Da you hender the wurruk." His eyes were full of water and Guy's were full of stars and of tears. Neither saw the fourth party near; but Yan did. There, not twenty yards away, stood William Raften, spectator of the whole affair—an expression not of anger but of infinite sorrow and disappointment on his face—not because they had quarrelled—no—he knew boy nature well enough not to give that a thought—but that *his* son, older and stronger than the other and backed by another boy, should be licked in fair fight by a thin, half-invalid.

It was as bitter a pill as he had ever had to swallow.

He turned in silence and disappeared, and never afterward alluded to the matter.

XV

The Peace of Minnie

THAT night the two avoided each other. Yan ate but little, and to Mrs. Raften's kindly solicitous questions he said he was not feeling well.

After supper they were sitting around the table, the men sleepily silent, Yan and Sam moodily so. Yan had it all laid out in his mind now. Sam would make a one-sided report of the affair; Guy would sustain him. Raften himself was witness of Yan's violence.

The merry days at Sanger were over. He was doomed, and felt like a condemned felon awaiting the carrying out of the sentence. There was only one lively member of the group. That was little Minnie. She was barely three, but a great chatterbox. Like all children, she dearly loved a "secret," and one of her favourite tricks was to beckon to some one, laying her pinky finger on her pinker lips, and then when they stooped she would whisper in their ear, "Don't tell." That was all. It was her idea of a "seek-it."

She was playing at her brother's knee. He picked her up and they whispered to each other, then she scrambled down and went to Yan. He lifted her with a tenderness that was born of the thought that she alone loved him now. She beckoned his head down, put her chubby arms around his neck and whispered, "*Don't tell,*" then slid down, holding her dear innocent little finger warningly before her mouth.

What did it mean? Had Sam told her to do that, or was it a mere repetition of her old trick? No matter, it brought a rush of warm feeling into Yan's heart. He coaxed the little cherub back and whispered, "No, Minnie, I'll never tell." He began to see how crazy he had been. Sam was such a good fellow, he was very fond of him, and he wanted to make up; but no—with Sam holding threats of banishment over him, he could not ask for forgiveness. No, he would do nothing but wait and see.

He met Mr. Raften again and again that evening and nothing was said. He slept little that night and was up early. He met Mr. Raften alone—rather tried to meet him alone. He wanted to have it over with. He was one of the kind not prayed for in the Litany that crave "sudden death." But Raften was unchanged. At breakfast Sam was as usual, except to Yan, and not very different to him. He had a swelling on his lip that he said he got "tusslin' with the boys somehow or nuther."

After breakfast Raften said:

"Yahn, I want you to come with me to the schoolhouse."

"It's come at last," thought Yan, for the schoolhouse was on the road to the railroad station. But why did not Raften say "the station"? He was not a man to mince words. Nothing was said about his handbag either, and there was no room for it in the buggy anyway.

Raften drove in silence. There was nothing unusual in that. At length he said:

"Yahn, what's yer father goin' to make of ye?"

"An artist," said Yan, wondering what this had to do with his dismissal.

"Does an artist hev to be bang-up eddicated?"

"They're all the better for it."

"Av coorse, av coorse, that's what I tell Sam. It's eddication that counts. Does artists make much money?"

"Yes, some of them. The successful ones sometimes make millions."

"Millions? I guess not. Ain't you stretchin' it just a leetle?"

"No, sir. Turner made a million. Titian lived in a palace, and so did Raphael."

"Hm. Don't know 'em, but maybe so—maybe so. It's wonderful what eddication does—that's what I tell Sam."

They now drew near the schoolhouse. It was holiday time, but the door was open and on the steps were two graybearded men. They nodded to Raften. These men were the school trustees. One of them was Char-less Boyle; the other was old Moore, poor as a church mouse, but a genial soul, and really put on the Board as a lubricant between Boyle and Raften.

Boyle was much the more popular. But Raften was always made trustee, for the people knew that he would take extremely good care of funds and school as well as of scholars.

This was a special meeting called to arrange for a new schoolhouse. Raften got out a lot of papers, including letters from the Department of Education. The School District had to find half the money; the Department would supply the other half if all conditions were complied with. Chief of these, the schoolhouse had to have a given number of cubic feet of air for each pupil. This was very important, but how were they to know in advance if they had the minimum and were not greatly over. It would not do to ask the Department that. They could not consult the teacher, for he was away now and probably would cheat them with more air than was needed. It was Raften who brilliantly solved this frightful mathematical problem and discovered a doughty champion in the thin, bright-eyed child.

"Yahn," he said, offering him a two-foot rule, "can ye tell me how many foot of air is in this room for every scholar when the seats is full?"

"You mean cubic feet?"

"Le's see," and Raften and Moore, after stabbing at the plans with huge forefingers and fumbling cumberously at the much-pawed documents, said together: "Yes, it says cubic feet." Yan quickly measured the length of the room and took the height with the map-lifter. The three graybeards gazed with awe and admiration as they saw how *sure* he seemed. He then counted the seats and said, "Do you count the teacher?" The men discussed this point, then decided, "Maybe ye better; he uses more wind than any of them. Ha, ha!"

Yan made a few figures on paper, then said, "Twenty feet, rather better."

"Luk at thot," said Raften in a voice of bullying and triumph; "jest agrees with the Gover'ment Inspector. I *towld* ye he could. Now let's put the new buildin' to test."

More papers were pawed over.

"Yahn, how's this—double as many children, one teacher an' the buildin' so an' so."

Yan figured a minute and said, "Twenty-five feet each."

"Thar, didn't I tell ye," thundered Raften; "didn't I say that that dhirty swindler of an architect was playing us into the conthractor's hands—thought we wuz simple—a put-up job, the hull durn thing. Luk at it! They're nothing but a gang of thieves."

Yan glanced at the plan that was being flourished in the air.

"Hold on," he said, with an air of authority that he certainly never before had used to Raften, "there's the lobby and cloak-room to come off." He subtracted their bulk and found the plan all right—the Government minimum of air.

Boyle's eye had now just a little gleam of triumphant malice. Raften seemed actually disappointed not to have found some roguery.

"Well, they're a shcaly lot, anyhow. They'll bear watchin'," he added, in tones of self-justification.

"Now, Yahn, last year the township was assessed at $265,000 an' we raised $265 with a school-tax of wan mill on the dollar. This year the new assessment gives $291,400; how much will the same tax raise if cost of collecting is same?"

"Two hundred and ninety-one dollars and forty cents," said Yan, without hesitation—and the three men sat back in their chairs and gasped.

It was the triumph of his life. Even old Boyle beamed in admiration, and Raften glowed, feeling that not a little of it belonged to him.

There was something positively pathetic in the simplicity of the three shrewd men and their abject reverence for the wonderful scholarship of this raw boy, and not less touching was their absolute faith in his infallibility as a mathematician.

Raften grinned at him in a peculiar, almost a weak way. Yan had never seen that expression on his face before, excepting once, and that was as he shook hands with a noted pugilist just after he had won a memorable fight. Yan did not know whether he liked it or not.

On the road home Raften talked with unusual freeness about his plans for his son. (Yan began to realize that the storm had blown over.) He harped on his favourite theme, "eddication." If Yan had only known, that was the one word of comfort that Raften found when he saw his big boy go down: "It's eddication done it. Oh, but he's fine eddicated." Yan never knew until years afterward, when a grown man and he and Raften were talking of the old days, that he had been for some time winning respect from the rough-and-ready farmer, but what finally

raised him to glorious eminence was the hip-throw that he served that day on Sam.

. . . .

Raften was all right, Yan believed, but what of Sam? They had not spoken yet. Yan wished to make up, but it grew harder. Sam had got over his wrath and wanted a chance, but did not know how.

He had just set down his two buckets after feeding the pigs when Minnie came toddling out.

"Sam! Sam! Take Minnie to 'ide," then seeing Yan she added, "Yan, you mate a tair, tate hold Sam's hand."

The queen must be obeyed. Sam and Yan sheepishly grasped hands to make a queen's chair for the little lady. She clutched them both around the neck and brought their heads close together. They both loved the pink-and-white baby between them, and both could talk to her though not to each other. But there is something in touch that begets comprehension. The situation was becoming ludicrous when Sam suddenly burst out laughing, then:

"Say, Yan, let's be friends."

"I—I want—to—be," stammered Yan, with tears standing in his eyes. "I'm awfully sorry. I'll never do it again."

"Oh, shucks! I don't care," said Sam. "It was all that dirty little sneak that made the trouble; but never mind, it's all right. The only thing that worries me is how you sent me flying. I'm bigger an' stronger an' older, I can heft more an' work harder, but you throwed me like a bag o' shavings. I only wish I knowed how you done it."

PART III

IN THE WOODS

I

Really in the Woods

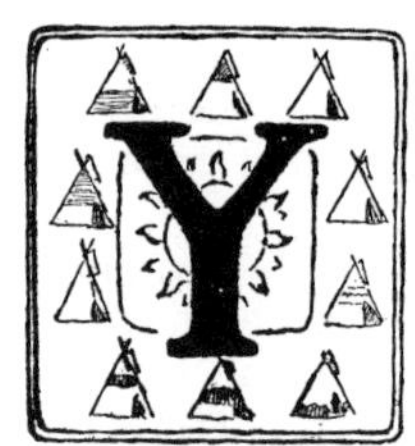

E seem to waste a powerful lot o' time goin' up an' down to yer camp; why don't ye stay thayer altogether?" said Raften one day, in the colourless style that always worried every one, for they did not know whether it was really meant or was mere sarcasm.

"Suits me. 'Tain't our choice to come home," replied his son.

"We'd like nothing better than to sleep there, too," said Yan.

"Well, why don't ye? That's what I'd do if I was a boy playin' Injun; I'd go right in an' play."

"*All right now*," drawled Sam (he always drawled in proportion to his emphasis), "that suits us; now we're a-going sure."

"All right, bhoys," said Raften; "but mind ye the pigs an' cattle's to be 'tended to every day."

"Is that what ye call lettin' us camp out—come home to work jest the same?"

"No, no, William," interposed Mrs. Raften; "that's not fair. That's no way to give them a holiday. Either do it or don't. Surely one of the men can do the chores for a month."

"Month—I didn't say nothin' about a month."

"Well, why don't you now?"

"Whoi, a month would land us into harvest," and William had the air of a man at bay, finding them all against him.

"I'll do Yahn's chores for a fortnight if he'll give me that thayer pictur he drawed of the place," now came in Michel's voice from the far end of the table—"except Sunday," he added, remembering a standing engagement, which promised to result in something of vast importance to him.

"Wall, I'll take care o' them Sundays," said Si Lee.

"Yer all agin me," grumbled William with comical perplexity. "But bhoys ought to be bhoys. Ye kin go."

"Whoop!" yelled Sam.

"Hooray!" joined in Yan, with even more interest though with less unrestraint.

"But howld on, I ain't through——"

"I say, Da, we want your gun. We can't go camping without a gun."

"Howld on, now. Give me a chance to finish. Ye can go fur two weeks, but ye got to *go;* no snakin' home nights to sleep. Ye can't hev no matches an' no gun. I won't hev a lot o' children foolin' wid a didn't-know-it-was-loaded, an' shootin' all the birds and squirrels an' each other, too. Ye kin hev yer bows an' arrows an' ye ain't likely to do no harrum. Ye kin hev all the mate an' bread an' stuff ye want, but ye must cook it yerselves, an' if I see any signs of settin' the woods afire I'll be down wid the rawhoide an' cut the very livers out o' ye."

The rest of the morning was devoted to preparation, Mrs. Raften taking the leading hand.

"Now, who's to be cook?" she asked.

"Sam"—"Yan"—said the boys in the same breath.

"Hm! You seem in one mind about it. Suppose you take it turn and turn about—Sam first day."

Then followed instructions for making coffee in the morning, boiling potatoes, frying bacon. Bread and butter enough they were to take with them—eggs, too.

"You better come home for milk every day or every other day, at least," remarked the mother.

"We'd ruther steal it from the cows in the pasture," ventured Sam, "seems naturaler to me Injun blood."

"If I ketch ye foolin' round the cows or sp'ilin' them the fur'll fly," growled Raften.

"Well, kin we hook apples and cherries?" and Sam added in explanation; "they're no good to us unless they're hooked."

"Take all the fruit ye want."

"An' potatoes?"

"Yes."

"An' aigs?"

"Well, if ye don't take more'n ye need."

"An' cakes out of the pantry? Indians do that."

"No; howld on now. That is a good place to draw the line. How are ye goin' to get yer stuff down thayer? It's purty heavy. Ye see thayer are yer beds an' pots an' pans, as well as food."

Didn't-Know-it-was-loaded Fool

"We'll have to take a wagon to the swamp and then carry them on our backs on the blazed trail," said Sam, and explained "our backs" by pointing to Michel and Si at work in the yard.

"The road goes as far as the creek," suggested Yan; "let's make a raft there an' take the lot in it down to the swimming-pond; that'd be real Injun."

"What'll ye make the raft of?" asked Raften.

"Cedar rails nailed together," answered Sam.

"No nails in mine," objected Yan; "that isn't Injun."

"An' none o' my cedar rails fur that. 'Pears to me it'd be less work an' more Injun to pack the stuff on yer backs an' no risk o' wettin' the beds."

So the raft was given up, and the stuff was duly carted to the creek's side. Raften himself went with it. He was a good deal of a boy at heart and he was much in sympathy with the plan. His remarks showed a mixture of interest, and doubt as to the wisdom of letting himself take so much interest.

"Hayre, load me up," he said, much to the surprise of the boys, as they came to the creek's edge. His broad shoulders carried half of the load. The blazed trail was only two hundred yards long, and in two trips the stuff was all dumped down in front of the teepee.

Sam noted with amusement the unexpected enthusiasm of his father. "Say, Da, you're just as bad as we are. I believe you'd like to join us."

'Moinds me o' airly days here," was the reply, with a wistful note in his voice. "Many a night me an' Caleb Clark slep' out this way on this very crick when them fields was solid bush. Do ye know how to make a bed?"

"Don't know a thing," and Sam winked at Yan. "Show us."

"I'll show ye the rale thing. Where's the axe?"

"Haven't any," said Yan. "There's a big tomahawk and a little tomahawk."

Raften grinned, took the big "tomahawk" and pointed to a small Balsam Fir. "Now there's a foine bed-tree."

"Why, that's a fire-tree, too," said Yan, as with two mighty strokes Raften sent it toppling down, then rapidly trimmed it of its flat green boughs. A few more strokes brought down a smooth young Ash and cut it into four pieces, two of them seven feet long and two of them five feet. Next he cut a

White Oak sapling and made four sharp pegs each two feet long.

"Now, boys, whayer do you want yer bed?" then stopping at a thought he added, "Maybe ye didn't want me to help—want to do everything yerselves?"

"Ugh, bully good squaw. Keep it up—wagh!" said his son and heir, as he calmly sat on a log and wore his most "Injun brave" expression of haughty approval.

The father turned with an inquiring glance to Yan, who replied:

"We're mighty glad of your help. You see, we don't know how. It seems to me that I read once the best place in the teepee is opposite the door and a little to one side. Let's make it here." So Raften placed the four logs for the sides and ends of the bed and drove in the ground the four stakes to hold them. Yan brought in several armfuls of branches, and Raften proceeded to lay them like shingles, beginning at the head-log of the bed and lapping them very much. It took all the fir boughs, but when all was done there was a solid mass of soft green tips a foot thick, all the butts being at the ground.

"Thayer," said Raften, "that's an *Injun feather bed* an' safe an' warrum. Slapin' on the ground's terrible dangerous, but that's all right. Now make your bed on that." Sam ana Yan did so, and when it was finished Raften said: "Now, fetch that little canvas I told yer ma to put in; that's to fasten to the poles fcr an inner tent over the bed."

Yan stood still and looked uncomfortable.

"Say, Da, look at Yan. He's got that tired look that he wears when the rules is broke."

"What's wrong," asked Raften.

"Indians don't have them that I ever heard of," said Little Beaver.

"Yan, did ye iver hear of a teepee linin' or a dew-cloth?"

"Yes," was the answer, in surprise at the unexpected knowledge of the farmer.

"Do ye know what they're like?"

"No—at least—no——"

"Well, *I do;* that's what it's like. That's something I do know, fur I seen old Caleb use wan."

"Oh, I remember reading about it now, and they are like that, and it's on them that the Indians paint their records. Isn't that bully," as he saw Raften add two long inner stakes which held the dew-cloth like a canopy.

"Say, Da, I never knew you and Caleb were hunting together. Thought ye were jest natural born enemies."

"Humph!" grunted Raften. "We wuz chums oncet. Never had no fault to find till we swapped horses."

"Sorry you ain't now, 'cause he's sure sharp in the woods."

"He shouldn't a-tried to make an orphan out o' you."

"Are you sure he done it?"

"If 'twasn't him I dunno who 'twas. Yan, fetch some of them pine knots thayer."

Yan went after the knots; it was some yards into the woods, and out there he was surprised to see a tall man behind a tree. A second's glance showed it to be Caleb. The Trapper laid one finger on his lips and shook his head. Yan nodded assent, gathered the knots, and went back to the camp, where Sam continued:

"You skinned him out of his last cent, old Boyle says."

"An' whoi not, when he throid to shkin me? Before that I was helpin' him, an' fwhat must he do but be ahfter swappin' horses. He might as well ast me to play poker and then squeal when I scooped the pile. Naybours is wan thing an' swappin' horses is another. All's fair in a horse trade, an' friends didn't orter swap horses widout they kin stand the shkinnin'. That's a game by itself. Oi would 'a' helped him jest the same afther that swap an' moore, fur he wuz good stuff, but he must nades shoot at me that noight as I come home wit the wad, so av coorse——

"I wish ye had a Dog now," said the farmer in the new tone of a new subject; "tramps is a nuisance at all toimes, an' a Dog is the best med'cine for them. I don't believe old Cap'd stay here; but maybe yer near enough to the house so they won't bother ye. An' now I guess the Paleface will go back to the settlement. I promised ma that I'd see that yer bed wuz all right, an' if ye sleep warrum an' dry an' hev plenty to ate ye'll take no harrum."

So he turned away, but as he was quitting the clearing he stopped,—the curious boyish interest was gone from his face, the geniality from his voice—then in his usual stern tones of command:

"Now, bhoys, ye kin shoot all the Woodchucks yer a mind ter, fur they are a nuisance in the field. Yer kin kill Hawks an' Crows an' Jays, fur they kill other birds, an' Rabbits an' Coons, fur they are fair game; but I don't want to hear of yer killin' any Squirrels or Chipmunks or Song-birds, an' if ye do I'll stop the hull thing an' bring ye back to wurruk, an' use the rawhoide on tap o' that."

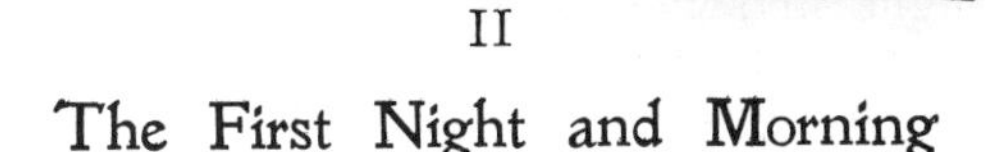

II

The First Night and Morning

IT was a strange new feeling that took possession of the boys as they saw Mr. Raften go, and when his step actually died away on the blazed trail they felt that they were really and truly alone in the woods and camping out. To Yan it was the realization of many dreams, and the weirdness of it was helped by the remembrance of the tall old man he had seen watching them from behind the trees. He made an excuse to wander out there, but of course Caleb was gone.

"Fire up," Sam presently called out. Yan was the chief expert with the rubbing-sticks, and within a minute or two he had the fire going in the middle of the teepee and Sam set about preparing the evening meal. This was supposed to be Buffalo meat and Prairie roots (beef and potatoes). It was eaten rather quietly, and then the boys sat down on the opposite sides of the fire. The conversation dragged, then died a natural death; each was busy with his thoughts, and there was, moreover, an impressive and repressive something or other all around them. Not a stillness, for there were many sounds, but beyond those a sort of voiceless background that showed up all the myriad voices. Some of these were evidently Bird, some Insect, and a few were recognized as Tree-frog notes. In the near stream were sounds of splashing or a little plunge.

"Must be Mushrat," whispered Sam to the unspoken query of his friend.

A loud, far "Oho-oho-oho" was familiar to both as the cry of the Horned Owl, but a strange long wail rang out from the trees overhead.

"What's that?"

"Don't know," was all they whispered, and both felt very uncomfortable. The solemnity and mystery of the night was on them and weighing more heavily with the waning light. The feeling was oppressive. Neither had courage enough to propose going to the house or their camping would have ended. Sam arose and stirred the fire, looked around for more wood, and, seeing none, he grumbled (to himself) and stepped outside in the darkness to find some. It was not till long afterward that he admitted having had to *dare* himself to step out into the darkness. He brought in some sticks and fastened the door as tightly as possible. The blazing fire in the teepee was cheering again. The boys perhaps did not realize that there was actually a tinge of home-sickness in their mood, yet both were thinking of the comfortable circle at the house. The blazing fire smoked a little, and Sam said:

"Kin you fix that to draw? You know more about it 'an me."

Yan now forced himself to step outside. The wind was rising and had changed. He swung the smoke poles till the vent was quartering down, then hoarsely whispered, "How's that?"

"That's better," was the reply in a similar tone, though there was no obvious difference yet.

He went inside with nervous haste and fastened up the entrance.

"Let's make a good fire and go to bed."

So they turned in after partly undressing, but not to sleep for hours. Yan in particular was in a state of nervous excitement. His heart had beaten violently when he went out that time, and even now that mysterious dread was on him. The fire was the one comfortable thing. He dozed off, but started up several times at some slight sound. Once it was a peculiar "*Tick, tick, scr-a-a-a-pe, lick-scra-a-a-a-a-pe*," down the teepee over his head. "*A Bear*" was his first notion, but on second thoughts he decided it was only a leaf sliding down the canvas. Later he was roused by a "*Scratch, scratch, scratch*" close to him. He listened silently for some time.· This was no leaf; it was an *animal!* Yes, surely—it was a Mouse. He slapped the

"If ye kill any Song-birds, I'll use the rawhoide on ye"

"Where's the axe?"

canvas violently and "hissed" till it went away, but as he listened he heard again that peculiar wail in the tree-tops. It almost made his hair sit up. He reached out and poked the fire together into a blaze. All was still and in time he dozed off. Once more he was wide awake in a flash and saw Sam sitting up in bed listening.

"What is it, Sam?" he whispered.

"I dunno. Where's the axe?"

"Right here."

"Let me have it on my side. You kin have the hatchet."

But they dropped off at last and slept soundly till the sun was strong on the canvas and filling the teepee with a blaze of transmitted light.

"Woodpecker! Woodpecker! Get up! Get up! Hi-e-yo! Hi-e-yo! Double-u-double-o-d-bang-fizz-whackety-whack-y-r-chuck-brrrrrrrrrrrrr-Woodpecker," shouted Yan to his sleepy chum, quoting a phrase that Sam when a child had been taught as the true spelling of his nickname.

Sam woke slowly, but knowing perfectly where he was, and drawled:

"Get up yourself. You're cook to-day, an' I'll take my breakfast in bed. Seems like my knee is broke out again."

"Oh, get up, and let's have a swim before breakfast."

"No, thank you, I'm too busy just now; 'sides, it's both cold and wet in that pond, this time o' day."

The morning was fresh and bright; many birds were singing; although it was July, a Red-eyed Vireo and a Robin were in full song; and as Yan rose to get the breakfast he wondered why he had been haunted by such strange feelings the night before. It was incomprehensible now. He wished that appalling wail in the tree-tops would sound again, so he might trace it home.

There still were some live coals in the ashes, and in a few minutes he had a blazing fire, with the pot boiling for coffee, and the bacon in the fryer singing sweetest music for the hungry.

Sam lay on his back watching his companion and making critical remarks.

"You may be an A1 cook—at least, I hope you are, but you don't know much about fire-wood," said he. "Now look at that," as one huge spark after another exploded from the fire and dropped on the bed and the teepee cover.

"How can I help it?"

"I'll bet Da's best cow against your jack-knife you got some Ellum or Hemlock in that fire."

"Well, I have," Yan admitted, with an air of surrender.

"My son," said the Great Chief Woodpecker, "no sparking allowed in the teepee. Beech, Maple, Hickory or Ash never spark. Pine knots an' roots don't, but they make smoke like—like—oh—you know. Hemlock, Ellum, Chestnut, Spruce and Cedar is public sparkers, an' not fit for dacint teepee sassiety. Big Injun heap hate noisy, crackling fire. Enemy hear that, an'—an'—it burns his bedclothes."

"All right, Grandpa," and the cook made a mental note, then added in tones of deadly menace, "You get up now, do you understand!" and he picked up a bucket of water.

"That might scare the Great Chief Woodpecker if the Great Chief Cook had a separate bed, but now he smiles kind o' scornful," was all the satisfaction he got. Then seeing that breakfast really was ready, Sam scrambled out a few minutes later. The coffee acted like an elixir—their spirits rose, and before the meal was ended it would have been hard to find two more hilarious and enthusiastic campers. Even the vague terrors of the night were now sources of amusement.

III

A Crippled Warrior and the Mud Albums

"SAY, Sam; what about Guy? Do we want him?"

"Well, it's just like this. If it was at school or any other place I wouldn't be bothered with the dirty little cuss, but out in the woods like this one feels kind o' friendly, an' three's better than two. Besides, he has been admitted to the Tribe already."

"Yes, that's what I say. Let's give him a *yell*."

So the boys uttered a long yell, produced by alternating the voice between a high falsetto and a natural tone. This was the "yell," and had never failed

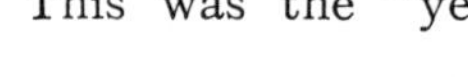

to call Guy forth to join them unless he had some chore on hand and his "Paw" was too near to prevent his renegading to the Indians. He soon appeared waving a branch, the established signal that he came as a friend.

He came very slowly, however, and the boys saw that he limped frightfully, helping himself along with a stick. He was barefoot, as usual, but his left foot was swaddled in a bundle of rags.

"Hello, Sappy; what happened? Out to Wounded Knee River?"

"Nope. Struck luck. Paw was bound I'd ride the Horse with the scuffler all day, but he gee'd too short an' I arranged to tumble off'n him, an' Paw scuffled me foot some. Law! how I did holler! You should 'a' heard me."

"Bet we did," said Sam. "When was it?"

"Yesterday about four."

"Exactly. We heard an awful screech and Yan says, says he, 'There's the afternoon train at Kelly's Crossing, but ain't she late?'

"'Train!' says I. 'Pooh. I'll bet that's Guy Burns getting a new licking.'"

"Guess I'll well up now," said War Chief Sapwood, so stripped his foot, revealing a scratch that would not have cost a thought had he got it playing ball. He laid the rags away carefully and with them every trace of the limp, then entered heartily into camp life.

The vast advantage of being astir early now was seen. There were Squirrels in every other tree, there were birds on every side, and when they ran to the pond a wild Duck spattered over the surface and whistled out of sight.

"What you got?" called Sam, as he saw Yan bending eagerly over something down by the pond.

Yan did not answer, and so Sam went over and saw him studying out a mark in the mud. He was trying to draw it in his note-book.

"What is it?" repeated Sam.

"Don't know. Too stubby for a Muskrat, too much claw for a Cat, too small for a Coon, too many toes for a Mink."

"I'll bet it's a Whangerdoodle."

Yan merely chuckled in answer to this.

"Don't you laugh," said the Woodpecker, solemnly. "You'd be more apt to cry if you seen one walk into the teepee blowing the whistle at the end of his tail.

Then it'd be, 'Oh, Sam, where's the axe?'"

"Tell you what I do believe it is," said Yan, not noticing this terrifying description; "it's a Skunk."

"Little Beaver, my son! I thought I would tell you, then I sez to meself, 'No; it's better for him to find out by his lone. Nothing like a struggle in early life to develop the stuff in a man. It don't do to help him too much,' sez I, an' so I didn't."

Here Sam condescendingly patted the Second War Chief on the head and nodded approvingly. Of course he did not know as much about the track as Yan did, but he prattled on:

"Little Beaver! you're a heap struck on tracks—— Ugh—good! You kin tell by them everything that passes in the night. Wagh! Bully! You're likely to be the naturalist of our Tribe. But you ain't got gumption. Now, in this yer hunting-ground of our Tribe there is only one place where you can see a track, an' that is that same mud-bank; all the rest is hard or grassy. Now, what I'd do if I was a Track-a-mist, I'd give the critters lots o' chance to leave tracks. I'd fix it all round with places so nothing could come or go 'thout givin' us his impressions of the trip. I'd have one on each end of the trail coming in, an' one on each side of the creek where it comes in an' goes out."

"Well, Sam, you have a pretty level head. I wonder I didn't think of that myself."

"My son, the Great Chief does the thinking. It's the rabble—that's you and Sappy—that does the work."

But all the same he set about it at once with Yan, Sappy following with a *slight limp now.* They removed the sticks and rubbish for twenty feet of the trail at each end and sprinkled this with three or four inches of fine black loam. They cleared off the bank of the stream at four places, one at each side where it entered the woods, and one at each side where it went into the Burns's Bush.

"Now," said Sam, "there's what I call visitors' albums like the one that Phil Leary's nine fatties started when they got their brick house and their swelled heads, so every one that came in could write their names an' something about 'this happy, happy, ne'er-to-be-forgotten visit them as could write. Reckon that's where our visitors get the start, for all of ours kin write that has feet."

"Wonder why I didn't think o' that," said Yan,

again and again. "But there's one thing you forget," he said. "We want one around the teepee."

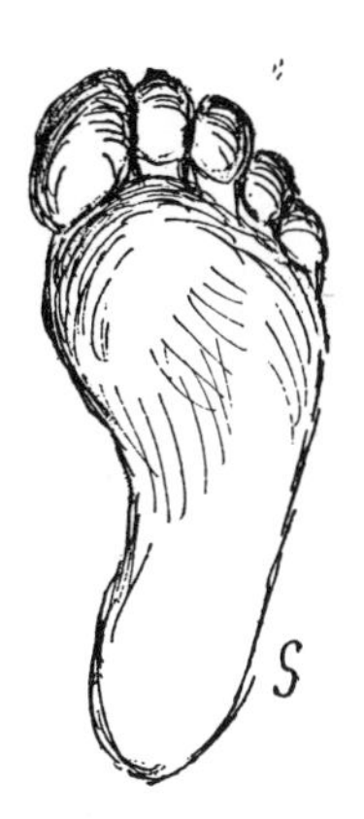

This was easily made, as the ground was smooth and bare there, and Sappy forgot his limp and helped to carry ashes and sand from the fire-hole. Then planting his broad feet down in the dust, with many snickers, he left some very interesting tracks.

"I call that a bare track," said Sam.

"Go ahead and draw it," giggled Sappy.

"Why not?" and Yan got out his book.

"Bet you can't make it life-size," and Sam glanced from the little note-book to the vast imprint.

After it was drawn, Sam said, "Guess I'll peel off and show you a human track." He soon gave an impression of his foot for the artist, and later Yan added his own; the three were wholly different.

"Seems to me it would be about right, if you had the ways the toes pointed and the distance apart to show how long the legs wuz."

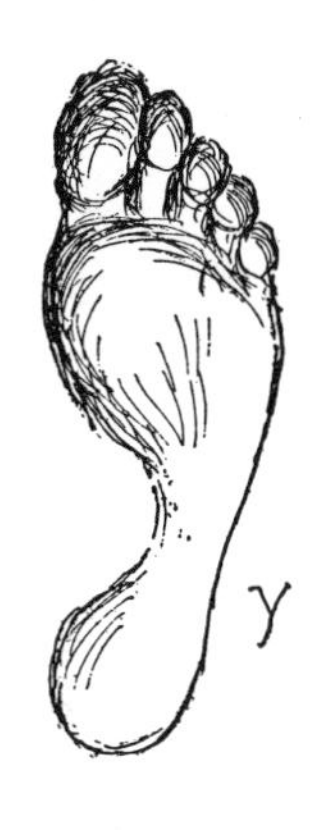

Again Sam had given Yan a good idea. From that time he noted these two points and made his records much better.

"Air you fellers roostin' here now?" said Sappy in surprise, as he noted the bed as well as the pots and pans.

"Yep."

"Well, I wanter, too. If I kin git hol' o' Maw 'thout Paw, it'll be O. K."

"You let on we don't want you and Paw'll let you come. Tell him Ole Man Raften ordered you off the place an' he'll fetch you here himself."

"I guess there's room enough in that bed fur three," remarked the Third War Chief.

"Well, I guess there ain't," said Woodpecker. "Not when the third one won first prize for being the dirtiest boy in school. You can get stuff an' make your own bed, across there on the other side the fire."

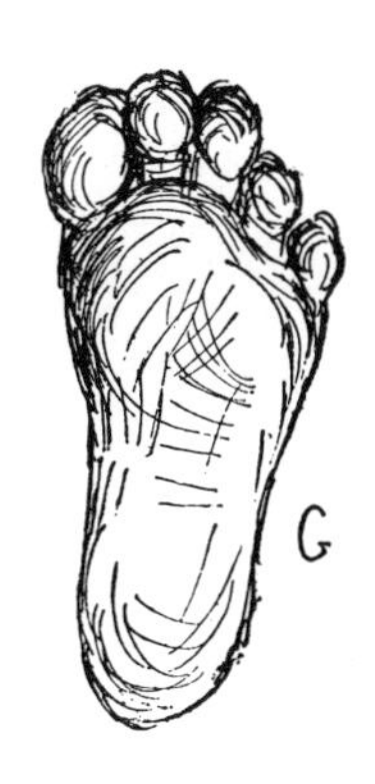

"Don't know how."

"We'll show you, only you'll have to go home for blankets an' grub."

The boys soon cut a Fir-bough bed, but Guy put off going home for the blankets as long as he could. He knew and they suspected that there was no chance of his rejoining them again that day. So after sundown he replaced his foot-rags and limped down the trail homeward, saying, "I'll be back in a few minutes," and the boys knew perfectly well that he would not.

The evening meal was over; they had sat around wondering if the night would repeat its terrors. An Owl "Hoo-hoo-ed" in the trees. There was a pleasing romance in the sound. The boys kept up the fire till about ten, then retired, determined that they would not be scared this time. They were barely off to sleep when the most awful outcry arose in the near woods, like "a Wolf with a sore throat," then the yells of a human being in distress. Again the boys sat up in fright. There was a scuffling outside—a loud and terrified "Hi—hi—hi—Sam!" Then an attack was made on the door. It was torn open, and in tumbled Guy. He was badly frightened; but when the fire was lighted and he calmed down a little he confessed that Paw had sent him to bed, but when all was still he had slipped out the window, carrying the bedclothes. He was nearly back to the camp when he decided to scare the boys by letting off a few wolfish howls, but he made himself very scary by doing it, and when a wild answer came from the tree-tops—a hideous, blaring screech—he lost all courage, dropped the bedding, and ran toward the teepee yelling for help.

The boys took torches presently and went nervously in search of the missing blankets. Guy's bed was made and in an hour they were once more asleep.

In the morning Sam was up and out first. From the home trail he suddenly called:

"Yan, come here."

"Do you mean me?" said Little Beaver, with haughty dignity.

"Yep, Great Chief; git a move on you. Hustle out here. Made a find. Do you see who was visiting us last night while we slept?" and he pointed to the "album" on the inway. "I hain't shined them shoes every week with soot off the bottom of the pot without knowin' that one pair of 'em was wore by Ma an' one of 'em by Da. But let's see how far they come. Why, I orter looked round the teepee before tramplin' round. They went back, and though the trails were much hidden by their own, they found enough around the doorway to show that during the night, or more likely late in the evening, the father and mother had paid them a visit in secret—had inspected the camp as they slept, but finding no one stirring and the boys breathing the deep breath of healthy sleep, they had left them undisturbed.

"Say, boys—I mean Great Chiefs—what we want in camp is a Dog, or one of these nights some one will steal our teeth out o' our heads an' we won't know a thing till they come back for the gums. All Injun camps have Dogs, anyway."

The next morning the Third War Chief was ordered out by the Council, first to wash himself clean, then to act as cook for the day. He grumbled as he washed, that "'Twan't no good—he'd be all dirty again in two minutes," which was not far from the truth. But he went at the cooking with enthusiasm, which lasted nearly an hour. After this he did not see any fun in it, and for once he, as well as the others, began to realize how much was done for them at home. At noon Sappy set out nothing but dirty dishes, and explained that so long as each got his own it was all right. His foot was very troublesome at meal time also. He said it was the moving round when he was hurrying that made it so hard to bear, but in their expedition with bows and arrows later on he found complete relief.

"Say, look at the Red-bird," he shouted, as a Tanager flitted onto a low branch and blazed in the sun. "Bet I hit him first shot!" and he drew an arrow.

"Here you, Saphead," said Sam, "quit that shooting at little birds. It's bad medicine. It's against the rules; it brings bad luck—it brings awful bad luck. I tell you there ain't no worse luck than Da's rawhide—that I know."

"Why, what's the good o' playin' Injun if we can't shoot a blame thing?" protested Sappy.

"You kin shoot Crows an' Jays if you like, an' Woodchucks, too."

"I know where there's a Woodchuck as big as a Bear."

"Ah! What size Bear?"

"Well, it is. You kin laugh all you want to. He has a den in our clover field, an' he made it so big that the mower dropped in an' throwed Paw as far as from here to the crick."

"An' the horses, how did they get out?"

"Well! It broke the machine, an' you should have heard Paw swear. My! but he was a socker. Paw offered me a quarter if I'd kill the old whaler. I borrowed a steel trap an' set it in the hole, but he'd dig out under it an' round it every time. I'll bet there ain't anything smarter'n an old Woodchuck."

"Is he there yet?" asked War Chief No. 2.

"You just bet he is. Why, he has half an acre of clover all eat up."

"Let's try to get him," said Yan. "Can we find him?"

"Well, I should say so. I never come by but I see the old feller. He's so big he looks like a calf, an' so old an' wicked he's gray-headed."

"Let's have a shot at him," suggested the Woodpecker. "He's fair game. Maybe your Paw'll give us a quarter each if we kill him."

Guy snickered. "Guess you don't know my Paw," then he giggled bubblously through his nose again.

Arrived at the edge of the clover, Sam asked, "Where's your Woodchuck?"

"Right in there."

"I don't see him."

"Well, he's always here."

"Not now, you bet."

"Well, this is the very first time I ever came here and didn't see him. Oh, I tell you, he's a fright. I'll bet he's a blame sight bigger'n that stump."

"Well, here's his track, anyway," said Woodpecker, pointing to some tracks he had just made unseen with his own broad palm.

"Now," said Sappy, in triumph. "Ain't he an old socker?"

"Sure enough. You ain't missed any cows lately, have you? Wonder you ain't scared to live anyways near!"

IV

A "Massacree" of Palefaces

SAY, fellers, I know where there's a stavin' Birch tree—do you want any bark?"

"Yes, I want some," said Little Beaver.

"But hold on; I guess we better not, coz it's right on the edge o' our bush, an' Paw's still at the turnips."

"Now if you want a real war party," said the Head Chief, "let's massacree the Paleface settlement up the crick and get some milk. We're just out, and I'd like to see if the place has changed any."

So the boys hid their bows and arrows and head-dresses, and, forgetting to take a pail, they followed in Indian file the blazed trail, carefully turning in their toes as they went and pointing silently to the track, making signs of great danger. First they crawled up, under cover of one of the fences, to the barn. The doors were open and men working at something. A pig wandered in from the barn-yard. Then the boys heard a sudden scuffle, and a squeal from the pig as it scrambled out again, and Raften's voice: "Consarn them pigs! Them boys ought to be here to herd them." This was sufficiently alarming to scare the Warriors off in great haste. They hid in the huge root-cellar and there held a council of war.

"Here, Great Chiefs of Sanger," said Yan, "behold I take three straws. That long one is for the Great Woodpecker, the middle size is for Little Beaver, and the short thick one with the bump on the end and a crack on top is Sappy. Now I will stack them up in a bunch and let them fall, then whichever way they point we must go, for this is Big Medicine."

So the straws fell. Sam's straw pointed nearly to the house; Yan's a little to the south of the house, and Guy's right back home.

"Aha, Sappy, you got to go home; the straw says so."

"I ain't goin' to believe no such foolishness."

"It's awful unlucky to go against it."

"I don't care, I ain't goin' back," said Guy doggedly.

"Well, my straw says go to the house; that means go scouting for milk, I reckon."

Yan's straw pointed toward the garden, and Guy's to the residence and grounds of "J. G. Burns, Esq."

"I don't care," said Sappy, "I ain't goin'. I am goin' after some of them cherries in your orchard, an' 'twon't be the first time, neither."

"We kin meet by the Basswood at the foot of the lane with whatever we get," said the First War Chief, as he sneaked into the bushes and crawled through the snake fence and among the nettles and manure heaps on the north side of the barnyard till he reached the woodshed adjoining the house. He knew where the men were, and he could guess where his mother was, but he was worried about the Dog. Old Cap might be on the front doorstep, or he might be prowling at just the wrong place for the Injun plan. The woodshed butted on the end of the kitchen. The milk was kept in the cellar, and one window of the cellar opened into a dark corner of the woodshed. This was easily raised, and Sam scrambled down into the cool damp cellar. Long rows of milk pans were in sight on the shelves. He lifted the cover of the one he knew to be the last put there and drank a deep, long draught with his mouth down to it, then licked the cream from his lips and remembered that he had come without a pail. But he knew where to get one. He went gently up the stairs, avoiding steps Nos. 1 and 7 because they were "creakers," as he found out long ago, when he used to "hook" maple sugar from the other side of the house. The door at the top was closed and buttoned, but he put his jack-knife blade through the crack and turned the button. After listening awhile and hearing no sound in the kitchen, he gently opened the squeaky old door. There was no one to be seen but the baby, sound asleep in her cradle. The outer door was open, but no Dog lying on the step as usual. Over the kitchen was a garret entered by a trap-door and a ladder. The ladder was up and the trap-door open, but all was still. Sam stood over the baby, grunted, "Ugh, Paleface papoose," raised his hand as if wielding a war club, aimed a deadly blow at the sleeping cherub, then stooped and kissed her rosy mouth so lightly that her pink fists went up to rub it at once. He now went to the pantry, took a large pie and a tin pail, then down into the cellar again. He, at first, merely closed the door behind him and was leaving it so, but remembered that Minnie might awaken and toddle around till she might toddle into the cellar; therefore he turned the button so that just a corner showed over the crack, closed the door and worked with his knife blade on that corner till the cellar was made as safe as before. He now escaped with his pie and pail.

Meanwhile his mother's smiling face beamed out of the dark loft. Then she came down the ladder. She had seen him come and enter the cellar; by chance she was in the loft when he reached the kitchen, but she had kept quiet to enjoy the joke.

Next time the Woodpecker went to the cellar he found a paper with this on it: "*Notice* to hostile Injuns—Next time you massacree this settlement, bring back the pail, and don't leave the covers off the milk pans."

Yan had followed the fence that ran south of the house. There was plenty of cover, but he crawled on hands and knees, going right down on his breast when he came to places more open than the rest. In this way he had nearly reached the garden when he heard a noise behind and, turning, he saw Sappy.

"Here, what are you following me for? Your straw pointed the other way. You ain't playing fair."

"Well, I don't care, I ain't going home. *You* fixed it up so my straw would point that way. It ain't fair, an' I won't do it."

"You got no right following me."

"I ain't following you, but you keep going just the place I want to go. It's you following me, on'y keepin' ahead. I told you I was after cherries."

"Well, the cherries are that way and I'm going this way, and I don't want you along."

"You couldn't get me if you wanted me."

"Erh——"

"Erh——"

So Sappy went cherryward and Yan waited awhile, then crawled toward the fruit garden. After twenty or thirty yards more, he saw a gleam of red, then under it a bright yellow eye glaring at him. He had chanced on a hen sitting on her nest. He came nearer, she took alarm and ran away, not clucking, but cackling loudly. There were a dozen eggs of two different styles, all bright and clean, and the hen's comb was bright red. Yan knew hens. This was easy to read: Two stray hens laying in one nest, and neither of them sitting yet.

"So ho! Straws show which way the hens go."

He gathered up the eggs into his hat and crawled back toward the tree where all had to meet.

But before he had gone far he heard a loud barking, then yells for help, and turned in time to see Guy scramble up a tree while Cap, the old Collie, barked savagely at him from below. Now that he was in no danger Sappy had the sense to keep quiet. Yan came back as quickly as possible. The Dog at once recognized and obeyed *him*, but doubtless was much puzzled to make out why he should be pelted back to the house when he had so nobly done his duty by the orchard.

"Now, you see, maybe next time you'll do what the medicine straw tells you. Only for me you'd been caught and fed to the pigs, sure."

"Only for you I wouldn't have come. I wasn't scared of your old Dog, anyway. Just in about two minutes more I was comin' down to kick the stuffin' out o' him myself."

"Perhaps you'd like to go back and do it now. I'll soon call him."

"Oh, I hain't got time now, but some other time—— Let's find Sam."

So they foregathered at the tree, and laden with their spoils, they returned gloriously to camp.

V

The Deer Hunt

THAT evening they had a feast and turned in to sleep at the usual hour. The night passed without special alarm. Once about daylight Sappy called them, saying he believed there was a Bear outside, but he had a trick of grinding his teeth in his sleep, and the other boys told him that was the Bear he heard.

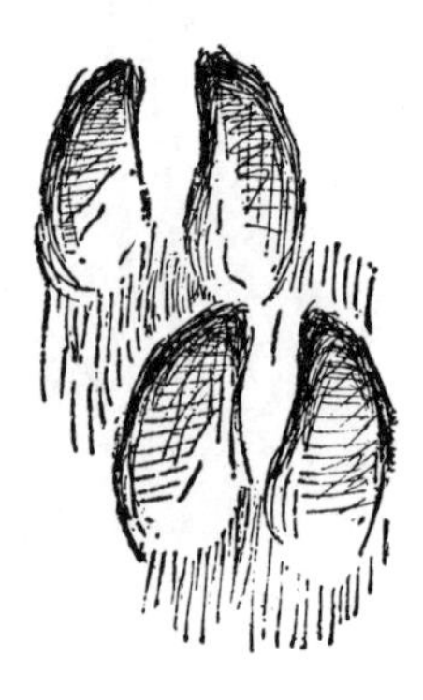

Yan went around to the mud albums and got some things he could not make out and a new mark that gave him a sensation. He drew it carefully. It was evidently the print of a small sharp hoof. This was what he had hungered for so long. He shouted, "Sam—Sam—Sapwood, come here; here's a *Deer track*."

The boys shouted back, "Ah, what you givin' us now!" "Call off your Dog!" and so forth.

But Yan persisted. The boys were so sure it was a trick that they would not go for some time, then the sun had risen high, shining straight down on the track instead of across, so it became very dim. Soon the winds, the birds and the boys themselves helped to wipe it out. But Yan had his drawing, and persisted in spite of the teasing that it was true.

At length Guy said aside to Sam: "Seems to me a feller that hunts tracks so terrible serious ought to see the critter *some time*. 'Tain't right to let him go on sufferin'. *I* think he ought to see that Deer. We ought to help him." Here he winked a volley or two and made signs for Sam to take Yan away.

This was easily done.

"Let's see if your Deer went out by the lower mud album." So they walked down that way, while Guy got an old piece of sacking, stuffed it with grass, and, hastily tying it in the form of a Deer's head, stuck it on a stick. He put in two flat pieces of wood for ears, took charcoal and made two black spots for eyes and one for a nose, then around each he drew a ring of blue clay from the bed of the brook. This soon dried and became white. Guy now set up this head in the bushes, and when all was ready he ran swiftly and silently through the wood to find Sam and Yan. He beckoned vigorously and called under his voice: "Sam—Yan—a Deer! Here's that there Deer that made them tracks, I believe."

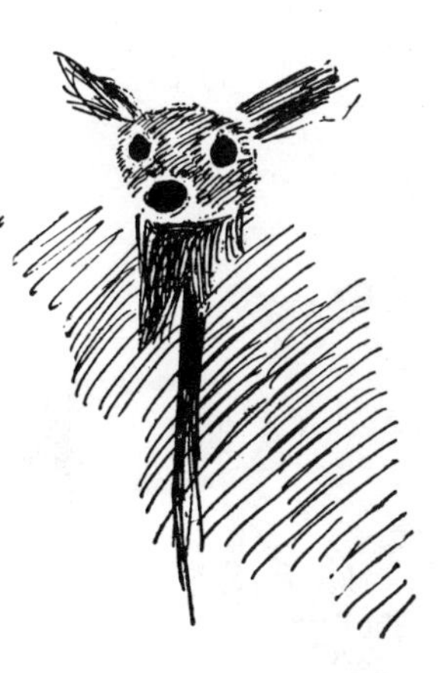

Guy would have failed to convince Yan if Sam had not looked so much interested. They ran back to the teepee, got their bows and arrows, then, guided by Guy, who, however, kept back, they crawled to where he had seen the Deer.

"There—there, now, ain't he a Deer? There—see him move!"

Yan's first feeling was a most exquisite thrill of pleasure. It was like the uplift of joy he had had the time he got his book, but was stronger. The savage impulse to kill came quickly, and his bow was in his hand, but he hesitated.

"Shoot! Shoot!" said Sam and Guy.

Yan wondered why *they* did not shoot. He turned, and in spite of his agitation he saw that they were making fun of him. He glanced at the Deer again, moved up a little closer and saw the trick.

Then they hooted aloud. Yan was a little crestfallen. Oh, it had been such an exquisite feeling! The drop was long and hard, but he rallied quickly.

"I'll shoot your Deer for you," he said, and sent an arrow close under it.

"Well, I kin beat that," and Sam and Guy both fired. Sam's arrow stuck in the Deer's nose. At that he gave a yell; then all shot till the head was stuck full of arrows, and they returned to the teepee to get dinner. They were still chaffing Yan about the Deer when he said slowly to Guy:

"Generally you are not so smart as you think you are, but this time you're smarter. You've given me a notion."

So after dinner he got a sack about three feet long and stuffed it full of dry grass; then he made a small sack about two and a half feet long and six inches thick, but with an elbow in it and pointed at one end. This he also stuffed with hay and sewed with a bone needle to the big sack. Next he cut four sticks of soft pine for legs and put them into the four corners of the big sack, wrapping them with bits of sacking to be like the rest. Then he cut two ears out of flat sticks; painted black eyes and nose with a ring of white around each, just as Sappy had done, but finally added a black spot on each side of the body, and around that a broad gray hand. Now he had completed what every one could see was meant for a Deer.

The other boys helped a little, but not did cease to chaff him.

"Who's to be fooled this time?" asked Guy.

"You," was the answer.

"I'll bet you'll get buck fever the first time you come across it," chuckled the Head Chief.

"Maybe I will, but you'll all have a chance. Now you fellers stay here and I'll hide the Deer. Wait till I come back."

The Deer

So Yan ran off northward with the dummy, then swung around to the east and hid it at a place quite out of the line that he first took. He returned nearly to where he came out, shouting "Ready!"

Then the hunters sallied forth fully armed, and Yan explained: "First to find it counts ten and has first shot. If he misses, next one can walk up five steps and shoot; if he misses, next walks five steps more, and so on until the Deer is hit. Then all the shooting must be done from the place where that arrow was fired. A shot in the heart counts ten; in the gray counts five; that's a body wound—and a hit outside of that counts one—that's a scratch. If the Deer gets away without a shot in the heart, then I count twenty-five, and the first one to find it is Deer for next hunt—twelve shots each is the limit."

The two hunters searched about for a long time.

Sam made disparaging remarks about the trail this Deer *did not* leave, and Guy sneaked and peaked in every thicket.

Sappy was not an athlete nor an intellectual giant, but his little piggy eyes were wonderfully sharp and clear.

"I see him," he yelled presently, and pointed out the place seventy-five yards away where he saw one ear and part of the head.

"Tally ten for Sappy," and Yan marked it down.

Guy was filled with pride at his success. He made elaborate preparation to shoot, remarking, "I could 'a' seen it twicet as far—if—if—if—it was—if I had a fair chance."

He drew his bow and left fly The arrow went little more than half way. So Sam remarked, "Five steps up I kin go. It don't say nothing about how long the steps?"

"No."

"Well, here goes," and he began the most wonderful Kangaroo hops that he could do. He covered about thirty feet in those five steps, and by swerving a little aside he got a good view of the Deer. He was now less than sixty-five yards away. He fired and missed. Now Guy had the right to walk up five steps. He also missed. Finally at thirty yards Sam sent an arrow close past a tree, deep in the Deer's gray flank.

"Bully shot! Body wound! Count five for the Great War Chief. All shooting from this spot now," said Yan, "and I don't know why I shouldn't shoot as well as the others."

"Coz you're the Deer and that'd be suicide," was Sam's objection. "But it's all right. You won't hit."

The objection was not sustained, and Yan tried his luck also. Two or three shots in the brown of the Deer's haunch, three or four into the tree that stood half way between, but nearly in line, a shot or two into the nose, then "Hooray!" a shot from Guy right into the Deer's heart put an end to the chase. Now they went up to draw and count the arrows.

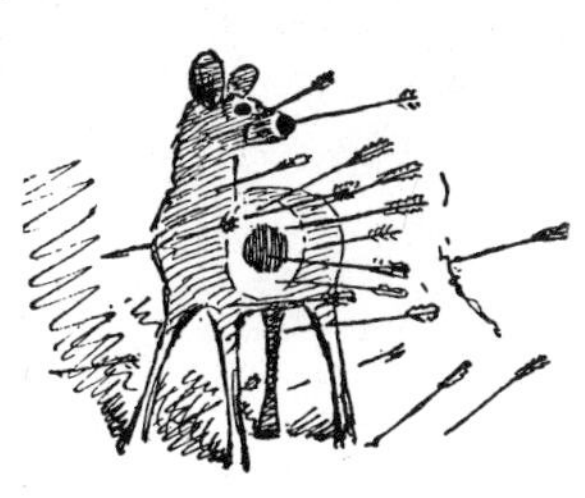

Guy was ahead with a heart shot, ten, a body wound, five, and a scratch, one, that's sixteen, with ten more for finding it—twenty-six points. Sam followed with two body wounds and two scratches—twelve points, and Yan one body wound and five scratches—ten points. The Deer looked like an old Porcupine when they came up to it, and Guy, bursting with triumph, looked like a young Emperor.

"I tell you it takes me to larn you fellers to Deer hunt. I'll bet I'll hit him in the heart first thing next time."

"I'll bet you won't, coz you'll be Deer and can't shoot till we both have."

Guy thought this the finest game he had ever played. He pranced away with the dummy on his back, scheming as he went to make a puzzle for the others. He hid the Deer in a dense thicket east of the camp, then sneaked around to the west of the camp and yelled "Ready!" They had a long, tedious search and had to give it up.

"Now what to do? Who counts?" asked the Woodpecker.

"When Deer escapes it counts twenty-five," replied the inventer of the game; and again Guy was ahead.

"This is the bulliest game I ever seen," was his ecstatic remark.

"Seems to me there's something wrong; that Deer ought to have a trail."

"That's so," assented Yan. "Wonder if he couldn't drag an old root!"

"If there was snow it'd be easy."

"I'll tell you, Sam; we'll tear up paper and leave a paper trail."

"Now you're talking." So all ran to camp. Every available scrap of wrapping paper was torn up small and put in a "scent bag."

Since no one found the Deer last time, Guy had the right to hide it again.

He made a very crooked trail and a very careful hide, so that the boys nearly walked onto the Deer before they saw it about fifteen yards away. Sam scored ten for the find. He fired and missed. Yan now stepped up his five paces and fired so hastily that he also missed. Guy now had a shot at it at five yards, and, of course, hit the Deer in the heart. This succession of triumphs swelled his head nearly to the bursting point, and his boasting passed all bounds. But it now became clear that there must be a limit to the stepping up. So the new rule was made, "No stepping up nearer than fifteen paces."

The game grew as they followed it. Its resemblance to real hunting was very marked. The boys found that they could follow the trail, or sweep the woods with their eyes as they pleased, and find the game, but the wisest way was a combination. Yan was too much for the trail, Sam too much for the general lookout, but Guy seemed always in luck. His little piglike eyes took in everything, and here at length he found a department in which he could lead. It looked as though the "dirty little cuss was really cut out for a hunter." He made a number of very clever hidings of the Deer. Once he led the trail to the pond, then across, and right opposite he put the Deer in full view, so that they saw it at once in the open; they were obliged either to shoot across the pond, or step farther away round the edge, or step into the deep water, and again Guy scored. It was found necessary to bar hiding the Deer on a ridge and among stones, because in one case arrows which missed were lost in the bushes and in the other they were broken.

They played this game so much that they soon found a new difficulty. The woods were full of paper trails, and there was no means of deciding which was the old and which the new. This threatened to end the fun altogether. But Yan hit on the device of a different colour of paper. This gave them a fresh start, but their supply was limited. There was paper everywhere in the woods now, and it looked as though the game was going to kill itself, when old Caleb came to pay them a visit. He always happened round as though it was an accident, but the boys were glad to see him, as he usually gave some help.

"Ye got some game, I see," and the old man's eye twinkled as he noted the dummy, now doing target duty on the forty-yard range. "Looks like the real thing. Purty good—purty good." He chuckled as he learned about the Deer hunt, and a sharp observer might have discerned a slight increase of interest when he found that it was not Sam Raften that was the "crack" hunter.

"Good fur you, Guy Burns. Me an' your Paw hev hunted Deer together on this very crik many a time."

When he learned the difficulty about the scent, he said "Hm," and puffed at his pipe for awhile in silence. Then at length:

"Say, Yan, why don't you and Guy get a bag o' wheat or Injun corn for scent; that's better than paper, an' what ye lay to-day is all clared up by

the birds and Squirrels by to-morrow."

"Bully!" shouted Sam. (He had not been addressed at all, but he was not thin-skinned.) Within ten minutes he had organized another "White massacree"—that is, a raid on the home barn, and in half an hour he returned with a peck of corn.

"Now, lemme be Deer," said Caleb. "Give me five minutes' start, then follow as fast as ye like. I'll show ye what a real Deer does."

He strode away bearing the dummy, and in five minutes as they set out on the trail he came striding back again. Oh, but that seemed a long run. The boys followed the golden corn trail—a grain every ten feet was about all they needed now, they were so expert. It was a straight run for a time, then it circled back till it nearly cut itself again (at X, page 145). The boys thought it did so, and claimed the right to know, as on a real Deer trail you could tell. So Caleb said, "No, it don't cut the old trail." Where, then, did it go? After beating about, Sam said that the trail looked powerful heavy, like it might be double.

"Bet I know," said Guy. "He's doubled back," which was exactly what he did do, though Caleb gave no sign. Yan looked back on the trail and found where the new one had forked. Guy gave no heed to the ground once he knew the general directions. He ran ahead (toward Y), so did Sam, but Guy glanced back to Yan on the trail to make sure of the line.

They had not gone far beyond the nearest bushes before Yan found another quirk in the trail. It doubled back at Z. He unravelled the double, glanced around, and at O he plainly saw the Deer lying on its side in the grass. He let off a triumphant yell, "Yi, yi, yi, *Deer!*" and the others came running back just in time to see Yan send an arrow straight into its heart.

VI

War Bonnet, Teepee and Coups

FORTY yards and first shot. Well, that's what the Injuns would call a '*grand coup*,'" and Caleb's face wore the same pleasant look as when he made the fire with rubbing-sticks.

"What's a *grand coup?*" asked Little Beaver.

"Oh, I suppose it's a big deed. The Injuns call a great feat a '*coup*,' an' an extra big one a '*grand coup.*' Sounds like French, an' maybe 'tis, but the Injuns says it. They had a regular way of counting their *coup*, and for each they had the right to an Eagle feather in their bonnet, with a red tuft of hair on the end for the extra good ones. At least, they used to. I reckon now they're forgetting it all, and any buck Injun wears just any feather he can steal and stick in his head."

"What do you think of our head-dresses?" Yan ventured.

"Hm! You ain't never seen a real one or you wouldn't go at them that way at all. First place, the feathers should all be white with black tips, an' fastened not solid like that, but loose on a cap of soft leather. Each feather, you see, has a leather loop lashed on the quill end for a lace to run through and hold it to the cap, an' then a string running through the middle of each feather to hold it—just so. Then there are ways of marking each feather to show how it was got. I mind once I was out on a war party with a lot of Santees—that's a brand of Sioux—an' we done a lot o' sneaking an' stealing an' scalped some of the enemy. Then we set out for home, and when we was still about thirty miles away we sent on an Injun telegram of good luck. The leader of our crowd set fire to the grass after he had sent two men half a mile away on each side to do the same thing, an' up went three big smokes. There is always some one watching round an Injun village, an' you bet when they seen them three smokes they knowed that we wuz a-coming back with scalps.

"The hull Council come out to meet us, but not too reckless, coz this might have been the trick of enemies to surprise them.

"Well, when we got there, maybe there wasn't a racket. You see, we didn't lose a man, and we brung in a hundred horses and seven scalps. Our leader never said a word to the crowd, but went right up to the Council teepee. He walked in—we followed. There was the Head Chief an' all the Council settin' smoking. Our leader give the '*How*,' an' then we all '*Howed*.' Then we sat an' smoked, an' the Chief called on our leader for an account

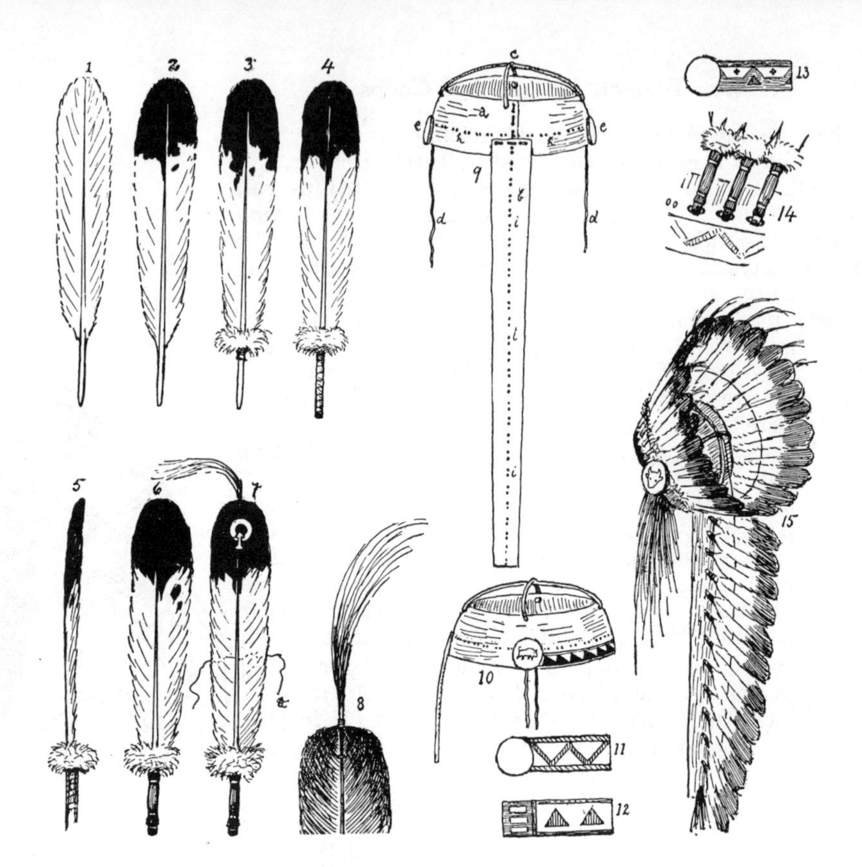

THE INDIAN WAR BONNET—HOW TO MAKE IT

1. **The plain white Goose or Turkey feather.**
2. **The same, with tip dyed black or painted with indelible ink.**
3. **The same, showing ruff of white down lashed on with wax end.**
4. **The same, showing leather loop lashed on for the holding lace.**
5. **The same, viewed edge on.**
6. **The same, with a red flannel cover sewn and lashed on the quill. This is a '*coup* feather.'**
7. **The same, with a tuft of red horsehair lashed on the top to mark a '*grand coup*' and (*a*) a thread through the middle of the rib to hold feather in proper place. This feather is marked with the symbol of a *grand coup* in target shooting. This symbol may be drawn on an oval piece of paper gummed on the top of the feather.**
8. **The tip of a feather showing how the red horsehair tuft is lashed on with fine waxed thread.**
9. **The groundwork of the war bonnet made of any soft leather,** (*a*) a broad band to go round the head, laced at the joint or seam behind; (*b*) a broad tail behind as long as needed to hold all the wearer's feathers; (*c*) two leather thongs or straps over the top; (*d*) leather string to tie under the chin; (*e*) the buttons, conchas or side ornaments of shells, silver, horn or wooden discs, even small mirrors and circles of beadwork were used, and sometimes the conchas were left out altogether; they may have the owner's totem on them, usually a bunch of ermine tails hung from each side of the bonnet just below the concha. A bunch of horsehair will answer as well; (*hh*) the holes in the leather for holding the lace of the feather; 24 feathers are needed for the full bonnet, without the tail, so they are put less than an inch apart; (*iii*) the lacing holes on the tail; this is as long as the **wearer's feathers call for; some never have any tail.**
10. Side view of the leather framework, showing a pattern sometimes used to decorate the front.

11, 12 and 13. Beadwork designs for front band of bonnet; all have white grounds. No. 11 (Arapaho) has green band at top and bottom with red zigzag. No. 12 (Ogallala) has blue band at top and bottom, red triangles; the concha is blue with three white bars and is cut off from the band by a red bar. No. 13 (Sioux) has narrow band above and broad band below blue, the triangle red, and the two little stars blue with yellow centre.

14. The bases of three feathers, showing how the lace comes out of the cap leather, through the eye or loop on the bottom of the quill, and in again.
15. The completed bonnet, showing how the feathers of the crown should spread out, also showing the thread that passes through the middle of each feather on inner side to hold it in place; another thread passes from the point where the two straps (*c* in 9) join, then down through each feather in the tail.

The Indians now often use the crown of a soft felt hat for the basis of a war bonnet.

of the little trip. He stood up an' made a speech.

"'Great Chief and Council of my Tribe,' says he. 'After we left the village and the men had purified themselves, we travelled seven days and came to the Little Muddy River. There we found the track of a travelling band of Arapaho. In two days we found their camp, but they were too strong for us, so we hid till night; then I went alone into their camp and found that some of them were going off on a hunt next day. As I left I met a lone warrior coming in. I killed him with my knife. For that I claim a *coup;* and I scalped him—for that I claim another *coup;* an' before I killed him I slapped his face with my hand—for this I claim a *grand coup;* and I brought his horse away with me—for that I claim another *coup*. Is it not so,' sez he, turning to us, and we all yelled '*How! How! How!*' For this fellow, 'Whooping Crane,' was awful good stuff. Then the Council agreed that he should wear three Eagle feathers, the first for killing and scalping the enemy in his own camp—that was a *grand coup*, and the feather had a tuft of red hair on it an' a red spot on the web. The next feather was for slapping the feller's face first, which, of course, made it more risky. This Eagle feather had a red tuft on top an' a red hand on the web; the one for stealing the horse had a horseshoe, but no tuft, coz it wasn't counted A1.

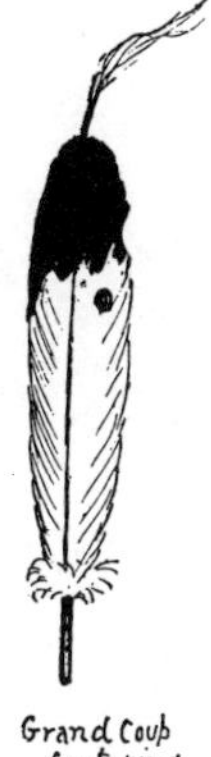

Grand Coup for taking Scalp in Enemy's Camp

"Then the other Injuns made their claims, an' we all got some kind of honours. I mind one feller was allowed to drag a Fox tail at each heel when he danced, an' another had ten horseshoe marks on an Eagle feather for stealing ten horses, an' I tell you them Injuns were prouder of them feathers than a general would be of his medals."

C. C. for slapping his face

Coup for Stealing his Horse

"My, I wish I could go out there and be with those fellows," and Yan sighed as he compared his commonplace lot with all this romantic splendour.

"Guess you'd soon get sick of it. I know *I* did," was the answer; "forever shooting and killing, never at peace, never more than three meals ahead of starvation and just as often three meals behind. No, siree, no more for me."

"I'd just like to see you start in horse-stealing for honours round here," observed Sam, "though I know who'd get the feathers if it was chicken stealing."

"Say, Caleb," said Guy, who, being friendly and of the country, never thought of calling the old man "Mr. Clark," "didn't they give feathers for good

Deer-hunting? I'll bet I could lick any of them at it if I had a gun."

"Didn't you hear me say first thing that that there shot o' Yan's should score a '*grand coup*'?"

"Oh, shucks! I kin lick Yan any time; that was just a chance shot. I'll bet if you give feathers for Deer-hunting I'll get them all."

"We'll take you up on that," said the oldest Chief, but the next interrupted:

"Say, boys, we want to play Injun properly. Let's get Mr. Clark to show us how to make a real war bonnet. Then we'll wear only what feathers we win."

"Ye mean by scalping the Whites an' horse-stealing?"

"Oh, no; there's lots of things we can do—best runner, best Deer hunter, best swimmer, best shot with bow and arrows."

"All right." So they set about questioning Caleb. He soon showed them how to put a war bonnet together, using, in spite of Yan's misgivings, the crown of an old felt hat for the ground work and white goose quills trimmed and dyed black at the tips for Eagle feathers. But when it came to the deeds that were to be rewarded, each one had his own ideas.

"If Sappy will go to the orchard and pick a peck of cherries without old Cap gettin' *him*, I'll give him a feather with all sorts of fixin's on it," suggested Sam.

"Well, I'll bet you can't get a chicken out of our barn 'thout our Dog gettin' *you*, Mr. Smarty."

"Pooh! I ain't stealing chickens. Do you take me for a nigger? I'm a noble Red-man and Head Chief at that, I want you to know, an' I've a notion to collect that scalp you're wearin' now. You know it belongs to me and Yan," and he sidled over, rolling his eye and working his fingers in a way that upset Guy's composure. "And I tell you a feller with one foot in the grave should have his thoughts on seriouser things than chicken-stealing. This yere morbid cravin' for excitement is rooinin' all the young fellers nowadays."

Yan happened to glance at Caleb. He was gazing off at nothing, but there was a twinkle in his eye that Yan never before saw there.

"Let's go to the teepee. It's too hot out here. Come in, won't you, Mr. Clark?"

" He soon appeared, waving a branch "

" The old Cat raged and tore "

"Hm. 'Tain't much cooler in here, even if it is shady," remarked the old Trapper. "Ye ought to lift one side of the canvas and get some air."

"Why, did the real Injuns do that?"

"I should say they did. There ain't any way they didn't turn and twist the teepee for comfort. That's what makes it so good. Ye kin live in it forty below zero an' fifty 'bove suffocation an' still be happy. It's the changeablest kind of a layout for livin' in. Real hot weather the thing looks like a spider with skirts on and held high, an' I tell you ye got to know the weather for a teepee. Many a hot night on the plains I've been woke up by hearing 'Tap-tap-tap' all around me in the still black night and wondered why all the squaws was working, but they was up to drop the cover and drive all the pegs deeper, an' within a half hour there never failed to come up a big storm. How they knew it was a-comin' I never could tell. One old woman said a Coyote told her, an' maybe that's true, for they do change their song for trouble ahead; another said it was the flowers lookin' queer at sundown, an' another had a bad dream. Maybe they're all true; it comes o' watchin' little things."

"Do they never get fooled?" asked Little Beaver.

"Oncet in awhile, but not near as often as a White-man would.

"I mind once seeing an artist chap, one of them there portygraf takers. He come out to the village with a machine an' took some of the little teepees. Then I said, 'Why don't you get Bull-calf's squaw to put up their big teepee? I tell you that's a howler.' So off he goes, and after dickering awhile he got the squaw to put it up for three dollars. You bet it was a stunner, sure—all painted red, with green an' yaller-animals an' birds an' scalps galore. It made that feller's eyes bug out to see it. He started in to make some portygrafs, then was taking another by hand, so as to get the colours, an' I bet it would have crowded him to do it, but jest when he got a-going the old squaw yelled to the other—the Chief hed two of them—an' lighted out to take down that there teepee. That artist he hollered to stop, said he had hired it to stay up an' a bargain was a bargain. But the old squaw she jest kept on a-jabberin' an' pintin' at the west. Pretty soon they had the hull thing down and rolled up an' that artist a-cussin' like a cow-puncher. Well, I mind it

Bull Calf's Teepee.

was a fine day, but awful hot, an before five minutes there come a little dark cloud in the west, then in ten minutes come a-whoopin' a regular small cyclone, an' it went through that village and wrecked all the teepees of any size. That red one would surely have gone only for that smart old squaw."

Under Caleb's directions the breezy side of the cover was now raised a little, and the shady side much more. This changed the teepee from a stifling hothouse into a cool, breezy shade.

"An' when ye want to know which way is the wind, if it's light, ye wet your finger so, an' hold it up. The windy side feels cool at once, and by that ye can set your smoke-flaps."

"I want to know about war bonnets," Yan now put in. "I mean about things to do to wear feathers—that is, things *we* can do."

"Ye kin have races, an' swimmin' an bownarrer shootin'. I should say if you kin send one o' them arrers two hundred yards that would kill a Buffalo at twenty feet. I'd think that was pretty good. Yes, I'd call that way up."

"What—a *grand coup?*"

"Yes, I reckon; an' if you fell short on'y fifty yards that'd still kill a Deer, an' we could call that a *coup*. If," continued Caleb, "you kin hit that old gunny-sack buck plunk in the heart at fifty yards first shot I'd call that away up; an' if you hit it at seventy-five yards in the heart no matter how many tries, I'd call you a shot. If you kin hit a nine-inch bull's-eye two out of three at forty yards every time an' no fluke, you'd hold your own among Injuns, though I must say they don't go in much for shooting at a target. They shoot at 'most anything they see in the woods. I've seen the little copper-coloured kids shooting away at butterflies. Then they have matches—they try who can have most arrers in the air at one time. To have five in the air at once is considered good. It means powerful fast work and far shooting. You got to hold a bunch handy in the left hand fur that. The most I ever seen one man have up at once was eight. That was reckoned 'big medicine,' an' any one that can keep up seven is considered swell."

"Do you know any other things besides bows and arrows that would do?"

"I think that a rubbing-stick fire ought to count," interrupted Sam. "I want that in coz Guy can't do it. Any one who kin do it at all gets a feather, an' any one who kin do it in one minute gets a swagger feather, or whatever you call it; that takes care of Yan and me an' leaves Guy out in the cold."

"I'll bet I kin hunt Deer all round you both, I kin."

"Oh, shut up, Sappy; we're tired a-hearing about your Deer hunting. We're going to abolish that game." Then Sam continued, apparently addressing Caleb, "Do you know any Injun games?"

But Caleb took no notice.

Presently Yan said, "Don't the Injuns play games, Mr. Clark?

"Well, yes, I kin show you two Injun games that will test your eyesight."

"I bet I kin beat any one at it," Guy made haste to tell. "Why, I seen that Deer before Yan could——"

"Oh, shut up, Guy," Yan now exclaimed. A peculiar sound—"*Wheet—wheet—wheet*"—made Sappy turn. He saw Sam with an immense knife, whetting it most vigorously and casting a hungry, fishy glance from time to time to the "yaller moss-tuft" on Guy's neck.

"Time has came," he said to nobody in particular.

"You better let me alone," whined Guy, for that horrible "*wheet—wheet*" jarred his nerves somehow. He looked toward Yan, and seeing, as he thought, the suggestion of a smile, he felt more comfortable, but a glance at Sam dispelled his comfort; the Woodpecker's face was absolutely inscrutable and perfectly demoniac with paint.

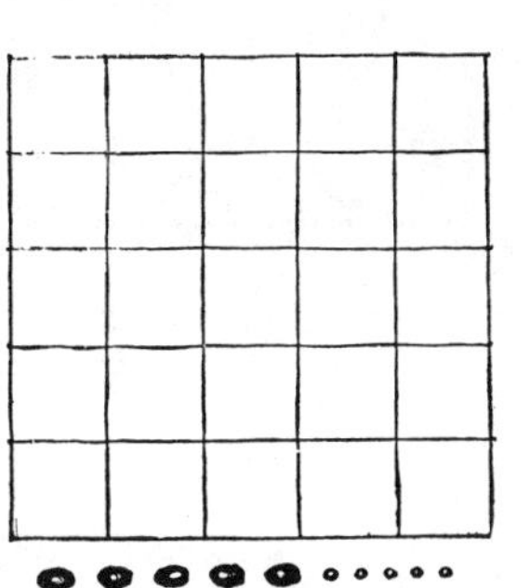
Counters (5 nuts & 5 pebbles) & Cards for Game of Quicksight

"Why don't you whet up, Little Beaver? Don't you want your share?" asked the Head Chief through his teeth.

"I vote we let him wear it till he brags again about his Deer-hunting. Then off she comes to the bone," was the reply. "Tell us about the Injun game, Mr. Clark."

"I pretty near forget it now, but le's see. They make two squares on the ground or on two skins; each one is cut up in twenty-five smaller squares with lines like that. Then they have, say, ten rings an' ten nuts or pebbles. One player takes five rings an' five nuts an' sets them around on the squares of one set, an' don't let the other see till all is ready; then the other turns an' looks at it while some one else sings a little song that one of the boys turned into:

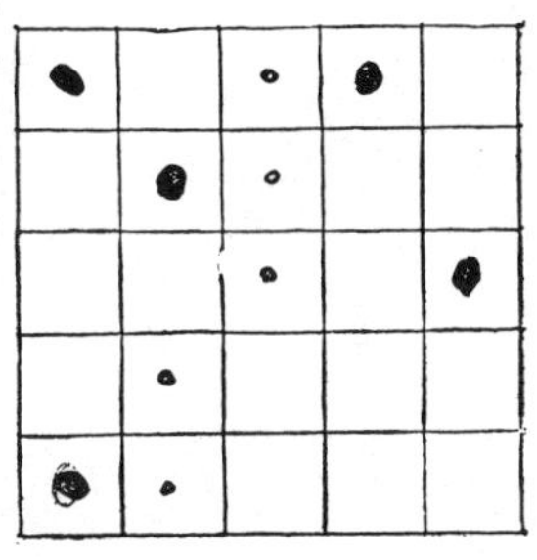

"'Ki yi ya—ki yi yee,
You think yer smart as ye kin be,
You think yer awful quick to see.

Spot-the-Rabbit or Farsight

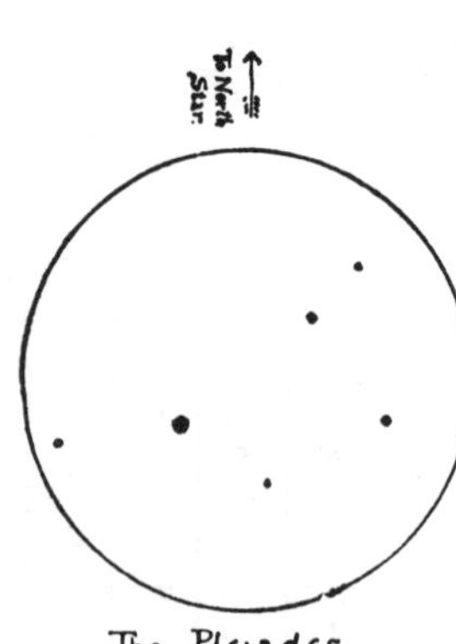

The Pleiades as seen by Ordinary Eyes

But yer not too quick for me,
Ki yi ya—ki yi yee.'

"Then the first square is covered with a basket or anything and the second player must cover the other skin with counters just the same from memory. For every counter he gets on the right square he counts one, and loses one for each on the wrong square."

"I'll bet I kin——" Guy began, but Sam's hand gripped his moss-tuft.

"Here, you let me alone. I ain't bragging. I'm only telling the simple truth."

"Ugh! Better tell some simple lies, then—much safer," said the Great Woodpecker, with horrid calm and meaning. "If ever I lift that scalp you'll catch cold and die, do ye know it?"

Again Yan could see that Caleb had to look far away to avoid taking an apparent interest.

"There's another game. I don't know as it's Injun, but it's the kind o' game where an Injun *could* win. They first made two six-inch squares of white wood or card, then on each they made rings like a target or squares like the quicksight game, or else two Rabbits the same on each. One feller takes six spots of black, half an inch across, an' sticks them on one, scattering anyhow, an' sets it up a hundred yards off; another feller takes same number of spots an' the other Rabbit an' walks up till he can see to fix his Rabbit the same. If he kin do it at seventy-five yards he's a swell; if he kin do it at sixty yards he's away up, but less than fifty yards is no good. I seen the boys have lots o' fun out o' it. They try to fool each other every way, putting one spot right on another or leaving some off. It's a sure 'nough test of good eyes."

"I'll bet——" began Sappy again, but a loud savage "Grrrr" from Sam, who knew perfectly well what was coming, put a stop to the bet, whatever it was.

"There was two other Injun tests of eyes that I mind now. Some old Buck would show the youngsters the Pleiades—them's the little stars that the Injuns call the Bunch—an' ask 'How many kin you see?' Some could sho'ly see five or six an' some could make out seven. Them as sees seven is mighty well off for eyes. Ye can't see the Pleiades now—they belong to the winter nights; but you kin see the Dipper the hull year round, turning about the North Star. The Injuns call this the 'Broken Back,' an' I've heard the old fellers ask the boys: 'You see the Old Squaw—that's the star second from the end, the one at the bend of the handle—well, she has a papoose on her back. Kin you see the papoose?' an' sure enough, when my eyes was real good I could see the little baby star tucked in by the big un. It's a mighty good test of eyes if you kin see that."

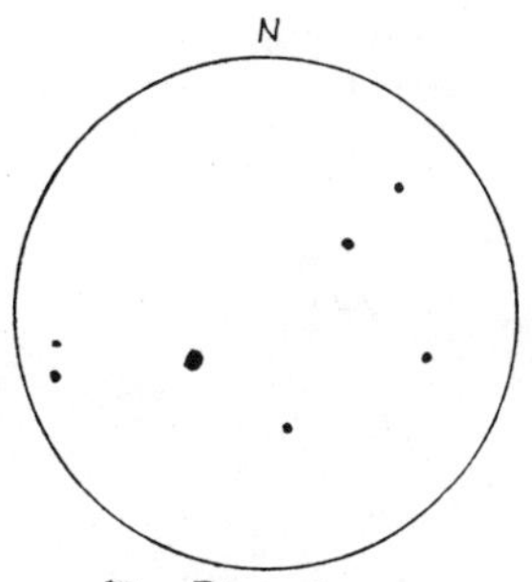

The Pleiades as seen by Good Eyes

"Eh——" began Guy.

But "Grrrrrrrrr" from Sam stopped him in time.

Again Caleb's eyes wandered afar. Then he stepped out of the teepee and Yan heard him mutter, "Consarn that whelp, he makes me laugh spite o' myself." He went off a little way into the woods and presently called "Yan! Guy! Come here." All three ran out. "Talking about eyes, what's that?" An opening in the foliage gave a glimpse of the distant Burns's clover field. "Looks like a small Bear."

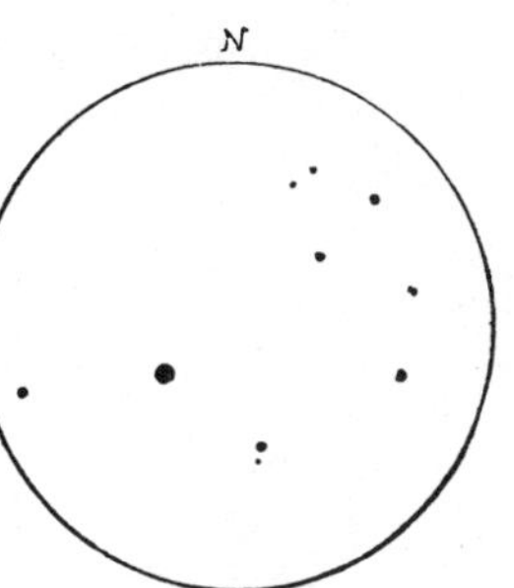

The Pleiades as seen by Extraordinary Eyes

"Woodchuck! That's our Woodchuck! That's the ole sinner that throwed Paw off'n the mower. Where's my bone-arrer?" and Guy went for his weapons.

The boys ran for the fence of the clover field, going more cautiously as they came near. Still the old Woodchuck heard something and sat up erect on his haunches. He was a monster, and out on the smooth clover field he did look like a very small Bear. His chestnut breast was curiously relieved by his unusually gray back and head.

"Paw says it's his sins as turned his head gray. He's a hoary headed sinner, an' he ain't repented o' none o' them so far, but *I'm* after him now."

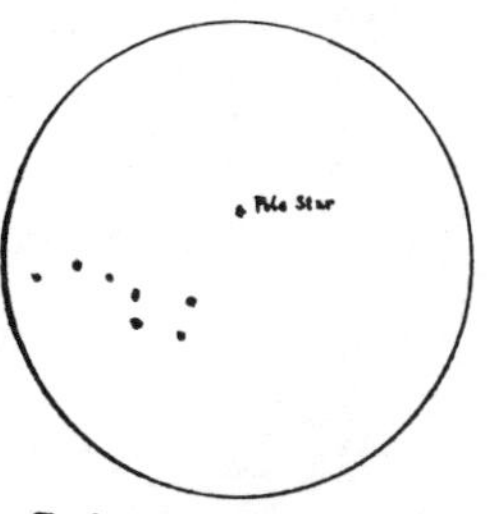

The Great Bear or Dipper pointing nearly to Pole Star. + The 2nd Star from left in handle of Dipper is the Squaw, & over it the little Pappoose

"Hold on! Start even!" said Sam, seeing that Guy was prepared to shoot.

So all drew together, standing in a row like an old picture of the battle of Crecy. The arrows scattered about the Woodchuck. Most went much too far, none went near because he was closer than they had supposed, but he scuttled away into his hole, there, no doubt, to plan a new trap for the man with the mower.

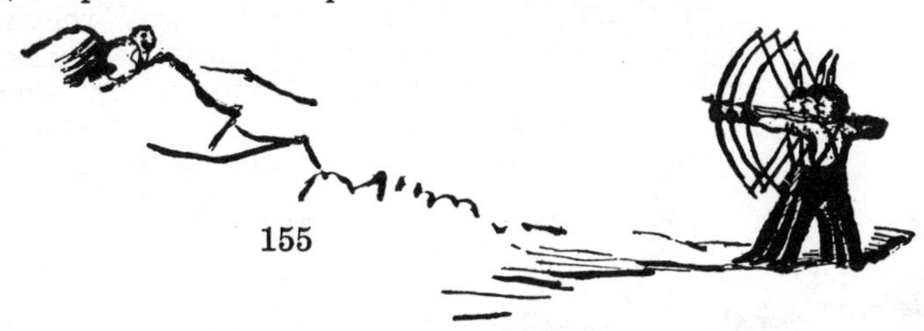

VII

Campercraft

"HOW'D you sleep, Sam?"

"Didn't sleep a durn bit."

"Neither did I. I was shivering all night. I got up an' put the spare blanket on, but it didn't do any good."

"Wonder if there was a chills-and-fever fog or something?"

"How'd you find it, Sappy?"

"All right."

"Didn't smell any fog?"

"Nope."

The next night it was even worse. Guy slept placidly, if noisily, but Sam and Yan tumbled about and shivered for hours. In the morning at dawn Sam sat up.

"Well, I tell you this is no joke. Fun's fun, but if I am going to have the shivers every night I'm going home while I'm able."

Yan said nothing. He was very glum. He felt much as Sam did, but was less ready to give up the outing.

Their blues were nearly dispelled when the warm sun came up, but still they dreaded the coming night.

"Wonder what it is," said Little Beaver.

"'Pears to me powerful like chills and fever and then again it don't. Maybe we drink too much swamp water. I believe we're p'isoned with Guy's cooking."

"More like getting scurvy from too much meat. Let's ask Caleb."

Caleb came around that afternoon or they would have gone after him. He heard Yan's story in silence, then, "Have ye sunned your blankets sense ye came?"

"No."

Caleb went into the teepee, felt the blankets, then grunted: "H-m! Jest so. They're nigh soppin'. You turn in night after night an' sweat an' sweat in them blankets an' wonder why they're damp. Hain't you seen your ma air the blankets every day at home? Every Injun squaw knows that much, an' every other day at least she gives the blankets a sun roast for three hours in the middle

of the day, or, failing that, dries them at the fire. Dry out your blankets and you won't have no more chills."

The boys set about it at once, and that night they experienced again the sweet, warm sleep of healthy youth.

There was another lesson they had to learn in campercraft. The Mosquitoes were always more or less of a plague. At night they forced the boys into the teepee, but they soon learned to smudge the insects with a wad of green grass on the hot fire. This they would throw on at sundown, then go outside, closing the teepee tight and eat supper around the cooking fire. After that was over they would cautiously open the teepee to find the grass all gone and the fire low, a dense cloud of smoke still in the upper part, but below it clear air. They would then brush off the Mosquitoes that had alighted on their clothes, crawl into the lodge and close the door tight. Not a Mosquito was left alive in it, and the smoke hanging about the smoke-vent was enough to keep them from coming in, and so they slept in peace. Thus they could baffle the worst pest of the woods. But there was yet another destroyer of comfort by day, and this was the Blue-bottle flies. There seemed more of them as time went on, and they laid masses of yellowish eggs on anything that smelled like meat or corruption. They buzzed about the table and got into the dishes; their dead, drowned and mangled bodies were polluting all the food, till Caleb remarked during one of his ever-increasing visits: "It's your own fault. Look at all the filth ye leave scattered about."

There was no blinking the fact; for fifty feet around the teepee the ground was strewn with scraps of paper, tins and food. To one side was a mass of potato peelings, bones, fish-scales and filth, and everywhere were the buzzing flies, to be plagues all day, till at sundown the Mosquitoes relieved them and took the night shift of the office of torment.

"I want to learn, especially if it's Injun," said Little Beaver. "What had we best do?"

"Wall, first ye could move camp; second, ye could clean this."

As there was no other available camp ground they had no choice, and Yan said with energy: "Boys, we got to clean this and keep it clean, too.

We'll dig a hole for everything that won't burn."

So Yan seized the spade and began to dig in the bushes not far from the teepee. Sam and Guy were gradually drawn in. They began gathering all the rubbish and threw it into the hole. As they tumbled in bones, tins and scraps of bread Yan said: "I just hate to see that bread go in. It doesn't seem right when there's so many living things would be glad to get it."

At this, Caleb, who was sitting on a log placidly smoking, said:

"Now, if ye want to be real Injun, ye gather all the eatables ye don't want—meat, bread and anything, an' every day put it on some high place. Most generally the Injuns has a rock—they call it *Wakan;* that means sacred medicine—an' there they leave scraps of food to please the good spirits. Av coorse it's the birds and Squirrels gets it all; but the Injun is content as long as it's gone, an' if ye argy with them that 'tain't the spirits gets it, but the birds, they say: 'That doesn't matter. The birds couldn't get it if the spirits didn't want them to have it,' or maybe the birds took it to carry to the spirits!"

Then the Grand Council went out in a body to seek the *Wakan Rock.* They found a good one in the open part of the woods, and it became a daily duty of one to carry the remnants of food to the rock. They were probably less acceptable to the wood creatures than they would have been half a year later, but they soon found that there were many birds glad to eat at the *Wakan;* and moreover, that before long there was a trail from the brook, only twenty-five yards away, that told of four-foots also enjoying the bounty of the good spirits.

Within three days of this the plague of Bluebottles was over, and the boys realized that, judging by its effects, the keeping of a dirty camp is a crime.

One other thing old Caleb insisted on: "Yan," said he, "you didn't ought to drink that creek water now; it ain't hardly runnin'. The sun hez it het up, an' it's gettin' too crawly to be healthy."

"Well, what are we going to do?" said Sam, though he might as well have addressed the brook itself.

"What can we do, Mr. Clark?"

"Dig a well!"

"Phew! We're out here for fun!" was Sam's reply.

"Dig an Injun well," Caleb said. "Half an hour will do it. Here, I'll show you."

He took the spade and, seeking a dry spot, about twenty feet from the upper end of the pond he dug a hole some two feet square. By the time he was down three feet the water was oozing in fast. He got it down about four feet and then had to stop, on account of inflow. He took a bucket and bailed the muddy stuff out right to the bottom, and let it fill up to be again bailed out. After three bailings the water came in cold, sweet, and pure as crystal.

"There," said he, "that water is from your pond, but it is filtered through twenty feet of earth and sand. That's the way to get cool, pure water out of the dirtiest of swamps. That's an Injun well."

VIII

The Indian Drum

**"Oh, that hair of horse and skin of sheep should
Have such power to move the souls of men."**

IF you were real Injun you'd make a drum of that," said Caleb to Yan, as they came to a Basswood blown over by a recent storm and now showing its weakness, for it was quite hollow—a mere shell.

"How do they do it? I want to know how."

"Get me the axe."

Yan ran for the axe. Caleb cut out a straight, unbroken section about two feet long. This they carried to camp.

"Coorse ye know," said Caleb, "ye can't have a drum without skins for heads."

"What kind of skins?"

"Oh, Horse, Dog, Cow, Calf—'most any kind that's strong enough."

"I got a Calfskin in our barn, an' I know where there's another in the shed, but it's all chawed up with Rats. Them's mine. I killed them Calves. Paw give me the skins for killin' an' skinnin' them. Oh, you jest ought to see me kill a Calf——"

Guy was going off into one of his autopanegyrics

when Sam who was now being rubbed on a sore place, gave a "Whoop!" and grabbed the tow-tuft with a jerk that sent the Third War Chief sprawling and ended the panegyric in the usual volley of "you-let-me-'lones."

"Oh, quit, Sam," objected Little Beaver. "You can't stop a Dog barking. It's his nature." Then to Guy: "Never mind, Guy; you are not hurt. I'll bet you can beat him hunting Deer, and you can see twice as far as he can."

"Yes, I kin; that's what makes him so mad. I'll bet I kin see three times as far—maybe five times," was the answer in injured tones.

"Go on now, Guy, and get the skins—that is, if you want a drum for the war dance. You're the only one in the crowd that's man enough to make the raise of a hide," and fired by this flattery, Guy sped away.

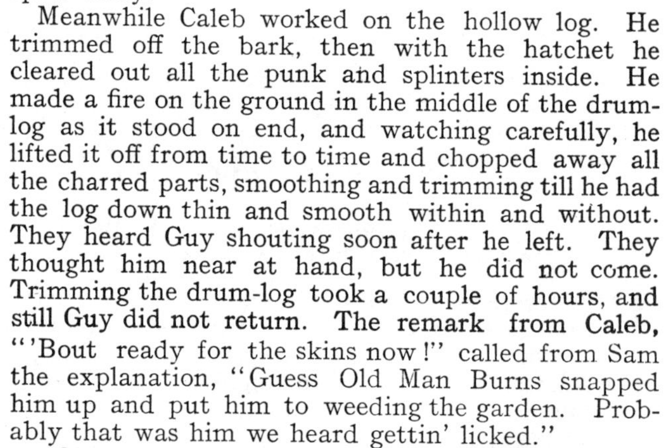

Meanwhile Caleb worked on the hollow log. He trimmed off the bark, then with the hatchet he cleared out all the punk and splinters inside. He made a fire on the ground in the middle of the drum-log as it stood on end, and watching carefully, he lifted it off from time to time and chopped away all the charred parts, smoothing and trimming till he had the log down thin and smooth within and without. They heard Guy shouting soon after he left. They thought him near at hand, but he did not come. Trimming the drum-log took a couple of hours, and still Guy did not return. The remark from Caleb, "'Bout ready for the skins now!" called from Sam the explanation, "Guess Old Man Burns snapped him up and put him to weeding the garden. Probably that was him we heard gettin' licked."

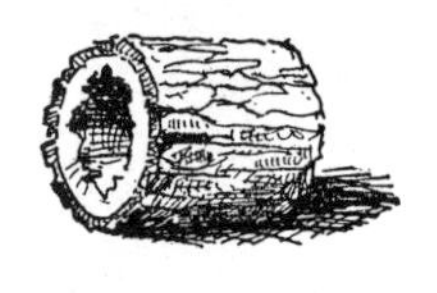

"Old Man Burns" was a poor and shiftless character, a thin, stoop-shouldered man. He was only thirty-five years of age, but, being married, that was enough to secure for him the title "Old Man." In Sanger, if Tom Nolan was a bachelor at eighty years of age he would still be Tom Nolan, "wan of the bhoys," but if he married at twenty he at once became "Old Man Nolan."

Mrs. Burns had produced the usual string of tow-tops, but several had died, the charitable neighbours said of starvation, leaving Guy, the eldest, his mother's darling, then a gap and four little girls, four, three, two and one years of age. She was a fat, fair, easy-going person, with a general sense of antagonism to her husband, who was, of course, the natural enemy of the children. Jim Burns cherished the ideal of bringing "that boy" up right—that is, getting all the work he could out of him—and Guy clung to his own ideal of doing as little work as possible. In this clash of ideals Guy's mother was his firm, though more or less secret, ally. He was without fault in her eyes: all that he did was right. His freckled visage and pudgy face were types of noble beauty, standards of comeliness and human excellence; his ways were ways of pleasantness and all his paths were peace; Margat Burns was sure of it.

Burns had a good deal of natural affection, but he was erratic; sometimes he would flog Guy mercilessly for nothing, and again laugh at some serious misdeed, so that the boy never knew just what to expect, and kept on the safe side by avoiding his "Paw" as much as possible. His visits to the camp had been thoroughly disapproved, partly because it was on Old Man Raften's land and partly because it enabled Guy to dodge the chores. Burns had been quite violent about it once or twice, but Mrs. Burns had the great advantage of persistence, and like the steady strain of the skilful angler on the slender line, it wins in the end against the erratic violence of the strongest trout. She had managed then that Guy should join the Injun camp, and gloried in his outrageously exaggerated accounts of how he could lick them all at anything, "though they wuz so much older'n bigger'n he wuz."

But on this day he was fallen in hard luck. His father saw him coming, met him with a "gad" and lashed him furiously. Knowing perfectly well that the flogging would not stop till the proper effect was produced, and that was to be gauged by the racket, Guy yelled his loudest. This was the uproar the boys had heard.

"Now, ye idle young scut! I'll larn ye to go round leaving bars down. You go an' tend to your work." So instead of hiking back gloriously laden with Calfskins, Guy was sent to ignominious and un-Injun toil in the garden.

Soon he heard his mother: "Guysie, Guysie." He dropped his hoe and walked to the kitchen.

"Where you goin'?" roared his father from afar. "Go back and mind your work."

"Maw wants me. She called me."

"You mind your work. Don't you dar' on your life to go thayer."

But Guy took no notice and walked on to his mother. He knew that at this post-thrashing stage of wrath his father was mouthy and harmless, and soon he was happy eating a huge piece of bread and jam.

"Poor dear, you must be hungry, an' your Paw was so mean to you. There, now, don't cry," for Guy began to weep again at the recollection of his wrongs. Then she whispered confidentially: "Paw's going to Downey's this afternoon, an' you can slip away as soon as he's gone, an' if you work well before that he won't be so awful mad after you come back. But be sure you don't let down the bars, coz if the pig was to get in Raften's woods dear knows what."

This was the reason of Guy's delay. He did not return to camp with the skins till late that day. As soon as he was gone, his foolish, doting mother, already crushed with the burden of the house, left everything and hoed two or three extra rows of cabbages, so "Paw" should find a great showing of work when he came back.

The Calfskins were hard as tin and, of course, had the hair on.

Caleb remarked, "It'll take two or three days to get them right," and buried them in a marshy, muddy pool in the full sunlight. "The warmer the better."

Three days later he took them out. Instead of being thin, hard, yellow, semi-transparent, they now were much thicker, densely white, and soft as silk. The hair was easily scraped off and the two pieces were pronounced all right for drum-heads.

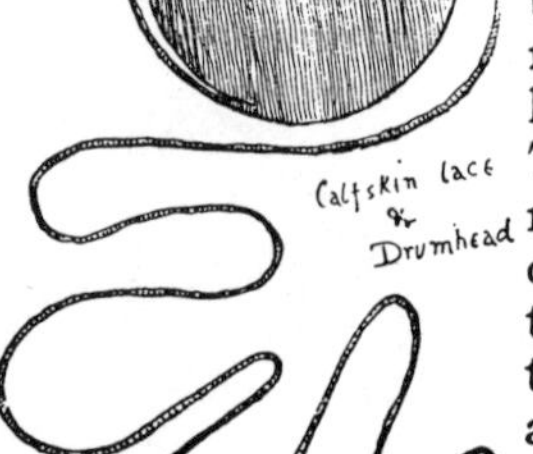

Caleb washed them thoroughly in warm water, with soap to clear off the grease, scraping them on both sides with a blunt knife; then he straightened the outer edge of the largest, and cut a thin strip round and round it till he had some sixty feet of raw-hide line, about three-quarters of an inch wide. This he twisted, rolled and stretched until it was nearly round, then he cut from the remainder a circular piece thirty inches across, and a second from the "unchawed" part of the other skin. He laid these one on the other, and with the sharp point of a knife he made a row of holes in both, one inch from the edge and two inches apart. Then he set one skin on the ground, the drum-log on that and the other skin on the top, and bound them together with the long lace, running it from hole No. 1 on the top to No. 2 on the bottom, then to No. 3 on the top, and No. 4 on the bottom, and so on twice around, till every hole had a lace through it and the crossing laces made a diamond pattern all around. At first this was done loosely, but tightened up when once around, and finally both the drum-heads were drawn tense. To the surprise of all, Guy promptly took possession of the finished drum. "Them's my Calfskins," which, of course, was true.

And Caleb said, with a twinkle in his eye, "The wood *seems* to go with the skins."

A drumstick of wood, with a piece of sacking lashed on to soften it, was made, and Guy was disgusted to find how little sound the drum gave out.

"'Bout like pounding a fur cap with a lamb's tail," Sam thought.

"You hang that up in the shade to dry and you'll find a change," said the Trapper.

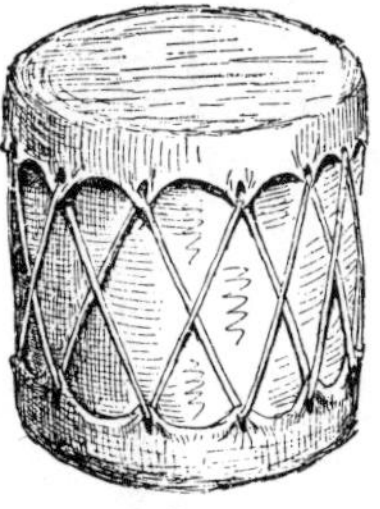
The Indian Drum–

It was quite curious to note the effect of the drying as the hours went by. The drum seemed to be wracking and straining itself in the agony of effort, and slight noises came from it at times. When perfectly dry the semi-transparency of the rawhide came back, and the sound now was one to thrill the Red-man's heart.

Caleb taught them a little Indian war chant, and they danced round to it as he drummed and sang, till their savage instincts seemed to revive. But above all it worked on Yan. As he pranced around in step his whole nature seemed to respond; he felt himself a part of that dance. It was in himself; it thrilled him through and through and sent his blood exulting. He would gladly have given up all the White-man's "glorious gains" to live with the feeling called up by that Indian drum.

IX

The Cat and the Skunk

SAM was away on a "massacree" to get some bread. Guy had been trapped by his natural enemy and was serving a term of hard labour in

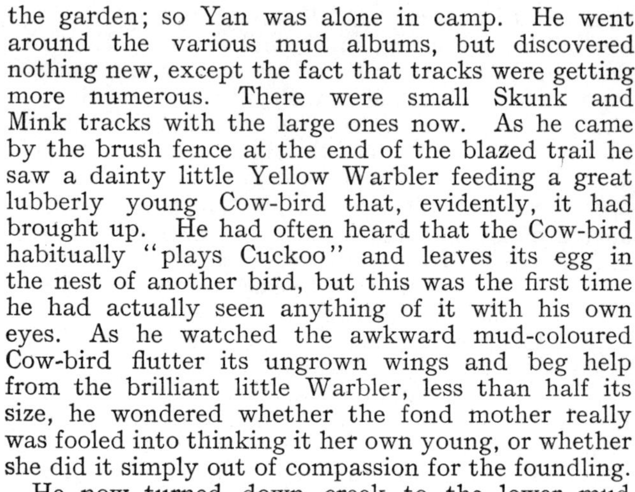

the garden; so Yan was alone in camp. He went around the various mud albums, but discovered nothing new, except the fact that tracks were getting more numerous. There were small Skunk and Mink tracks with the large ones now. As he came by the brush fence at the end of the blazed trail he saw a dainty little Yellow Warbler feeding a great lubberly young Cow-bird that, evidently, it had brought up. He had often heard that the Cow-bird habitually "plays Cuckoo" and leaves its egg in the nest of another bird, but this was the first time he had actually seen anything of it with his own eyes. As he watched the awkward mud-coloured Cow-bird flutter its ungrown wings and beg help from the brilliant little Warbler, less than half its size, he wondered whether the fond mother really was fooled into thinking it her own young, or whether she did it simply out of compassion for the foundling.

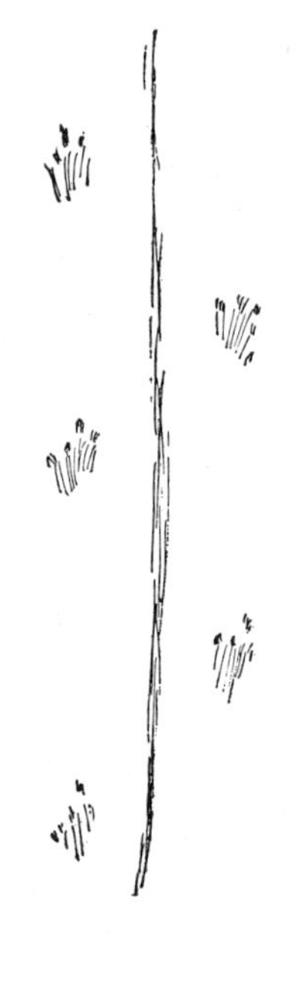

He now turned down creek to the lower mud album, and was puzzled by a new track like this. He sketched it, but before the drawing was done it dawned on him that this must be the track of a young Mud-turtle. He also saw a lot of very familiar tracks, not a few being those of the common Cat, and he wondered why they should be about so much and yet so rarely seen. Of course the animals were chiefly nocturnal, but the boys were partly so, and always on the ground now, so that explanation was not satisfactory. He lay down on his breast at the edge of the brook, which had here cut in a channel with steep clay walls six feet high and twenty feet apart. The stream was very small now —a mere thread of water zigzagging over the level muddy floor of the "cañon," as Yan loved to call it. A broad, muddy margin at each side of the water made a fine place of record for the travelling Four-foots, and tracks new and old were there in abundance.

The herbage on the bank was very rank and full of noisy Grasshoppers and Crickets. Great masses of orange Jewelweed on one side were variegated with some wonderful Cardinal flowers. Yan viewed all this with placid content. He knew their names now, and thus they were transferred from the list of tantalizing mysteries to that of engaging and wonderful friends. As he lay there on his breast his thoughts wandered back to the days when he did not know the names of any flowers or birds—when

all was strange and he alone in his hunger to know them, and Bonnerton came back to him with new, strange force of reminder. His father and mother, his brother and schoolmates were there. It seemed like a bygone existence, though only two months ago. He had written his mother to tell of his arrival, and once since to say that he was well. He had received a kind letter from his mother, with a scripture text or two, and a postscript from his father with some sound advice and more scripture texts. Since then he had not written. He could not comprehend how he could so completely drift away, and yet clearly it was because he had found here in Sanger the well for which he had thirsted.

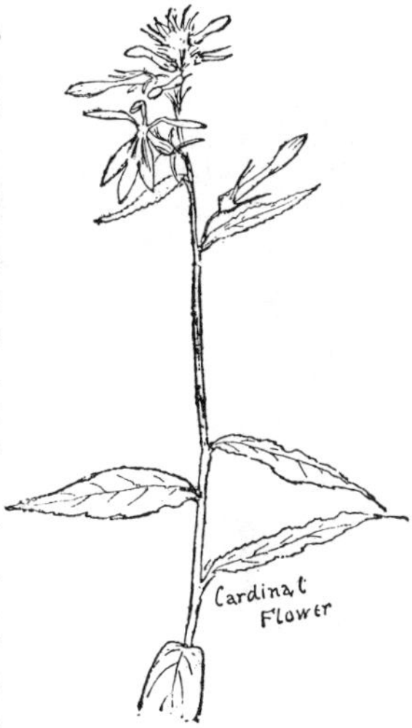

As he lay there thinking, a slight movement nearer the creek caught his eye. A large Basswood had been blown down. Like most of its kind, it was hollow. Its trunk was buried in the tangle of rank summer growth, but a branch had been broken off and left a hole in the main stem. In the black cavern of the hole there appeared a head with shining green eyes, then out there glided onto the log a common gray Cat. She sat there in the sunshine, licked her paws, dressed her fur generally, stretched her claws and legs after the manner of her kind, walked to the end of the log, then down the easy slope to the bottom of the cañon. Here she took a drink, daintily shook the water from her paws, and set the hair just right with a stroke. Then to Yan's amusement she examined all the tracks much as he had done, though it seemed clear that her nose, not her eyes, was judge. She walked down stream, leaving some very fine impressions that Yan mentally resolved to have in his note-book very soon, suddenly stopped, looked upward and around, a living picture of elegance, sleekness and grace, with eyes of green fire, then deliberately leaped from the creek bed to the tangle of the bank and disappeared.

This seemed a very commonplace happening, but the fact of a house Cat taking to the woods lent her unusual interest, and Yan felt much of the thrill that a truly wild animal would have given him, and had gone far enough in art to find exquisite pleasure in the series of pictures the Cat had presented to his eyes.

He lay there for some minutes expecting her to reappear; then far up the creek he heard slight rattling of the gravel. He turned and saw, not the

Cat, but a very different and somewhat larger animal. Low, thick-set, jet black, with white marks and an immense bushy tail—Yan recognized the Skunk at once, although he had never before met a wild one in daylight. It came at a deliberate waddle, nosing this way and that. It rounded the bend and was nearly opposite Yan, when three little Skunks of this year's brood came toddling after the mother.

Cat Tracks

The old one examined the tracks much as the Cat had done, and Yan got a singular sense of brotherhood in seeing the wild things at his own study.

Then the old Skunk came to the fresh tracks of the Cat and paused so long to smell them that the three young ones came up and joined in. One of the young ones went to the bank where the Cat came down. As it blew its little nose over the fresh scent, the old Skunk waddled to the place, became quite interested, then climbed the bank. The little ones followed in a disjointed procession, varied by one of them tumbling backward from the steep trail.

The old Skunk reached the top of the bank, then mounted the log and followed unerringly the Cat's back trail to the hole in the trunk. Down this she peered a minute, then, sniffing, walked in, till nothing could be seen but her tail. Now Yan heard loud, shrill mewing from the log, "*Mew, mew, m-e-u-w, m-e-e-u-w,*" and the old Skunk came backing out, holding a small gray Kitten.

The little thing mewed and spit energetically, holding on to the inside of the log. But the old Skunk was too strong—she dragged it out. Then holding it down with both paws, she got a good firm grip of its neck and turned to carry it down to the bed of the brook. The Kitten struggled vigorously, and at last got its claws into the Skunk's eye and gave such a wrench that the ill-smelling villain loosened its hold a little and so gave the Kitten another chance to squeal, which it did with a will, putting all its strength into a succession of heartrending *mee-ow—mee-ows*. Yan's heart was touched. He was about to dash to the rescue when there was a scrambling in the far grass, a rush of gray, and the Cat—the old mother Cat was on the scene, a picture of demon rage, eyes ablaze, fur erect, ears back. With the spring of a Deer and the courage of a Lion she made for the black murderer. Eye could not follow the flashings of her paws. The Skunk recoiled and stared stupidly, but not long; nothing was "long"

about it. Her every superb muscle was tingling with force and mad with hate as the mother Cat closed like a swooping Falcon. The Skunk had no time to aim that dreadful gun, and in the excitement fired a volley of the deadly musky spray backward, drenching her own young as they huddled in the trail.

Tooth and claw and deadly grip—the old Cat raged and tore, the black fur flew in every direction, and the Skunk for once lost her head and fired random shots of choking spray that drenched herself as well as the Cat. The Skunk's head and neck were terribly torn. The air was suffocating with the poisonous musk. The Skunk was desperately wounded and threw herself backward into the water. Blinded and choking, though scarcely bleeding, the old Cat would have followed even there, but the Kitten, wedged under the log, mewed piteously and stayed the mother's fury. She dragged it out un-unharmed but drenched with musk and carried it quickly to the den in the hollow log, then came out again and stood erect, blinking her blazing eyes—for they were burning with the spray—lashing her tail, the image of a Tigress eager to fight either part or all the world for the little ones she nursed. But the old Skunk had had more than enough. She scrambled off down the cañon. Her three young ones had tumbled over each other to get out of the way when they got that first accidental charge of their mother's battery. She waddled away, leaving a trail of blood and smell, and they waddled after, leaving an odour just as strong.

Yan was thrilled by the desperate fight of the heroic old Cat. Her whole race went up higher in his esteem that day; and the fact that the house Cat really could take to the woods and there maintain herself by hunting was all that was needed to give her a place in his list of animal heroes.

Pussy walked uneasily up and down the log, from the hole where the Kittens were to the end overlooking the cañon. She blinked very hard and was evidently suffering severely, but Yan knew quite well that there was no animal on earth big enough or strong enough to frighten that Cat from her post at the door of her home. There is no courage more indomitable than that of a mother Cat who is guarding her young.

At length all danger of attack seemed over, and

Pussy, shaking her paws and wiping her eyes, glided into her hole. Oh, what a shock it must have been to the poor Kittens, though partly prepared by their brother's unsavoury coming back. There was the mother, whose return had always been heralded by a delicious odour of fresh Mouse or bird, interwoven with a loving and friendly odour of Cat, that was in itself a promise of happiness. Scent is the main thing in Cat life, and now the hole was darkened by a creature that was rank with every nasal guarantee of deadly enmity. Little wonder that they all fled puffing and spitting to the dark corners. It was a hard case; all the little stomachs were upset for a long time. They could do nothing but make the best of it and get used to it. The den never ceased to stink while they were there, and even after they grew up and lived elsewhere many storms passed overhead before the last of the Skunk smell left them.

X

The Adventures of a Squirrel Family

I'LL bet I kin make a Woodpecker come out of that hole," said Sapwood, one day as the three Red-men proceeded, bow in hand, through a far corner of Burns's Bush. He pointed to a hole in the top of a tall dead stub, then going near he struck the stub a couple of heavy blows with a pole. To the surprise of all there flew out, not a Woodpecker, but a Flying Squirrel. It scrambled to the top of the stub, looked this way and that, then spread its legs, wings and tail and sailed downward, to rise slightly at the end of its flight against a tree some twenty feet away. Yan bounded to catch it. His fingers clutched on its furry back, but he got such a cut from its sharp teeth that he was glad to let it go. It scrambled up the far side of the trunk and soon was lost in the branches.

Guy was quite satisfied that he had carried out his promise of bringing a Woodpecker out of the hole, "For ain't a Flying Squirrel a kind of Wood-

pecker?" he argued. He was, in consequence, very "cocky" the rest of the day, proposing to produce a Squirrel whenever they came to a stub with a hole in it, and at length, after many failures, had the satisfaction of driving a belated Woodpecker out of its nest.

The plan was evidently a good one for discovering living creatures. Yan promptly adopted it, and picking up a big stick as they drew near another stub with holes, he gave three or four heavy thumps. A Red Squirrel scrambled out of a lower hole and hid in an upper one; another sharp blow made it pop out and jump to the top of the stub, but eventually back into the lower hole.

The boys became much excited. They hammered the stub now without making the Squirrel reappear.

"Let's cut it down," said Little Beaver.

"Show you a better trick than that," replied the Woodpecker. He looked about and got a pole some twenty feet long. This he placed against a rough place high up on the stub and gave it a violent push, watching carefully the head of the stub. Yes! It swayed just a little. Sam repeated the push, careful to keep time with the stub and push always just as it began to swing away from him. The other boys took hold of the pole and all pushed together, as Sam called, "Now—now—now——"

A single push of 300 or 400 pounds would scarcely have moved the stub, but these little fifty-pound pushes at just the right time made it give more and more, and after three or four minutes the roots, that had begun to crack, gave way with a craunching sound, and down crashed the great stub. Its hollow top struck across a fallen log and burst open in a shower of dust, splinters and rotten wood. The boys rushed to the spot to catch the Squirrel, if possible. It did not scramble out as they expected it would, even when they turned over the fragments. They found the front of the stub with the old Woodpecker hole in it, and under that was a mass of finely shredded cedar bark, evidently a nest. Yan eagerly turned it over, and there lay the Red Squirrel, quite still and unharmed apparently, but at the end of her nose was a single drop of blood. Close beside her were five little Squirrels, evidently a very late brood, for they were naked, blind and helpless. One of them had at its nose a drop of blood and it lay as still as the mother. At first the hunters thought the old one was playing 'Possum, but the stiffness of death soon set in.

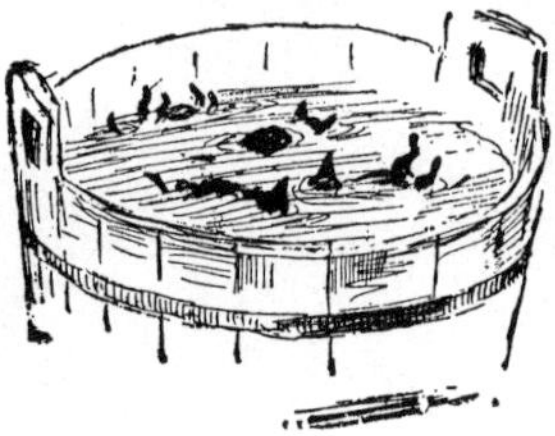

Now the boys felt very guilty and sorry. By thoughtlessly giving way to their hunting instincts they had killed a harmless mother Squirrel in the act of protecting her young, and the surviving little ones had no prospect but starvation.

Yan had been the most active in the chase, and now was far more conscience-stricken than either of the others.

"What are we going to do with them?" asked the Woodpecker. "They are too young to be raised for pets."

"Better drown them and be done with them," suggested Sappy, recalling the last honours of several broods of Kittens at home.

"I wish we could find another Squirrel's nest to put them into," said Little Beaver remorsefully, and then as he looked at the four squirming, helpless things in his hand the tears of repentance filled his eyes. "We might as well kill them and end their misery. We can't find another Squirrel's nest so late as this." But after a little silence he added: "I know some one who will put them out of pain. She may as well have them. She'd get them anyway, and that's the old gray wild Cat. Let's put them in her nest when she's away."

This seemed a reasonable, simple and merciful way of getting rid of the orphans. So the boys made for the "cañon" part of the brook. At one time of the afternoon the sun shone so as to show plainly all that was in the hole. The boys went very quietly to Yan's lookout bank, and seeing that only the Kittens were there, Yan crept across and dropped the young Squirrels into the nest, then went back to his friends to watch, like Miriam, the fate of the foundlings.

They had a full hour to wait for the old Cat, and as they were very still all that time they were rewarded with a sight of many pretty wild things.

A Humming-bird "boomed" into view and hung in a misty globe of wings before one Jewel-flower after another.

"Say, Beaver, you said Humming-birds was something or other awful beautiful," said Woodpecker, pointing to the dull grayish-green bird before them.

"And I say so yet. Look at that," as, with a turn in the air, the hanging Hummer changed its jet-black throat to flame and scarlet that silenced the critic.

After the Humming-bird went away a Field-mouse was seen for a moment dodging about in the grass, and shortly afterward a Shrew-mole, not so big as the Mouse, was seen in hot pursuit on its trail.

Later a short-legged brown animal, as big as a Rabbit, came nosing up the dry but shady bed of the brook, and as it went beneath them Yan recognized by its little Beaver-like head and scaly oar-shaped tail that it was a Muskrat, apparently seeking for water.

There was plenty in the swimming-pond yet, and the boys realized that this had become a gathering place for those wild things that were "drowned out by the drought," as Sam put it.

The Muskrat had not gone more than twenty minutes before another deep-brown animal appeared. "Another Muskrat; must be a meeting," whispered the Woodpecker. But this one, coming close, proved a very different creature. As long as a Cat, but lower, with broad, flat head and white chin and throat, short legs, in shape a huge Weasel, there was no mistaking it; this was a Mink, the deadly enemy of the Muskrat, and now on the track of its prey. It rapidly turned the corner, nosing the trail like a Hound. If it overtook the Muskrat before it got to the pond there would be a tragedy. If the Muskrat reached the deep water it might possibly escape. But just as sure as the pond became a gathering place for Muskrats it would also become a gathering place for Mink.

Not five minutes had gone since the Mink went by before a silent gray form flashed upon the log opposite. Oh, how sleek and elegant it looked! What perfection of grace she seemed after the waddling, hunchy Muskrat and the quick but lumbering Mink. There is nothing more supple and elegant than a fine Cat, and men of science the world over have taken the Cat as the standard of perfection in animal make-up. Pussy glanced about for danger. She had brought no bird or Mouse, for the Kittens were yet too young for such training. The boys watched her with intensest interest. She glided along the log to the hole—the Skunk-smelling hole—uttered her low "*purrow, purrow,*" that always sets the hungry Kittens agog, and was curling in around them, when she discovered the pink Squirrel-babies among her own. She stopped licking the nearest Kitten, stared at a young Squirrel, and smelled it. Yan wondered what help that could be when everything smelled of Skunk. But it did seem to decide her, for she licked it a moment, then lying down she gathered them all in her four-legged embrace, turned her chin up in the air and Sappy announced gleefully that "The little Squirrels were feeding with the little Cats."

The boys waited a while longer, then having made sure that the little Squirrels had been lovingly adopted by their natural enemy, they went quietly back to camp. Now they found a daily pleasure in watching the mixed family.

And here it may be as well to give the rest of the story. The old gray Cat faithfully and lovingly nursed those foundlings. They seemed to prosper, and Yan, recalling that he had heard of a Cat actually raising a brood of Rabbits, looked forward to the day when Kittens and Squirrelets should romp together in the sun. After a week Sappy maintained that only one Squirrel appeared at the breakfast table, and in ten days none. Yan stole over to the log and learned the truth. All four were dead in the bottom of the nest. There was nothing to tell why. The old Cat had done her best—had been all love and tenderness, but evidently had not been able to carry out her motherly intentions.

XI

How to See the Woodfolk

THE days went merrily now, beginning each morning with a hunting of the Woodchuck. The boys were on terms of friendship with the woods that contrasted strongly with the feelings of that first night.

This was the thought in Sam's mind when he one day remarked, "Say, Yan, do you remember the night I slep' with the axe an' you with the hatchet?"

The Indians had learned to meet and conquer all the petty annoyances of camp life, and so forgot them. Their daily routine was simplified. Their acquaintance with woodfolk and wood-ways had grown so fast that now they were truly at home. The ringing "*Kow—Kow—Kow*" in the tree-tops was no longer a mere wandering voice, but the summer song of the Black-billed Cuckoo. The loud, rattling, birdy whistle in the low trees during dull weather Yan had traced to the Tree-frog.

Tree-frog

The long-drawn "*Pee—re-e-e-e*" of hot afternoons was the call of the Wood-peewee, and a vast number of mysterious squeaks and warbles had been traced home to the ever-bright and mischievous Blue Jay.

The nesting season was now over, as well as the song season; the birds, therefore, were less to be seen, but the drying of the streams had concentrated much life in the swimming-pond. The fence had been arranged so that the cattle could reach one end of it to drink, but the lower parts were safe from their clumsy feet, and wild life of many kinds were there in abundance.

The Muskrats were to be seen every evening in the calm pool, and fish in great numbers were in the deeper parts. Though they were small, the boys found them so numerous and so ready to bite that fishing was great sport, and more than one good meal they had from that pond. There were things of interest discovered daily. In a neighbour's field Sam had found another Woodchuck with a "price on his head." Rabbits began to come about the camp at night, especially when the moon was bright, and frequently of late they had heard a querulous, yelping bark that Caleb said was made by a Fox, "probably that old rascal that lives in Callahan's woods."

The gray Cat in the log was always interesting. The boys went very regularly to watch from a distance, but for good reasons did not go near. First, they did not wish to scare her; second, they knew that if they went too close she would not hesitate to attack them.

One of the important lessons that Yan learned was this: In the woods *the silent watcher sees the most.* The great difficulty in watching was how to pass the time, and the solution was to sit and *sketch.* Reading would have done had books been at hand, but not so well as sketching, because then the eyes are fixed on the book instead of the woods, and the turning of the white pages is apt to alarm the shy woodfolk.

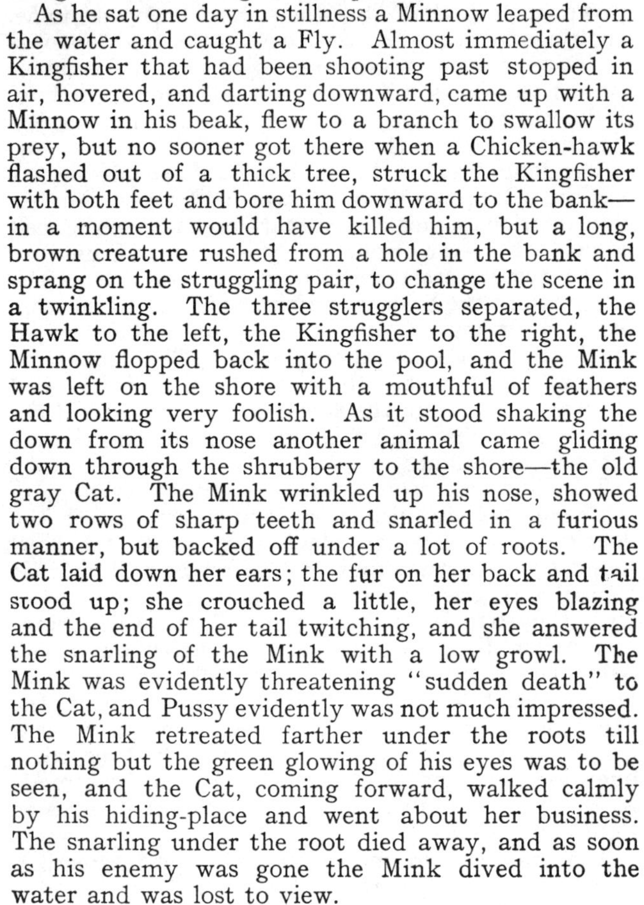

Thus Yan put in many hours making drawings of things about the edge of the pond.

As he sat one day in stillness a Minnow leaped from the water and caught a Fly. Almost immediately a Kingfisher that had been shooting past stopped in air, hovered, and darting downward, came up with a Minnow in his beak, flew to a branch to swallow its prey, but no sooner got there when a Chicken-hawk flashed out of a thick tree, struck the Kingfisher with both feet and bore him downward to the bank—in a moment would have killed him, but a long, brown creature rushed from a hole in the bank and sprang on the struggling pair, to change the scene in a twinkling. The three strugglers separated, the Hawk to the left, the Kingfisher to the right, the Minnow flopped back into the pool, and the Mink was left on the shore with a mouthful of feathers and looking very foolish. As it stood shaking the down from its nose another animal came gliding down through the shrubbery to the shore—the old gray Cat. The Mink wrinkled up his nose, showed two rows of sharp teeth and snarled in a furious manner, but backed off under a lot of roots. The Cat laid down her ears; the fur on her back and tail stood up; she crouched a little, her eyes blazing and the end of her tail twitching, and she answered the snarling of the Mink with a low growl. The Mink was evidently threatening "sudden death" to the Cat, and Pussy evidently was not much impressed. The Mink retreated farther under the roots till nothing but the green glowing of his eyes was to be seen, and the Cat, coming forward, walked calmly by his hiding-place and went about her business. The snarling under the root died away, and as soon as his enemy was gone the Mink dived into the water and was lost to view.

These two animals had a second meeting, as Yan had the luck to witness from his watching-place. He had heard the "plop" of a deft plunge, and looked in time only to see the spreading rings near the shore. Then the water was ruffled far up in the pond. A brown spot showed and was gone. A second appeared, to vanish as the first had done. Later, a Muskrat crawled out on the shore, waddled along for twenty feet, then, plunging in, swam below, came up at the other bank, and crawled under a lot of overhanging roots. A minute later the Mink appeared, his hair all plastered close till he looked like a four-legged Snake. He landed where the Muskrat had come out, followed the trail so that it was lost, then galloped up and down the shore, plunged in, swam across, and beat about the other shore. At last he struck the trail and followed. Under the root there were sounds of a struggle, the snarling of the Mink, and in two or three minutes he appeared dragging out the body of the Muskrat. He sucked its blood and was eating the brains when again the gray Cat came prowling up the edge of the pond and, not ten feet off, stood face to face with the Mink, as she had done before.

The Water Weasel saw his enemy but made no attempt to escape from her. He stood with forepaws on his victim and snarling a warning and defiance to the Cat. Pussy, after glaring for a few seconds, leaped lightly to the high bank, passed above the Mink, then farther on leaped down, and resumed her journey up the shore.

Why should the Mink fear the Cat the first time, and the Cat the Mink the second? Yan believed that ordinarily the Cat could "lick," but that now the Mink had right on his side; he was defending his property, and the Cat, knowing that, avoided a quarrel; whereas the same Cat would have faced a thousand Mink in defense of her Kittens.

These two scenes did not happen the same day, but are told together because Yan always told them together afterward to show that the animals understand something of right and wrong.

But later Yan had another experience with the Muskrats. He and Sam were smoothing out the lower album for the night, when a long stream of water came briskly down the middle of the creek bed, which had been dry for more than a week.

"Hallo," said Woodpecker, "where's that from?"

"A leak in the dam," said Little Beaver, with fear in his voice.

The boys ran up to the dam and learned that the guess was right. The water had found an escape round the end of the dam, and a close examination showed that it had been made by a burrowing Muskrat.

It was no little job to get it tightly closed up. But the spade was handy, and a close-driven row of stakes with plenty of stiff clay packed behind not only stopped the leak but gave a guarantee that in future that corner at least would be safe.

When Caleb heard of the Muskrat mischief he said:

"Now ye know why the Beavers are always so dead sore on the Muskrats. They know the Rats are liable to spoil their dams any time, so they kill them whenever they get the chance."

Little Beaver rarely watched an hour without seeing something of interest in the swamp. The other warriors had not the patience to wait so long and they were not able to make a pastime of sketching.

Yan made several hiding-places where he found that living things were most likely to be seen. Just below the dam was a little pool where various Crawfish and thread-like Eels abounding proved very attractive to Kingfisher and Crow, while little Tipups or Teetering Snipe would wiggle their latter end on the level dam, or late in the day the never-failing Muskrat would crawl out on a flat stone and sit like a fur cap. The cañon part of the creek was another successful hiding-place, but the very best was at the upper end of the pond, for the simple reason that it gave a view of more different kinds of land. First the water with Muskrats and occasionally a Mink, next the little marsh, always there, but greatly increased now by the back-up of the water. Here one or two Field-mice and a pair of Sora Rails were at home. Close at hand was the thick woods, where Partridges and Black Squirrels were sometimes seen.

Yan was here one day sketching the trunk of a Hemlock to pass the watching time, but also because he had learned to love that old tree. He never sketched because he loved sketching; he did not; the motive always was love of the thing he was drawing.

A Black-and-white Creeper had crawled like a Lizard over all the trunks in sight. A Downy Woodpecker had digged a worm out of a log by labour that most birds would have thought ill-paid by a dozen such worms. A Chipmunk had come nearer and nearer till it had actually run over his foot and then scurried away chattering in dismay at its own rashness; finally, a preposterous little Cock Chickadee sang "*Spring soon—spring soon*," as though any one were interested in the gratuitous and unconvincing fib, when a brown, furry form hopped noiselessly from the green leaves by the pond, skipped over a narrow bay without wetting its feet, paused once or twice, then in the middle of the open glade it sat up in plain view—a Rabbit. It sat so long and so still that Yan first made a sketch that took three or four minutes, then got out his watch and timed it for three minutes longer before it moved in the least. Then it fed for some time, and Yan tried to make a list of the things it ate and the things it shunned, but could not do so with certainty.

A noisy Flicker came out and alighted close by on a dried branch. The Rabbit, or really a Northern Hare, "froze"—that is, became perfectly still for a moment—but the Flicker marks were easy to read and had long ago been learned as the uniform of a friend, so the Rabbit resumed his meal, and when the Flicker flew again he paid no heed. A Crow passed over, and yet another. "No; no danger from them." A Red-shouldered Hawk wailed in the woods; the Rabbit heard that and every other sound, but the Red-shoulder is not dangerous and he knew it. A large Hawk with *red tail* circled silently over the glade, and the Rabbit froze on the instant. That same red tail was the mark of a dreaded foe. How well Bunny had learned to know them all!

A bunch of clover tempted him to a full repast, after which he hopped into a tussock in the midst of the glade and there turned himself into a moss-bump, his legs swallowed up in his fur, and his ears laid over his back like a pair of empty gloves or a couple of rounded shingles; his nose-wabblings reduced in number, and he seemed to be sleeping in the last warm rays of the sun. Yan was very anxious to see whether his eyes were open or not; he had been told that Rabbits sleep with open eyes, but at this distance he could not be sure. He had no field-glass and Guy was not at hand, so the point remained in doubt.

The last sun-blots had gone from the trail and the pond was all shadowed by the trees on the western side. A Robin began its evening hymn on a tall tree, where it could see the red sun going down, and a Veery was trilling his *weary, weary, weary* in the Elder thicket along the brook, when another, a larger animal, loomed up in the distant trail and glided silently toward Yan. Its head was low, and he could not make out what it was. As it stood there for a few seconds Yan wet his finger in his mouth and held it up. A slight coolness on the side next the coming creature told Yan that the breeze was from it to him and would not betray him. It came on, seeming to grow larger, turned a little to one side, and then Yan saw plainly by the sharp nose and ears and the bushy tail that it was nothing less than a Fox, probably the one that often barked near camp at night.

It was trotting away at an angle, knowing nothing of the watching boy nor of the crouching Rabbit, when Yan, merely to get a better look at the cunning one, put the back of his hand to his mouth and by sucking made a slight Mouse-like squeak, sweetest music, potent spellbinder, to a hungry Fox, and he turned like a flash. For a moment he stood, head erect, full of poise and force in curb; a second squeak—he came slowly back toward the sound and in so doing passed between Yan and the Rabbit. He had crossed its old trail without feeling much interest, but now the breeze brought its *body scent.* Instantly the Fox gave up the Mouse hunt—no hunter goes after Mice when big game is at hand—and began an elaborate and beautiful stalk of the Rabbit—the Rabbit that he had not seen. But his nose was his best guide. He cautiously zig-zagged up the wind, picking his steps with the greatest care, and pointing with his nose like a Pointer Dog.

Each step was bringing him nearer to Bunny as it slept or seemed asleep in the tussock. Yan wondered whether he ought not to shout out and end the stalk before the Rabbit was caught, but as a naturalist he was eager to see the whole thing out and learn how the Fox would make the capture. The red-furred gentleman was now within fifteen feet of the tussock and still the gray one moved not. Now he was within twelve feet—and no move; ten feet—and Bunny seemed in tranquil sleep; eight feet—and now the Fox for the first time seemed to actually see his victim. Yan had hard work to keep from shouting a warning; six feet—and now the Fox was plainly preparing for a final spring.

"Is it right to let him?" and Yan's heart beat with excitement.

The Fox brought his feet well under him, tried the footing till it was perfect, gathered all his force, then with silent, vicious energy sprung straight for the sleeper. Sleeping? Oh, no! Not at all. Bunny was playing his own game. The moment the Fox leaped, he leaped with equal vigour the opposite way and out under his enemy, so Reynard landed on the empty bunch of grass. Again he sprang, but the Rabbit had rebounded like a ball in the other direction, and continued this bewildering succession of marvellous erratic hops. The Fox in vain tried to keep up, for these wonderful side jumps are the Rabbit's strength and the Fox's weakness; and Bunny went zigzag—hop—skip—into the thicket, and was gone before the Fox could get his heavier body under speed at all.

Had the Rabbit bounded out as soon as he saw the Fox coming he might have betrayed himself unnecessarily; had he gone straight away when the Fox leaped for him he might have been caught in three or four leaps, for the enemy was under full speed, but by biding his time he had courted no danger, and when it did come he had played the only possible offset, and "lives in the greenwood still."

The Fox had to seek his supper somewhere else, and Yan went to camp happy in having learned another of the secrets of the woods.

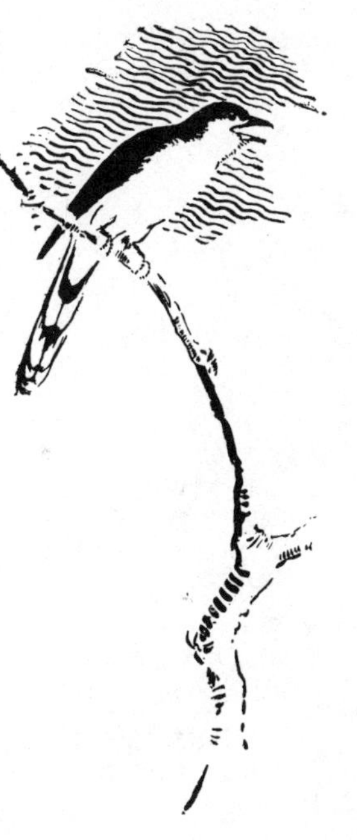

XII

Indian Signs and Getting Lost

"WHAT do you mean when you say Indian signs, Mr. Clark?"

"Pretty near anything that shows there's Injuns round: a moccasin track, a smell of smoke, a twig bent, a village, one stone a-top of another or a white settlement scalped and burned—they all are Injun signs. They all mean something, and the Injuns read them an' make them, too, jest as you would writing."

"You remember the other day you told us three smokes meant you were coming back with scalps."

"Well, no; it don't har'ly mean that. It means 'Good news'—that is, with some tribes. Different tribes uses 'em different."

"Well, what does one smoke mean?"

"As a rule just simply '*Camp is here.*'"

"And two smokes?"

"Two smokes means '*Trouble*'—may mean, '*I am lost.*'"

"I'll remember that; *double for trouble.*"

"Three means good news. *There's luck in odd numbers.*"

"And what is four?"

"Well, it ain't har'ly ever used. If I seen fo smokes in camp I'd know *something big* was on—maybe a Grand Council."

"Well, if you saw five smokes what would you think?"

"I'd think some blame fool was settin' the hull place a-blaze," Caleb replied with the sniff end of a laugh.

"Just now you said one stone on another was a sign. What does it mean?"

"Course I can't speak for all Injuns Some has it for one thing an' some for another, but usually in the West two stones or 'Buffalo chips' settin' one on the other means 'This is the trail'; and a little stone at the left of the two would mean 'Here we turned off to the left'; and at the other side, 'Here we turned to the right.' Three stones settin' one on top of another means, 'This is sure enough the trail,' 'Special' or 'Particular' or 'Look out'; an' a pile of stones just throwed together means 'We camped here 'cause some one was sick.' They'd be the stones used for giving the sick one a steam bath."

"Well, what would they do if there were no stones?"

"Ye mean in the woods?"

"Yes, or smooth prairie."

Indian Sign
Pile of Stones =
"We camped here because one of us was sick"

"Well, I pretty near forget, it's so long ago, but le's see now," and Yan worried Caleb and Caleb threshed his memory till they got out a general scheme, or Indian code, though Caleb was careful to say that "some Injuns done it differently."

Yan must needs set about making a signal fire at once, and was disappointed to find that a hundred yards away the smoke could not be seen above the tree-tops, till Caleb showed him the difference between a clear fire and a smoke or smudge fire.

"Begin with a clear fire to get the heat, then smother it with green grass and rotten wood. There, now you see the difference," and a great crooked, angling pillar of smoke rolled upward as soon as the grass and punk began to sizzle in the glow of embers.

"I bet ye kin see that ten miles away if ye'r on a high place to look for it."

INDIAN SIGNS

Signs in Stones

This is the Trail

Turn to the Right

Turn to the Left

Important • Warning.

Signs in Twigs

This is the Trail

Turn to the Right

Turn to the Left

Important . Warning.

Signs in Grass

This is the Trail

Turn to the Right

Turn to the Left

Important • Warning.

Signs in Blazes

This is the Trail

Turn to the Right

Turn to the Left

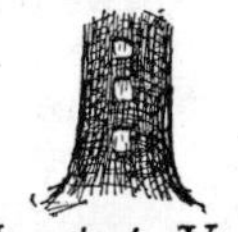
Important - Warning.

Code for Smoke Signals

Camp is Here

I am lost. Help!

Good News

All come to Council

Some Special Blazes used by Hunters & Surveyors

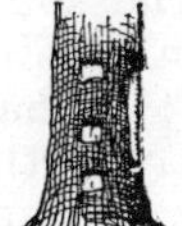
A Trap to Right

A Trap to Left

Camp is to Right

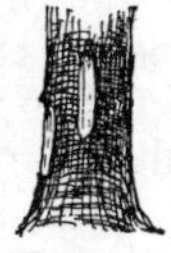
Camp is to Left

Special

Adirondack Special

Surveyor's Line Here

"I bet I could see it twenty miles," chirped in Guy.

"Mr. Clark, were you ever lost?" continued the tireless asker.

"Why, course I was, an' more than once. Every one that goes in the woods is bound to get lost once in awhile."

"What—do the Indians?"

"Of course! Why not? They're human, an' I tell you when you hear a man brag that he never was lost, I know he never was far from his mother's apron string. Every one is bound to get lost, but the real woodsman gets out all right; that's the difference."

"Well, what would you do if you got lost?"

"Depends on where. If it was a country that I didn't know, and I had friends in camp, after I'd tried my best I'd jest set right down and make two smoke fires. 'Course, if I was alone I'd try to make a bee line in the likeliest direction, an' this is easy to make if ye kin see the sun and stars, but stormy weather 'tain't possible. No man kin do it, an' if ye don't know the country ye have to follow some stream; but I'm sorry for ye if ever ye have to do that, for it's the worst walking on earth. It will surely bring ye out some place—that is, it will keep ye from walking in a circle—but ye can't make more than four or five miles a day on it."

"Can't you get your direction from moss on the tree trunks?"

"*Naw!* Jest try it an' see; moss on the north side of a tree and rock; biggest branches on the south of a trunk; top of a Hemlock pointing to east; the biggest rings of growth on the south side of a stump, an' so on. It fits a tree standin' out by itself in the open—the biggest ring is in the south but it don't fit a tree on the south side of an opening then the biggest rings is on the north. If ye have a compass in hand it's all kind o' half true—that is, just a little bit true; but it ain't true; it's on'y a big lie, when ye'r scared out o' your wits an' needin' to know. I never seen but one good compass plant, an' that was the prairie Golden Rod. Get a bunch of them in the open and the most of them point north, but under cover of taller truck they jest point every which way for Sunday.

"If ye find a beaten game trail, ye follow that an' it'll bring ye to water—that is, if ye go the right way, an' that ye know by its gettin' stronger. If it's peterin' out, ye'r goin' in the wrong direction. A flock of Ducks or a Loon going over is sure to be pointing for water. Y're safe to follow.

"If ye have a Dog or a Horse with ye he kin bring ye home all right. Never knew them to fail but oncet, an' that was a fool Horse; there is sech oncet in awhile, though there's more fool Dogs.

"But come right down to it, the compass is the safest thing. The sun and stars is next, an' if ye know your friends will come ye'r best plan is to set right down and make two smoke fires, keep them a-going, holler every little while, and keep calm. Ye won't come to no harm unless ye'r a blame fool, an' such ought to stay to hum, where they'll be nursed."

XIII

Tanning Skins and Making Moccasins

SAM had made a find. A Calf had been killed and its skin hung limp on a beam in the barn. His father allowed him to carry this off, and now he appeared with a "fresh Buffalo hide to make a robe."

"I don't know how the Injuns dress their robes," he explained, "but Caleb does, and he'll tell you, and, of course, I'll pay no attention."

The old Trapper had nothing to do, and the only bright spots in his lonely life, since his own door was shut in his face, were visits to the camp. These had become daily, so it was taken as a matter of course when, within an hour after Sam's return, he "happened round."

"How do the Indians tan furs and robes?" Yan asked at once.

"Wall, different ways——"

But before he could say more Hawkeye reappeared and shouted:

"Say, boys, Paw's old Horse died!" and he grinned joyfully, merely because he was the bearer of news.

"Sappy, you grin so much your back teeth is

gettin' sunburned," and the Head Chief eyed him sadly.

"Well, it's so, an' I'm going to skin out his tail for a scalp. I bet I'll be the Injunest one of the crowd."

"Why don't you skin the hull thing, an' I'll show you how to make lots of Injun things of the hide," Caleb added, as he lighted his pipe.

"Will you help me?"

"It's same as skinnin' a Calf. I'll show you where to get the sewing sinew after the hide's off."

So the whole camp went to Burns's field. Guy hung back and hid when he saw his father there drawing the dead Horse away with the plough team.

"Good-day, Jim," was Caleb's greeting, for they were good friends. "Struck hard luck with the Horse?"

"No! Not much. Didn't cost nothing; got him for boot in a swap. Glad he's dead, for he was foundered."

"We want his skin, if you don't."

"You're welcome to the hull thing."

"Well, just draw it over by the line fence an' we'll bury what's left when we're through."

"All right. You hain't seen that durn boy o' mine, have you?"

"Why, yes; I seen him not long ago," said Sam. "He was p'inting right for home then."

"H-m. Maybe I'll find him at the house."

"Maybe you will." Then Sam added under his breath, "I don't think."

So Burns left them, and a few minutes later Guy sneaked out of the woods to take a secondary part in the proceedings.

Caleb showed them how to split the skin along the under side of each leg and up the belly. It was slow work skinning, but not so unpleasant as Yan feared, since the animal was fresh.

Caleb did the most of the work; Sam and Yan helped. Guy assisted with reminiscences of his own Calf-skinning and with suggestions drawn from his vast experiences.

When the upper half of the skin was off, Caleb remarked: "Don't believe we can turn him over, and when the Injuns didn't have a Horse at hand to turn over the Buffalo they used to cut the skin in two down the line of the back. I guess we better do that. We've got all the rawhide we need, anyhow."

So they cut off the half they had skinned, took the tail and the mane for "scalps," and then Caleb sent Yan for the axe and a pail.

He cut out a lump of liver and the brains of the Horse. "That," said he, "is for tanning, an' here is where the Injun woman gits her sewing thread."

He made a deep cut alongside the back bone from the middle of the back to the loin, then forcing his fingers under a broad band of whitish fibrous tissue, he raised it up, working and cutting till it ran down to the hip bone and forward to the ribs. This sewing sinew was about four inches wide, very thin, and could easily be split again and again till it was like fine thread.

"There," he said, "is a hank o' thread. Keep that. It'll dry up, but can be split at any time, and soaking in warm water for twenty minutes makes it soft and ready for use. Usually, when she's sewing, the squaw keeps a thread soaking in her mouth to be ready. Now we've got a Horse skin and a Calfskin I guess we better set up a tan-yard."

"Well, how do you tan furs, Mr. Clark?"

"Good many different ways. Sometimes just scrape and scrape till I get all the grease and meat off the inside, then coat it with alum and salt and leave it rolled up for a couple of days till the alum has struck through and made the skin white at the roots of the hair, then when this is half dry pull and work it till it is all soft.

"But the Injuns don't have alum and salt, and they make a fine tan out of the liver and brains, like I'm going to do with this."

"Well, I want to do it the Indian way."

"All right, you take the brains and liver of your Calf."

"Why not some of the Horse brains and liver?"

"Oh, I dunno. They never do it that way that I've seen. Seems like it went best with its own brains."

"Now," remarked the philosophical Woodpecker, "I call that a wonderful provision of nature, always to put Calf brains and liver into a Calfskin, and just enough to tan it."

"First thing always is to clean your pelt, and while you do that I'll put the Horsehide in the mud to soak off the hair." He put it in the warm mud to soak there a couple of days, just as he had done the Calfskin for the drum-heads, then came to super-

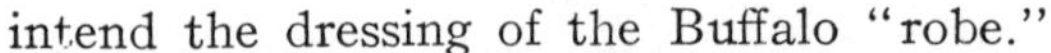

intend the dressing of the Buffalo "robe."

Sam first went home for the Calf brains and liver, then he and Yan scraped the skin till they got out a vast quantity of grease, leaving the flesh side bluish-white and clammy, but not greasy to the touch. The liver of the Calf was boiled for an hour and then mashed up with the raw brains into a tanning "dope" or mash and spread on the flesh side of the hide, which was doubled, rolled up and put in a cool place for two days. It was then opened out, washed clean in the brook and hung till nearly dry. Then Caleb cut a hardwood stake to a sharp edge and showed Yan how to pull and work the hide over the edge till it was all soft and leathery.

The treatment of the Horsehide was the same, once the hair was removed, but the greater thickness needed a longer soaking in the "tan dope."

After two days the Trapper scraped it clean and worked it on the sharp-edged stake. It soon began to look like leather, except in one or two spots. On examining these he said:

"H-m. Tanning didn't strike right through every place." So he buttered it again with the mash and gave it a day more; then worked it as before over the angle of the pole till it was soft and fibrous.

"There," said he, "that's Injun tan leather. I have seen it done by soaking the hide for a few days in liquor made by boiling Hemlock or Balsam bark in water till it's like brown ink, but it ain't any better than that. Now it needs one thing more to keep it from hardening after being wet. It has to be smoked."

So he made a smoke fire by smothering a clear fire with rotten wood; then fastening the Horsehide into a cone with a few wooden pins, he hung it in the dense smoke for a couple of hours, first one side out, then the other, till it was all of a rich smoky-tan colour and had the smell so well known to those who handle Indian leather.

"There it is; that's Injun tan, an' I hope you see that elbow grease is the main thing in tannin'."

"Now, will you show us how to make moccasins and war-shirts?" asked Little Beaver, with his usual enthusiasm.

"Well, the moccasins is easy, but I won't promise about the war-shirts. That's pretty much a case of following the pattern of your own coat, with the front in one piece, but cut down just far enough for your head to go through, instead of all the way, and fixed with tie-strings at the throat and fringes at the seams and at the bottom; it hain't easy to do. But any one kin larn to make moccasins. There is two styles of them—that is, two main styles. Every Tribe has its own make, and an Injun can tell what language another speaks as soon as he sees his footgear. The two best known are the Ojibwa, with soft sole—sole and upper all in one, an' a puckered instep —that's what Ojibwa means—'puckered moccasin.' The other style is the one most used in the Plains. You see, they have to wear a hard sole, 'cause the country is full of cactus and thorns as well as sharp stones."

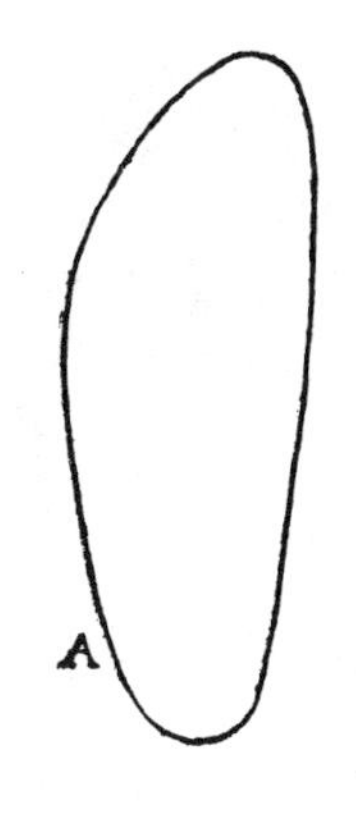

"I want the Sioux style. We have copied their teepee and war bonnet—and the Sioux are the best Indians, anyway."

"Or the worst, according to what side you're on,' was Caleb's reply. But he went on: "Sioux Injuns are Plains Injuns and wear a hard sole. Let's see, now. I'll cut you a pair."

"No, make them for *me*. It's my Horse," said Guy.

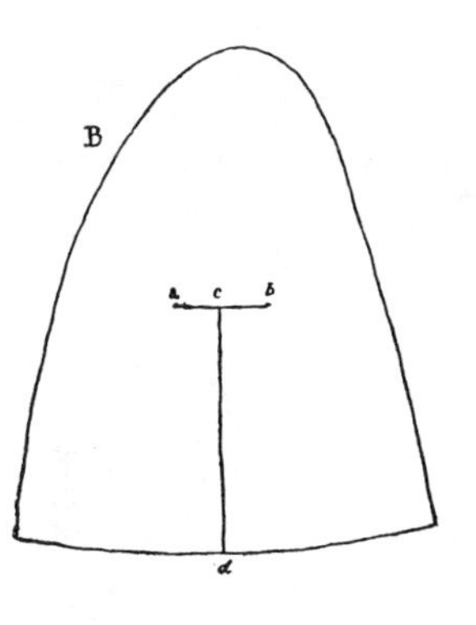

"No, you don't. Your Paw give that to me." Caleb's tone said plainly that Guy's laziness had made a bad impression, so he had to stand aside while Yan was measured. Caleb had saved a part of the hide untanned though thoroughly cleaned. This was soaked in warm water till soft. Yan's foot was placed on it and a line drawn around the foot for a guide; this when cut out made the sole of one moccasin (A, cut above), and by turning it underside up it served as pattern to cut the other.

Now Caleb measured the length of the foot and added one inch, and the width across the instep, adding half an inch, and with these as greatest length and breadth cut out a piece of soft leather (B). Then in this he made the cut *a b* on the middle line one way and *c d* on the middle line the other way. A second piece the reverse of this was cut, and next a piece of soft leather for inside tongue (C) was sewn to the large piece (B), so that the edge *a b* of C was fast to *a b* of B. A second piece was sewn to the other leather (B reversed).

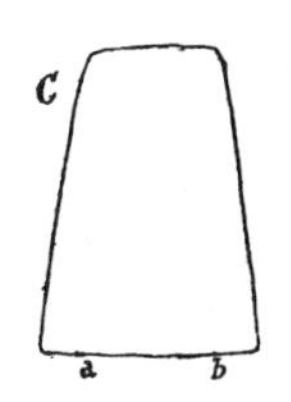

"Them's your vamps for uppers. Now's the time to bead 'em if you want to."

"Don't know how."

"Well, I can't larn you that; that's a woman's

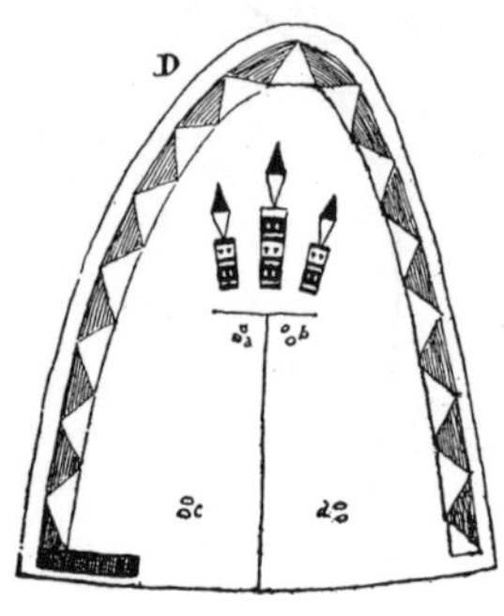

work. But I kin show you the pattern of the first pair I ever wore; I ain't likely to forget 'em, for I killed the Buffalo myself and seen the hull making." He might have added that he subsequently married the squaw, but he did not.

"There's about the style" [D]. "Them three-cornered red and white things all round is the hills where the moccasins was to carry me safely; on the heel is a little blue pathway with nothing in it: that is behind—it's past. On the instep is three red, white and blue pathways where the moccasin was to take me: they're ahead—in the future. Each path has lots of things in it, mostly changes and trails, an' all three ends in an Eagle feather—that stands for an honour. Ye kin paint them that way after they're made. Well, now, we'll sew on the upper with a good thick strand of sinew in the needle—or if you have an awl you kin do without a needle on a pinch—and be sure to bring the stitches out the edge of the sole instead of right through, then they don't wear off. That's the way." [E.]

So they worked away, clumsily, while Guy snickered and sizzled, and Sam suggested that Si Lee would make a better squaw than both of them.

The sole as well as the upper being quite soft allowed them to turn the moccasin inside out as often as they liked—and they did like; it seemed necessary to reverse it every few minutes. But at length the two pieces were fastened together all around, the seam gap at the heel was quickly sewn up, four pairs of lace holes were made (*a*, *b*, *c*, *d*, in D), and an eighteen-inch strip of soft leather run through them for a lace.

Now Yan painted the uppers with his Indian paints in the pattern that Caleb had suggested, and the moccasins were done.

A squaw would have made half a dozen good pairs while Yan and Caleb made the one poor pair, but she would not have felt so happy about it.

XIV

Caleb's Philosophy

THE tracks of Mink appeared from time to time on Yan's creekside mud albums, and at length another of these tireless watchers, placed at the Wakan Rock, reported to him that Mink as well as Skunks came there now for a nightly feast.

The Mink was a large one, judging by the marks, and Caleb was asked to help in trapping it.

"How do you trap Mink, Mr. Clark?" was the question.

"Don't trap 'em at all this time o' year, for they're no good till October," was the answer.

"Well, how do you trap them when they are in season?"

"Oh, different ways."

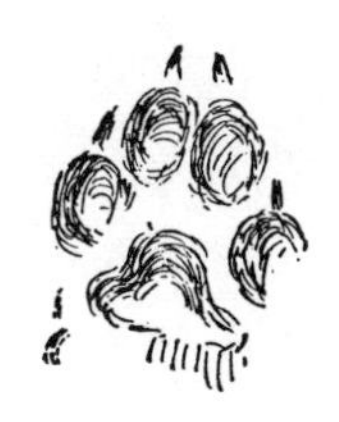

It was slow work, but Yan kept on and at length got the old man going.

"Airly days we always used a deadfall for Mink. That's made like this, with a bird or a Partridge head for bait. That kills him sure, sudden and merciful. Then if it's cold weather he freezes and keeps O. K. till you come around to get him; but in warm weather lots o' pelts are spoiled by being kept too long, so ye have to go round pretty often to save all you kill. Then some one brought in them new-fangled steel traps that catches them by the foot and holds them for days and days, sometimes, till they jest starve to death or chaw their foot off to get free. I mind once I ketched a Mink with only two legs left. He had been in a steel trap twice before and chawed off his leg to get away. Them traps save the trapper going round so often, but they're expensive, and heavy to carry, and you have got to be awful hard-hearted before ye kin use 'em. I tell ye, when I thought of all the sufferin' that Mink went through it settled me for steel traps. Since then, says I, if ye must trap, use a deadfall or a ketchalive, one or other; no manglin' an' tormentin' for days. I tell ye that thar new Otter trap that grabs them in iron claws ought to be forbid by law; it ain't human.

"Same way about huntin'. Huntin's great sport, an' it can't be bad, 'cause I can't for the life of me see that it makes men bad. 'Pears to me men as hunt is humaner than them as is above it; as for the cruelty—wall, we know that no wild animal dies easy abed. They all get killed soon or late, an' if it's any help to man to kill them I reckon he has as good a right to do it as Wolves an' Wildcats. It don't hurt any more—yes, a blame sight less—to be killed by a rifle ball than to be chawed by Wolves. The on'y thing I says is don't do it cruel—an' don't wipe out the hull bunch. If ye never kill a thing that's no harm to ye 'live an' no good to ye dead nor more than the country kin stand, 'pears to me ye won't do much harm, an' ye'll have a lot o' real fun to think about afterward.

"But I mind a feller from Europe, some kind o' swell, that I was guidin' out West. He had crippled a Deer so it couldn't get away. Then he sat down to eat lunch right by, and every few moments he'd fire a shot into some part or another, experimentin' an' aimin' not to kill it for awhile. I heard the shootin' an' blattin', an' when I come up I tell ye it set my blood a-boilin'. I called him some names men don't like, an' put that Deer out o' pain quick as I could pull trigger. That bu'st up our party—I didn't want no more o' him. He come pretty near lyin' by the Deer that day. It makes me hot yet when I think of it.

"If he'd shot that Deer down runnin' an' killed it as quick as he could it wouldn't 'a' suffered more than if it had been snagged a little, 'cause bullets of right weight numb when they hit. The Deer wouldn't have suffered more than he naturally would at his finish, maybe less, an' he'd 'a' suffered it at a time when he could be some good to them as hunted him. An' these yer new repeatin' guns is a curse. A feller knows he has lots of shot and so blazes away into a band o' Deer as long as he can see, an' lots gets away crippled, to suffer an' die; but when a feller has only one shot he's going to place it mighty keerful. Ef it's sport ye want, get a single-shot rifle; ef it's destruction, get a Gatling-gun. Sport's good, but I'm agin this yer wholesale killin' an' cruelty. Steel traps, light-weight bullets an' repeatin' guns ain't human. I tell ye it's them as makes all the sufferin'."

This was a long speech for Caleb, but it was really less connected than here given. Yan had to keep him going with occasional questions. This he followed up.

"What do you think about bows and arrows, Mr. Clark?"

"The Two Smokes"

1. Shelldrake 2. Red-breasted Merganser 3. Hooded Merganser

The Fish-Ducks, Sawbills or Mergansers

4. Mallard 5. Black Duck 6. Gadwell

7. Widgeon 9. Blue-winged Teal

10. Shoveller 11. Pintail 12. Wood Duck

The River Ducks

Far-sketches showing common Ducks as seen on the water at about 50 yards distance. The pair is shown in each square, the male above.

N. B. The wings are rarely seen when the bird is swimming.

THE FISH-DUCK, SAWBILLS OR MERGANSERS

Largely white and all are crested, wings with large white areas in flight.

1. The Shelldrake or Goosander (*Merganser americanus*). Bill, feet and eye red.
2. The Sawbill or Red-breasted Merganser (*Merganser serrator*). Bill and feet red.
3. Hooded Merganser (*Lophodytes cucullatus*). Bill and feet dark; paddle-box buff.

THE RIVER DUCKS

The males usually with shining green and black on head and wings, the females streaky gray-brown.

4. Mallard (*Anas boschas*). Red feet; male has pale, greenish bill. Known in flight by white tail feathers and thin white bar on wing.
5. Black Duck or Dusky Duck (*Anas obscura*). Dark bill, red feet, no white except in flight, then shows white lining of wings.
6. Gadwall or Gray Duck (*Anas strepera*). Beak flesh-coloured on edges, feet reddish, a white spot on wing showing in flight.
7. Widgeon or Baldpate (*A. americana*). Bill and feet dull blue; a large white spot on wing in flight; female has sides reddish.
8. Green-winged Teal (*A. carolinensis*). Bill and feet dark.
9. Blue-winged Teal (*A. discors*). Bill and feet dark.
10. Shoveller (*Spatula clypeata*). Bill dark, feet red, eye yellow-orange; a white patch on wings showing in flight.
11. Pintail or Sprigtail (*Dafila acuta*). Bill and feet dull blue.
12. Wood Duck or Summer Duck (*Aix sponsa*). Bill of male red, paddle-box buff, bill of female and feet of both dark.

"I wouldn't like to use them on big game like Bear and Deer, but I'd be glad if shotguns was done away with and small game could be killed only with arrows. They are either sure death or clear miss. There's no cripples to get away and die. You can't fire an arrow into a flock of birds and wipe out one hundred, like you can with one of them blame scatterguns. It's them things that is killing off all the small game. Some day they'll invent a scattergun that is a pump repeater like them new styles, and when every fool has one they'll wonder where all the small game has gone to.

"No, sir, I'm agin them. Bows and arrows is less destructful an' calls for more Woodcraft an' give more sport—that is, for small game. Besides, they don't make that awful racket, an' you know who is the party that owns the shot, for every arrow is marked."

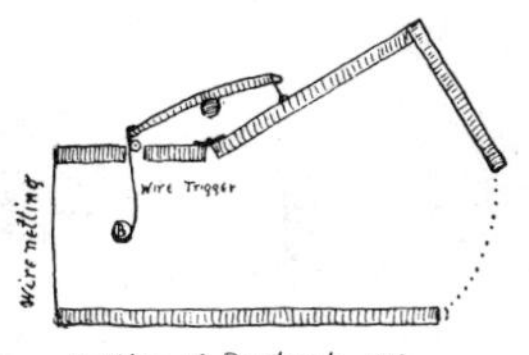

Section of Boxtrap or 'Ketchalive'

Yan was sorry that Caleb did not indorse the arrow for big game, too.

The Trapper was well started now; he seemed ready enough with information to-day, and Yan knew enough to "run the rapids on the freshet."

"How do you make a ketchalive?"

"What for?"

"Oh, Mink."

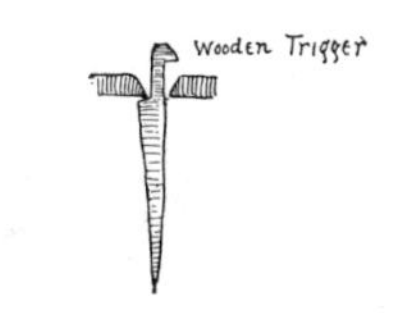

"They ain't fit to catch now, and the young ones need the mothers."

"I wouldn't keep it. I only want to make a drawing."

"Guess that won't harm it if you don't keep it too long. Have ye any boards? We used to chop the whole thing out of a piece of Balsam wood or White Pine, but the more stuff ye find ready-made the easier it is. Now I'll show you how to make a ketchalive if ye'll promise me never to miss a day going to it while it is set."

Ketchalive (set)

The boys did not understand how any one could miss a day in visiting a place of so much interest, and readily promised.

So they made a ketchalive, or box-trap, two feet long, using hay wire to make a strong netting at one end.

"Now," said the trapper, "that will catch Mink, Muskrat, Skunk, Rabbit—'most anything, 'cording to where you put it and how you bait it."

"Seems to me the Wakan Rock will be a good place to try."

So the trap was baited with a fish head firmly

lashed on the wire trigger.

In the morning, as Yan approached, he saw that it was sprung. A peculiar whining and scratching came from it and he shouted in great excitement: "Boys, boys, I've got him! I've got the Mink!"

They seized the trap and held it cautiously up for the sunlight to shine through the bars, and there saw to their disgust that they had captured only the old gray Cat. As soon as the lid was raised she bounded away, spitting and hissing, no doubt to hurry home to tell the Kittens that it was all right, although she had been away so long.

XV

A Visit from Raften

SAM, I must have another note-book. It's no good getting up a new 'massacree' of Whites, 'cause there ain't any note-books there, but maybe your father would get one the next time he drove to Downey's Dump. I suppose I'll have to go on a peace party to ask him."

Sam made no answer, but looked and listened out toward the trail, then said: "Talk of the er—angels, here comes Da."

When the big man strode up Yan and Guy became very shy and held back. Sam, in full war-paint, prattled on in his usual style.

"Morning, Da; I'm yer kid. Bet ye'r in trouble an' want advice or something."

Raften rolled up his pendulous lips and displayed his huge yellow tusks in a vast purple-and-yellow grin that set the boys' hearts at ease.

"Kind o' thought you'd be sick av it before now."

"Will you let us stay here till we are?" chimed in Sam, then without awaiting the reply that he did not want, "Say, Da, how long is it since there was any Deer around here?"

"Pretty near twenty years, I should say."

"Well, look at that now," whispered the Woodpecker.

Raften looked and got quite a thrill, for the dummy, half hidden in the thicket, looked much like a real Deer.

"Don't you want to try a shot?" ventured Yan.

Raften took the bow and arrow and made such a poor showing that he returned them with the remark, "Sure, a gun's good enough for me," then, "Ole Caleb been around since?"

"Old Caleb? I should say so; why, he's our stiddy company."

"'Pears fonder o' you than he is o' me."

"Say, Da, tell us about that. How do you know it was Caleb shot at you?"

"Oh, I don't know it to prove it in a coort o' law, but we quarr'led that day in town after the Horse trade an' he swore he'd fix me an' left town. His own stepson, Dick Pogue, stood right by and heard him say it; then at night when I come along the road by the green bush I was fired at, an' next day we found Caleb's tobacco pouch and some letters not far away. That's about all I know, an' all I want to know. Pogue served him a mean trick about the farm, but that's none o' my business. I 'spect the old fellow will have to get out an' scratch for himself pretty soon."

"He seems kind-hearted," said Yan.

"Ah, he's got an awful temper, an' when he gets drunk he'd do anything. Other times he's all right."

"Well, how is it about the farm?" Sam asked. "Doesn't he own it?"

"No, I guess not now. I don't r'aly know. I only hear them say. Av coorse, Saryann ain't his own daughter. She's nowt o' kin, but he has no one else, and Dick was my hired man—a purty slick feller with his tongue; he could talk a bird off a bush; but he was a good worker. He married Sary and persuaded the old man to deed them the place, him to live in comfort with them to the end of his days. But once they got the place, 'twas aisy to see that Dick meant to get rid o' Caleb, an' the capsheaf was put last year, about his Dog, old Turk. They wouldn't have him 'round. They said he was scaring the hens and chasing sheep, which is like

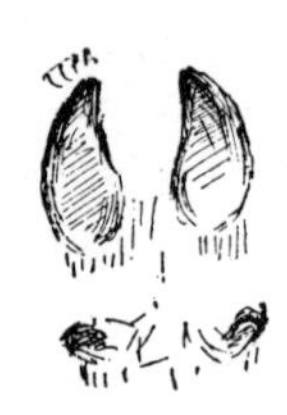

enough, for I believe he killed wan ov my lambs, an' I'd give ten dollars to have him killed—making sure 'twas him, av coorse. Rather than give up the Dog, Caleb moved out into the shanty on the creek at the other end of the place. Things was better then, for Dick and Saryann let up for awhile an' sent him lots o' flour an' stuff, but folks say they're fixin' it to put the old man out o' that and get shet of him for good. But I dunno; it's none o' my business, though he does blame me for putting Dick up to it."

"How's the note-book?" as Raften's eye caught sight of the open sketch-book still in Yan's hand.

"Oh, that reminds me," was the reply. "But what is this?" He showed the hoof-mark he had sketched. Raften examined it curiously.

"H-m, I dunno'; 'pears to me moighty loike a big Buck. But I guess not; there ain't any left."

"Say, Da," Sam persisted, "wouldn't you be sore if you was an old man robbed and turned out?"

"Av coorse; but I wouldn't lose in a game of swap-horse, an' then go gunnin' after the feller. If I had owt agin him I'd go an' lick him or be licked, an' take it all good-natured. Now that's enough. We'll talk about something else."

"Will you buy me another note-book next time you go to Downey's Dump? I don't know how much it will cost or I'd give you the money," said Yan, praying mentally that it be not more than the five or ten cents which was all his capital.

"Shure; I'll charge it up. But ye needn't wait till next week. Thayer's one back at the White settlement ye can have for nothin'."

"Say, Mr. Raften," Guy broke in, "I kin lick them all at Deer-hunting."

Sam looked at Yan and Yan looked at Sam, then glanced at Guy, made some perfectly diabolical signs, seized each a long knife and sprung toward the Third War Chief, but he dodged behind Raften and commenced his usual "Now you let me 'lone——"

Raften's eye twinkled. "Shure, I thought ye was all wan Tribe an' paceable."

"We've got to suppress crime," retorted his son.

"Make him let me 'lone," whimpered Sapwood.

"We'll let ye off this time if ye find that Wood-chuck. It's near two days since we've had a skirmish."

"All right," and he went. Within five minutes he came running back, beckoning. The boys got their bows and arrows, but fearing a trick they held back. Guy dashed for his own weapons with unmistakable and reassuring zest; then all set out for the field. Raften followed, after asking if it would be safe for him to come along.

The grizzly old Woodchuck was there feeding in a bunch of clover. The boys sneaked under the fence, crawling through the grass in true Injun fashion, till the Woodchuck stood up to look around, then they lay still; when he went down they crawled again, and all got within forty yards. Now the old fellow seemed suspicious, so Sam said, "Next time he feeds we all fire together." As soon, then, as the Woodchuck's breast was replaced by the gray back, the boys got partly up and fired. The arrows whizzed around Old Grizzly, but all missed, and he had scrambled to his hole before they could send a second volley.

"Hallo, why didn't you hit him, Sappy?"

"I'll bet I do next time."

When they returned to Raften he received them with ridicule.

"But ye'r a poor lot o' hunters. Ye'd all starve if it wasn't for the White settlement nearby. Faith, if ye was rale Injun ye'd sit up all night at that hole till he come out in the morning, then ye'd get him; an' when ye get through with that one I've got another in the high pasture ye kin work on."

So saying, he left them, and Sam called after him:

"Say, Da; where's that note-book for Yan? He's the Chief of the 'coup-tally,' and I reckon he'll soon have a job an' need his book. I feel it in my bones."

"I'll lave it on yer bed." Which he did, and Yan and Sam had the pleasure of lifting it out of the window with a split stick.

XVI

How Yan Knew the Ducks Afar

ONE day as the great Woodpecker lay on his back in the shade he said in a tone of lofty command:

"Little Beaver, I want to be amused. Come hyar. Tell me a story."

"How would you like a lesson in Tutnee?" was the Second Chief's reply, but he had tried this before, and he found neither Sam nor Guy inclined to take any interest in the very dead language.

"Tell me a story, I said," was the savage answer of the scowling and ferocious Woodpecker.

"All right," said Little Beaver. "I'll tell you a story of such a fine boy—oh, he was the noblest little hero that ever wore pantaloons or got spanked in school. Well, this boy went to live in the woods, and he wanted to get acquainted with all the living wild things. He found lots of difficulties and no one to help him, but he kept on and on—oh! he was so noble and brave—and made notes, and when he learned anything new he froze on to it like grim death. By and by he got a book that was some help, but not much. It told about some of the birds as if you had them *in your hand*. But this heroic youth only saw them at a distance and he was stuck. One day he saw a wild Duck on a pond so far away he could only see some spots of colour, but he made a sketch of it, and later he found out from that rough sketch that it was a Whistler, and then this wonderful boy had an idea. All the Ducks are different; all have little blots and streaks that are their labels, or like the uniforms of soldiers. 'Now, if I can put their uniforms down on paper I'll know the Ducks as soon as I see them on a pond a long way off.' So he set to work and drew what he could find. One of his friends had a stuffed Wood-duck, so the 'Boy-that-wanted-to-know' drew that from a long way off. He got another from an engraving and two more from the window of a taxidermist shop. But he knew perfectly well that there are twenty or thirty different kinds of Ducks, for he often saw others at a distance and made far-sketches, hoping some day he'd find out what they were. Well, one day the 'Boy-that-wanted-to-know' sketched a new Duck on a pond, and he saw it again and again, but couldn't find out what it was, and there was his b-e-a-u-t-i-f-u-l sketch, but no one to tell him its name, so when he saw that he just had to go into the teepee and steal the First War Chief's last apple and eat it to hide his emotion."

Here Yan produced an apple and began to eat it with an air of sadness.

Without changing a muscle, the Great Woodpecker continued the tale:

"Then when the First War Chief heard the harrowing tale of a blighted life, he said: 'Shucks, I didn't want that old apple. It was fished out of the swill-barrel anyway, but 'pears to me when a feller sets out to do a thing an' don't he's a 'dumb failure,' which ain't much difference from a 'durn fool.'

"Now, if this heroic youth had had gumption enough to come out flat-footed, an' instead of stealing rotten apples that the pigs has walked on, had told his trouble to the Great Head War Chief, that native-born noble Red-man would 'a' said: 'Sonny, quite right. When in doubt come to Grandpa. You want to get sharp on Duck. Ugh! Good'—then he'd 'a' took that simple youth to Downey's Hotel at Downey's Dump an' there showed him every kind o' Duck that ever was born, an' all tagged an' labelled. Wah! I have spoken."

And the Great Woodpecker scowled ferociously at Guy, who was vainly searching his face for a clue, not sure but what this whole thing was some subtle mockery. But Yan had been on the lookout for this. Sam's face throughout had shown nothing but real and growing interest. The good sense of this last suggestion was evident, and the result was an expedition was formed at once for Downey's Dump, a little town five miles away, where the railroad crossed a long bog on the Skagbog River. Here Downey, the contractor, had carried the railroad dump across a supposed bottomless morass, and by good luck had soon made a bottom and in consequence a small fortune, with which he built a hotel, and was now the great man of the town for which he had done so much.

"Guess we'll leave the Third War Chief in charge of camp," said Sam, "an' I think we ought to go disguised as Whites."

"You mean to go back to the Settlement and join the Whites?"

"Yep, an' take a Horse an' buggy, too. It's five miles."

That was a jarring note. Yan's imagination had

pictured a foot expedition through the woods, but this was more sensible, so he yielded.

They went to the house to report and had a loving reception from the mother and little Minnie. The men were away. The boys quickly harnessed a Horse and, charged also with some commissions from the mother, they drove to Downey's Dump.

On arriving they went first to the livery-stable to put up the horse, then to the store, where Sam delivered his mother's orders, and having made sure that Yan had pencil, paper and rubber, they went into Downey's. Yan's feelings were much like those of a country boy going for the first time to a circus—now he is really to see the things he has dreamed of so long; now all heaven is his.

And, curiously enough, he was not disappointed. Downey was a rough, vigorous business man. He took no notice of the boys beyond a brief "Morning, Sam," till he saw that Yan was making very fair sketches. All the world loves an artist, and now there was danger of too much assistance.

The cases could not be opened, but were swung around and shades raised to give the best light. Yan went at once to the bird he had "far-sketched" on the pond. To his surprise, it was a female Wood-duck. He put in the whole afternoon drawing those Ducks, male and female, and as Downey had more than fifty specimens Yan felt like Aladdin in the Fairy Garden—overpowered with abundance of treasure. The birds were fairly well labelled with the popular names, and Yan brought away a lot of sketches, which made him very happy. These he afterward carefully finished and put together in a Duck Chart that solved many of his riddles about the Common Ducks.

When they got back to camp at dusk they found a surprise. On the trail was a white thing, which on investigation proved to be a ghost, evidently made by Guy. The head was a large puff-ball carved like a skull, and the body a newspaper.

But the teepee was empty. Guy probably felt too much reaction after the setting up of the ghost to sit there alone in the still night.

XVII

Sam's Woodcraft Exploit

SAM'S "long suit," as he put it, was axemanship. He was remarkable even in this land of the axe, and, of course, among the "Injuns" he was a marvel. Yan might pound away for half an hour at some block that he was trying to split and make no headway, till Sam would say, "Yan, hit it right there," or perhaps take the axe and do it for him; then at one tap the block would fly apart. There was no rule for this happy hit. Sometimes it was above the binding knot, sometimes beside it, sometimes right in the middle of it, and sometimes in the end of the wood away from the binder altogether—often at the unlikeliest places. Sometimes it was done by a simple stroke, sometimes a glancing stroke, sometimes with the grain or again angling, and sometimes a compound of one or more of each kind of blow; but whatever was the right stroke, Sam seemed to know it instinctively and applied it to exactly the right spot, the only spot where the hard, tough log was open to attack, and rarely failed to make it tumble apart as though it were a trick got ready beforehand. He did not brag about it. He simply took it for granted that he was the master of the art, and as such the others accepted him.

On one occasion Yan, who began to think he now had some skill, was whacking away at a big, tough stick till he had tried, as he thought, every possible combination and still could make no sign of a crack. Then Guy insisted on "showing him how," without any better result.

"Here, Sam," cried Yan, "I'll bet this is a baffler for you."

Sam turned the stick over, selected a hopeless-looking spot, one as yet not touched by the axe, set the stick on end, poured a cup of water on the place, then, when that had soaked in, he struck with all his force a single straight blow at the line where the grain spread to embrace the knot. The aim was true to a hair and the block flew open.

"Hooray!" shouted Little Beaver in admiration.

"Pooh!" said Sapwood. "That was just chance. He couldn't do that again."

"Not to the same stick!" retorted Yan. He recognized the consummate skill and the cleverness of knowing that the cup of water was just what was needed to rob the wood of its spring and turn the balance.

But Guy continued contemptuously, "I had it started for him."

"*I* think that should count a *coup*," said Little Beaver.

"Coup nothin'," snorted the Third War Chief, in scorn. "I'll give you something to do that'll try it you can chop. Kin you chop a six-inch tree down in three minutes an' throw it up the wind?"

"What kind o' tree?" asked the Woodpecker.

"Oh, any kind."

"I'll bet you five dollars I kin cut down a six-inch White Pine in *two* minutes an' throw it any way I want to. You pick out the spot for me to lay it. Mark it with a stake an' I'll drive the stake."

"I don't think any of the Tribe has five dollars to bet. If you can do it we'll give you a *grand coup* feather," answered Little Beaver.

"No spring pole," said Guy, eager to make it impossible.

"All right," replied the Woodpecker; "I'll do it without using a spring pole."

So he whetted up his axe, tried the lower margin of the head, found it was a trifle out of the true—that is, its under curve centred, not on the handle one span down, but half an inch out from the handle. A nail driven into the point of the axe-eye corrected this and the chiefs went forth to select a tree. A White Pine that measured roughly six inches through was soon found, and Sam was allowed to clear away the brush around it. Yan and Guy now took a stout stake and, standing close to the tree, looked up the trunk. Of course, every tree in the woods leans one way or another, and it was easy to see that this leaned slightly southward. What wind there was came from the north, so Yan decided to set the stake due north.

Sam's little Japanese eyes twinkled. But Guy, who, of course, knew something of chopping, fairly exploded with scorn. "Pooh! What do you know? That's easy; any one can throw it straight up the wind. Give him a cornering shot and let him try. There, now," and Guy set the stake off to the north-west. "Now, smarty. Let's see you do that."

"All right. You'll see me. Just let me look at it a minute."

Sam walked round the tree, studied its lean and the force of the wind on its top, rolled up his sleeves, slipped his suspenders, spat on his palms, and, standing to west of the tree, said "*Ready.*"

Yan had his watch out and shouted "*Go.*"

Two firm, unhasty strokes up on the south side of the tree left a clean nick across and two inches deep in the middle. The chopper then stepped forward one pace and on the north-northwesterly side, eighteen inches lower down than the first cut, after reversing his hands—which is what few can do—he rapidly chopped a butt-kerf. Not a stroke was hasty; not a blow went wrong. The first chips that flew were ten inches long, but they quickly dwindled as the kerf sank in. The butt-kerf was two-thirds through the tree when Yan called "One minute up." Sam stopped work, apparently without cause, leaned one hand against the south side of the tree and gazed unconcernedly up at its top.

"Hurry up, Sam. You're losing time!" called his friend. Sam made no reply. He was watching the wind pushes and waiting for a strong one. It came—it struck the tree-top. There was an ominous crack, but Sam had left enough and pushed hard to make sure; as soon as the recoil began he struck in very rapid succession three heavy strokes, cutting away all the remaining wood on the west side and leaving only a three-inch triangle of uncut fibre All the weight was now northwest of this. The tree toppled that way, but swung around on the uncut part; another puff of wind gave help, the swing was lost, the tree crashed down to the northwest and drove the stake right out of sight in the ground.

"Hooray! Hooray! Hooray! One minute and forty-five seconds!" How Yan did cheer. Sam was silent, but his eyes looked a little less dull and stupid than usual, and Guy said "Pooh! That's nothin'."

Yan took out his pocket rule and went to the stump. As soon as he laid it on, he exclaimed "Seven and one-half inches through where you cut," and again he had to swing his hat and cheer.

"Well, old man, you surely did it that time. That's a grand coup if ever I saw one," and so, notwithstanding Guy's proposal to "leave it to Caleb," Sam got his grand Eagle feather as Axeman A1 of the Sanger Indians.

XVIII

The Owls and the Night-School

ONE night Sam was taking a last look at the stars before turning in. A Horned Owl had been hooting not far away.

"*Hoo—hohoo-hoho—hoooooo.*"

And as he looked, what should silently sail to the top of the medicine pole stuck in the ground twenty yards away but the Owl.

"Yan! Yan! Give me my bow and arrow, quick. Here's a Cat-Owl—a chicken stealer; he's fair game."

"He's only codding you, Yan," said Guy sleepily from his blanket. "I wouldn't go."

But Yan rushed out with his own and Sam's weapons.

Sam fired at the great feathery creature, but evidently missed, for the Owl spread its wings and sailed away.

"There goes my best arrow. That was my 'Sure-death.'"

"Pshaw!" growled Yan, as he noted the miss. "You can't shoot a little bit."

But as they stood, there was a fluttering of broad wings, and there, alighting as before on the medicine pole, was the Owl again.

"My turn now!" exclaimed Yan in a gaspy whisper. He drew his bow, the arrow flew, and the Owl slipped off unharmed as it had the first time.

"Yan, you're no good. An easy shot like that. Why, any idiot could hit that. Why didn't you fetch her?"

"'Cause I'm not an idiot, I suppose. I hit the same place as you did, anyway, and drew just as much blood."

"Ef he comes back again you call me," piped Guy in his shrill voice. "I'll show you fellers how to shoot. You're no good at all 'thout me. Why, I mind the time I was Deer-shooting——" but a fierce dash of the whole Tribe for Sappy's bed put a stop to the reminiscent flow and replaced it with whines of "Now you let me alone. I ain't doin' nothin' to you."

During the night they were again awakened by the screech in the tree-tops, and Yan, sitting up, said, "Say, boys, that's nothing but that big Cat-Owl."

"So it is," was Sam's answer; "wonder I didn't think of that before."

"I did," said Guy; "I knew it all the time."

In the morning they went out to find their arrows. The medicine pole was a tall pole bearing a feathered shield, with the tribal totem, a white Buffalo, which Yan had set up to be in Indian fashion. Sighting in line from the teepee over this, they walked on, looking far beyond, for they had learned always to draw the arrow to the head. They had not gone twenty-five feet before Yan burst out in unutterable astonishment: "Look! Look at that—and *that*——"

There on the ground not ten feet apart were two enormous Horned Owls, both shot fairly through the heart, one with Sam's "Sure-death" arrow, the other with Yan's "Whistler"; both shots had been true, and the boys could only say, "Well, if you saw that in print you would say it was a big lie!" It was indeed one of those amazing things which happen only in real life, and the whole of the Tribe with one exception voted a *grand coup* to each of the hunters.

Guy was utterly contemptuous. "They got so close they hit by chance an' didn't know they done it. If he had been shooting," etc., etc., etc.

"How about that screech in the tree-tops, Guy?"

"Errrrh."

What a fascination the naturalist always finds in a fine Bird. Yan revelled in these two. He measured their extent of wing and the length from beak to tail of each. He studied the pattern on their quills; he was thrilled by their great yellow eyes and their long, powerful claws, and he loved their every part. He hated to think that in a few days these wonderful things would be disgusting and fit only to be buried.

"I wish I knew how to stuff them," he said.

"Why don't you get Si Lee to show you," was Sam's suggestion. "Seems to me I often seen pictures of Injun medicine men with stuffed birds," he added shrewdly and happily.

"Well, that's just what I will do."

Then arose a knotty question. Should he go to Si Lee and thereby turn "White" and break the charm of the Indian life, or should he attempt the task of persuading Si to come down there to work without proper conveniences. They voted to bring Si to camp. "Da might think we was backing out." After all, the things needed were easily carried, and Si, having been ambushed by a scout, consented to come and open a night-school in taxidermy.

The tools and things that he brought were a bundle of tow made by unravelling a piece of rope, some cotton wool, strong linen thread, two long darning needles, arsenical soap worked up like cream, corn-meal, some soft iron wire about size sixteen and some of stovepipe size, a file, a pair of pliers, wire cutters, a sharp knife, a pair of stout scissors, a gimlet, two ready-made wooden stands, and last of all a good lamp. The boys hitherto had been content with the firelight.

Thus in the forest teepee Yan had his first lesson in the art that was to give him so much joy and some sorrow in the future.

Guy was interested, though scornful; Sam was much interested; Yan was simply rapt, and Si Lee was in his glory. His rosy red cheeks and his round figure swelled with pride; even his semi-nude head and fat, fumbling fingers seemed to partake of his general elation and importance.

First he stuffed the Owls' throats and wounds with cotton wool.

Then he took one, cut a slit from the back of the breast-bone nearly to the tail (*A* to *B*, Fig. 1, page 206), while Yan took the other and tried faithfully to follow his example.

He worked the skin from the body chiefly by the use of his finger nails, till he could reach the knee of each leg and cut this through at the joint with the knife (*Kn*, Fig. 1, page 206). The flesh was removed from each leg-bone down to the heel-joint (*Hl*, *Hl*, Fig. 1), leaving the leg and skin as in *Lg*, Figure 2. Then working back on each side of the tail, he cut the "pope's nose" from the body and left it as part of the skin, with the tail feathers in it, and this, Si explained, was a hard place to get around. Sam called it "rounding Cape Horn." As the flesh was exposed Si kept it powdered thickly with corn-meal, and this saved the feathers from soiling.

Once around Cape Horn it was easy sailing. The skin was rapidly pushed off till the wings were reached. These were cut off at the joint deep in the breast (under *J J*, Fig. 1, or seen on the back, *W J*, Fig. 2), the first bone of each wing was cleared of meat, and the skin, now inside out and well mealed, was pushed off the neck up to the head.

Here Si explained that in most birds it would slip easily over the head, but in Owls, Woodpeckers, Ducks and some others one had sometimes to help it by a lengthwise slit on the nape (*Sn*, Fig. 2). "Owls is hard, anyway," he went on, "though not so bad as Water-fowl. If ye want a real easy bird for a starter, take a Robin or a Blackbird, or any land Bird about that size except Woodpeckers."

When the ears were reached they were skinned and pulled out of the skull without cutting, then, after the eyes were passed, the skin and body looked as in Figure 2. Now the back of the head with the neck and body was cut off (*Ct*, Fig. 2), and the first operation of the skinning was done.

Yan got along fairly well, tearing and cutting the skin once or twice, but learning very quickly to manage it.

Now began the cleaning of the skin.

The eyes were cut clean out and the brains and flesh carefully scraped away from the skull.

The wing bones were already cleaned of meat down to the elbow joint, where the big quill feathers began, and the rest of the wing had to be cleared of flesh by cutting open the under side of the next joint (*H* to *El*, Fig. 1). The "pope's nose" and the skin generally was freed from meat and grease by scraping with a knife and rubbing with the meal.

Then came the poisoning. Every part of the bones and flesh had to be painted with the creamy arsenical soap, then the head was worked back into its place and the skin turned right side out.

When this was done it was quite late. Guy was asleep, Sam was nearly so, and Yan was thoroughly tired out.

"Guess I'll go now," said Si. "Them skins is in good shape to keep, only don't let them dry," so they were wrapped up in a damp sack and put away in a tin till next night, when Si promised to return and finish the course in one more lesson.

While they were so working Sam had busied himself opening the Owls' stomachs—"looking up their records," as he called it. He now reported that one had lynched a young Partridge and the other had killed a Rabbit for its latest meal.

Next night Si Lee came as promised, but brought bad news. He had failed to find the glass Owl eyes he had hoped were in his trunk. His ingenuity, however, was of the kind that is never balked in a small matter. He produced some black and yellow oil paints, explaining, "Guess we'll make wooden eyes do for the present, an' when you get to town you can put glass ones in their place." So Sam was set to

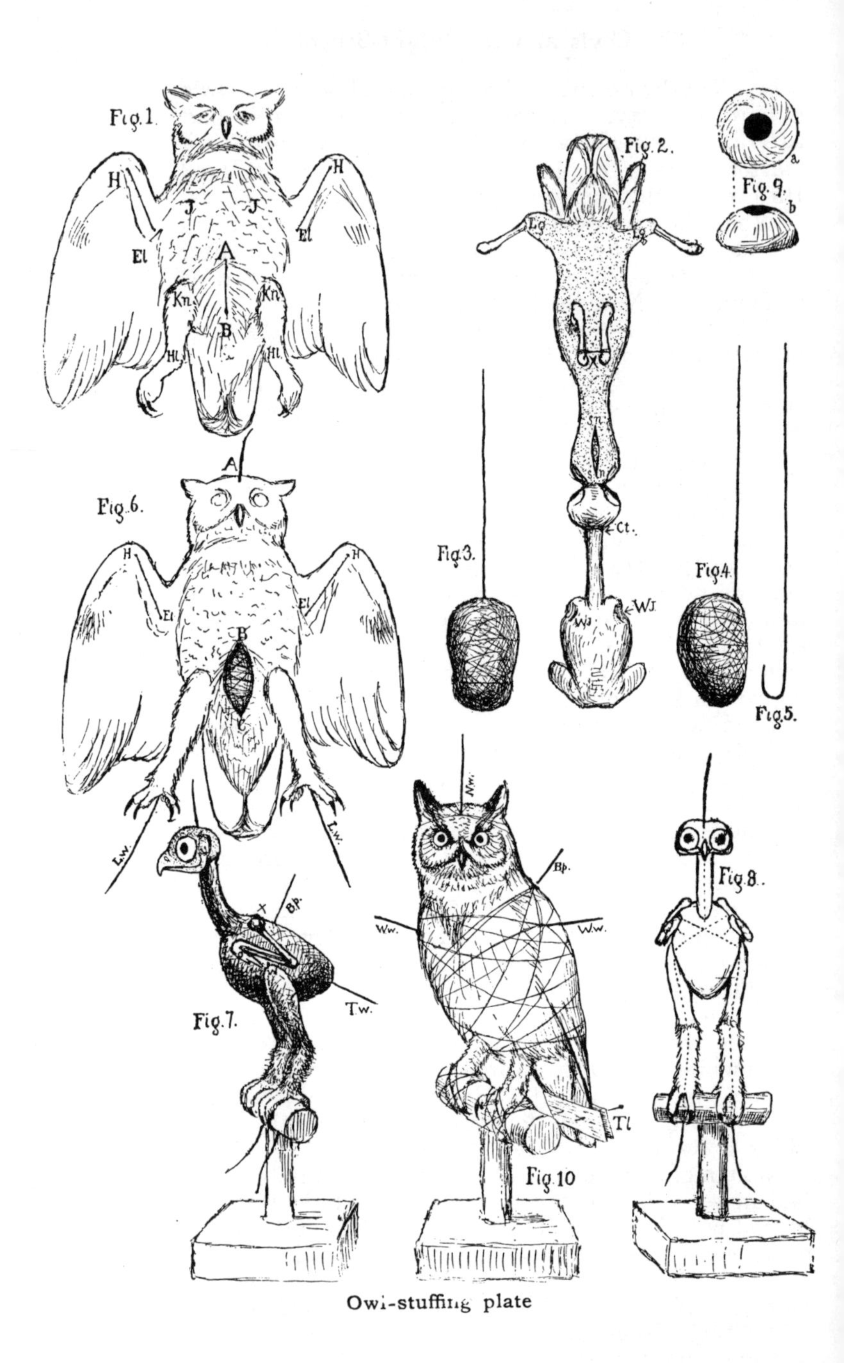

Owl-stuffing plate

work whittling four wooden eyes the shape of well-raised buns and about three-quarters of an inch across. When whittled, scraped and smooth, Si painted them brilliant yellow with a central black spot and put them away to dry (shown on a large scale on page 206, Fig. 9, *a* and *b*).

Meanwhile, he and Yan got out the two skins. The bloody feathers on the breasts were washed clean in a cup of warm water, then dried with cotton and dusted all over with meal to soak up any moisture left. The leg and wing bones were now wrapped with as much tow as would take the place of the removed meat. The eye sockets were partly filled with cotton, then a long soft roll of tow about the length and thickness of the original neck was worked up into the neck skin and into the skull and left hanging. The ends of the two wing bones were fastened two inches apart with a shackle of strong string (*X*, Fig. 2 and Fig. 7). Now the body was needed.

For this Si rolled and lashed a wad of tow with strong thread until he made a dummy of the same size and shape as the body taken out, squeezing and sewing it into a hard solid mass. Next he cut about two and a half feet of the large wire, filed both ends sharp, doubled about four inches of one end back in a hook (Fig. 5), then drove the long end through the tow body from the tail end out where the neck should join on (Figs. 3 and 4). This was driven well in so that the short end of the hook was buried out of sight. Now Si passed the projecting ends of the long wire up the neck in the middle of the tow roll or neck already there, worked it through the skull and out at the top of the Owl's head, and got the

OWL-STUFFING PLATE

Fig. 1. The dead Owl, showing the cuts made in skinning it: A to B, for the body; El to H, on each wing, to remove the meat of the second joint.

Fig. 2. After the skinning is done the skull remains attached to the skin, which is now inside out, the neck and body are cut off at Ct. Sn to Sn shows the slit in the nape needed for Owls and several other kinds.

Fig. 3. Top view of the tow body, neck end up, and neck wire projecting.

Fig. 4. Side view of the tow body, with the neck wire put through it; the tail end is downward.

Fig. 5. The heavy iron wire for neck.

Fig. 6. The Owl after the body is put in; it is now ready to close up, by stitching up the slit on the nape, the body slit B to C and the two wing slits El to H, on each wing.

Fig. 7. A dummy as it *would look* if all the feathers were off; this shows the proper position for legs and wings on the body. At W is a glimpse of the leg wire entering the body at the middle of the side.

Fig. 8. Another view of the body without feathers; the dotted lines show the wires of the legs through the hard body, and the neck wire.

Fig. 9. Two views of one of the wooden eyes; these are on a much larger scale than the rest of the figures in this plate.

Fig. 10. The finished Owl, with the thread wrappings on and the wires still projecting; Nw is end of the neck-wire; Bp is back-pin—that is, the wire in the center of the back; Ww and Ww are the wing wires; Tl are the cards pinned on the tail to hold it flat while it dries. The last operation is to remove the threads and cut all these wires off close so that the feathers hide what remains.

tow body properly placed in the skin with the string that bound the wing bones across the back (*X*, Fig. 7).

Two heavy wires each eighteen inches long and sharp at one end were needed for the legs. These were worked up one through the sole of each foot under the skin of the leg behind (*Lw*, Fig. 6), then through the tow body at the middle of the side (*W*, Fig. 7), after which the sharp end was bent with pliers into a hook and driven back into the hard body (after the manner of the neck wire, Fig. 4).

Another wire was sharpened and driven through the bones of the tail, fastening that also to the tow body (*Tw*, Fig. 7).

Now a little soft tow was packed into places where it seemed needed to fit the skin on, and it remained to sew up the opening below (*Bc* in Fig. 6), the wing slits (*El*, *H*, Fig. 6 and Fig. 1), and the slit in the nape (*Sn Sn*, Fig. 2) with half a dozen stitches, always putting the needle into the skin from the flesh side.

The projecting wires of the feet were put through gimlet holes in the perch and made firm, and Si's Owls were ready for their positions. They were now the most ridiculous looking things imaginable, wings floppy, heads hanging.

"Here is where the artist comes in," said Si proudly, conscious that this was himself. He straightened up the main line of the body by bending the leg wires and set the head right by hunching the neck into the shoulders. "An Owl always looks over its shoulder," he explained, but took no notice of Sam's query as to "whose shoulder he expected it to look over." He set two toes of each foot forward on the perch and two back to please Yan, who insisted that that was Owly, though Si had his doubts. He spread the tail a little by pinning it between two pieces of card (*Tl*, Fig. 10), gave it the proper slant, and now had the wings to arrange.

They were drooping like those of a clucking hen. A sharp wire of the small size was driven into the bend of each wing (*O*, Fig. 7), nailing it in effect to the body (*Ww* and *Ww*, Fig. 10). A long pin was set in the middle of the back (*Bp*, Fig. 10), then using these with the wing wires and head wire as lashing points, Si wrapped the whole bird with the thread (Fig. 10), putting a wad of cotton here or a bit of stick there under the wrapping till he had the position and "feathering" perfect, as he put it.

"We can put in the eyes now," said he, "or later, if we soften the skin around the eye-sockets by putting wet cotton in them for twenty-four hours."

Yan had carefully copied Si's method with the second Owl, and developed unusual quickness at it.

His teacher remarked, "Wall, I larned lots o' fellows to stuff birds, but you ketch on the quickest I ever seen."

Si's ideas of perfection might differ from those of a trained taxidermist; indeed, these same Owls afforded Yan no little amusement in later years, but for the present they were an unmitigated joy.

They were just the same in position. Si knew only one; all his birds had that. But when they had dried fully, had their wrappings removed, the wires cut off flush and received the finishing glory of their wooden eyes, they were a source of joy and wonder to the whole Tribe of Indians.

XIX

The Trial of Grit

THE boys had made war bonnets after the "really truly" Indian style learned from Caleb. White Turkey tail-feathers and white Goose wing-feathers dyed black at the tips made good Eagle feathers. Some wisps of red-dyed horsehair from an old harness tassel; strips of red flannel from an old shirt, and some scraps of sheepskin supplied the remaining raw material. Caleb took an increasing interest, and helped them not only to make the bonnet, but also to decide on what things should count *coup* and what *grand coup*. Sam had a number of feathers for shooting, diving, "massacreeing the Whites," and his grand tufted feathers for felling the pine and shooting the Cat-Owl.

Among other things, Yan had counted coup for trailing. The Deer hunt had been made still more real by having the "Deer-boy" wear a pair of sandals made from old boots; on the sole of each they put two lines of hobnails in V shape, pointing forward. These made hooflike marks wherever the Deer went. One

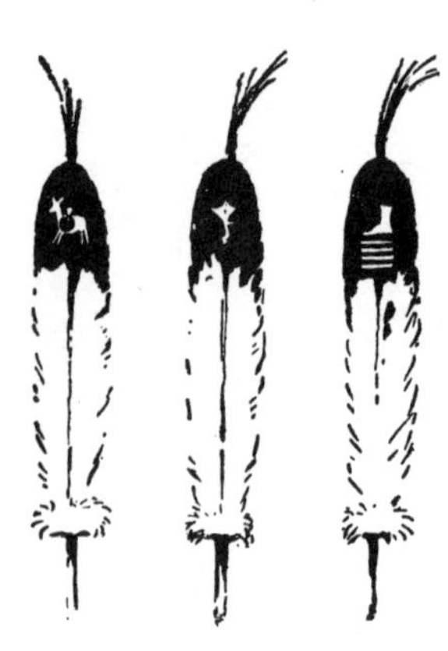

of the difficulties with the corn was that it gave no clue to the direction or doubling of the trail, but the sandals met the trouble, and with a very little corn to help they had an ideal trail. All became very expert, and could follow fast a very slight track, but Yan continued the best, for what he lacked in eyesight he more than made up in patience and observation. He already had a *grand coup* for finding and shooting the Deer in the heart, that time, at first shot before the others came up even, and had won six other *grand coups*—one for swimming 200 yards in five minutes, one for walking four measured miles in one hour, one for running 100 yards in twelve seconds, one for knowing 100 wild plants, one for knowing 100 birds, and the one for shooting the Horned Owl.

Guy had several good *coups*, chiefly for eyesight. He could see "the papoose on the squaw's back," and in the Deer hunt he had several times won *coups* that came near being called *grand coup*, but so far fate was against him, and even old Caleb, who was partial to him, could not fairly vote him a *grand coup*.

"What is it that the Injuns most likes in a man: I mean, what would they druther have, Caleb?" asked Sappy one day, confidently expecting to have his keen eyesight praised.

"Bravery," was the reply. "They don't care what a man is if he's brave. That's their greatest thing—that is, if the feller has the stuff to back it up. An' it ain't confined to Injuns; I tell you there ain't anything that anybody goes on so much. Some men pretends to think one thing the best of all, an' some another, but come right down to it, what every man, woman an' child in the country loves an' worships is pluck, clear grit, well backed up."

"*Well, I tell you,*" said Guy, boiling up with enthusiasm at this glorification of grit, "*I* ain't scared o' nothin'."

"Wall, how'd you like to fight Yan there?"

"Oh, that ain't fair. He's older an' bigger'n I am."

"Say, Sappy, I'll give you one. Suppose you go to the orchard alone an' get a pail of cherries. All the men'll be away at nine o'clock."

"Yes, and have old Cap chaw me up."

"Thought you weren't scared of anything, an' a poor little Dog smaller than a yearling Heifer scares you."

"Well, I don't like cherries, anyhow."

"Here, now, Guy, I'll give you a real test. You see that stone?" and Caleb held up a small round stone with a hole in it. "Now, you know where old Garney is buried?"

Garney was a dissolute soldier who blew his head off, accidentally, his friends claimed, and he was buried on what was supposed to be his own land just north of Raften's, but it afterward proved to be part of the highway where a sidepath joined in, and in spite of its diggers the grave was at the *crossing of two roads*. Thus by the hand of fate Bill Garney was stamped as a suicide.

The legend was that every time a wagon went over his head he must groan, but unwilling to waste those outcries during the rumbling of the wheels, he waited till midnight and rolled them out all together. Anyone hearing should make a sympathetic reply or they would surely suffer some dreadful fate. This was the legend that Caleb called up to memory and made very impressive by being properly impressed himself.

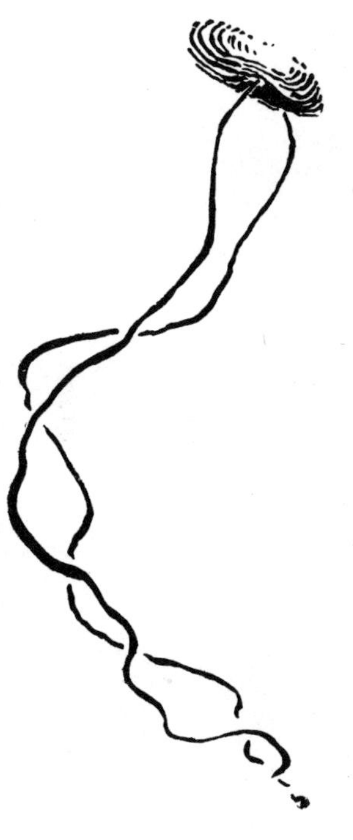

"Now," said he, "I am going to hide this stone just behind the rock that marks the head of Garney's grave, an' I'll send you to git it some night. Air ye game?"

"Y-e-s, I'll go," said the Third War Chief without visible enthusiasm.

"If he's so keen for it now, there'll be no holding him back when night comes," remarked the Woodpecker.

"Remember, now," said Caleb, as he left them to return to his own miserable shanty, "this is the chance to show what you're made of. I'll tie a cord to the stone to make sure that you get it."

"We're just going to eat. Won't you stay and jine with us," called Sam, but Caleb strode off without taking notice of the invitation.

In the middle of the night the boys were aroused by a man's voice outside and the scratching of a stick on the canvas.

"Boys! Guy—Yan! Oh, Guy!"

"Hello! Who is it?"

"Caleb Clark! Say, Guy, it's about half-past eleven now. You have just about time to go to Garney's grave by midnight an' get that stone, and if you can't find the exact spot *you listen for the groaning—that'll guide you.*"

This cheerful information was given in a hoarse whisper that somehow conveyed the idea that the old man was as scared as he could be.

"I—I—I—" stammered Guy, "I can't see the way."

"This is the chance of your life, boy. You get that stone and you'll get a *grand coup* feather, top honours fur grit. I'll wait here till you come back."

"I—I—can't find the blamed old thing on such a dark night. I—I—ain't goin'."

"Errr—you're scared," whispered Caleb.

"I ain't scared, on'y what's the use of goin' when I couldn't find the place? I'll go when it's moonlight."

"Err—anybody here brave enough to go after that stone?"

"I'll go," said the other two at the same time, though with a certain air of "But I hope I don't have to, all the same."

"You kin have the honour, Yan," said the Woodpecker, with evident relief.

"Of course, I'd like the chance—but—but—I don't want to push ahead of you—you're the oldest; that wouldn't be square," was the reply.

"Guess we'd better draw straws for it."

So Sam sought a long straw while Yan stirred up the coals to a blaze. The long straw was broken in two unequal pieces and hidden in Sam's hand. Then after shuffling he held it toward Yan, showing only the two tips, and said, "Longest straw takes the job." Yan knew from old experience that a common trick was to let the shortest straw stick out farthest, so he took the other, drew it slowly out and out—it seemed endless. Sam opened his hand and showed that the short straw remained, then added with evident relief: "You got it. You are the luckiest feller I ever did see. Everything comes your way."

If there had been any loophole Yan would have taken it, but it was now clearly his duty to go for that stone. It was pride rather than courage that carried him through. He dressed quietly and nervously; his hands trembled a little as he laced his shoes. Caleb waited outside when he heard that it was Yan who was going. He braced him up by telling him: "You're the stuff. I jest love to see grit. I'll go with you to the edge of the woods—'twouldn't be fair to go farther—and wait there till you come back. It's easy to find. Go four panels of fence past the little Elm, then right across on the other side

21. Black Scoter 22. White-winged Scoter 23. Surf Duck

The Sea Ducks

THE SEA DUCKS

Chiefly black and white in colour; the female brownish instead of black; most have yellow or orange eye, and more or less white on wings which does not show as they swim.

13. Red-head (*Aythya americana*). Head and neck bright red; eye of male yellow, bill and feet blue.
14. Canvasback (*A. vallisneria*). Head and neck dark-red, eye of male red, bill and feet of both dark or bluish.
15. Ring-necked Bluebill (*A. collaria*). Bill and feet bluish.
16. Big Bluebill (*A. marila*). Bill and feet bluish.
17. Little Bluebill (*A. affinis*). Same colour as the preceding.
18. Whistler or Goldeneye (*Clangula clangula americana*). Feet orange.
19. Bufflehead or Butterball (*Charitonetta albeola*).
20. Old-Squaw or Longtail (*Harelda hyemalis*). This is its winter plumage, in which it is mostly seen.
21. Black Scoter (*Oidemia americana*). A jet-black Duck with orange bill; no white on it anywhere.
22. White-winged Scoter (*O. deglandi*). A black Duck with white on cheek and wing; feet and bill orange; much white on wing shows as they fly, sometimes none as they swim.
23. Surf Duck or Sea Coot (*O. perspicillata*). A black Duck with white on head, but none on wings; bill and feet orange.
24. Ruddy Duck or Stiff-tailed Duck (*Erismatura jamaicensis*). Bill and feet bluish; male is in general a dull red with white face.

"Guy gave a leap of terror and fell"

of the road is the big stone. Well, on the side next the north fence you'll find the ring pebble. The coord is lying kind o' cross the big white stone, so you'll find it easy; and here, take this chalk; if your grit gives out, you mark on the fence how far you did get, but don't you worry about that groaning—it's nothing but a yarn—don't be scairt."

"I am afraid I am scared, but still I'll go."

"That's right," said the Trapper with emphasis. "Bravery ain't so much not being scairt as going ahead when you are scairt, showing that you kin boss your fears."

So they talked till they struck out of the gloom of the trees to the comparative light of the open field.

"It's just fifteen minutes to midnight," said Caleb, looking at his watch with the light of a match. "You'll make it easy. I'll wait here."

Then Yan went on alone.

It was a somber night, but he felt his way along the field fence to the line fence and climbed that into the road that was visible as a less intense darkness on the black darkness of the grass. Yan walked on up the middle cautiously. His heart beat violently and his hands were cold. It was a still night, and once or twice little mousey sounds in the fence corner made him start, but he pushed on. Suddenly in the blackness to the right of the road he heard a loud "whisk," then he caught sight of a white thing that chilled his blood. It was the shape of a man wrapped in white, but lacked a head, just as the story had it. Yan stood frozen to the ground. Then his intellect came to the rescue of his trembling body. "What nonsense! It must be a white stone." But no, it moved. Yan had a big stick in his hand. He shouted: "Sh, sh, sh!" Again the "corpse" moved. Yan groped on the road for some stones and sent one straight at the "white thing." He heard a "whooff" and a rush. The "white thing" sprang up and ran past him with a clatter that told him he had been scared by Granny de Neuville's white-faced cow.

At first the reaction made him weak at the knees, but that gave way to a better feeling. If a harmless old Cow could lie out there all night, why should he fear? He went on more quietly till he neared the rise in the road. He should soon see the little Elm. He kept to the left of the highway and peered into the gloom, going more slowly. He was not so near as he had supposed, and the tension of the early part of the expedition was coming back more than ever. He wondered if he had not passed the Elm—should he go back? But no, he could not bear the idea; that would mean retreat. Anyhow, he would put his chalk mark here to show how far he did get. He sneaked cautiously toward the fence to make it, then to his relief made out the Elm not twenty-five feet away. Once at the tree, he counted off the four panels westward and knew that he was opposite the grave of the suicide. It must now be nearly midnight. He thought he heard sounds not far away, and there across the road he saw a whitish thing—the headstone. He was greatly agitated as he crawled quietly as possible toward it. Why quietly he did not know. He stumbled through the mud of the shallow ditch at each side, reached the white stone, and groped with clammy, cold hands over the surface for the string. If Caleb had put it there it was gone now. So he took his chalk and wrote on the stone "Yan."

Oh, what a scraping that chalk made! He searched about with his fingers around the big boulder. Yes, there it was; the wind, no doubt, had blown it off. He pulled it toward him. The pebble was drawn across the boulder with another and louder rasping that sounded fearfully in the night. Then at once a gasp, a scuffle, a rush, a splash of something in mud, or water—horrible sounds of a being choking, strangling or trying to speak. For a moment Yan sank down in terror. His lips refused to move. But the remembrance of the cow came to help him. He got up and ran down the road as fast as he could go, a cold sweat on him. He ran so blindly he almost ran into a man who shouted "Ho, Yan; is that you?" It was Caleb coming to meet him. Yan could not speak. He was trembling so violently that he had to cling to the Trapper's arm.

"What was it, boy? I heard it, but what was it?"

"I—I—don't know," he gasped; "only it was at the g-g-grave."

"Gosh! I heard it, all right," and Caleb showed no little uneasiness, but added, "We'll be back in camp in ten minutes."

He took Yan's trembling hand and led him for a little while, but he was all right when he came to the blazed trail. Caleb stepped ahead, groping in the darkness.

Yan now found voice to say, "I got the stone all right, and I wrote my name on the grave, too."

Good boy! You're the stuff!" was the admiring response.

They were very glad to see that there was a fire in the teepee when they drew near. At the edge of the clearing they gave a loud "*O-hoo—O-hoo—O-hoo-oo,*" the Owl cry that they had adopted because it is commonly used by the Indians as a night signal, and they got the same in reply from within.

"All right," shouted Caleb; "he done it, an' he's bully good stuff and gets an uncommon *grand coup.*"

"Wish I had gone now," said Guy. "I could 'a' done it just as well as Yan."

"Well, go on now."

"Oh, there ain't any stone to get now for proof."

"You can write your name on the grave, as I did."

"Ah, that wouldn't prove nothin'," and Guy dropped the subject.

Yan did not mean to tell his adventure that night, but his excitement was evident, and they soon got it out of him in full. They were a weird-looking crowd as they sat around the flickering fire, experiencing as he told it no small measure of the scare he had just been through.

When he had finished Yan said, "Now, Guy, don't you want to go and try it?"

"Oh, quit," said Guy; "I never saw such a feller as you for yammering away on the same subjek."

Caleb looked at his watch now, as though about to leave, when Yan said:

"Say, Mr. Clark, won't you sleep here? There's lots o' room in Guy's bed."

"Don't mind if I do, seein' it's late."

XX

The White Revolver

IN the morning Caleb had the satisfaction of eating a breakfast prepared by the son of his enemy, for Sam was cook that day.

The Great Woodpecker expressed the thought of the whole assembly when after breakfast he said: "Now I want to go and see that grave. I believe

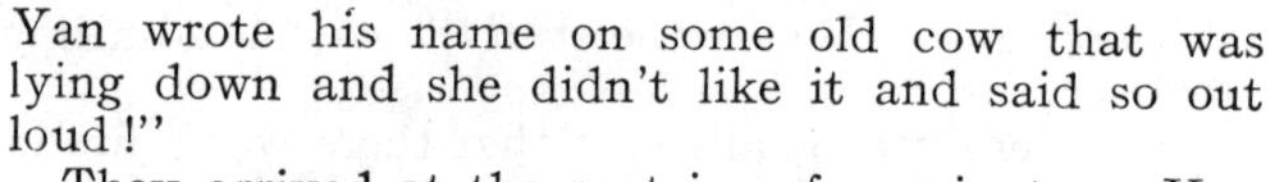

Yan wrote his name on some old cow that was lying down and she didn't like it and said so out loud!"

They arrived at the spot in a few minutes. Yes, there it was plainly written on the rude gravestone, rather shaky, but perfectly legible—"Yan."

"Pretty poor writing," was Guy's remark.

"Well, you sure done it! Good boy!" said Sam warmly. "Don't believe I'd 'a' had the grit."

"Bet I would," said Guy.

"Here's where I crossed the ditch. See my trail in the mud? Out there is where I heard the yelling. Let's see if ghosts make tracks. Hallo, what the——"

There were the tracks in the mud of a big man. He had sprawled, falling on his hands and knees. Here was the print of his hands several times, and in the mud, half hidden, something shining—Guy saw it first and picked it up. It was a white-handled Colt's revolver.

"Let's see that," said Caleb. He wiped off the mud. His eye kindled. "That's my revolver that was stole from me 'way back, time I lost my clothes and money." He looked it over and, glancing about, seemed lost in thought. "This beats me!" He shook his head and muttered from time to time, "This beats me!" There seemed nothing more of interest to see, so the boys turned homeward.

On the way back Caleb was evidently thinking hard. He walked in silence till they got opposite Granny de Neuville's shanty, which was the nearest one to the grave. At the gate he turned and said: "Guess I'm going in here. Say, Yan, you didn't do any of that hollering last night, did you?"

"No, sir; not a word. The only sound I made was dragging the ring-stone over the boulder."

"Well, I'll see you at camp," he said, and turned in to Granny's.

"The tap o' the marnin' to ye, an' may yer sowl rest in pace," was the cheery old woman's greeting. "Come in—come in, Caleb, an' set down. An' how is Saryann an' Dick?"

"They seem happy an' prosperin'," said the old man with bitterness. "Say, Granny, did you ever hear the story about Garney's grave out there on the road?"

"For the love av goodness, an' how is it yer after askin' me that now? Sure an' I heard the story many a time, an' I'm atter hearin' the ghost last night, an' it's a-shiverin' yit Oi am."

"What did you hear, Granny?"

"Och, an' it was the most divilish yells iver let out av a soul in hell. Shure the Dog and the Cat both av thim was scairt, and the owld white-faced cow come a-runnin' an' jumped the bars to get aff av the road."

Here was what Caleb wanted, and he kept her going by his evident interest. After she tired of providing more realistic details of the night's uproar, Caleb deliberately tapped another vintage of tittle-tattle in hope of further information leaking out.

"Granny, did you hear of a robbery last week down this side of Downey's Dump?"

"Shure an' I did not," she exclaimed, her eyes ablaze with interest—neither had Caleb, for that matter; but he wanted to start the subject—"An' who was it was robbed?"

"Don't know, unless it was John Evans's place."

"Shure an' I don't know him, but I warrant he could sthand to lose. Shure an' it's when the raskils come after me an' Cal Conner the moment it was talked around that we had sold our Cow; then sez I, it's gittin' onraisonable, an' them divils shorely seems to know whin a wad o' money passes."

"That's the gospel truth. But when wuz you robbed, Granny?"

"Robbed? I didn't say I wuz robbed," and she cackled. "But the robbers had the best av intintions when they came to me," and she related at length her experience with the two who broke in when her Cow was reported sold. She laughed over their enjoyment of the Lung Balm, and briefly told how the big man was sulky and the short, broad one was funny. Their black beards, the "big wan" with his wounded head, his left-handedness and his accidental exposure of the three fingers of the right hand, all were fully talked over.

"When was it, Granny?"

"Och, shure an' it wuz about three years apast."

Then after having had his lungs treated, old Caleb left Granny and set out to do some very hard thinking.

There had been robberies all around for the last four years. There was no clue but this: They were all of the same character; nothing but cash was taken, and the burglars seemed to have inside knowledge of the neighbourhood, and timed all their visits to happen just after the householder had come into possession of a roll of bills.

As soon as Caleb turned in at the de Neuville

gate, Yan, acting on a belated thought, said:

"Boys, you go on to camp; I'll be after you in five minutes. He wanted to draw those tracks in the mud and try to trail that man, so went back to the grave.

He studied the marks most carefully and by opening out the book he was able to draw the boot tracks life-size, noting that each had three rows of small hobnails on the heel, apparently put in at home because so irregular, while the sole of the left was worn into a hole. Then he studied the hand tracks, selected the clearest, and was drawing the right hand when something odd caught his attention. Yes! It appeared in all the impressions of that hand—the middle finger was gone.

Yan followed the track on the road a little way, but at the corner it turned southward and was lost in the grass.

As he was going back to camp he overtook Caleb also returning.

"Mr. Clark," he said. "I went back to sketch those tracks, and do you know—that man had only three fingers on his right hand?"

"Consarn me!" said Caleb. "Are you sure?"

"Come and see for yourself."

Yes! It surely was true, and Caleb on the road back said, "Yan, don't say a word of this to the others just now."

The old Trapper went to the Pogue house at once. He found the tracks repeated in the dust near the door, but they certainly were not made by Dick. On a line was a pair of muddy trousers drying.

From this night Yan went up and Guy went down in the old man's opinion, for he spoke his own mind that day when he gave first place to grit. He invited Yan to come to his shanty to see a pair of snow-shoes he was making. The invitation was vague and general, so the whole Tribe accepted. Yan had not been there since his first visit. The first part of their call was as before. In answer to their knock there was a loud baying from the Hound, then a voice ordering him back. Caleb opened the door, but now said "Step in." If he was displeased with the others coming he kept it to himself. While Yan was looking at the snow-shoes Guy discovered something much more interesting on the old man's bunk; that was the white revolver, now cleaned up and in perfect order. Caleb's delight at its recovery, though not very apparent, was boundless. He had not been able to buy himself another, and this was as warmly welcomed back as though a long-lost only child.

"Say, Caleb, let's try a shot. I bet I kin beat the hull gang," exclaimed Sapwood.

Caleb got some cartridges and pointed to a white blaze on a stump forty yards away. Guy had three or four shots and Yan had the same without hitting the stump. Then Caleb said, "Lemme show you."

His big rugged. hand seemed to swallow up the little gun-stock. His long knobbed finger fitted around the lock in a strange but familiar way. Caleb was a bent-arm shot, and the short barrel looked like his own forefinger pointing at the target as he pumped away six times in quick succession. All went into the blaze and two into the charcoal spot that marked the centre.

"By George! Look at that for shooting!" and the boys were loud in their praise.

"Well, twenty year ago I used to be a pretty good shot," Caleb proceeded to explain with an air of unnecessary humility and a very genial expression on his face. "But that's dead easy. I'll show you some real tricks."

Twenty-five feet away he set up three cartridges in a row, their caps toward him, and exploded them in succession with three rapid shots. Then he put the revolver in the side pocket of his coat, and recklessly firing it without drawing, much less sighting or even showing it, he peppered a white blaze at twenty yards. Finally he looked around for an old fruit tin. Then he cocked the revolver, laid it across his right hand next the thumb and the tin across the fingers. He then threw them both in the air with a jerk .that sent the revolver up ten feet and the tin twenty. As the revolver came down he seized it and shot a hole through the tin before it could reach the ground.

The boys were simply dumbfounded. They had used up all their exclamations on the first simple target trial.

Caleb stepped into the shanty to get a cleaning-rag for his darling, and Sam burst out:

"Well, now I know he never shot at Da, for if he did he'd 'a' got him sure."

It was not meant for Caleb's ears, but it reached him, and the old Trapper came to the door at once with a long, expressive "H-m-m-mrr."

Thus was broken the dam of silent scorn, for it

was the first time Caleb had addressed himself to Sam. The flood had forced the barrier, but it still left plenty of stuff in the channel to be washed away by time and wear, and it was long before he talked to Sam as freely as to the others, but still in time he learned.

There was an air of geniality on all now, and Yan took advantage of this to ask for something he had long kept in mind.

"Mr. Clark, will you take us out for a Coon hunt? We know where there are lots of Coons that feed in a corn patch up the creek."

If Yan had asked this a month ago he would have got a contemptuous refusal. Before the visit to Garney's grave it might have been, "Oh, I dunno —I ain't got time," but he was on the right side of Caleb now, and the answer was:

"Well, yes! Don't mind if I do, first night it's coolish, so the Dog kin run."

XXI

The Triumph of Guy

THE boys had hunted the Woodchuck quite regularly since first meeting it. Their programme was much the same—each morning about nine or ten they would sneak out to the clover field. It was usually Guy who first discovered the old Grizzly, then all would fire a harmless shot, the Woodchuck would scramble into his den and the incident be closed for the day. This became as much a part of the day's routine as getting breakfast, and much more so than the washing of the dishes. Once or twice the old Grizzly had narrow escapes, but so far he was none the worse, rather the better, being wiser. The boys, on the other hand, gained nothing, with the possible exception of Guy. Always quick-sighted, his little washed-out optics developed a marvellous keenness. At first it was as often Yan or Sam who saw the old Grizzly, but later it was always Guy.

One morning Sam approached the game from one point, Guy and Yan from another some yards away. "No Woodchuck!" was the first opinion, but suddenly Guy called "I see him." There in a little hollow fully sixty yards from his den, and nearly a hundred from the boys, concealed in a bunch of clover, Guy saw a patch of gray fur hardly two inches square. "That's him, sure."

Yan could not see it at all. Sam saw but doubted. An instant later the Woodchuck (for it was he) stood up on his hind legs, raised his chestnut breast above the clover, and settled all doubt.

"By George!" exclaimed Yan in admiration. "*That is great.* You have the most wonderful eyes I ever did see. Your name ought to be 'Hawkeye' —that should be your name."

"All right," shrilled out Guy enthusiastically. "Will you—will you, Sam, will you call me Hawkeye? I think you ought to," he added pleadingly.

"I think so, Sam," said the Second Chief. "He's turned out great stuff, an' it's regular Injun."

"We'll have to call a Council and settle that. Now let's to business."

"Say, Sapwood, you're so smart, couldn't you go round through the woods to your side and crawl through the clover so as get between the old Grizzly and his den?" suggested the Head Chief.

"I bet I can, an' I'll bet a dollar——"

"Here, now," said Yan, "Injuns don't have dollars."

"Well, I'll bet my scalp—my black scalp, I mean—against Sam's that I kill the old Grizzly first."

"Oh, let me do it first—you do it second," said Sam imploringly.

"Errr—yer scared of yer scalp."

"I'll go you," said Sam.

Each of the boys had a piece of black horsehair that he called his scalp. It was tied with a string to the top of his head—and this was what Guy wished to wager.

Yan now interfered: "Quit your squabbling, you Great War Chiefs, an' 'tend to business. If Woodpecker kills old Grizzly he takes Sapwood's scalp; if Sappy kills him he takes the Woodpecker's scalp, an' the winner gets a grand feather, too."

Sam and Yan waited impatiently in the woods while Guy sneaked around. The Woodchuck seemed unusually bold this day. He wandered far from his den and got out of sight in hollows at times. The boys saw Guy crawl through the fence, though the Woodchuck did not. The fact was, that he had always had the enemy approach him from the other side, and was not watching eastward.

Guy, flat on his breast, worked his way through the clover. He crawled about thirty yards and now was between the Woodchuck and his den. Still old Grizzly kept on stuffing himself with clover and watching toward the Raften woods. The boys became intensely excited. Guy could see them, but not the Woodchuck. They pointed and gesticulated. Guy thought that meant "Now shoot." He got up cautiously. The Woodchuck saw him and bounded straight for its den—that is, toward Guy. Guy fired wildly. The arrow went ten feet over the Grizzly's head, and, that "huge, shaking mass of fur" bounding straight at him, struck terror to his soul. He backed up hastily, not knowing where to run. He was close to the den. The Woodchuck chattered his teeth and plunged to get by the boy, each as scared as could be. Guy gave a leap of terror and fell heavily just as the Woodchuck would have passed under him and home. But the boy weighed nearly 100 pounds, and all that weight came with crushing force on old Grizzly, knocking the breath out of his body. Guy scrambled to his feet to run for his life, but he saw the Woodchuck lying squirming, and plucked up courage enough to give him a couple of kicks on the nose that settled him. A loud yell from the other two boys was the first thing that assured Guy of his victory. They came running over and found him standing like the hunter in an amateur photograph, holding his bow in one hand and the big Woodchuck by the tail in the other.

"Now, I guess you fellers will come to me to larn you how to kill Woodchucks. Ain't he an old socker? I bet he weighs fifty pounds—yes, near sixty." [It weighed about ten pounds.]

"Good boy! Bully boy! Hooray for the Third War Chief! Hooray for Chief Sapwood!" and Guy had no cause to complain of lack of appreciation on the part of the others.

He swelled out his chest and looked proud and haughty. "Wished I knew where there was some more Woodchucks," he said. "*I* know how to get them, if the rest don't."

"Well, that should count for a *grand coup*, Sappy."

"You tole me you wuz goin' to call me 'Hawkeye' after this morning."

"We'll have to have a Grand Council to fix that up," replied the Head Chief.

"All right; let's have it this afternoon, will you?"

"All right."

"'Bout four o'clock?"

"Why, yes; any time."

"And you'll fix me up as 'Hawkeye,' and give me a dandy Eagle feather for killing the Woodchuck, at four o'clock?"

"Yes, sure; only, why do you want it at four o'clock?"

But Guy seemed not to hear, and right away after dinner he disappeared.

"He's dodging the dishwashing again," suggested the Woodpecker.

"No, he isn't," said the Second Chief. "I believe he's going to bring his folks to see him in his triumph."

"That's so. Let's chip right in and make it an everlasting old blowout—kind of a new date in history. You'll hear me lie like sixty to help him out."

"Good enough. I'm with you. You go and get your folks. I'll go after old Caleb, and we'll fix it up to call him 'Hawkeye' and give him his *grand coup* feather all at once."

"'Feard my folks and Caleb wouldn't mix," replied Sam, "but I believe for a splurge like this Guy'd ruther have my folks. You see, Da has the mortgage on their place."

So it was agreed Sam was to go for his mother, while Yan was to prepare the Eagle feather and skin the Woodchuck.

It was not "as big as a bear," but it was a very large Woodchuck, and Yan was as much elated over the victory as any of them. He still had an hour or more before four o'clock, and eager to make Guy's triumph as Indian as possible, he cut off all the Woodchuck's claws, then strung them on a string, with a peeled and pithed Elder twig an inch long between each two. Some of the claws were very, very small, but the intention was there to make a Grizzly-claw necklace.

Guy made for home as fast as he could go. His father hailed him as he neared the garden and evidently had plans of servitude, but Guy darted into the dining-room-living-room-bedroom-kitchen-room, which constituted nine-tenths of the house.

"Oh, Maw, you just ought to seen me; you just want to come this afternoon—I'm the Jim Dandy of the hull Tribe, an' they're going to make me Head Chief. I killed that whaling old Woodchuck that pooty nigh killed Paw. They couldn't do a thing without me—them fellers in camp. They tried an' tried more'n a thousand times to get that old Woodchuck—yes, I bet they tried a million times, an' I just waited till they was tired and give up, then I says, 'Now, I'll show you how.' First I had to point him out. Them fellers is no good to see things. Then I says, 'Now, Sam and Yan, you fellers stay here, an' just to show how easy it is when you know how, I'll leave all my bosenarrers behind an' go with nothing.' Wall, there they stood an' watched me, an' I s-n-e-a-k-e-d round the fence an' c-r-a-w-l-e-d in the clover just like an Injun till I got between him an' his hole, and then I hollers and he come a-snortin' an' a-chatterin' his teeth at me to chaw me up, for he seen I had no stick nor nothin', an' I never turned a hair; I kep' cool an' waited till jest as he was going to jump for my throat, then I turned and gave him one kick on the snoot that sent him fifty feet in the air, an' when he come down he was deader'n Kilsey's hen when she was stuffed with onions. Oh, Maw, I'm just the bully boy; they can't do nothin' in camp 'thout me. I had to larn 'em to hunt Deer an' see things—an'—an'—an'—lots o' things, so they are goin' to make me Head Chief of the hull Tribe, an' call me 'Hawkeye,' too; that's the way the Injuns does. It's to be at four o'clock this afternoon, an' you got to come."

Burns scoffed at the whole thing and told Guy to get to work at the potatoes, and if he left down the bars so that the Pig got out he'd skin him alive; he would have no such fooling round his place. But Mrs. Burns calmly informed him that *she* was going. It was to her much like going to see a university degree conferred on her boy.

Since Burns would not assist, the difficulty of the children now arose. This, however, was soon settled. They should go along. It was two hours' toil for the mother to turn the four brown-limbed, nearly naked, dirty, happy towsle-tops into four little martyrs, befrocked, beribboned, becombed and bebooted. Then they all straggled across the field, Mrs. Burns carrying the baby in one arm and a pot of jam in the other. Guy ran ahead to show the way, and four-year-old, three-year-old and two-year-old, hand in hand, formed a diagonal line in the wake of the mother.

They were just a little surprised on getting to camp to find Mrs. Raften and Minnie there in holiday clothes. Marget's first feeling was resentment, but her second thought was a pleasant one. That "stuck-up" woman, the enemy's wife, should see her boy's triumph, and Mrs. Burns at once seized on the chance to play society cat.

"How do ye do, Mrs. Raften; hope you're well," she said with a tinge of malicious pleasure and a grand attempt at assuming the leadership.

"Quite well, thank you. We came down to see how the boys were getting on in camp."

"They've got on very nicely *sense my boy j'ined them*," retorted Mrs. Burns, still fencing.

"So I understand; the other two have become very fond of him," returned Mrs. Raften, seeking to disarm her enemy.

This speech had its effect. Mrs. Burns aimed only to forestall the foe, but finding to her surprise that the enemy's wife was quite gentle, a truce was made, and by the time Mrs. Raften had petted and praised the four tow-tops and lauded Guy to the utmost the air of latent battle was replaced by one of cordiality.

The boys now had everything ready for the grand ceremony. On the Calfskin rug at one end was the Council; Guy, seated on the skin of the Woodchuck and nearly hiding it from view, Sam on his left hand and Yan with the drum, on his right. In the middle the Council fire blazed. To give air, the teepee cover was raised on the shady side and the circle of visitors was partly in the teepee and partly out.

The Great War Chief first lighted the peace pipe, puffed for a minute, then blew off the four smokes to the four winds and handed it to the Second and Third War Chiefs, who did the same.

Little Beaver gave three thumps on the drum for silence, and the Great Woodpecker rose up:

"Big Chiefs, Little Chiefs, Braves, Warriors, Councillors, Squaws, and Papooses of the Sanger Indians: When our Tribe was at war with them—them—them—other Injuns—them Birchbarks, we took prisoner one of their warriors and tortured him to death two or three times, and he showed such unusual stuff that we took him into our Tribe——"

Loud cries of "How—How—How," led by Yan.

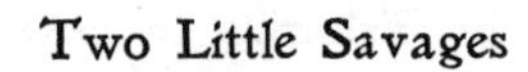

"We gave a sun-dance for his benefit, but he didn't brown—seemed too green—so we called him Sapwood. From that time he has fought his way up from the ranks and got to be Third War Chief——"

"How—How—How."

"The other day the hull Tribe j'ined to attack an' capture a big Grizzly and was licked bad, when the War Chief Sapwood came to the rescue an' settled the owld baste with one kick on the snoot. Deeds like this is touching. A feller that kin kick like that didn't orter be called Sapwood nor Saphead nor Sapanything. No, sirree! It ain't right. He's the littlest Warrior among the War Chiefs, but he kin see farder an' do it oftener an' better than his betters. He kin see round a corner or through a tree. 'Cept maybe at night, he's the swell seer of the outfit, an' the Council has voted to call him 'Hawkeye.'"

"How—How—How—How—How——"

Here Little Beaver handed the Head War Chief a flat white stick on which was written in large letters "Sapwood."

"Here's the name he went by before he was great an' famous, an' this is the last of it." The Chief put the stick in the fire, saying, "Now let us see if you're too green to burn." Little Beaver now handed Woodpecker a fine Eagle feather, red-tufted, and bearing in outline a man with a Hawk's head and an arrow from his eye. "This here's a swagger Eagle feather for the brave deed he done, and tells about him being Hawkeye, too" (the feather was stuck in Guy's hair and the claw necklace put about his neck amid loud cries of "How—How—" and thumps of the drum), "and after this, any feller that calls him Sapwood has to double up and give Hawkeye a free kick."

There was a great chorus of "How—How." Guy tried hard to look dignified and not grin, but it got beyond him. He was smiling right across and half way round. His mother beamed with pride till her eyes got moist and overflowed.

Every one thought the ceremony was over, but Yan stood up and began: "There is something that has been forgotten, Chiefs, Squaws and Pappooses of the Sanger Nation: When we went out after this Grizzly I was witness to a bargain between two of the War Chiefs. According to a custom of our Tribe, they bet their scalps, each that he would be the one to kill the Grizzly. The Head Chief Woodpecker was one and Hawkeye was the other.

Hawkeye, you can help yourself to Woodpecker's scalp."

Sam had forgotten about this, but he bowed his head. Guy cut the string, and holding up the scalp, he uttered a loud, horrible war-whoop in which every one helped with some sort of noise. It was the crowning event. Mrs. Burns actually wept for joy to see her heroic boy properly recognized at last.

Then she went over to Sam and said, "Did you bring your folks here to see my boy get praised?"

Sam nodded and twinkled an eye.

"Well, I don't care who ye are, Raften or no Raften, you got a good heart, an' it's in the right place. I never did hold with them as says 'There ain't no good in a Raften.' I always hold there's some good in every human. I know your Paw *did* buy the mortgage on our place, but I never did believe your Maw stole our Geese, *an' I never will*, an' next time I hear them runnin' on the Raftens I'll jest open out an' tell what I know."

The picture on the Teepee Lining, to record Guys Exploit.

XXII

The Coon Hunt

YAN did not forget the proposed Coon hunt—in fact, he was most impatient for it, and within two days the boys came to Caleb about sundown and reminded him of his promise. It was a sultry night, but Yan was sure it was just right for a Coon hunt, and his enthusiasm carried all before it. Caleb was quietly amused at the "*cool night*" selected, but reckoned it would be "better later."

"Set down—set down, boys," he said, seeing them standing ready for an immediate start. "There's no hurry. Coons won't be running for three or four hours after sundown."

So he sat and smoked, while Sam vainly tried to get acquainted with old Turk; Yan made notes on some bird wings nailed to the wall, and Guy got out the latest improved edition of his exploits in Deer-hunting and Woodchuck killing, as well as enlarged on his plans for gloriously routing any Coon they might encounter.

By insisting that it would take an hour to get to the place, Yan got them started at nine o'clock, Caleb, on a suggestion from Guy, carrying a small axe. Keeping old Turk well in hand, they took the highway, and for half an hour tramped on toward the "Corners." Led by Sam, they climbed a fence, crossed a potato field, and reached the corn patch by the stream.

"Go ahead, Turk. Sic him! Sic him! Sic him!" and the company sat in a row on the fence to await developments.

Turk was somewhat of a character. He hunted what he pleased and when he pleased. His master could bring him on the Coon grounds, but he couldn't make him hunt Coon nor anything else unless it suited his own fancy. Caleb had warned the boys to be still, and they sat along the fence in dead silence, awaiting the summons from the old Hound. He had gone off beating and sniffing among the cornstalks. His steps sounded very loud and his sniffs like puffs of steam. It was a time of tense attention; but the Hound wandered farther away, and even his noisy steps were lost.

They had sat for two long minutes, when a low yelp from a distant part of the field, then a loud "*bow-wow*" from the Hound, set Yan's heart jumping.

"Game afoot," said Sam in a low voice.

"Bet I heered him first," piped Guy.

Yan's first thought was to rush pell-mell after the Dog. He had often read of the hunt following furiously the baying of the Hounds, but Caleb restrained him.

"Hold on, boy; plenty of time. Don't know yet what it is."

For Turk, like most frontier Hounds, would run almost any trail—had even been accused of running on his own—and it rested with those who knew him best to discover from his peculiar style of tonguing just what the game might be. But they waited long and patiently without getting another bay from the Hound. Presently a rustling was heard and Turk came up to his master and lay down at his feet.

"Go ahead, Turk; put him up," but the Dog stirred not. "Go ahead," and Caleb gave him a rap with a small stick. The Dog dodged away, but lay down again, panting.

"What was it, Mr. Clark?" demanded Yan.

"Don't hardly know. Maybe he only spiked himself on a snag. But this is sure; there's no Coons here to-night. There won't be after this. We come too early, and it's too hot for the Dog, anyway."

"We could cross the creek and go into Boyle's bush," suggested the Woodpecker. "We're like to strike anything there. Larry de Neuville swears he saw a Unicorn there the night he came back from Garney's wake."

"How can you tell the kind of game by the Dog's barking?" asked Yan.

"H-m!" answered Caleb, as he put a fresh quid in his lantern jaw. "You surely can if you know the country an' the game an' the Dog. Course, no two Dogs is alike; you got to study your Dog, an' if he's good he'll larn you lots about trailing."

The brook was nearly dry now, so they crossed where they would. Then feeling their way through the dark woods with eyes for the most part closed, they groped toward Boyle's open field, then across it to the heavy timber. Turk had left them at the brook, and, following its course till he came to a pool, had had a bath. As they entered the timber tract he joined them, dripping wet and ready for business.

"Go ahead, Turk," and again all sat down to await the opinion of the expert.

It came quickly. The old Hound, after circling about in a way that seemed to prove him independent of daylight, began to sniff loudly, and gave a low whine. He followed a little farther, and now his tail was heard to '*tap*, *tap*, *tap*' the brush as he went through a dry thicket.

"Hear that? He's got something this time," said Caleb in a low voice. "Wait a little."

The Hound was already working out a puzzle, and when at last he got far enough to be sure, he gave a short bark. There was another spell of sniffing, then another bark, then several little barks at intervals, and at last a short bay; then the baying recommenced, but was irregular and not full-chested. The sounds told that the Hound was running in a circle about the forest, but at length ceased moving, for all the barking was at one place. When the hunters got there they found the Dog half-way in a hole under a stump, barking and scratching.

"Humph," said Caleb; "nothing but a Cotton-tail. Might 'a' knowed that by the light scent an' the circling without treeing."

So Turk was called off and the company groped through the inky woods in quest of more adventures.

"There's a kind of swampy pond down the lower end of the bush—a likely place for Coons on a Frog-hunt," suggested the Woodpecker.

So the Hound was again "turned on" near the pond. The dry woods were poor for scent, but the damp margin of the marsh proved good, and Turk became keenly interested and very sniffy. A preliminary "*Woof!*" was followed by one or two yelps and then a full-chested "*Boooow!*" that left no doubt he had struck a hot trail at last. Oh, what wonderfully thrilling horn-blasts those were! Yan for the first time realized the power of the "full cry," whose praises are so often sung.

The hunters sat down to await the result, for, as Caleb pointed out, there was "no saying where the critter might run."

The Hound bayed his fullest, roundest notes at quick intervals, but did not circle. The sound of his voice told them that the chase was straight away, out of the woods, easterly across an open field, and at a hot pace, with regular, full bellowing, unbroken by turn or doubt.

"I believe he's after the old Callaghan Fox," said the Trapper. "They've tried it together before now, an' there ain't anything but a Fox will run so straight and fetch such a tune out of Turk."

The baying finally was lost in the distance, probably a mile away, but there was nothing for it but to wait. If Turk had been a full-bred and trained Foxhound he would have stuck to that trail all night, but in half an hour he returned, puffing and hot, to throw himself into the shallow pond.

"Everything scared away now," remarked Caleb. "We might try the other side of the pond." Once or twice the dog became interested, but decided that there was nothing in it, and returned to pant by his master's feet."

They had now travelled so far toward home that a very short cut across fields would bring them into their own woods.

The moon arose as they got there, and after their long groping in the murky darkness this made the night seem very bright and clear.

They had crossed the brook below Granny de Neuville's, and were following the old timber trail that went near the stream, when Turk stopped to sniff, ran back and forth two or three times, then stirred the echoes with a full-toned bugle blast and led toward the water.

"*Bow—bow—bow—bow*," he bawled for forty yards and came to a stop. The baying was exactly the same that he gave on the Fox trail, but the course of the animal was crooked, and now there was a break.

They could hear the dog beating about close at hand and far away, but silent so far as tongue was concerned.

"What is it, Caleb?" said Sam with calm assurance, forgetting how recent was their acquaintance.

"Dunno," was the short reply.

"'Tisn't a Fox, is it?" asked Yan.

But a sudden renewal of "*Bow—bow—bow—*" from the Hound one hundred yards away, at the fence, ended all discussion. The dog had the hot trail again. The break had been along the line of a fence that showed, as Caleb said, "It was a Coon, 'cept it might be some old house Cat maybe; them was the only things that would run along top of a fence in the night time."

It was easy to follow now; the moonlight was good, and the baying of the Hound was loud and regular. It led right down the creek, crossing several pools and swamps.

"That settles it," remarked the Trapper decisively. "Cats don't take to the water. That's a Coon," and as they hurried they heard a sudden change in the dog's note, no longer a deep rich '*B-o-o-w-w.*' It became an outrageous clamour of mingled yelps, growls and barks.

"Ha—heh. That means he's right on it. That is what he does when he *sees* the critter."

But the "view halloo" was quickly dropped and the tonguing of the dog was now in short, high-pitched yelps *at one place*.

"Jest so! He's treed! That's a Coon, all right!"

and Caleb led straight for the place.

The Hound was barking and leaping against a big Basswood, and Caleb's comment was: "Hm, never knowed a Coon to do any other way—always gets up the highest and tarnalest tree to climb in the hull bush. Now who's the best climber here?"

"Yan is," volunteered Sam.

"Kin ye do it, Yan?"

"I'll try."

"Guess we'll make a fire first and see if we can't see him," said the Woodpecker.

"If it was a Woodchuck I'd soon get him for you," chimed in Hawkeye, but no one heeded.

Sam and Yan gathered stuff and soon had a flood of flickering red light on all the surrounding trees. They scanned the big Basswood without getting sight of their quarry. Caleb took a torch and found on the bark some fresh mud. By going back on the trail to where it had crossed the brook they found the footprint—undoubtedly that of a large Coon.

"Reckon he's in some hollow; he's surely up that tree, and Basswood's are always hollow."

Yan now looked at the large trunk in doubt as to whether he could manage it.

Caleb remarked his perplexity and said: "Yes; that's so. You ain't fifteen foot spread across the wings, are you? But hold on——"

He walked to a tall thin tree near at hand, cut it through with the axe in a few minutes, and threw it so as to rest against the lowest branch of the big Basswood. Up this Yan easily swarmed, carrying a stout Elm stick tied behind. When he got to the great Basswood he felt lost in the green mass, but the boys below carried torches so as to shed light on each part in turn. At first Yan found neither hole in the trunk nor Coon, but after long search in the upper branches he saw a great ball of fur on a high crotch and in it two glowing eyes that gave him a thrill. He yelled: "Here he is! Look out below." He climbed up nearer and tried to push the Coon off, but it braced itself firmly and defied him until he climbed above it, when it leaped and scrambled to a lower branch.

Yan followed it, while his companions below got greatly excited, as they could see nothing, and only judged by the growling and snarling that Yan and the Coon were fighting. After another passage at arms the Coon left the second crotch and scrambled down the trunk till it reached the leaning sapling, and there perched, glaring at the hunters below. The old Hound raised a howl when he saw the quarry, and Caleb, stepping to one side, drew his revolver and fired. The Coon fell dead into their midst. Turk sprang to do battle, but he was not needed, and Caleb fondly and proudly wiped the old white pistol as though it alone were to be thanked for the clever shot.

Yan came down quickly, though he found it harder to get down than up. He hurried excitedly into the ring and stroked the Coon with a mixture of feelings—admiring its fur—sorry, after all, that it was killed, and triumphant that he had led the way. *It was his Coon*, and all admitted that. Sam "hefted" it by one leg and said, "Weighs thirty pounds, I bet."

Guy said: "Pooh! 'Tain't half as big as that there big Woodchuck I killed, an' you never would have got him if I hadn't thought of the axe."

Yan thought it would weigh thirty-five pounds. Caleb guessed it at twenty-five (and afterward they found out that it barely weighed eighteen). While they were thus talking the Dog broke into an angry barking such as he gave for strangers—his "human voice," Caleb called it—and at once there stepped into the circle William Raften. He had seen the lights in the woods, and, dreading a fire at this dry season, had dressed and come out.

"Hello, Da; why ain't you in bed, where you ought to be?"

Raften took no notice of his son, but said sneeringly to Caleb: "Ye ain't out trying to get another shot at me, air ye?" 'Tain't worth your while; I hain't got no cash on me to-night."

"Now see here, Da," said Sam, interrupting before Caleb could answer, "you don't play fair. I know, an' you ought to know, that's all rot about Caleb shooting at you. If he had, he'd 'a' got you sure. I've seen him shoot."

"Not when he was drunk."

"Last time I was drunk we was in it together," said Caleb fiercely, finding his voice.

"Purty good for a man as swore he had no revolver," and Raften pointed to Caleb's weapon. "I seen you with that ten years ago. An' sure I'm not scairt of you an' yer revolver," said Raften, seeing Caleb fingering his white pet; "an' I tell ye this. I won't have ye and yer Sheep-killing cur ramatacking

through my woods an' making fires this dry saison."

"D—— you, Raften, I've stood all I'm goin' to stand from you." The revolver was out in a flash, and doubtless Caleb would have lived up to his reputation, but Sam, springing to push his father back, came between, and Yan clung to Caleb's revolver arm, while Guy got safely behind a tree.

"Get out o' the way, you kids!" snarled Caleb.

"By all manes," said Raften scoffingly; "now that he's got me unarrumed again. You dhirty coward! Get out av the way, bhoys, an Oi'll settle him," for Raften was incapable of fear, and the boys would have been thrust aside and trouble follow, but that Raften as he left the house had called his two hired men to follow and help fight the fire, and now they came on the scene. One of them was quite friendly with Caleb, the other neutral, and they succeeded in stopping hostilities for a time, while Sam exploded:

"Now see here, Da, 'twould just 'a' served you right if you'd got a hole through you. You make me sick, running on Caleb. He didn't make that fire; 'twas me an' Yan, an' we'll put it out safe enough. You skinned Caleb an' he never done you no harm. You run on him just as Granny de Neuville done on you after she grabbed your groceries. You ought to be ashamed of yourself. 'Tain't square, an' 'tain't being a man. When you can't prove nothin' you ought to shut up."

Raften was somewhat taken aback by this outburst, especially as he found all the company against him. He had often laughed at Granny de Neuville's active hatred against him when he had done her nothing but good. It never occurred to him that he was acting a similar part. Most men would have been furious at the disrespectful manner of their son, but Raften was as insensitive as he was uncowardly. His first shock of astonishment over, his only thought of Sam was, "Hain't he got a cheek! My! but he talks like a lawyer, an' he sasses right back like a fightin' man; belave I'll make him study law instid of tooth-pullin'."

The storm was over, for Caleb's wrath was of the short and fierce kind, and Raften, turning away in moral defeat, growled: "See that ye put that fire out safe. Ye ought all to be in yer beds an' aslape, like dacint folks."

"Well, ain't you dacint?" retorted Sam.

Raften turned away, heeding neither that nor

Guy's shrill attempt to interpolate some details of his own importance in this present hunt—"Ef it hadn't been for me they wouldn't had no axe along, Mr. Raften"—but William had disappeared.

The boys put out the fire carefully and made somewhat silently for camp. Sam and Yan carried the Coon between them on a stick, and before they reached the teepee they agreed that the carcass weighed at least eighty pounds.

Caleb left them, and they all turned in at once and slept the sleep of the tired camper.

XXIII

The Banshee's Wail and the Huge Night Prowler

NEXT day while working on the Coon-skin Sam and Yan discussed thoroughly the unpleasant incident of the night before, but they decided that it would be unwise to speak of it to Caleb unless he should bring up the subject, and Guy was duly cautioned.

That morning Yan went to the mud albums on one of his regular rounds and again found, first that curious hoof-mark that had puzzled him before, and down by the pond album the track of a very large bird—much like a Turkey track, indeed. He brought Caleb to see them. The Trapper said that one was probably the track of a Blue Crane (Heron), and the other, "Well, I don't hardly know; but it looks to me mighty like the track of a big Buck—only there ain't any short of the Long Swamp, and that's ten miles at least. Of course, *when there's only one it ain't a track;* it's an accident."

"Yes; but I've found lots of them—a trail every time, but not quite enough to follow.

That night after dark, when he was coming to

camp with the product of a "massacree," Yan heard a peculiar squawking, guttural sound that rose from the edge of the pond and increased in strength, drawing nearer, till it was a hideous and terrifying uproar. It was exactly the sound that Guy had provoked on that first night when he came and tried to frighten the camp. It passed overhead, and Yan saw for a moment the form of a large slow-flying bird.

Next day it was Yan's turn to cook. At sunrise, as he went for water, he saw a large Blue Heron rise from the edge of the pond and fly on heavy pinions away over the tree-tops. It was a thrilling sight. The boy stood gazing after it, absolutely rapt with delight, and when it was gone he went to the place where it rose and found plenty of large tracks just like the one he had sketched. Unquestionably it was the same bird as on the night before, and the mystery of the Wolf with the sore throat was solved. This explanation seemed quite satisfactory to everybody but Guy. He had always maintained stoutly that the woods were full of Bears right after sundown. Where they went at other times was a mystery, but he "reckoned he hadn't yet run across the bird that could scare him—no, nor the beast, nuther."

Caleb agreed that the grating cry must be that of the Blue Crane, but the screech and wail in the tree-tops at night he could shed no light on.

There were many other voices of the night that became more or less familiar. Some of them were evidently birds; one was the familiar Song-Sparrow, and high over the tree-tops from the gloaming sky they often heard a prolonged sweet song. It was not till years afterward that Yan found out this to be the night-song of the Oven-bird, but he was able to tell them at once the cause of the startling outcry that happened one evening an hour after sundown.

The Woodpecker was outside, the other two inside the teepee. A peculiar sound fell on his ear. It kept on—a succession of long whines, and getting stronger. As it gave no sign of ending, Sam called the other boys. They stood in a row there and heard this peculiar "*whine*, *whine*, *whine*" develop into a loud, harsh "*whow*, *whow*, *whow*."

"It must be some new Heron cry," Yan whispered.

But the sound kept on increasing till it most resembled the yowling of a very strong-voiced Cat, and still grew till each separate "*meow*" might have been the yell of a Panther. Then at its highest

and loudest there was a prolonged "*meow*" and silence, followed finally by the sweet chant of the Song-sparrow.

A great light dawned on Little Beaver. Now he remembered that voice in Glenyan so long ago, and told the others with an air of certainty:

"Boys, that's the yelling of a Lynx," and the next day Caleb said that Yan was right.

Some days later they learned that another lamb had been taken from the Raften flock that night.

In the morning Yan took down the tom-tom for a little music and found it flat and soft.

"Hallo," said he; "going to rain."

Caleb looked up at him with an amused expression. "You're a reg'lar Injun. It's surely an Injun trick that. When the tom-tom won't sing without being warmed at the fire they allus says 'rain before night.'"

The Trapper stayed late that evening. It had been cloudy all the afternoon, and at sundown it began to rain, so he was invited to supper. The shower grew heavier instead of ending. Caleb went out and dug a trench all round the teepee to catch the rain, then a leader to take it away. After supper they sat around the campfire in the teepee; the wind arose and the rain beat down. Yan had to go out and swing the smoke poles, and again his ear was greeted with *the screech*. He brought in an armful of wood and made the inside of the teepee a blaze of cheerful light. A high wind now came in gusts, so that the canvas flopped unpleasantly on the poles.

"Where's your anchor rope?" asked the Trapper.

Sam produced the loose end; the other was fastened properly to the poles above. It had never been used, for so far the weather had been fine; but now Caleb sunk a heavy stake, lashed the anchor rope to that, then went out and drove all the pegs a little deeper, and the Tribe felt safe from any ordinary storm.

There was nothing to attract the old Trapper to his own shanty. His heirs had begun to forget that he needed food, and what little they did send was of vilest quality. The old man was as fond of human society as any one, and was easily persuaded now to stay all night, "if you can stand Guy for a bed-feller." So Caleb and Turk settled down for a comfortable evening within, while the storm raged without.

"Say, don't you touch that canvas, Guy; you'll make it leak."

"What, me? Oh, pshaw! How can it leak for a little thing like that?" and Guy slapped it again in bravado.

"All right; it's on your side of the bed," and sure enough, within two minutes a little stream of water was trickling from the place he had rubbed, while elsewhere the canvas turned every drop.

This is well known to all who have camped under canvas during a storm, and is more easily remembered than explained.

The smoke hung heavy in the top of the teepee and kept crowding down until it became unpleasant.

"Lift the teepee cover on the windward side, Yan. There, that's it—but hold on," as a great gust came in, driving the smoke and ashes around in whirlwinds. "You had ought to have a lining. Give me that canvas: that'll do." Taking great care not to touch the teepee cover, Caleb fastened the lining across three pole spaces so that the opening under the canvas was behind it. This turned the draught from their backs and, sending it over their heads, quickly cleared the teepee of smoke as well as kept off what little rain entered by the smoke hole.

"It's on them linings the Injuns paint their records and adventures. They mostly puts their totems on the outside an' their records on the lining."

"Bully," said Sam; "now there's a job for you, Little Beaver; by the time you get our adventures on the inside and our totems on the out I tell you we'll be living in splendour."

"I think," answered Yan indirectly, "we ought to take Mr. Clark into the Tribe. Will you be our Medicine Man?" Caleb chuckled in a quiet way, apparently consenting. "Now I have four totems to paint on the outside," and this was the beginning of the teepee painting that Yan carried out with yellow clay, blue clay dried to a white, yellow clay burned to red, and charcoal, all ground in Coon grease and Pine gum, to be properly Indian. He could easily have gotten bright colours in oil paint, but scorned such White-man's truck, and doubtless the general effect was all the better for it.

"Say, Caleb," piped Guy, "tell us about the Injuns—about their bravery. Bravery is what *I* like," he added with emphasis, conscious of being now on his own special ground. "Why, I mind the time that old Woodchuck was coming roaring at me—I bet some fellers would just 'a' been so scared——"

"*Hssh!*" said Sam.

The Banshee's Wail and the Huge Night Prowler

Caleb smoked in silence. The rain pattered on the teepee without; the wind heaved the cover. They all sat silently. Then sounded loud and clear a terrifying "*scrrrrrr—oouwurr*." The boys were startled—would have been terrified had they been outside or alone.

"That's it—that's the Banshee," whispered Sam.

Caleb looked up sharply.

"What is it?" queried Yan. "We've heard it a dozen times, at least."

Caleb shook his head, made no reply, but turned to his Dog. Turk was lying on his side by the fire, and at this piercing screech he had merely lifted his head, looked backward over his shoulder, turned his big sad eyes on his master, then laid down again.

"Turk don't take no stock in it."

"Dogs never hear a Banshee," objected Sam, "no more than they can see a ghost; anyway, that's what Granny de Neuville says." So the Dog's negative testimony was the reverse of comforting.

"Hawkeye," said the Woodpecker, "you're the bravest one of the crowd. Don't you want to go out and try a shot at the Banshee? I'll lend you my Witch-hazel arrow. We'll give you a *grand coup* feather if you hit him. Go ahead, now—you know bravery is what *you* like."

"Yer nothin' but a passel o' blame dumb fools," was the answer, "an' I wouldn't be bothered talking to ye. Caleb, tell us something about the Indians."

"What the Injuns love is bravery," said the Medicine Man with a twinkle in his eye, and everybody but Guy laughed, not very loudly, for each was restrained by the thought that *he* would rather not be called upon to show his bravery to-night.

"I'm going to bed," said Hawkeye with unnecessary energy.

"Don't forget to roost under the waterspout you started when you got funny," remarked the Woodpecker.

Yan soon followed Guy's example, and Sam, who had already learned to smoke, sat up with Caleb. Not a word passed between them until after Guy's snore and Yan's regular puffs told of sound sleep, when Sam, taking advantage of a long-awaited chance, opened out rather abruptly:

"Say, Caleb, I ain't going to side with no man against Da, but I know him just about as well as he knows me. Da's all right; he's plumb and square, and way down deep he's got an awful kind heart;

it's pretty deep, grant you, but it's there, O. K. The things he does on the quiet to help folks is done on the quiet and ain't noticed. The things he does to beat folks—an' he does do plenty—is talked all over creation. But I know he has a wrong notion of you, just as you have of him, and it's got to be set right."

Sam's good sense was always evident, and now, when he laid aside his buffoonery, his voice and manner were very impressive—more like those of a grown man than of a fifteen-year-old boy.

Caleb simply grunted and went on smoking, so Sam continued, "I want to hear your story, then Ma an' me'll soon fix Da."

The mention of "Ma" was a happy stroke. Caleb had known her from youth as a kind-hearted girl. She was all gentleness and obedience to her husband except in matters of what she considered right and wrong, and here she was immovable. She had always believed in Caleb, even after the row, and had not hesitated to make known her belief.

"There ain't much to tell," replied Caleb bitterly. "He done me on that Horse-trade, an' crowded me on my note so I had to pay it off with oats at sixty cents, then he turned round and sold them within half an hour for seventy-five cents. We had words right there, an' I believe I did say I'd fix him for it. I left Downey's Dump early that day. He had about $300 in his pocket—$300 of my money—the last I had in the world. He was too late to bank it, so was taking it home, when he was fired at in going through the "green bush." My tobacco pouch and some letters addressed to me was found there in the morning. Course he blamed me, but I didn't have any shootin'-iron then; my revolver, the white one, was stole from me a week before—along with them same letters, I expect. I consider they was put there to lay the blame on me, an' it was a little overdone, most folks would think. Well, then your Da set Dick Pogue on me, an' I lost my farm—that's all."

Sam smoked gravely for awhile, then continued:

"That's true about the note an' the oats an' the Horse-trade—just what Da would do; that's all in the game: but you're all wrong about Dick Pogue—that's too dirty for Da."

"*You* may think so, but *I don't*."

Sam made no answer, but after a minute laid his hand on Turk, who responded with a low growl. This made Caleb continue: "Down on me, down on my Dog. Pogue says he kills Sheep 'an' every one is ready to believe it. I never knowed a Hound turn Sheep-killer, an' I never knowed a Sheep-killer kill at home, an' I never knowed a Sheep-killer content with one each night, an' I never knowed a Sheep-killer leave no tracks, an' Sheep was killed again and again when Turk was locked up in the shanty with me."

"Well, whose Dog is it does it?"

"I don't know as it's any Dog, for part of the Sheep was eat each time, they say, though I never seen one o' them that was killed or I could tell. It's more likely a Fox or a Lynx than a Dog."

There was a long silence, then outside again the hair-lifting screech to which the Dog paid no heed, although the Trapper and the boy were evidently startled and scared.

They made up a blazing fire and turned in silently for the night.

The rain came down steadily, and the wind swept by in gusts. It was the Banshee's hour, and two or three times, as they were dropping off, that fearful, quavering human wail, "like a woman in distress," came from the woods to set their hearts a-jumping, not Caleb and Sam only, but all four.

In the diary which Yan kept of those times each day was named after its event; there was Deer day, Skunk-and-Cat day, Blue Crane day, and this was noted down as the night of the Banshee's wailing.

Caleb was up and had breakfast ready before the others were fully awake. They had carefully kept and cleaned the Coon meat, and Caleb made of it a "prairie pie," in which bacon, potatoes, bread, one small onion and various scraps of food were made important. This, warmed up for breakfast and washed down with coffee, made a royal meal, and feasting they forgot the fears of the night.

The rain was over, but the wind kept on. Great blockish clouds were tumbling across the upper sky. Yan went out to look for tracks. He found none but those of raindrops.

The day was spent chiefly about camp, making arrows and painting the teepee.

Again Caleb was satisfied to sleep in the camp. The Banshee called once that night, and again Turk seemed not to hear, but half an hour later there was a different and much lower sound outside, a light, nasal "*wow.*" The boys scarcely heard it, but Turk sprang up with bristling hair, growling, and forcing his way out under the door, he ran, loudly barking, into the woods.

"He's after something now, all right," said his master; "and now he's treed it," as the Dog began his high-pitched yelps.

"Good old Dog; he's treed the Banshee," and Yan rushed out into the darkness. The others followed, and they found Turk barking and scratching at a big leaning Beech, but could get no hint of what the creature up it might be like.

"How does he usually bark for a Banshee?" asked the Woodpecker, but got no satisfaction, and wondering why Turk should bother himself so mightily over a little squeal and never hear that awful scream, they retired to camp.

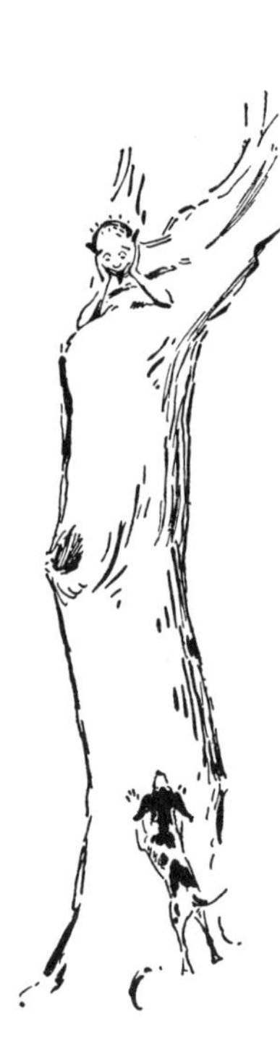

Next morning in the mud not far from the teepee Yan found the track of a common Cat, and shrewdly guessed that this was the prowler that had been heard and treed by the Dog; probably it was his old friend of the Skunk fight. The wind was still high, and as Yan pored over the tracks he heard for the first time in broad daylight the appalling screech. It certainly was *loud*, though less dreadful than at night, and peering up Yan saw *two large limbs that crossed and rubbed each other, when the right puff of wind came.* This was the Banshee that did the wailing that had scared them all—*all but the Dog.* His keener senses, unspoiled by superstition, had rightly judged the awful sound as the harmless scraping of two limbs in the high wind, but the lower, softer noise made by the prowling Cat he had just as truly placed and keenly followed up.

Guy was the only one not convinced. He clung to his theory of Bears.

Late in the night the two Chiefs were awakened by Guy. "Say, Sam—Sam, Yan—Yan—Yan—Yan, get up; that big Bear is 'round again. I told you there was a Bear, an' you wouldn't believe me."

There was a loud champing sound outside, and occasionally growls or grumbling.

"There's surely something there, Sam. I wish Turk and Caleb were here now."

The boys opened the door a little and peered out. There, looming up in the dim starlight, was a huge black animal, picking up scraps of meat and digging up the tins that were buried in the garbage hole. All doubts were dispelled. Guy had another triumph, and he would have expressed his feelings to the full but for fear of the monster outside.

"What had we better do?"

"Better not shoot him with arrows. That'll only rile him. Guy, you blow up the coals and get a blaze.

All was intense excitement now. "Oh, why haven't we got a gun!"

"Say, Sam, while Sap—I mean Hawkeye—makes a blaze, let's you and me shoot with blunt arrows, if the Bear comes toward the teepee." So they arranged themselves, Guy puttering in terror at the fire and begging them not to shoot.

"What's the good o' riling him? It—it—it's croo-oo-el."

Sam and Yan stood with bows ready and arrows nocked.

Guy was making a failure of the fire, and the Bear began nosing nearer, champing his teeth and grunting. Now the boys could see the great ears as the monster threw up its head.

"Let's shoot before he gets any nearer." At this Guy promptly abandoned further attempts to make a fire and scrambled up on a cross-stick that was high in the teepee for hanging the pot. He broke out into tears when he saw Sam and Yan actually drawing their bows.

"He'll come in and eat us, he will."

But the Bear was coming anyway, and having the two tomahawks ready, the boys let fly. At once the Bear wheeled and ran off, uttering the loud, unmistakable squeal of an old Pig—Burns's own Pig—for young Burns had again forgotten to put up the bars that crossed his trail from the homestead to the camp.

Guy came down quickly to join in the laugh. "I tole you fellers not to shoot. I just believed it was our old Hog, an' I couldn't help crying when I thought how mad Paw'd be when he found out."

"I s'pose you got up on that cross pole to see if Paw was coming, didn't you?"

"No; he got up there to show how brave he was."

This was the huge night prowler that Guy had seen, and in the morning one more mystery was explained, for careful examination of Yan's diary of the big Buck's track showed that it was nothing more than the track of Burns's old Hog. Why had Caleb and Raften both been mistaken? First, because it was a long time since they had seen a Buck track, and second, because this Pig happened to have a very unpiggy foot—one as much like that of a Buck as of a Hog.

XXIV

Hawkeye Claims Another Grand Coup

"*WA wa wa wa wa! Wa wa wa wa wa! Wa wa wa wa wa!*" Three times it echoed through the woods—a loud, triumphant cry.

"That's Hawkeye with a big story of bravery; let's hide."

So Sam and Yan scrambled quickly into the teepee, hid behind the lining and watched through an "arrow hole." Guy came proudly stepping, chin in air, uttering his war-whoop at intervals as he drew near, and carrying his coat bundled up under one arm.

"*Coup! Grand coup! Wa wa wa wa!*" he yelled again and again, but looked simple and foolish when he found the camp apparently deserted.

So he ceased his yells and, walking deliberately into the teepee, pulled out the sugar box and was stuffing a handful into his mouth when the other two Chiefs let off their wildest howls and, leaping from their concealment, chased him into the woods—not far, for Yan laughed too much, and Sam had on but one boot.

This was their re-gathering after a new search for adventures. Early in the morning, as he wiped off the breakfast knives by sticking them into the sod, the Second War Chief had suggested: "Say, boys, in old days Warriors would sometimes set out in different directions in search of adventure, then agree to meet at a given time. Let's do that to-day and see what we run across."

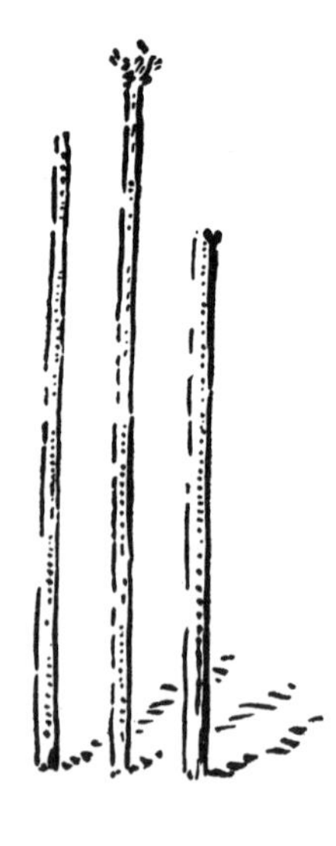

"Get your straws," was Woodpecker's reply, as he returned from putting the scraps on the Wakan Rock.

"No you don't," put in Hawkeye hastily; "at least, not unless you let me hold the straws. I know you'll fix it so I'll have to go home."

"All right. You can hold the three straws; long one is Woodpecker—that's his head with a bit of red flannel to prevent mistakes; the middle-sized thin one is me; and the short fat one is you. Now let them drop. Sudden death and no try over."

The straws fell, and the two boys gave a yell as Hawkeye's fate pointed straight to the Burns homestead.

"Oh, get out; that's no good. We'll take the other end," he said angrily, and persisted in going the opposite way.

"Now we all got to go straight till we find something, and meet here again when that streak of sunlight gets around in the teepee to that pole."

As the sunstreak, which was their Indian clock, travelled just about one pole for two hours, this gave about four hours for adventures.

Sam and Yan had been back some minutes, and now Guy, having recovered his composure, bothered not to wipe the stolen sugar from his lips, but broke out eagerly:

"Say, fellers, I bet I'm the bully boy. I bet you I——"

"Silence!" roared Woodpecker. "You come last."

"All right; I don't care. I bet I win over all of you. I bet a million dollars I do."

"Go ahead, Chief Woodpecker-settin'-on-the-edge."

So Sam began:

"I pulls on my boots" [he went barefooted half the time]. "Oh, I tell you I know when to wear my boots—an' I set out following my straw line straight out. I don't take no back track. *I'm* not scared of the front trail," and he turned his little slit eyes sadly on Guy, "and I kep' right on, and when I came to the dry bed of the creek it didn't turn *me*; no, not a dozen rods; and I kept right till I came to a Wasp's nest, and I turned and went round that coz it's cruel to go blundering into a nest of a lot of poor innocent little Wasps—and I kep' on, till I heard a low growl, and I looked up and didn't see a thing. Then the growling got louder, and I seen it was a hungry Chipmunk roaring at me and jest getting ready to spring. Then when I got out my bonearrer he says to me, he says, as bold as brass: 'Is your name Woodpecker?' Now that scared me, and so I told a lie—my very first. I says, says I: 'No,' says I. 'I'm Hawkeye.' Well, you should 'a' seen him. He just turned pale; every stripe on his back faded *when I said that name*, and he made for a hollow log and got in. Now I was mad, and tried to get him out, but when I'd run to one end he'd run to the other, so we ran up and down till I had a deep-worn trail alongside the log, an' he had a deep-worn trail inside the log, an' I was figgerin' to have him wear it right through at the bottom so the log'd open, but all of a sudden I says, 'I know what to do for you.' I took off my boot and stuffs the leg into one end of the log. Then I rattles a stick at the other end and I heard him run into the boot. Then I squeezes in the leg and ties a string around it an' brings him home, me wearing one boot and the Chipmunk the other, and there he is in it now," and Sam curled up his free bunch of

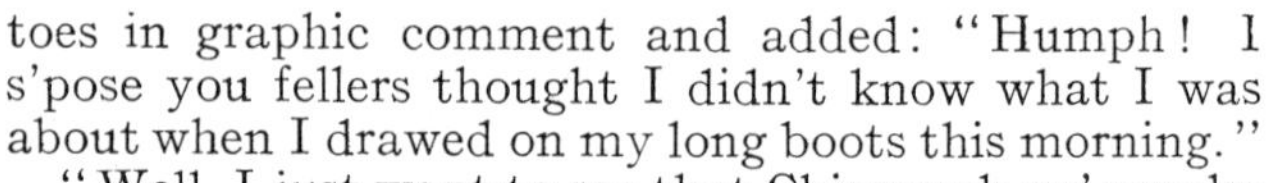

toes in graphic comment and added: "Humph! I s'pose you fellers thought I didn't know what I was about when I drawed on my long boots this morning."

"Well, I just want to see that Chipmunk an' maybe I'll believe you."

"In there hunting for a loose patch," and Sam held up the boot.

"Let's turn him out," suggested the Second Chief.

So the string was cut and the Chipmunk scrambled out and away to a safer refuge.

"Now, sonny," said Sam, as it disappeared, "don't tell your folks what happened you or they'll swat you for a liar."

"Oh, shucks! That's no adventure. Why, I——"

"Hold on, Hawkeye; Little Beaver next."

"Well, I don't care. I bet I——"

Sam grabbed his knife and interrupted: "Do you know what Callahan's spring lamb did when it saw the old man gathering mint? Go ahead, Little Beaver."

"I hadn't much of an adventure, but I went straight through the woods where my straw pointed and ran into a big dead stub. It was too old and rotten for Birds to use now, as well as too late in the season, so I got a pole and pushed it over, and I found the whole history of a tenement in that stub. First of all, a Flicker had come years ago and dug out a fine big nesting-place, and used it maybe two or three times. When he was through, or maybe between seasons, the Chickadees made a winter den of it, for there were some Chickadee tail-feathers in the bottom. Next a Purple Blackbird came and used the hole, piling up a lot of roots with mud on them. Next year it seems it came again and made another nest on top of the last; then that winter the Chickadees again used it for a cubby-hole, for there were some more Chickadee feathers. Next year a Blue Jay found it out and nested there. I found some of her egg-shells among the soft stuff of the nest. Then I suppose a year after a pair of Sparrow-hawks happened on the place, found it suited them, and made their nest in it and hatched a brood of little Sparrow-hawks. Well, one day this bold robber brought home to his little ones a Shrew."

"What's that?"

"Oh, a little thing like a Mouse, only it isn't a Mouse at all; it is second cousin to a Mole."

"I allus thought a Mole *was* a Mouse specie," remarked Hawkeye, not satisfied with Yan's distinction.

"Oh, you!" interrupted Sam. "You'll try to make out the Burnses is some kin to the Raftens next."

"I bet I won't!" and for once Guy got even.

"Well," Yan continued, "it so happened—about the first time in about a million years—the little Hawks were not hungry just then. The Shrew wasn't gobbled up at once, and though wounded, it set to work to escape as soon as it was free of the old one's claws. First it hid under the little ones, then it began to burrow down through the feather-bed of the Sparrow-hawk's nest, then through the Blue Jay's nest, then through the soft stuff of the Blackbird's nest and among the old truck left by the Chickadees till it struck the hard mud floor of the Blackbird's nest, and through that it could not dig. Its strength gave out now, and it died there and lay hidden in the lowest nest of the house, till years after I came by and broke open the old stub and made it tell me a sad and mournful story—that—maybe—never happened at all. But there's the drawing I made of it at the place, showing all the nests just as I found them, and there's the dried up body of the little Shrew."

Sam listened with intense interest, but Guy was at no pains to conceal his contempt. "Oh, pshaw! That's no adventure—just a whole lot of 's'posens' without a blame thing doing. Now I'll tell you what I done. I——"

"Now, Hawkeye," Sam put in, "please don't be rough about it. Leave out the awful things: I ain't well to-day. You keep back the scary parts till to-morrow."

"I tell you I left here and went straight as a die, an' I seen a Woodchuck, but he wasn't in line, so I says: 'No; some other day. I kin get you *easy* any time.' Then I seen a Hawk going off with a Chicken, but that was off my beat, an' I found lots o' old stumps an' hundreds o' Chipmunks an' wouldn't be bothered with them. Then I come to a farmhouse an'—an' I went around that so's not to scare the Dog, an' I went pretty near as far as Downey's Dump—yes, a little a-past it—only to one side—when up jumps a Partridge as big as a Turkey, an' a hull gang of young ones—about thirty or forty. I bet I seen them forty rod away, an' they all flew, but one that lighted on a tree as far as—oh, 'cross that field, anyway. I bet you fellers wouldn't 'a' seen it at all. Well, I jest hauled off as ca'm as ca'm an' let him have it. I aimed straight for his eye—an' that's where I hit him. *Now who gets a grand coup, for there he is!*" Hawkeye unrolled his coat and turned out a bobtailed young Robin in the speckled plumage, shot through the body.

"So that's your Partridge. I call that a young Robin," said the First Chief with slow emphasis. "Rules is broke. Killed a Song-bird. Little Beaver, arrest the criminal."

But Hawkeye struggled with all the ferocity born of his recent exploit, and had to be bound hand and foot while a full Council was called to try the case. The angry protests weakened when he found how serious the Councillors were. Finally he pleaded "guilty" and was condemned to wear a black feather of disgrace and a white feather for cowardice for three days, as well as wash the dishes for a week. They would also have made him cook for that term, but that they had had some unhappy experiences with some dishes of Guy's make.

"Well, I won't do it, that's all," was the prisoner's defiant retort. "I'll go home first."

"And hoe the garden? Oh, yes; I think I see you."

"Well, I won't do it. You better let me 'lone."

"Little Beaver, what do they do when an Injun won't obey the Council?"

"Strip him of his honours. Do you remember that stick we burned with 'Sapwood' on it?"

"Good idee. We'll burn Hawkeye for a name and dig up the old one."

"No, you won't, you dirty mean Skunks! Ye promised me you'd never call me that again. I *am* Hawkeye. I kin see farder'n—n——" and he began to weep.

"Well, will you obey the Council?"

"Yes; but I won't wear no white feather—I'm *brave*, boohoo!"

"All right. We'll leave that off; but you must do the other punishments.

"Will I still be Hawkeye?"

"Yes."

"All right. I'll do it."

XXV

The Three-Fingered Tramp.

BROAD-SHOULDERED, beetle-browed, brutal and lazy was Bill Hennard, son of a prosperous settler. He had inherited a fine farm, but he was as lazy as he was strong, and had soon run through his property and followed the usual course from laziness to crime. Bill had seen the inside of more than one jail. He was widely known in the adjoining township of Emolan; many petty thefts were traced to him, and it was openly stated that but for the help of a rich and clever confederate he would certainly be in the penitentiary. It was darkly hinted, further, that this confederate was a well-to-do Sangerite who had many farms and a wife and son and a little daughter, and his first name was William, and his second name Ra—— "But never mind; and don't for the world say I told you." Oh, it's easy to get rich—if you know how. Of course, these rumours never reached the parties chiefly concerned.

Hennard had left Downey's Dump the evening before, and avoiding the roads, had struck through the woods, to visit his partner, with important matters to arrange—very important for Hennard. He was much fuddled when he left Downey's, the night was cloudy, and consequently he had wandered round and round till he was completely lost. He slept under a tree (a cold, miserable sleep it was), and in the sunless morning he set out with little certainty to find his "pal." After some time he stumbled on the trail that led him to the boys' camp. He was now savage with hunger and annoyance, and reckless with bottle assistance, for he carried a flask. No longer avoiding being seen, he walked up to the teepee just as Little Beaver was frying meat for the noonday meal he expected to eat alone. At the sound of footsteps Yan turned, supposing that one of his companions had come back, but there instead was a big, rough-looking tramp.

"Well, sonny, cookin' dinner? I'll be glad to j'ine ye," he said with an unpleasant and fawning smile.

His manner was as repulsive as it could be, though he kept the form of politeness.

"Where's your folks, sonny?"

"Haven't any—here," replied Yan, in some fear, remembering now the tramps of Glenyan.

"H-m—all alone—camped all alone, are ye?"

"The other fellers are away till the afternoon."

"Wall, how nice. Glad to know it. I'll trouble you to hand me that stick," and now the tramp's manner changed from fawning to command, as he pointed to Yan's bow hanging unstrung.

"That's my bow!" replied Yan, in fear and indignation.

"I won't tell ye a second time—hand me that stick, or I'll spifflicate ye."

Yan stood still. The desperado strode forward, seized the bow, and gave him two or three blows on the back and legs.

"Now, you young Pup, get me my dinner, and be quick about it, or I'll break yer useless neck."

Yan now realized that he had fallen into the power of the worst enemy of the harmless camper, and saw too late the folly of neglecting Raften's advice to have a big Dog in camp. He glanced around and would have run, but the tramp was too quick for him and grabbed him by the collar. "Oh, no you don't; hold on, sonny. I'll fix you so you'll do as you're told." He cut the bowstring from its place, and violently throwing Yan down, he tied his feet so that they had about eighteen inches' play.

"Now rush around and get my dinner; I'm hungry. An' don't you spile it in the cooking or I'll use the gad on you; an' if you holler or cut that cord I'll kill ye. See that?" and he got out an ugly-looking knife.

Tears of fear and pain ran down Yan's face as he limped about to obey the brute's orders.

"Here, you move a little faster!" and the tramp turned from poking the fire with the bow to give another sounding blow. If he had looked down the trail he would have seen a small tow-topped figure that turned and scurried away at the sound.

Yan was trained to bear punishment, but the tyrant seemed careless of even his life.

"Are you going to kill me?" he burst out, after another attack for stumbling in his shackles.

"Don't know but I will when I've got through with ye," replied the desperado with brutal coolness. "I'll take some more o' that meat—an' don't you let it burn, neither. Where's the sugar for the coffee? I'll get a bigger club if ye don't look spry," and so the tramp was served with his meal. "Now bring me some tobaccer."

Yan hobbled into the teepee and reached down Sam's tobacco bag.

"Here, what's that box? Bring that out here,"

and the tramp pointed to the box in which they kept some spare clothes. Yan obeyed in fear and trembling. "Open it."

"I can't. It's locked, and Sam has the key."

"He has, has he? Well, I have a key that will open it," and so he smashed the lid with the axe; then he went through the pockets, got Yan's old silver watch and chain, and in Sam's trousers pocket he got two dollars.

"Ha! That's just what I want, sonny," and the tramp put them in his own pockets. "'Pears to me the fire needs a little wood," he remarked, as his eye fell on Yan's quiverful of arrows, and he gave that a kick that sent many of them into the blaze.

"Now, sonny, don't look at me quite so hard, like you was taking notes, or I may have to cut your throat and put you in the swamp hole to keep ye from telling tales."

Yan was truly in terror of his life now.

"Bring me the whetstone," the tyrant growled, "an' some more coffee." Yan did so. The tramp began whetting his long knife, and Yan saw two things that stuck in his memory: first, the knife, which was of hunting pattern, had a brass Deer on the handle; second, the hand that grasped it had only three-fingers.

"What's that other box in there?"

"That's—that's—only our food box."

"You lie to me, will ye?" and again the stick descended. "Haul it out."

"I can't."

"Haul it out or I'll choke ye."

Yan tried, but it was too heavy.

"Get out, you useless Pup!" and the tramp walked into the teepee and gave Yan a push that sent him headlong out on the ground.

The boy was badly bruised, but saw his only chance. The big knife was there. He seized it, cut the cord on his legs, flung the knife afar in the swamp and ran like a Deer. The tramp rushed out of the teepee yelling and cursing. Yan might have gotten away had he been in good shape, but the tramp's cruelty really had crippled him, and the brute was rapidly overtaking him. As he sped down the handiest, the south trail, he sighted in the trees ahead a familiar figure, and yelling with all his remaining strength, "Caleb! Caleb!! Caleb Clark!!!" he fell swooning in the grass.

There is no mistaking the voice of dire distress.

Caleb hurried up, and with one impulse he and the tramp grappled in deadly struggle. Turk was not with his master, and the tramp had lost his knife, so it was a hand-to-hand conflict. A few clinches, a few heavy blows, and it was easy to see who must win. Caleb was old and slight. The tramp, strong, heavy-built, and just drunk enough to be dangerous, was too much for him, and after a couple of rounds the Trapper fell writhing with a foul blow. The tramp felt again for his knife, swore savagely, looked around for a club, found only a big stone, and would have done no one knows what, when there was a yell from behind, another big man crashed down the trail, and the tramp faced William Raften, puffing and panting, with Guy close behind. The stone meant for Caleb he hurled at William, who dodged it, and now there was an even fight. Had the tramp had his knife it might have gone hard with Raften, but fist to fist the farmer had the odds. His old-time science turned the day, and the desperado went down with a crusher "straight from the shoulder.

It seemed a veritable battle-field—three on the ground and Raften, red-faced and puffing, but sturdy and fearless, standing in utter perplexity.

"Phwhat the divil does it all mane?"

"I'll tell you, Mr. Raften," chirped in Guy, as he stole from his safe shelter.

"Oh, ye're here, are ye, Guy? Go and git a rope at camp—quick now," as the tramp began to move.

As soon as the rope came Raften tied the fellow's arms safely.

"'Pears to me Oi've sane that hand befoore," remarked Raften, as the three fingers caught his eye.

Yan was now sitting up, gazing about in a dazed way. Raften went over to his old partner and said: "Caleb, air ye hurrt? It's me—it's Bill Raften. Air ye hurrt?"

Caleb rolled his eyes and looked around.

Yan came over now and knelt down. "Are you hurt, Mr. Clark?"

He shook his head and pointed to his chest.

"He's got his wind knocked out," Raften explained; "he'll be all right in a minute or two. Guy, bring some wather."

Yan told his story and Guy supplied an important chapter. He had returned earlier than expected, and was near to camp, when he heard the tramp beating Yan. His first impulse to run home to his puny father was replaced with the wiser one to go for brawny Mr. Raften.

The tramp was now sitting up and grumbling savagely.

"Now, me foine feller," said William. "We'll take ye back to camp for a little visit before we take ye to the 'Pen.' A year in the cooler will do ye moore good, Oi'm thinkin', than anny other tratement. Here, Guy, you take the end av the rope and fetch the feller to camp, while I help Caleb."

Guy was in his glory. The tramp was forced to go ahead; Guy followed, jerking the rope and playing Horse, shouting, "Ch'—ch'—ch'—get up, Horsey," while William helped old Caleb with a gentleness that recalled a time long ago when Caleb had so helped him after a falling tree had nearly killed him in the woods.

At camp they found Sam. He was greatly astonished at the procession, for he knew nothing of the day's events, and fearfully disappointed he was on learning what he had missed.

Caleb still looked white and sick when they got him to the fire, and Raften said, "Sam, go home and get your mother to give you a little brandy."

"You don't need to go so far," said Yan, "for that fellow has a bottle in his pocket."

"I wouldn't touch a dhrap of annything he has, let alone give it to a *sick friend*," was William's reply.

So Sam went for the brandy and was back with it in half an hour.

"Here now, Caleb," said William, "drink that now an' ye'll feel better," and as he offered the cup he felt a little reviving glow of sympathy for his former comrade.

When Sam went home that morning it was with a very clear purpose. He had gone straight to his mother and told all he knew about the revolver and the misunderstanding with Caleb, and they two had had a long, unsatisfactory interview with the father. Raften was brutal and outspoken as usual. Mrs. Raften was calm and clear-witted. Sam was shrewd. The result was a complete defeat for William—a defeat that he would not acknowledge; and Sam came back to camp disappointed for the time being, but now to witness the very thing he had been striving for—his father and the Trapper reconciled; deadly enemies two hours ago, but now made friends through a fight. Though overpowered in argument,

Raften's rancour was not abated, but rather increased toward the man he had evidently misused, until the balance was turned by the chance of his helping that man in a time of direst straits.

XXVI

Winning Back the Farm

OH, the magic of the campfire! No unkind feeling long withstands its glow. For men to meet at the same campfire is to come closer, to have better understanding of each other, and to lay the foundations of lasting friendship. "He and I camped together once!" is enough to explain all cordiality between the men most wide apart, and Woodcraft days are days of memories happy, bright and lifelong.

To sit at the same camp fireside has always been a sacred bond, and the scene of twenty years before was now renewed in the Raften woods, thanks to that campfire lit a month before—the sacred fire! How well it had been named! William and Caleb were camped together in good fellowship again, marred though it was with awkwardness as yet, but still good fellowship.

Raften was a magistrate. He sent Sam with an order to the constable to come for the prisoner. Yan went to the house for provisions and to bring Mrs. Raften, and Guy went home with an astonishing account of his latest glorious doings. The tramp desperado was securely fastened to a tree; Caleb was in the teepee lying down. Raften went in for a few minutes, and when he came out the tramp was gone. His bonds were cut, not slipped. How could he have gotten away without help?

"Never mind," said Raften. "That three-fingered hand is aisy to follow. Caleb, ain't that Bill Hennard?"

"I reckon."

The men had a long talk. Caleb told of the loss of his revolver—he was still living in the house with the Pogues then—and of its recovery. They both remembered that Hennard was close by at the time of the quarrel over the Horse-trade. There was much that explained itself and much of mystery that remained.

But one thing was clear. Caleb had been tricked out of everything he had in the world, for it was just a question of days now before Pogue would, in spite of Saryann, throw off all pretense and order Caleb from the place to shift for himself.

Raften sat a long time thinking, then said:

"Caleb, you do exactly as Oi tell ye and ye'll get yer farrum back. First, Oi'll lend ye wan thousand dollars for wan week."

A thousand dollars! ! ! Caleb's eyes opened, and what was next he did not then learn, for the boys came back and interrupted, but later the old Trapper was fully instructed.

When Mrs. Raften heard of it she was thunderstruck. A thousand dollars in Sanger was like one hundred thousand dollars in a big city. It was untold wealth, and Mrs. Raften fairly gasped.

"A thousand dollars, William! Why! isn't that a heavy strain to put on the honesty of a man who thinks still that he has some claim on you? Is it safe to risk it?"

"Pooh!" said William. "Oi'm no money-lender, nor spring gosling nayther. Thayer's the money Oi'll lend him," and Raften produced a roll of counterfeit bills that he as magistrate had happened to have in temporary custody. "Thayer's maybe five hundred or six hundred dollars, but it's near enough."

Caleb, however, was allowed to think it real money, and fully prepared, he called at his own—the Pogue house—the next day, knocked, and walked in.

"Good-morning, father," said Saryann, for she had some decency and kindness.

"What do you want here?" said Dick savagely; "bad enough to have you on the place, without forcing yerself on us day and night."

"Hush now, Dick; you forget——"

"Forget—I don't forget nothin'," retorted Dick, interrupting his wife. "He had to help with the chores an' work, an' he don't do a thing and expects to live on me."

"Oh, well, you won't have me long to bother you," said Caleb sadly, as he tottered to a chair. His face was white and he looked sick and shaky.

"What's the matter, father?"

"Oh, I'm pretty bad. I won't last much longer.

You'll be quit o' me before many days."

"Big loss!" grumbled Dick.

"I—I give you my farm an' everything I had——"

"Oh, shut up. I'm sick of hearing about it."

"At least—'most—everything. I—I—I—didn't say nothing about a little wad o'—o'—bills I had stored away. I—I—" and the old man trembled violently—"I'm so cold."

"Dick, do make a fire," said his wife.

"I won't do no sich fool trick. It's roastin' hot now."

"'Tain't much," went on the trembling old man, "only fif—fif—teen hundred—dollars. I got it here now," and he drew out the roll of greenbacks.

FIFTEEN HUNDRED DOLLARS! Twice as much as the whole farm and stock were worth! Dick's eyes fairly popped out, and Caleb was careful to show also the handle of the white revolver.

"Why, father," exclaimed Saryann, "you are ill! Let me go get you some brandy. Dick, make a fire. Father is cold as ice."

"Yes—please—fire—I'm all of—a—tremble—with—cold."

Dick rushed around now and soon the big fireplace was filled with blaze and the room unpleasantly warm.

"Here, father, have some brandy and water," said Dick, in a very different tone. "Would you like a little quinine?"

"No, no—I'm better now; but I was saying—I only got a few days to live, an' having no legal kin—this here wad'd go to the gover'ment, but I spoke to the lawyer, an' all I need do—is—add—a word to the deed o' gift—for the farm—to include this—an' it's very right you should have it, too." Old Caleb shook from head to foot and coughed terribly.

"Oh, father, let me send for the doctor," pleaded Saryann, and Dick added feebly, "Yes, father, let me go for the doctor."

"No, no; never mind. It don't matter. I'll be better off soon. Have you the deed o' gift here?"

"Oh, yes, Dick has it in his chest." Dick ran to get the deed, for these were the days before registration in Canada; possession of the deed was possession of the farm, and to lose the deed was to lose the land.

The old man tremblingly fumbled over the money, seeming to count it—"Yes—just—fif-teen hun'erd,"

QUININE
O.D.V.
FEVER
CHILLS

as Dick came clumping down the ladder with the deed.

"Have you got a—pen—and ink——"

Dick went for the dried-up ink bottle while Saryann hunted for *the* pen. Caleb's hand trembled violently as he took the parchment, glanced carefully over it—yes, this was it—the thing that had made him a despised pauper. He glanced around quickly. Dick and Saryann were at the other end of the room. He rose, took one step forward, and stuffed the deed into the blazing fire. Holding his revolver in his right hand and the poker in the left, he stood erect and firm, all sign of weakness gone; his eyes were ablaze, and with voice of stern command he hissed "*Stand back!*" and pointed the pistol as he saw Dick rushing to rescue the deed. In a few seconds it was wholly consumed, and with that, as all knew, the last claim of the Pogues on the property, for Caleb's own possessory was safe in a vault at Downey's.

"Now," thundered Caleb, "you dirty paupers, get out of my house! Get off my land, and don't you dare touch a thing belonging to me."

He raised his voice in a long "halloo" and rapped three times on the table. Steps were heard outside. Then in came Raften with two men.

"Magistrate Raften, clear my house of them interlopers, if ye please."

Caleb gave them a few minutes to gather up their own clothes, then they set out on foot for Downey's, wild with helpless rage, penniless wanderers in the world, as they had meant to leave old Caleb.

Now he was in possession of his own again, once more comfortably "fixed." After the men had had their rough congratulations and uproarious laughter over the success of the trick, Raften led up to the question of money, then left a blank, wondering what Caleb would do. The good old soul pulled out the wad.

"There it is, Bill. I hain't even counted it, and a thousand times obliged. If ever you need a friend, call on me."

Raften chuckled, counted the greenbacks and said "All right!" and to this day Caleb doesn't know that the fortune he held in his hand that day was nothing but a lot of worthless paper.

A week later, as the old Trapper sat alone getting his evening meal, there was a light rap at the door.

"Come in."

A woman entered. Turk had sprung up growling, but now wagged his tail, and when she lifted a veil Caleb recognized Saryann.

"What do you want?" he demanded savagely.

"'Twasn't my doing, father; you know it wasn't; and now he's left me for good." She told him her sorrowful story briefly. Dick had not courted Saryann, but the farm, and now that that was gone he had no further use for her. He had been leading a bad life, "far worse than any one knew," and now he had plainly told her he was done with her.

Caleb's hot anger never lasted more than five minutes. He must have felt that her story was true, for the order of former days was reëstablished, and with Saryann for housekeeper the old man had a comfortable home to the end of his days.

Pogue disappeared; folks say he went to the States. The three-fingered tramp never turned up again, and about this time the serious robberies in the region ceased. Three years afterward they learned that two burglars had been shot while escaping from an American penitentiary. One of them was undoubtedly Dick Pogue, and the other was described as a big dark man with three fingers on the right hand.

XXVII

The Rival Tribe

THE winning back of the farm, according to Sanger custom must be celebrated in a "sociable" that took the particular form of a grand house-warming, in which the Raftens, Burnses and Boyles were fully represented, as Char-less was Caleb's fast friend. The Injun band was very prominent, for Caleb saw that it was entirely owing to the meetings at the camp that the glad event had come about

Caleb acted as go-between for Char-less Boyle and William Raften, and their feud was forgotten—for the time at least—as they related stories of their early hunting days, to the delight of Yan and the Tribe. There were four other boys there whom Little Beaver met for the first time. They were Wesley Boyle, a dark-skinned, low-browed, active boy of Sam's age; his brother Peter, about twelve, hair, fat and freckled, and with a marvellous squint; and their cousin Char-less Boyle, Jr., good-natured, giggly, and of spongy character; also Cyrus Digby, a smart city boy, who was visiting "the folks," and who usually appeared in white cuffs and very high stand-up collar. These boys were greatly interested in the Sanger Indian camp, and one outcome of the meeting at Caleb's was the formation of another Tribe of Indians, composed of the three Boyle boys and their town friend.

Since most of these were Boyles and the hunting-ground was the Boyles woods about that marshy pond, and especially because they had read of a band of Indians named Boilers or Stoneboilers (Assineboines), they called themselves the "Boilers." Wesley was the natural leader. He was alert as well as strong, and eager to do things, so made a fine Chief. His hooked nose and black hair and eyes won for him the appropriate name of "Blackhawk." The city boy being a noisy "show-off," who did little work, was called "Bluejay." Peter Boyle was "Peet-weet," and Char-less, from his peculiar snickering and showing two large front teeth, was called "Red-squirrel."

They made their camp as much as possible like that of the Sangers, and adopted their customs; but a deadly rivalry sprang up between them from the first. The Sangers felt that they were old and experienced Woodcrafters. The Boilers thought they knew as much and more, and they outnumbered the Sangers. Active rivalry led to open hostilities. There was a general battle with fists and mud; that proved a draw. Then a duel between leaders was arranged, and Blackhawk won the fight and the Woodpecker's scalp. The Boilers were wild with enthusiasm. They proposed to take the whole Sanger camp, but in a hand-to-hand fight of both tribes it was another draw. Guy, however, scored a glorious triumph over Char-less and secured his scalp at the moment of victory.

Now Little Beaver sent a challenge to Blackhawk. It was scornfully accepted. Again the Boiler Chief was victor and won another scalp, while Little Beaver got a black eye and a bad licking, but the enemy retired.

Yan had always been considered a timid boy at Bonnerton, but that was largely the result of his repressive home training. Sanger was working great changes. To be treated with respect by the head of the house was a new and delightful experience. It developed his self-respect. His wood life was making him wonderfully self-reliant, and improved health helped his courage, so next day, when the enemy appeared in full force, every one was surprised when Yan again challenged Blackhawk. It really cost him a desperate and mighty effort to do so, for it is one thing to challenge a boy that you think you can "lick" and another to challenge one the very day after he has licked you. Indeed, if the truth were known, Yan did it in fear and trembling, and therein lay the courage—in going ahead when fear said "Go back."

It is quite certain that a year before he would not have ventured in such a fight, and he only did it now because he had realized that Blackhawk was left-handed, and a plan to turn this to account had suggested itself. Every one was much surprised at the challenge, but much more so when, to the joy of his tribe, Little Beaver won a brilliant victory.

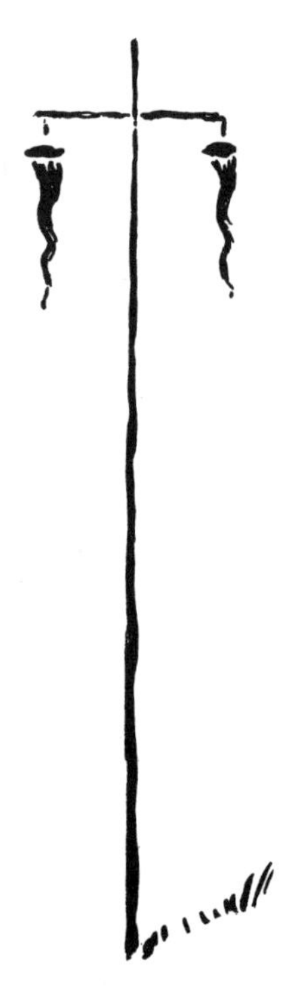

Inspired by this, they drove the Boilers from the field, scored a grand triumph, and Sam and Yan each captured a scalp.

The Sangers held a Council and scalp-dance in celebration that night around an outdoor fire. The Medicine Man was sent for to be in it.

After the dance, Chief Beaver, his face painted to hide his black eye, made a speech. He claimed that the Boilers would surely look for reinforcements and attempt a new attack, and that, therefore, the Sangers should try to add to their number, too.

"I kin lick Char-less any time," piped in Guy proudly, and swung the scalp he had won.

But the Medicine Man said: "If I were you boys I'd fix up a peace. Now you've won you ought to ask them to a big pow-wow."

These were the events that led to the friendly meeting of the two Tribes in full war-paint.

Chief Woodpecker first addressed them: "Say, fellers—Brother Chiefs, I mean—this yere quar'lin' don't pay. We kin have more fun working together. Let's be friends an' join in one Tribe. There's more fun when there's a crowd."

"All right," said Blackhawk; "but we'll call the tribe the 'Boilers,' coz we have the majority, and leave me Head Chief."

"You are wrong about that. Our Medicine Man makes us even number and more than even weight. We've got the best camp—have the swimming-pond, and we are the oldest Tribe, not to speak of the success we had in a certain leetle business not long ago which the youngest of us kin remember," and Guy grinned in appreciation of this evident reference to his exploit.

As a matter of fact, it was the swimming-pond that turned the day. The Boilers voted to join the Sangers. Their holiday was only ten days, the Sangers had got a week's extension, and all knew that they could get most out of their time by going to the pond camp. The question of a name was decided by Little Beaver.

"Boiler Warriors," said he, "it is the custom of the Indians to have the Tribes divided in clans. We are the Sanger clan. You are the Boiler clan. But as we all live in Sanger we are all Sanger Indians."

"Who's to be Head Chief?"

Blackhawk had no notion of submitting to Woodpecker, whom he had licked, nor would Woodpecker accept a Chief of the inferior tribe. One suggested that Little Beaver be Chief, but out of loyalty to his friend, the Woodpecker, Yan declined.

"Better leave that for a few days till you get acquainted," was the Medicine Man's wise suggestion.

That day and the next were spent in camp. The Boilers had their teepee to make and beds to prepare. The Sangers merrily helped, making a "bee" of it.

Bow and arrow making were next to do. Little Beaver had not fully replaced his own destroyed by the robber. A hunt of the Burlap Deer was a pleasant variation of the second day, though there were but two bows for all, and the Boilers began to realize that they were really far behind the Sangers in knowledge of Woodcraft.

At swimming Blackhawk was easily first. Of course, this greatly increased his general interest in the swimming-pond, and he chiefly was responsible for the making of a canoe later on.

The days went on right merrily—oh, so fast! Little Beaver showed all the things of interest in his kingdom. How happy he was in showing them—playing experienced guide as he used to dream it! Peetweet took a keen interest; so did the city boy. Char-less took a little interest in it all, helped a little, was generally a little in everything, and giggled a good deal. Hawkeye was disposed to bully Char-less, since he found him quite lickable. His tone was high and haughty when he spoke to him—not at all like his whining when addressing the others. He volunteered to discipline Char-less if he should ill-treat any of the others, and was about to administer grievous personal punishment for some trifling offense, when Blackhawk gave him a warning that had good effect.

Yan's note-book was fully discussed and his drawings greatly admired. He set to work at once with friendly enthusiasm to paint the Boilers' teepee. Not having any adventures that seemed important, except, perhaps, Blackhawk's defeat of Woodpecker and Little Beaver, subjects that did not interest the artist, the outside decorations were the totem of the clan and its members.

XXVIII

White-Man's Woodcraft

BLACKHAWK was the introducer of a new game which he called "judging."

"How far is it from here to that tree?" he would ask, and when each had written down his guess they would measure, and usually it was Woodpecker or Blackhawk that came nearest to the truth. Guy still held the leadership "for far sight," for which reason he suggested that game whenever a change of amusement was wanted.

Yan, following up Blackhawk's suggestion, brought in the new game of "White-man's Woodcraft."

"Can you," asked he, "tell a Dog's height by its track?"

"No; nor you nor any one else," was the somewhat scornful reply.

"Oh, yes, I can. Take the length in inches of his forefoot track, multiply it by 8, and that gives his height at the shoulder. You try it and you'll see. A little Dog has a 2¼-inch foot and stands about 18 inches, a Sheep Dog with a 3-inch track stands 24 inches, and a Mastiff or any big Dog with a 4-inch track gives 30 to 32 inches."

"You mean every Dog is 8 feet high?" drawled Sam, doubtfully, but Yan went on. "And you can tell his weight, too, by the track. You multiply the width of his forefoot in inches by the length, and multiply that by 5, and that gives pretty near his weight in pounds. I tried old Cap. His foot is 3½ by 3; that equals 10½, multiplied by 5 equals 52½ pounds: just about right."

"I'll bet I seen a Dog at the show that that wouldn't work on," drawled Sam. "He was as long as my two arms, he had feet as big as a young Bear, an' he wasn't any higher than a brick. He was jest about the build of a Caterpiller, only he didn't have but four legs at the far ends. They was so far apart he couldn't keep step. He looked like he was raised under a bureau. I think when they was cutting down so on his legs they might have give him more of them; a row in the middle would 'a' been 'bout right."

"Yes, I know him. That's a Dachshund. But you can't reckon on freaks; nothing but straight Dog. It works on wild animals, too—that is, on Wolves and Foxes and maybe other things," then changing the subject Beaver continued:

"Can you tell the height of a tree by its shadow?"

"Never thought of that. How do you do it?"

"Wait till your own shadow is the same length as yourself—that is, about eight in the morning or four in the afternoon—then measure the tree's shadow. That gives its length."

"You'd have to wait all day to work that, and you can't do it at all in the woods or on a dull day," objected Blackhawk. "I'd rather do it by guess."

"I'll bet my scalp against yours I can tell the height of that tree right now without climbing it, and get closer than you can by guessing," said Little Beaver.

"No, I won't bet scalps on that—but I'll bet who's to wash the dishes."

"All right. To the top of that tree, how much is it?"

"Better not take the top, 'cause we can't get there to measure it, but say that knot," was the rejoinder. "Here, Woodpecker, you be judge."

"No, I want to be in this guessing. The loser takes the next turn of dishwashing for each of the others."

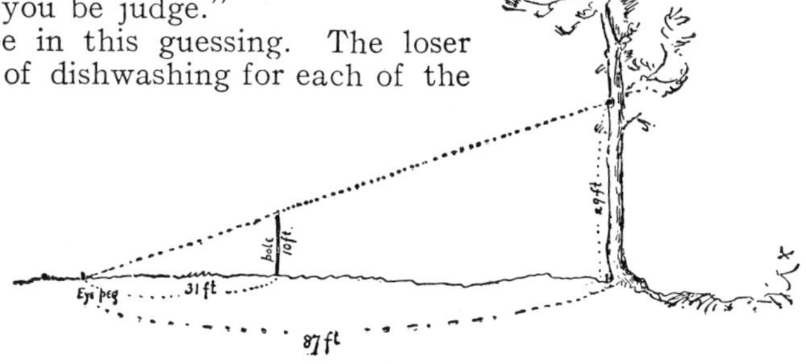

So Blackhawk studied the knot carefully and wrote down his guess—Thirty-eight feet.

Sam said, "Blackhawk! Ground's kind of uneven. I'd like to know the exact spot under the tree that you'd measure to. Will you mark it with a peg?"

So Blackhawk went over and put in a white peg, at the same time unwittingly giving Woodpecker what he wanted—a gauge, for he knew Blackhawk was something more than five feet high; judging then as he stood there Sam wrote down Thirty-five feet.

Now it was Yan's turn to do it by "White-man's Woodcraft," as he called it. He cut a pole exactly ten feet long, and choosing the smoothest ground, he walked about twenty yards from the tree, propped the pole upright, then lay down so that his eye was level with the tree base and in line with the top of the pole and the knot on the tree. A peg marked the spot.

Now he measured from this "eye peg" to the foot of the pole; it was 31 feet. Then from the eye peg to the peg under the tree; it was 87 feet. Since the 10-foot pole met the line at 31 feet, then 31 is to 10 as 87 is to the tree—or 28 feet. Now one of the boys climbed and measured the height of the knot. It was 29 feet, and Yan had an easy victory.

"Here, you close guessers, do you want another try, and I'll give you odds this time. If you come within ten feet you'll win. I want only two feet to come and go on."

'All right. Pick your trees."

"'Tisn't a tree this time, but the distance across that pond, from this peg (H, page 265) to that little Hemlock (D). You put down your guesses and I'll show you another trick."

Sam studied it carefully and wrote Forty feet. Wes put down Forty-five.

"Here, I want to be in this. I'll show you fellers how," exclaimed Guy in his usual scornful manner, and wrote down Fifty feet.

"Let's all try it for scalps," said Char-less, but this was ruled too unimportant for scalps, and again the penalty of failure was dishwashing, so the other boys came and put down their guesses close to that of their Chief—Forty-four, Forty-six and Forty-nine feet.

"Now we'll find out exactly," and Little Beaver, with an air of calm superiority, took three straight poles of exactly the same length and pegged them together in a triangle, leaving the pegs sticking up.

He placed this triangle on the bank at *A B C*, sighting the line *A B* for the little Hemlock *D*, and put three pegs in the ground exactly under the three pegs where the triangle was; moved the triangle to *E F G* and placed it so that *F G* should line with *A C* and *E G* with *D*. Now *A G D* also must be an equilateral triangle; therefore, according to arithmetic, the line *D H* must be seven-eighths of *A G*. *A G* was easily measured—70 feet. Seven-eighths of 70 equals 61¼ feet. The width of the pond—they measured it with tape line—was found to be 60 feet, so Yan was nearest, but Guy claimed that 50 feet was within 10 feet of it, which was allowed. Thus there were two winners—two who escaped dish-washing; and Hawkeye's bragging became insufferable. He never again got so close in a guess, but no number of failures could daunt him after such a success.

Sam was interested in the White-man's Woodcraft chiefly on Yan's account, but Blackhawk was evidently impressed with the study itself, and said:

"Little Beaver, I'll give you one more to do. Can you measure how far apart those two trees are on that bank, without crossing?"

"Yes," said Yan; "easily." So he cut three poles 6, 8 and 10 feet long and pegged them together in a triangle (below). "Now," said he, "*A B C* is a right angle; it must be, when the legs of the triangle are 6, 8 and 10; that's a law."

He placed this on the shore, the side *A B* pointing to the inner side of the first tree, and the side *B C* as nearly as possible parallel with the line between the two

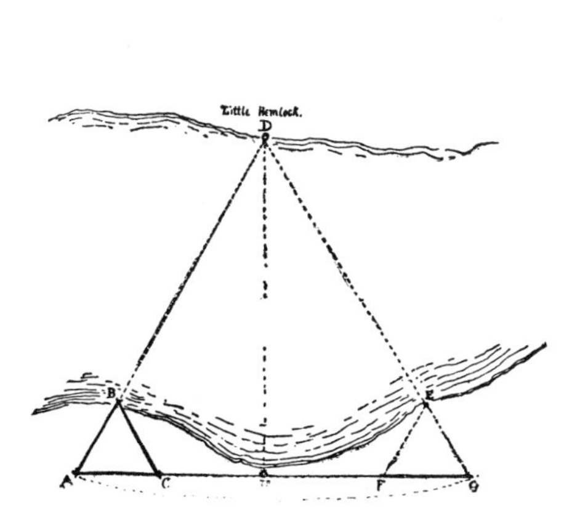

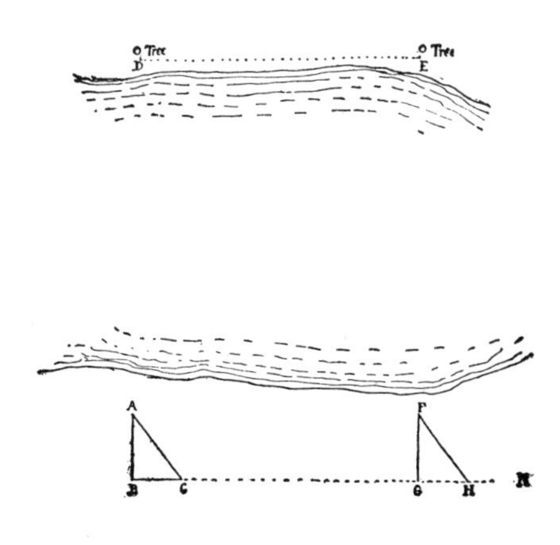

trees. Then he put in a stake at *B*, another at *C*, and continued this line toward *K*. Now he slid his triangle along this till the side *G F* pointed to *E*, and the side *H G* in line with *C B*. The distance from *D* to *E*, of course, is equal to *B G*, which can be measured, and again the tape line showed Yan to be nearly right.

This White-man's Woodcraft was easy for him, and he volunteered to teach the other Indians, but they thought it looked "too much like school." They voted him a *coup* on finding how well he could do it. But when Raften heard of it he exclaimed in wonder and admiration, "My, but that's mightiful!" and would not be satisfied till the *coup* was made a *grand coup*.

"Say, Beaver," said Woodpecker, sadly harking back, "if a Dog's front foot is 3½ inches long and 3 inches wide, what colour is the end of his tail?"

"White," was the prompt reply; "'cause a Dog with feet that size and shape is most likely to be a yaller Dog, and a yaller Dog always has some white hairs in the end of his tail."

"Well, this 'un hadn't, 'cause his tail was cut off in the days of his youth!"

XXIX

The Long Swamp

THE union of the tribes, however, was far from complete. Blackhawk was inclined to be turbulent. He was heavier than Beaver. He could not understand how that slighter, younger boy could throw him, and he wished to try again. Now Yan was growing stronger every day. He was quick and of very wiry build. In the first battle, which was entirely fisty, he was worsted; on the try-over, which cost him such an effort, he had arranged "a rough-and-tumble," as they called it, and had won chiefly by working his only trick. But now Blackhawk was not satisfied, and while he did not care to offer another deadly challenge, by way of a feeler he offered, some days after the peace, to try a friendly throw for scalps.

"Fists left out!" Just what Beaver wanted, and the biggest boy was sent flying. "If any other Boiler would like to try I'd be pleased to oblige him," said Yan, just a little puffed up, as he held up the second scalp he had won from Blackhawk.

Much to his surprise, Bluejay, the city boy, accepted, and he was still more surprised when the city boy sent *him* down in the dust.

"Best out of three!" shouted Woodpecker quickly, in the interest of his friend, taking advantage of an unwritten law that when it is not stated to be in one try, usually called "sudden death," it is "best two out of three" that counts.

Yan knew now that he had found a worthy foe. He dodged, waiting for an opening—gripped—locked—and had him on the hip, he thought, but the city boy squirmed in time, yielding instead of resisting, and both went down tight-gripped. For a minute it was doubtful.

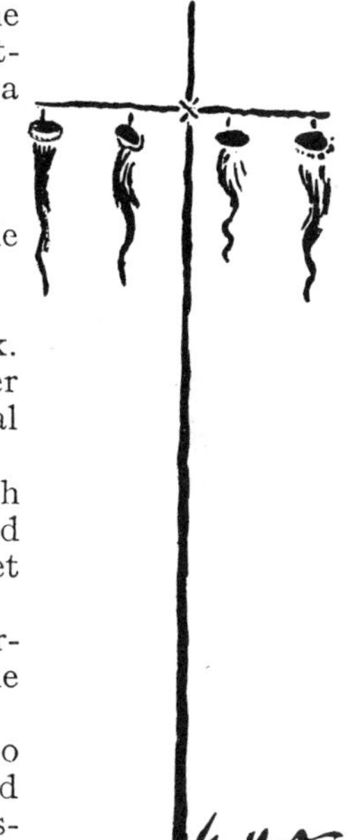

"Go it, Yan."

"Give it to him, Bluejay."

But Yan quickly threw out one leg, got a little purchase, and threw the city boy on his back.

"Hooray for Little Beaver!"

"One try more! So far even!" cried Blackhawk.

They closed again, but Yan was more than ever careful. The city boy was puffing hard. The real trial was over and Cy went down quite easily.

"Three cheers for Little Beaver!" A fourth scalp was added to his collection, and Sam patted him on the back, while Bluejay got out a pocket mirror and comb and put his hair straight.

But this did not help out in the matter of leadership, and when the Medicine Man heard of the continued deadlock he said:

"Boys, you know when there is a doubt about who is to lead the only way is for all Chiefs to resign and have a new election." The boys acted on this suggestion but found another deadlock. Little Beaver refused to be put up. Woodpecker got three votes, Blackhawk four, and Guy one (his own), and the Sangers refused to stand by the decision.

"Let's wait till after the 'hard trip'—that will show who is the real Chief—then have a new election," suggested Little Beaver, with an eye to Woodpecker's interest, for this hard trip was one that had been promised them by Caleb—a three-days' expedition in the Long Swamp.

This swamp was a wild tract, ten miles by thirty, that lay a dozen miles north of Sanger. It was swampy only in parts, but the dry places were mere rocky ridges, like islands in the bogs. The land on these was worthless and the timber had been ruined by fire, so Long Swamp continued an uninhabited wilderness.

There was said to be a few Deer on the hardwood ridges. Bears and Lynx were occasionally seen, and Wolves had been heard in recent winters. Of course there were Foxes, Grouse and Northern Hare. The streams were more or less choked with logs, but were known to harbour a few Beavers and an occasional Otter. There were no roads for summer use, only long, dim openings across the bogs, known as winter trails and timber roads. This was the region that the boys proposed to visit under Caleb's guidance.

Thus at last they were really going on an "Indian trip"—to explore the great unknown, with every probability of adventure.

At dawn Yan tapped the tom-tom. It sang a high and vibrant note, in guarantee of a sunny day.

They left camp at seven in the morning, and after three hours' tramp they got to the first part of the wilderness, a great tract of rocky land, disfigured with blackened trees and stumps, but green in places with groves of young Poplars or quaking-Aspen.

The Indians were very ready to camp now, but the Medicine Man said, "No; better keep on till we find water." In another mile they reached the first stretch of level Tamarack bog and a welcome halt for lunch was called. "Camp!" shouted the leader, and the Indians ran each to do his part. Sam got wood for the fire and Blackhawk went to seek water, and with him was Bluejay, conspicuous in a high linen collar and broad cuffs, for Caleb unfortunately had admitted that he once saw an Indian Chief in high hat and stand-up collar.

Beaver was just a little disappointed to see the Medicine Man light the fire with a match. He wanted it all in truly Indian style, but the Trapper remarked, "Jest as well to have some tinder and a thong along when you're in the woods, but matches is handier than rubbing-sticks."

Blackhawk and Bluejay returned with two pails of dirty, tepid, swampy water.

"Why, that's all there is!" was their defense.

"Yan, you go and show them how to get good

water," said Caleb, so the Second Sanger Chief, remembering his training, took the axe and quickly made a wooden digger, then went to the edge of the swamp, and on the land twenty feet from the bog he began to dig a hole in the sandy loam. He made it two feet across and sunk it down three feet. The roily water kept oozing in all around, and Bluejay was scornful. "Well, I'd rather have what we got." Beaver dug on till there was a foot of dirty water in the hole. Then he took a pail and bailed it all out as fast as possible, left it to fill, bailed it out a second time, and ten minutes later cautiously dipped out with a cup a full pail of crystal-clear cold water, and thus the Boilers learned how to make an Indian well and get clear water out of a dirty puddle.

After their simple meal of tea, bread and meat Caleb told his plan. "You never get the same good of a trip if you jest wander off; better have a plan—something to do; and do it without a guide if ye want adventures. Now eight is too many to travel together; you'd scare everything with racket and never see a livin' thing. Better divide in parties. I'll stay in camp and get things ready for the night."

Thus the leaders, Sam and Yan, soon found themselves paired with Guy and Peetweet. Wes felt bound to take care of his little cousin Char-less.

Bluejay, finding himself the odd man, decided to stay with Caleb, especially as the swamp evidently was without proper footpaths.

"Now," said Caleb, "northwest of here there is a river called the Beaver, that runs into Black River. I want one of you to locate that. It's thirty or forty feet wide and easy to know, for it's the only big stream in the swamp. Right north there is an open stretch of plain, with a little spring creek, where there's a band of Injuns camped. Somewhere northeast they say there's a tract of Pine bush not burned off, and there is some Deer there. None of the places is ten miles away except, maybe, the Injuns' camp. I want ye to go scoutin' and report. You kin draw straws to say who goes where."

So the straws were marked and drawn. Yan drew the timber hunt. He would rather have had the one after the Indians. Sam had to seek the river, and Wesley the Indian camp. Caleb gave each of them a few matches and this parting word:

"I'll stay here till you come back. I'll keep up a fire, and toward sundown I'll make a smoke with rotten wood and grass so you kin find your way back.

Remember, steer by the sun; keep your main lines of travel; don't try to remember trees and mudholes; and if you get lost, you make *two smokes* well apart and stay right there and holler every once in awhile; some one will be sure to come."

So about eleven o'clock the boys set out eagerly. As they were going Blackhawk called to the others, First to carry out his job wins a *grand coup!*"

"Let the three leaders stake their scalps," said the Woodpecker.

"All right. First winner home gets a scalp from each of the others and saves his own."

"Say, boys, you better take along your hull outfit, some grub an' your blankets," was the Medicine Man's last suggestion. "You may have to stay out all night."

Yan would rather have had Sam along, but that couldn't be, and Peetweet proved a good fellow, though rather slow. They soon left the high ground and came to the bog—flat and seemingly endless and with a few tall Tamaracks. There were some Cedar-birds catching Flies on the tall tree-tops, and a single Flycatcher was calling out: "*Whoit—whoit—whoit!*" Yan did not know until long after that it was the Olive-side. A Sparrow-hawk sailed over, and later a Bald Eagle with a Sparrow-hawk in hot and noisy pursuit. But the most curious thing was the surface of the bog. The spongy stretch of moss among the scattering Tamaracks was dotted with great masses of Pitcher Plant, and half concealed by the curious leaves were thousands of Droseræ, or fly-eating plants, with their traps set to secure their prey.

The bog was wonderful, but very bad walking. The boys sank knee-deep in the soft moss, and as they went farther, steering only by the sun, they found the moss sank till their feet reached the water below and they were speedily wet to the knees. Yan cut for each a long pole to carry in the hand; in case the bog gave way this would save them from sinking. After two miles of this Peetweet wanted to go back, but was scornfully suppressed by Little Beaver.

Shortly afterward they came to a sluggish little stream in the bog with a peculiar red-and-yellow scum along its banks. It was deep and soft-bottomed. Yan tried it with the pole—did not dare to wade, so they walked along its course till they found a small tree lying from bank to bank, then crossed on this. Half a mile farther on the bog got dryer, and a mass of green ahead marked one of the islands of high

"Well, sonny, cookin' dinner?"

"He nervously fired and missed"

land. Over this they passed quickly, keeping the northwest course. They now had a succession of small bogs and large islands. The sun was hot here, and Peetweet was getting tired. He was thirsty, too, and persisted in drinking the swamp water whenever he found a hole.

"Say, Peetweet, you'll suffer for that if you don't quit; that water isn't fit to drink unless you boil it."

But Peetweet complained of burning thirst and drank recklessly. After two hours' tramp he was very tired and wanted to turn back. Yan sought a dry island and then gathered sticks for a fire, but found all the matches they had were soaking wet with wading through the bog. Peetweet was much upset by this, not on account of fire now, but in case they should be out all night.

"You wait and see what an Indian does," said Little Beaver. He sought for a dried Balsam Fir, cut the rubbing-sticks, made a bow of a slightly bent branch, and soon had a blazing fire, to Peter's utter amazement, for he had never seen the trick of making a fire by rubbing-sticks.

After drinking some tea and eating a little, Pete felt more encouraged.

"We have travelled more than six miles now, I reckon," said the Chief; "an hour longer and we shall be in sight of the forest if there is one," and Yan led off across swamps more or less open and islands of burned timber.

Pete began to be appalled by the distance they were putting between them and their friends. "What if we should get lost? They never could find us."

"We won't get lost," said Yan in some impatience; "and if we did, what of it? We have only to keep on straight north or south for four or five hours and we reach some kind of a settlement."

After an hour's tramp northeast they came to an island with a tall tree that had branches right to the ground. Yan climbed up. A vast extent of country lay all about him—open flat bogs and timber islands, and on far ahead was a long, dark mass of solid evergreen—surely the forest he sought. Between him and it he saw water sparkling.

"Oh, Pete, you ought to be up here," he shouted joyfully; "it's worth the climb to see this view."

"I'd ruther see our own back-yard," grumbled Pete.

Yan came down, his face aglow with pleasure, and

exclaimed: "It's close to, now! I saw the Pine woods. Just off there."

"How far?"

"Oh, a couple of miles, at most."

"That's what you have been saying all along."

"Well, I saw it this time; and there is water out there. I saw that, too."

He tramped on, and in half an hour they came to the water, a deep, clear, slow stream, fringed with scrub willows, covered with lily-pads, and following the middle of a broad, boggy flat. Yan had looked for a pond, and was puzzled by the stream. Then it struck him. "Caleb said there was only one big stream through this swamp. This must be it. This is Beaver River."

The stream was barely forty feet across, but it was clearly out of the question to find a pole for a bridge, so Yan stripped off, put all his things in a bundle, and throwing them over, swam after them. Pete had to come now or be left.

As they were dressing on the northern side there was a sudden loud "*Bang—swish!*" A torrent of water was thrown in the air, with lily-pads broken from their mooring, the water pattered down, the wavelets settled, and the boys stood in astonishment to see what strange animal had made this disturbance; but nothing more of it was seen, and the mystery remained unsolved.

Then Yan heard a familiar "*Quack!*" down the stream. He took his bow and arrow, while Pete sat gloomily on a hummock. As soon as he peered through the rushes in a little bay he saw three Mallard close at hand. He waited till two were in line, then fired, killing one instantly, and the others flew away. The breeze wafted it within reach of a stick, and he seized it and returned in triumph to Pete, but found him ready to cry. "I want to go home!" he said miserably. The sight of the Mallard cheered him a little, and Yan said: "Come now, Pete, don't spoil everything, there's a good fellow. Brace up,

and if I don't show you the Pine woods in twenty minutes I'll turn and take you home."

As soon as they got to the next island they saw the Pine wood—a solid green bank not half a mile away, and the boys gave a little cheer, and felt, no doubt, as Mungo Park did when first he sighted the Niger. In fifteen minutes they were walking in its dry and delightful aisles.

"Now we've won," said Yan, "whatever the others do, and all that remains is to get back."

"I'm awfully tired," said Pete; "let's rest awhile."

Yan looked at his watch. "It's four o'clock. I think we'd better camp for the night."

"Oh, no; I want to go home. It looks like rain."

It certainly did, but Yan replied, "Well, let's eat first." He delayed as much as possible so as to compel the making of a camp, and the rain came unexpectedly, before he even had a fire. Yet to his own delight and Peter's astonishment he quickly made a rubbing-stick fire, and they hung up their wet clothes about it. Then he dug an Indian well and took lots of time in the preparation, so it was six o'clock before they began to eat, and seven when finished—evidently too late to move out even though the rain seemed to be over. So Yan collected firewood, made a bed of Fir boughs and a windbreak of bushes and bark. The weather was warm, and with the fire and two blankets they passed a comfortable night. They heard their old friend the Horned Owl, a Fox barked his querulous "*Yap-yurr!*" close at hand, and once or twice they were awakened by rustling footsteps in the leaves, but slept fairly well.

At dawn Yan was up. He made a fire and heated some water for tea. They had very little bread left, but the Mallard was untouched.

Yan cleaned it, rolled it in wet clay hid it in the ashes and covered it with glowing coals. This is an Indian method of cooking, but Yan had not fully mastered it. In half an hour he opened his clay pie and found the Duck burned on one side and very raw on the other. Part of it was good, however, so he called his companion to breakfast. Pete sat up white-faced and miserable, evidently a sick boy. Not only had he caught cold, but he was upset by the swamp water he had taken. He was paying the penalty of his indiscretion. He ate a little and drank some tea, then felt better, but clearly was unable to travel that day. Now for the first time Yan felt a qualm of fear. Separated by a dozen miles of swamp from all help, what could he do with a sick boy? He barked a small dead tree with a knife, then on the smooth surface wrote with a pencil, "Yan Yeoman and Pete Boyle camped here August 10, 18—"

He made Pete comfortable by the fire, and, looking for tracks, he found that during the night two Deer had come nearly into the camp; then he climbed a high tree and scanned the southern horizon for a smoke sign. He saw none there, but to the north-west, beyond some shining yellow hills, he discovered a level plain dotted over with black Fir clumps; from one of these smoke went up, and near it were two or three white things like teepees.

Yan hurried down to tell Pete the good news, but when he confessed that it was two miles farther from home Pete had no notion of going to the Indian camp; so Yan made a smoke fire, and knife-blazing the saplings on two sides as he went, he set out alone for the Indian camp. Getting there in half an hour, he found two log shanties and three teepees. As he came near he had to use a stick to keep off the numerous Dogs. The Indians proved shy, as usual, to White visitors. Yan made some signs that he had learned from Caleb. Pointing to himself, he held up two fingers—meaning that he was two. Then he pointed to the Pine woods and made sign of the other lying down, and added the hungry sign by pressing in his stomach with the edges of the hands, meaning "I am cut in two here." The Chief Indian offered him a Deer-tongue, but did not take further interest. Yan received it thankfully, made a hasty sketch of the camp, and returned to find Pete much better, but thoroughly alarmed at being so long alone. He was able and anxious now to go back. Yan led off, carrying all the things of the outfit, and his comrade followed slowly and peevishly When they came to the river, Pete held back in fear, believing that the loud noise they had heard was made by some monster of the deep, who would seize them.

Yan was certain it could be only an explosion of swamp gas, and forced Pete to swim across by setting the example. What the cause really was they never learned.

They travelled very fast now for a time. Pete was helped by the knowledge that he was really going home. A hasty lunch of Deer-tongue delayed them but little. At three they sighted Caleb's smoke signal, and at four they burst into camp with yells of triumph.

Caleb fired off his revolver, and Turk bayed his basso profundo full-cry Fox salute. All the others had come back the night before.

Sam said he had "gone ten mile and never got a sight of that blamed river." Guy swore they had gone forty miles, and didn't believe there was any such river.

"What kind o' country did you see?"

"Nothin' but burned land and rocks."

"H-m, you went too far west—was runnin' parallel with Beaver River."

"Now, Blackhawk, give an account of yourself to Little Beaver," said Woodpecker. "Did you two win out?"

"Well," replied the Boiler Chief, "if Hawkeye travelled forty miles, we must have gone sixty. We pointed straight north for three hours and never saw a thing but bogs and islands of burned timber—never a sign of a plain or of Indians. I don't believe there are any."

"Did you see any sandhills?" asked Little Beaver.

"No."

"Then you didn't get within miles of it."

Now he told his own story, backed by Pete, and he was kind enough to leave out all about Peetweet's whimpering. His comrade responded to this by giving a glowing account of Yan's Woodcraft, especially dwelling on the feat of the rubbing-stick fire in

the rain, and when they finished Caleb said:

"Yan, you won, and you more than won, for you found the green timber you went after, you found the river Sam went after, an' the Injuns Wesley went after. Sam and Wesley, hand over your scalps."

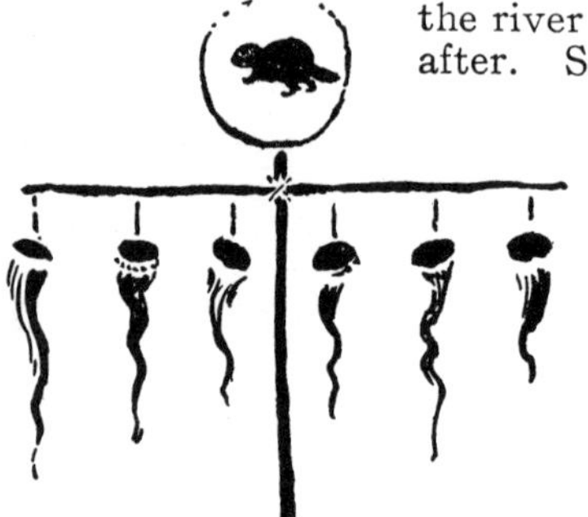

XXX

A New Kind of Coon

A MERRY meal now followed, chaffing and jokes passed several hours away, but the boys were rested and restless by nine o'clock and eager for more adventures.

"Aren't there any Coons 'round here, Mr. Clark?"

"Oh, I reckon so. Y-e-s! Down a piece in the hardwood bush near Widdy Biddy Baggs's place there's lots o' likely Cooning ground."

That was enough to stir them all, for the place was near at hand. Peetweet alone was for staying in camp, but when told that he might stay and keep house by himself he made up his mind to get all the fun he could. The night was hot and moonless, Mosquitoes abundant, and in trampling and scrambling through the gloomy woods the hunters had plenty of small troubles, but they did not mind that so long as Turk was willing to do his part. Once or twice he showed signs of interest in the trail, but soon decided against it.

Thus they worked toward the Widdy Baggs's till they came to a dry brook bed. Turk began at once to travel up this, while Caleb tried to make him go down. But the Dog recognized no superior officer when hunting. After leading his impatient army a quarter of a mile away from the really promising heavy timber, Turk discovered what *he* was after, and that was a little muddy puddle. In this he calmly lay down, puffing, panting and lapping with energy, and his humble human followers had nothing to do but sit on a log and impatiently await his lordship's pleasure. Fifteen minutes went by, and Turk was still enjoying himself, when Sam ventured at last:

"'Pears to me if I owned a Dog I'd own him."

"There's no use crowdin' him," was the answer. "He's runnin' this hunt, an' he knows it. A Dog without a mind of his own is no 'count."

So when Turk had puffed like a Porpoise, grunted and wallowed like a Hog, to his heart's content and to the envy of the eight who sat sweltering and impatient, he arose, all dribbling ooze, probably to seek a new wallowing place, when his nose discovered something on the bank that had far more effect than all the coaxings and threats of the "waiting line," and he gave a short bark that was a note of joy for the boys. They were all attention now, as the old Hound sniffed it out, and in a few moments stirred the echoes with an opening blast of his deepest strain.

"Turk's struck it rich!" opined Caleb.

The old Dog's bawling was strong now, but not very regular, showing that the hunted animal's course was crooked. Then there was a long break in it, showing possibly that the creature had run a fence or swung from one tree to another.

"That's a Coon," said Yan eagerly, for he had not forgotten any detail of the other lesson.

Caleb made no reply.

The Hound tongued a long way off, but came back to the pond and had one or two checks.

"It's a great running for a Coon," Yan remarked, at length in doubt. Then to Caleb, "What do you think?"

Caleb answered slowly: "I dunno what to think. It runs too far for a Coon, an' 'tain't treed yet; an' I kin tell by the Dog's voice he's mad. If you was near him now you'd see all his back hair stannin' up."

Another circle was announced by the Dog's baying, and then the long, continuous, high-pitched yelping told that the game was treed at last.

"Well, that puts Fox and Skunk out of it," said the Trapper, "but it certainly don't act like a Coon on the ground."

"First there gets the Coon!" shouted Blackhawk, and the boys skurried through the dark woods, getting many a scratch and fall. As it was, Yan and Wesley arrived together and touched the tree at the same moment. The rest came straggling up, with Char-less last and Guy a little ahead of him. Guy wanted to relate the full particulars of his latest glorious victory over Char-less, but all attention was now on old Turk, who was barking savagely up the tree.

"Don't unnerstan' it at all, at all," said Caleb.

"Coony kind o' tree, but Dog don't act Coony."

"Let's have a fire," said the Woodpecker, and the two crowds of boys began each a fire and strove hard to get theirs first ablaze.

The firelight reached far up into the night, and once or twice the hunters thought they saw the shining eyes of the Coon.

"Now who's to climb?" asked the Medicine Man.

"I will, I will," etc., seven times repeated; even Guy and Char-less chimed in.

"You're mighty keen hunters, but I want you to know I can't tell what it is that's up that tree. It may be a powerful big Coon, but seems to me the Dog acts a little like it was a Cat, and 'tain't so long since there was Painter in this county. The fact of him treeing for Turk don't prove that he's afraid of a Dog; lots of animals does that 'cause they don't want to be bothered with his noise. If it's a Cat, him as climbs is liable to get his face scratched. Judging by the actions of the Dog, *I think it's something dangerous*. Now who wants the job?"

For awhile no one spoke. Then Yan, "I'll go if you'll lend me the revolver."

"So would I," said Wesley quickly.

"Well, now, we'll draw straws"—and Yan won. Caleb felled a thin tree against the big one and Yan climbed as he had done once before.

There was an absence of the joking and chaffing that all had kept up when on the other occasion Yan went after the Coon. There was a tension that held them still and reached the climber to thrill him with a weird sense of venturing into black darkness to face a fearful and mysterious danger. The feeling increased as he climbed from the leaning tree to the great trunk of the Basswood, to lose sight of his comrades in the wilderness of broad leaves and twisted tree-arms. The dancing firelight sent shadow-blots and light-spots in a dozen directions with fantastic effect. Some of the feelings of the night at Garney's grave came back to him, but this time with the knowledge of real danger. A little higher and he was out of sight of his friends below. The danger began to appal him; he wanted to go back, and to justify the retreat he tried to call out, "No Coon here!" but his voice failed him, and, as he clung to the branch, he remembered Caleb's words, "There's nothing ahead of grit, an' grit ain't so much not bein' scairt as it is goin' straight ahead when you *are* scairt." No; he would go on, come what would.

"Find anything?" drawled a cheery voice below, just at the right time.

Yan did not pause to answer, but continued to climb into the gloom. Then he thought he heard a Coon snarl above him. He swung to a higher branch and shouted, "Coon here, all right!" but the moment he did so a rattling growl sounded close to him, and looking down he saw a huge grey beast spring to a large branch between him and the ground, then come climbing savagely toward him. As it leaped to a still nearer place Yan got a dim view of a curious four-cornered face, shaggy and striped, like the one he saw so long ago in Glenyan—it was an enormous *Lynx*.

Yan got such a shock that he nearly lost his hold but quickly recovering, he braced himself in a crotch, and got out the revolver just as the Lynx with a fierce snarl leaped to a side branch that brought it nearly on a level with him. He nervously cocked the pistol, and scarcely attempting to sight in the darkness, he fired and missed. The Lynx recoiled a little and crouched at the report. The boys below raised a shout and Turk outdid them all in racket.

"A Lynx!" shouted Yan, and his voice betrayed his struggle with fear.

"Look out!" Caleb called. "You better not let him get too close."

The Lynx was growling ferociously. Yan put forth all his will-power to control his trembling hand, took more deliberate aim, and fired. The fierce beast was struck, but leaped wildly at the boy. He threw up his arm and it buried its teeth in his flesh, while Yan clung desperately to the tree with the other arm. In a moment he knew he would be dragged off and thrown to the ground, yet felt less fear now than he had before. He clutched for the revolver with the left hand, but it found only the fur of the Lynx, and the revolver dropped from his grasp. Now he was indeed without hope, and dark fear fell on him. But the beast was severely wounded. Its hind quarters were growing heavy. It loosed its hold of Yan and struggled to get on the limb. A kick from his right foot upset its balance; it slipped from the tree and flopped to the ground below, wounded, but full of fight. Turk rushed at it, but got a blow from its armed paw that sent him off howling.

A surge of reaction came over Yan. He might have fainted, but again he remembered the Trapper's words, "Bravery is keeping on even when you *are* skairt." He pulled himself together and very cautiously worked his way back to the leaning tree. Hearing strange sounds, yells, growls, sounds of conflict down below, expecting every moment to hear the Lynx scramble up the trunk again, to finish him, dimly hearing but not comprehending the shouts, he rested once at the leaning tree and breathed freely.

"Hurry up, Yan, with that revolver," shouted Blackhawk.

"I dropped it long ago."

"Where is it?"

Yan slid down the sapling without making reply. The Lynx had gone, but not far. It would have got away, but Turk kept running around and bothering it so it could not even climb a tree, and the noise they made in the thicket was easy to follow.

"Where's the revolver?" shouted Caleb, with unusual excitement.

"I dropped it in the fight."

"I know; I heard it fall in the bushes," and Sam soon found it.

Caleb seized it, but Yan said feebly, "Let me! Let me! It's my fight!"

Caleb surrendered the pistol, said "Look out for the Dog!" and Yan crawled through the bushes till that dark moving form was seen again. Another shot and another. The sound of combat died away, and the Indians raised a yell of triumph—all but Little Beaver. A giddiness came over him; he trembled and reeled, and sank down on a root. Caleb and Sam came up quickly.

"What's the matter, Yan?"

"I'm sick—I——"

Caleb took his arm. It was wet. A match was struck.

"Hallo, you're bleeding."

"Yes, he had me—he caught me up the tree. I—I—thought I was a goner."

All interest was now turned from the dead Lynx to the wounded boy.

"Let's get him to the water."

"Guess the camp well is the nearest."

Caleb and Sam took care of Yan, while the others brought the Lynx. Yan grew better as they moved slowly homeward. He told all about the attack of the Lynx.

"Gosh! I'd 'a' been scared out o' my wits," said Sam.

"Guess I would, too," added Caleb, to the surprise of the Tribe; "up there, helpless, with a wounded Lynx—I tell you!"

"Well, I *was* scared—just as scared as I could be," admitted Yan.

At camp a blazing fire gave its lurid light. Cold water was handy and Yan's bleeding arm was laid bare. He was shocked and yet secretly delighted to see what a mauling he had got, for his shirt sleeve was soaked with blood, and the wondering words of his friends was sweetest music to his ears.

Caleb and the city boy dressed his wounds, and when washed they did not look so very dreadful.

They were too much excited to sleep for an hour at least, and as they sat about the fire—that they did not need but would not dream of doing without—Yan found no lack of enthusiasm in the circle, and blushed with pleasure to be the hero of the camp. Guy didn't see anything to make so much fuss about, but Caleb said, "I knowed it; I always knowed you was the stuff, after the night you went to Garney's grave.

XXXI

On the Old Camp Ground

IT was threatening to rain again in the morning and the Indians expected to tramp home heavy laden in the wet. But their Medicine Man had a surprise in store. "I found an old friend not far from here and fixed it up with him to take us all home in his wagon." They walked out to the edge of the rough land and found a farm wagon with two horses and a driver. They got in, and in little less than a hour were safely back to the dear old camp by the pond.

The rain was over now, and as Caleb left for his own home he said:

"Say, boys, how about that election for Head Chief? I reckon it's due now. Suppose you wait till to-morrow afternoon at four o'clock an' I'll show you how to do it."

That night Yan and his friend were alone in their teepee. His arm was bound up, and proud he was of those bandages and delighted with the trifling red spots that appeared yet on the last layer; but he was not in pain, nor, indeed, the worse for the adventure, for, thanks to his thick shirt, there was no poisoning. He slept as usual till long after midnight, then awoke in bed with a peculiar feeling of well-being and clearness of mind. He had no bodily sense; he seemed floating alone, not in the teepee nor in the woods, but in the world—not dreaming, but wide awake—more awake than ever in his life before, for all his life came clearly into view as never before: his stern, religious training; his father, refined and well-meaning, but blind, compelling him to embark in a profession to which he was little inclined, and to give up the one thing next his heart—his Woodcraft lore.

Then Raften stepped into view, loud-voiced, externally coarse, but blessed with a good heart and a sound head. The farmer suffered sadly in contrast with the father, and yet Yan had to suppress the wish that Raften were his father. What had they in common? Nothing; and yet Raften had given him two of the dearest things in life. He, the head of the house, a man of force and success, had treated Yan with respect. Yan was enough like his own father to glory in the unwonted taste; and like that other rugged stranger long ago in Glenyan, Raften had also given him sympathy. Instead of considering his Woodcraft pursuits mere trifling, the farmer had furthered them, and even joined to follow for a time. The thought of Bonnerton came back. Yan knew he must return in a year at most; he knew that his dearest ambition of a college course in zoölogy was never to be realized, for his father had told him he must go as errand boy at the first opening. Again his rebellious spirit was stirred, to what purpose he did not know. He would rather stay here on the farm with the Raftens. But his early Scriptural training was not without effect. "Honour thy father and thy mother" was of lasting force. He felt it to be a binding duty. He could not rebel if he would. No, he would obey; and in that resolution new light came. In taking him from college and sending him to the farm his father had apparently cut off his hope of studies next his heart. Instead of suffering loss by this obedience, he had come to the largest opportunity of his life.

Yes! He would go back—be errand boy or anything to make a living, but in his hours of freedom he would keep a little kingdom of his own. The road to it might lie through the cellar of a grocer's shop, but he would not flinch. He would strive and struggle as a naturalist. When he had won the insight he was seeking, the position he sought would follow, for every event in the woodland life had shown him—had shown them all, that his was the kingdom of the Birds and Beasts and the power to comprehend them.

And he seemed to float, happy in the fading of all doubt, glad in the sense of victory. There was a noise outside. The teepee door was forced gently; a large animal entered. At another time Yan might have been alarmed, but the uplift of his vision was on him still. He watched it with curious unalarm. It gently came to his bed, licked his hand and laid down beside him. It was old Turk, and this was the first time he had heeded any of them but Caleb.

XXXII

The New War Chief

CALEB had been very busy all the day before, doing no one knew what, and Saryann was busy, too. She had been very busy for long, but now she was bustling. Then, it seems, Caleb had gone to Mrs. Raften, and she was very busy, and Guy made a flying visit to Mrs. Burns, and she had become busy. Thus they turned the whole neighbourhood into a "bee."

For this was Sanger, where small gatherings held the same place as the club, theatre and newspaper do in the lives of city folk. No matter what the occasion, a christening, wedding or funeral, a logging, a threshing, a home-coming or a parting, the finishing of a new house or the buying of a new harness or fanning-mill, any one of these was ample grounds for one of their "talking bees"; so it was easy to set the wheels a-running.

At three o'clock three processions might have been seen wending through the woods. One was from Burns's, including the whole family; one from Raften's, comprising the family and the hired men; one from Caleb's, made up of Saryann and many of the Boyles. All brought baskets.

They were seated in a circle on the pleasant grassy bank of the pond. Caleb and Sam took charge of the ceremonies. First, there were foot-races, in which Yan won in spite of his wounded arm, the city boy making a good second; then target-shooting and "Deer-hunting," that Yan could not take part in. It was not in the programme, but Raften insisted on seeing Yan measure the height of a knot in a tree without going to it, and grinned with delight when he found it was accurate.

"Luk at that for eddication, Sam!" he roared. "When will ye be able to do the like? Arrah, but ye're good stuff, Yan, an' I've got something here'll plase ye."

Raften now pulled out his purse and as magistrate paid over with evident joy the $5 bounty due for killing the Lynx. Then he added: "An' if it turns out as ye all claim" [and it did] "that this yer beast is the Sheep-killer instid av old Turk, I'll add that other tin."

Thus Yan came into the largest sum he had ever owned in his life.

Then the Indians went into their teepees. Caleb set up a stake in the ground and on that a new shield of wood covered with rawhide; over the rawhide was lightly fastened a piece of sacking.

The guests were in a circle around this; at one side were some skins—Yan's Lynx and Coon—and the two stuffed Owls.

Then the drum was heard, "Túm-tum—túm-tum—túm-tum—túm-tum——" There was a volley of war-whoops, and out of the teepees dashed the Sanger Indians in full war paint.

"Ki ki—ki yi—ki yi yi yi
Ki yi—ki yi—ki yi yi yi!"

They danced in exact time to the two-measure of the drum that was pounded by Blackhawk. Three times round the central post with the shield they danced, then the drum stopped, and they joined in a grand final war-whoop and squatted in a circle within that of the guests.

The New War Chief

The Great Woodpecker now arose—his mother had to be told who it was—and made a characteristic speech:

"Big Chiefs, Little Chiefs, and Squapooses of the Sanger Indians: A number of things has happened to rob this yer nation of its noble Head Chief; they kin never again expect to have his equal, but this yer assembly is for to pick out a new one. We had a kind of whack at it the other day, but couldn't agree. Since then we had a hard trip, and things has cleared up some, same as puttin' Kittens in a pond will tell which one is the swimmer, an' we're here to-day to settle it."

Loud cries of "How—how—how—how——" while Blackhawk pounded the drum vigorously.

"O' course different ones has different gifts. Now who in all this Tribe is the best runner? That's Little Beaver."

("How—how—how—how—how—" and drum.)

"That's my drum, Ma!" said Guy aside, forgetting to applaud.

"Who is the best trailer and climber? Little Beaver, again, I reckon."

("How—how—how—how—" and drum.)

("He can't see worth a cent!" whispered Guy to his mother.)

"Who was it won the trial of grit at Garney's grave? Why, it was Little Beaver."

("An' got pretty badly scared doin' it!" was Guy's aside.)

"But who was it shot the Cat-Owl plumb in the heart, an' fit the Lynx hand to hand, not to speak of the Coon? Little Beaver every time."

("Hen ever killed a Woodchuck in his life, Ma!")

"Then, again, which of us can lay all the others on his back? Little Beaver, I s'pose."

("Well, I can lick Char-less, any time," was Guy's aside.)

"Which of us has most *grand coups* and scalps?"

"Ye're forgittin' his eddication," put in Raften, to be scornfully ignored; even Little Beaver resented this as un-Indian.

"Which has most scalps?" Sam repeated with sternness. "Here's a scalp won in battle with the inimy," Woodpecker held it up, and the Medicine Man fastened it on the edge of the shield that hung from the post.

"Here is one tuk from the Head Chief of the hostiles," and Caleb fastened that to the shield. "Here

is another tuk from the Second Chief of the hostiles," and Caleb placed it. "Here is one tuk from the Great Head War Chief of the Sangers, and here is one from the Head Chief of the Boilers, and another tuk in battle. Six scalps from six famous warriors. This yere is the record for the whole Tribe, an' Little Beaver done it; besides which, he draws pictures, writes poethry and cooks purty good, an' I say Little Beaver is the one for Chief! What says the rest?" and with one voice they shouted, "Hoorah for Little Beaver!"

"How—how—how—how—how — *thump, thump, thump, thump.*"

"Any feller anything to say agin it?"

"I eh——" Guy began.

—"has got to lick the Chief," Sam continued, and Guy did not complete his objection, though he whispered to his mother, "If it was Char-less I bet I'd show him."

Caleb now pulled the cover off the shield that he fastened the scalps to, and it showed the white Buffalo of the Sangers with a Little Beaver above it. Then he opened a bundle lying near and produced a gorgeous war-shirt of buff leather, a pair of leggins and moccasins, all fringed, beaded and painted, made by Saryann under Caleb's guidance. They were quickly put on the new Chief; his war bonnet, splendid with the plumes of his recent exploits, was all ready; and proud and happy in his new-found honours, not least of which were his wounds, he stepped forward. Caleb viewed him with paternal pride and said: "I knowed ye was the stuff the night ye went to Garney's grave, an' I knowed it again when ye crossed the Big Swamp. Yan, ye could travel anywhere that man could go," and in that sentence the boy's happiness was complete. He surely was a Woodcrafter now. He stammered in a vain attempt to say something appropriate, till Sam relieved him by: "Three cheers for the Head War Chief!" and when the racket was over the women opened their baskets and spread the picnic feast. Raften, who had been much gratified by his son's flow of speech, recorded a new vow to make him study law, but took advantage of the first gap in the chatter to say:

"Bhise, ye'r two weeks' holiday with wan week extension was up at noon to-day. In wan hour an' a half the Pigs is fed."